THE LEAPING

Tom Fletcher

D1531195

Quercus

First published in 2010 by

Quercus
21 Bloomsbury Square
London
WC1A 2NS

A CIP catalogue record for this book is available
from the British Library

ISBN 978 1 84916 135 0

10 9 8 7 6 5 4 3 2 1

Typeset by Ellipsis Books Limited, Glasgow

Printed and bound in Great Britain by Clays Ltd, St Ives plc

For Beth

PROLOGUE

ERIN

The wind wakes me up in the early hours and I confuse the present with a memory; one summer, years ago, we were kept awake by the wind, because it was really strong, powerful. I remember hearing the slates coming off the roof and imagining them whipping through the air like huge lethal crows, and hoping that they wouldn't land on either of my parents. I don't know why they would have been outside. Maybe it was that fear that kept me awake, not the wind. In the morning, when it got light, we found that the whole of the village had been covered in this red, dusty film, making windows and windscreens dirty and thick. It was sand from the Sahara blown over by some high, snaking wind, high above the clouds and the cities that I used to believe were in the clouds, and oh, our white car. The car wash at the garage, all that sand, all that sand from the hot, dry, red desert, down the drain at the petrol station. My mum said that it had happened once before, when she was very young, and there had been this other time, she

1

said, when she woke up one night, and the sky was dark red. The sun hadn't come up, and it was the middle of the night, but the sky was brick-red, cold, dead, barren, and she had never known what that was, and her parents hadn't been able to explain it, and it had scared her. She had been four or five or something, and her hair was a huge big knotty ball around her head. She'd said it scared her, since she was only a kid, but I think it would have scared anybody.

My bedroom is dark still, and I should get back to sleep because I'm in work at nine. It's only when I close my eyes again and listen to the wind that I remember I was dreaming. I was dreaming about a red sky. The way things can connect in your head without you knowing about it – it makes me shudder. I was dreaming about a place with no people, like a desert or the moon or something. And the sky was all red. A deep red, like a sunset, but more complete. Just completely red. And there was somebody walking towards me. Some sort of giant, huge he was, gradually blocking out the sky as he got nearer, but he was only ever a black silhouette. His knees were bent the wrong way.

Mum said that when I was little I would ask what was at the end of the sky. And she'd say space, the universe, and I'd ask what was at the end of the universe, and she'd say nothing, nothing, and I'd say, but what's actually *there*? And she'd say OK, OK then, Erin, OK, a big brick wall. A big brick wall. A big red brick-red wall.

Is there a door, I'd say.

No, she'd say.

No door.

PART ONE

JACK

Ice Bar was quite full, but we managed to get standing room near the tiny, comfy bit with the sofas – separated from the rest of the club by a pair of heavy curtains – so that when the sofas became free we could just hop on. The walls and floor were brown and the sofas were cream and there were low, black tables with little tea-lights on each one and the music was too bland even for me to be able to say what genre it was.

'I hope he's OK,' Erin said. 'He said his mother sounded a bit fretful on the phone.'

'Sure he'll be fine,' Graham said. 'Francis thinks everybody's down all the time. He always thinks there's something wrong.'

'But still,' Erin said. 'I hope they're all OK.' She drew deeply on the straw that protruded from her Long Island Iced Tea and her large, green eyes scanned the small, dark room for Taylor. 'Where's Taylor?' she asked.

'He'll be here soon,' I said. 'He wasn't finishing work until eleven.'

'He'll be properly fucking some monumentally screwed-up fresher in her *Playboy* shit-pit of a bedroom,' Graham said. 'I bet.'

'Shut up, Graham,' Erin said. 'You're such a rapist.'

'It's hardly going to be a fresher,' I said. 'I mean, we're not even at university any more.'

Graham just shrugged and downed his Stella, spilling a little into his massive blond beard. 'Just a joke,' he said, and looked around hungrily.

'Taylor told me he likes you, Erin,' I said.

'Yeah, but I want him to tell *me*,' she said.

'You know Taylor,' I said. 'He's not the most forthcoming of people. Why don't you tell him that you like him?'

'Oh, I don't know!' She smiled and laughed. Her face was surrounded by thick, red curls. Her skin was pale and smooth and her high cheeks were lightly freckled.

Taylor is lucky, I thought, he's a lucky boy or, rather, a lucky man, but I didn't say it. He probably knew it, but was one of those people who pretty much kept his thoughts to himself.

'This is shit,' Graham said. 'What are we doing? What's the plan? Are we going to go anywhere good?'

'We're waiting for Taylor,' I said. 'Remember?'

'Oh yeah,' he said. 'Hey! Those dickheads are going. Quick – get the sofas!'

'Have you taken anything tonight, Graham?' I asked. 'You seem jumpy.'

'Just the usual,' he said. 'Just a pill.'

*

Taylor was tall and dark-haired and thin-faced and looked a little bit like a young Richard E. Grant, which Erin liked, and that's what mattered, I suppose. He emerged from between the curtains and, spotting us immediately, made his way over to us, picking his way through a maze of soft leather beanbags and amorous couples.

'Evening,' he said. 'You all OK?'

'Yes, thank you,' Erin said, quickly.

'I'll be better once I've got about ten more drinks inside me,' Graham said. 'Either that or some fit girl's finger.'

'I'm all right, thank you,' I said. 'How was work?'

'You know better than to ask that,' Taylor said.

We all worked at the same place. A monolithic building that was a multi-storey call centre somewhere near the middle of Manchester, comprising of floor upon floor of old, unreliable computers, broken spirits and bowed heads connected via black, curly wires to telephones that crouched like bulbous insects on the dirty desks, the humming of tonnes of electrical equipment, the frustration of bad maths, the pure panic of not knowing all the answers all the time, right now, come on, what are they paying you for, you been to school or what? The slimish scorn of the nation, dripping through earpieces and trickling into our open ears like warm, lumpy milk. You heard people say all kinds of things. The building towered up into the greenish city sky and burrowed down, it seemed like, burrowed down and down all the way to hell. There was something of the hell-wain about it. The hell-wain was a vehicle, an old coach that reputedly rattled around transporting the souls of the dead. The call centre had that kind of lifeless, limbo-esque feeling to it. The place was open twenty-four hours a day, seven days a week, and we all worked varying shifts.

The pay was low, but with five of us living together we got by with enough left over for a social life.

'Sorry,' I said.

'It was terrible,' Taylor said. 'It was as terrible as ever. I won't go on about it though. Ended up getting a bus over here with Kenny Hicks. He's here somewhere.' Kenny was a manager. He was a little man with a mouth too big for his head that flapped open and shut like a cat-flap in the wind, spilling all kinds of rubbish.

'All the more reason for us to be leaving, then,' Graham said. 'Come on. Let's go somewhere good.'

'Graham,' Taylor said, 'when are you going to realise that all of these clubs are essentially the same? It doesn't make any difference where we go. They're like super-markets or music television channels. Besides. I've just bought a drink. And I don't drink fast.'

'Jesus Christ,' Graham said. 'I could be at home watching porn.'

'I'm going to get a drink,' I said. 'Anybody want one?'

'Same again, please,' Erin said.

'I'm coming with you,' Graham said. 'I want to assess the situation.'

'What situation?' I said.

'The female situation,' he said.

Taylor shook his head and rolled his eyes. I stood up, and gestured for Taylor to sit down next to Erin.

'Just tell her,' I whispered, as we passed each other. 'For goodness' sake.'

I saw Kenny standing at the other end of the bar, but he didn't appear to have noticed me so I made sure not to make eye contact. Kenny was there, then, and Kenny – he had this big, weird grin, like his facial muscles relaxed into it, like the widest possible smile was the natural at-rest state of his face.

Graham lingered beside me, looking about desperately, his big, shaggy, dirty-blonde head twisting and turning like the head of a mop being rolled between somebody's hands. He was tall and broad and scruffy, with bright blue eyes and a fair-sized beard and bit of a beer-gut. He ate women with his eyes.

'Why don't girls want to sleep with me, do you think?' he said.

'I really don't know,' I said. 'What are you drinking?'

'Double Jack Daniels, Jack. Jack Jack. Ha. And a Stella, please.'

I looked at him. 'You're drinking a lot. And you're taking a fair few drugs.'

'Well,' he said. 'I like it. It takes the edge off.'

'Takes the edge off what?'

He shrugged.

We got served, eventually, and as we turned away from the bar with our drinks in hand I risked a glance in Kenny's direction. Typically, he saw me, and grinned ghoulishly. It was as if he were just looking me directly in the eyes whilst smiling at something in his memory, not at me at all. The expression put me in mind of some twisted little sprite, some Puck, thinking up a nasty practical joke.

When we got back, Erin and Taylor were having an in-depth conversation about Milton Friedman and Iraq, which I didn't fully understand. They looked up as we passed them their drinks.

'Hello again,' I said.

'Hi, you two,' Erin said, and then finished what she was saying to Taylor.

'I was hoping they'd be kissing or something,' I whispered to Graham.

'I know,' he said. 'I wish they'd fucking get on with it.'

Later on, we were near the club, outside a fast-food place called Chicken Jack's, adrift in a tide of confused, randy drunkards, taxis, take-away wrappers and neon. It could have been one of a hundred or more such streets across cities all over the country, all of them pretty much the same. Sometimes I would forget that we were in Manchester, and I would allow myself to think that we kept stumbling into some other dimension, some sort of shared space, which everybody mistook for a specific loca-tion. I would often get the feeling in supermarkets.

We were eating chips, looking around ourselves, trying to decide whether to get a taxi or just walk. Taylor was charming the girls with long, elaborate jokes, of which he seemed to have an inexhaustible supply.

Next to Chicken Jack's there was a small, dark alleyway

that didn't appear to have a name, and I could hear some-thing, some noise coming from its dark mouth. It sounded like there was somebody up there laughing, or coughing. After a moment I could tell that it was definitely coughing, so I drifted towards the alley, away from the others, concerned. As I got closer it started to sound worse, like an asthma attack or some sort of fit.

The alleys that branched off the main street all joined up together behind the scenes, forming a complex warren inhabited largely by homeless people. I pictured them living in a kind of cardboard city made out of empty Chicken Jack's pizza boxes, which was probably a little romantic, but it made me feel better about never having any change on me when I walked past them on the pavement.

Looking around the corner, I saw somebody up there, or at least I saw the shape of a person, somebody leaning against the filthy brick wall, coughing and throwing up. It wasn't that unusual to see people in that state, of course, at that time of day in that kind of place at the weekend, but this sounded worse, somehow, more unhealthy, more *difficult.*

I edged down the alley, and I was a bit scared, to be honest, but once I'd seen them and convinced myself that they probably needed help I couldn't very well just turn around and forget about it. The ground was almost completely covered in old newspapers, flattened boxes, polystyrene trays, chicken bones, broken glass.

'Hey,' I said. 'Hey! You OK?'

The figure didn't say anything, but stopped vomiting,

11

and if they could stop at will they must have been all right, I supposed. They looked up at me and I *thought* that they looked male, but it was still too dark to tell for sure. Then they bent over and an obscene amount of wet matter poured from their face, splashing all down the wall and piling up on the floor, substantially enough for me to see it from where I was standing, so there must have been a horrendous volume of the stuff.

I don't like this, I thought. There's something deeply wrong with you.

The figure looked up again, but this time a car performing a 180-degree turn on the main road behind me shone its headlights directly down the alley and the person's face was clearly illuminated. I would have been difficult to identify, silhouetted as I was, and their body remained hidden, obscured by my shadow, but the face. *That face.*

Kenny. Kenny Hicks. All the car gave me was a split second, but that was all I needed to identify the dead eyes, the huge mouth, the sharp, broken nose, and it also revealed thick, dark blood running from his lips, smeared across his cheek and throat, flowing from the weird smile that bisected his face.

He was moving towards me.

I turned and sprinted down the alley, shooting from its mouth like I was being spat out.

'We have to go,' I said, wheeling on the others, shaking. 'In a taxi. Come on. Let's go. Now.'

FRANCIS

So my dad arrives in his old white Metro. There is moss growing in the mirrors. There is moss growing along the bottoms of the windows. The whole thing is covered in rust spots and mud splats. But he couldn't care less. Neither could I. I've never understood what people find interesting about cars. But then, a lot of people don't understand what I find so interesting about crap films.

He pulls up. I make my way round to the passenger side. Open the door and duck in. I sling my backpack into the back seat. I try not to gag at the intense scent of stale tobacco smoke.

'Alright, Dad,' I say.

'Alright, Son,' he says.

'How are you?'

'Alright,' he says. 'Alright.'

'You look tired,' I say. He doesn't look well.

'I am quite tired,' he says. 'Was out late last night. Making the most of these clear skies. Perfect for watching, they are.'

'UFOs?'

'Yep. UFOs. Haven't seen any, though.'

'There's a surprise.'

'Don't start that, Son,' he says. 'Not tonight.'

'What's all this about, anyway?'

'What do you mean?'

'Is there something up? You've got some bad news or something?'

'What?' he looks at me, briefly. He looks back out of the windscreen. He sets off. 'No, of course not. You always think the worst. Why would we have some bad news? No.' He shakes his head. 'Just been a while since we saw you. That's all.'

'Right,' I say. 'OK.'

'You've got to drop this thing you have. About getting ill. Won't do you any good, you know.'

'I know, Dad,' I say.

We are encased in a bubble of light. The car. It traverses these tiny roads. We are surrounded by that pale countryside dark. Mossy cobble walls on either side rush past at speed. This is all we see. Walls and road and naked trees.

'Best moment of my life,' he says, 'was seeing a UFO over Scafell Pike.'

'What?' I say. 'Really?'

'Well,' he says. 'Apart from marrying your mother, of course. And her giving birth to you.' He glances at me sideways. Kind of smiling.

'Well, I don't know. I didn't mean that. I meant – what, seriously? Seeing a UFO?'

14

'Yep.'

'Why was that so good?'

'Because I couldn't *explain* it,' he says. 'When was the last time that you saw something that you couldn't explain?'

'I saw an aeroplane yesterday,' I say. 'And I can't explain that. How it was working, I mean.'

He shakes his head.

'You know, though, that the aeroplane was built by men and women,' he says. '*People*. People who understood how the thing was going to fly. What I saw that night, that was different. Just seeing it evoked a feeling, I don't know how to describe it, it was so strange. I feel like I can't really describe it using human words, Francis. It was completely *other*.'

'I bet I could describe it,' I say. 'I bet I could describe it now. 'It looked kind of like a helicopter in the fog.' Would that be accurate?'

'You know,' Dad says, 'I've seen a helicopter in the fog. And that thing over Scafell Pike looked nothing like it. I'm telling you now. The sight of it, just the way it looked, placed it well outside our understanding.'

'No,' I say. 'You can't ever know that. All you can ever know is that it's outside of *your* understanding. That's all you can definitely say! That's what I meant about the aeroplane, see. You don't know that the thing you saw wasn't built by people.'

'One day,' Dad says, 'you'll see something. Or hear something. Or feel something. And you'll know exactly what I'm talking about.'

Well. That would be nice, I guess.

'You want to stop somewhere to do some watching?' he asks.

'No,' I say. 'No thanks.'

My parents live in a small terrace on a small road that sticks out from a small village in the Lake District. It's a pretty nice house, actually. All nice grey stone and flowers. They bought it years ago. When they were younger than I am now. Dad turns off the engine.

'Here we are,' he says. But doesn't move.

'OK then,' I say. 'Thanks, Dad.'

I reach back for my backpack and open the car door. He still doesn't move. He's staring into space. Literally. His eyes pointing upwards through the windscreen. He gazes absently at the actually pretty amazing starscape.

'Dad,' I say. 'You getting out?'

'Yeah.' He seems to come back. Shakes his head slightly. 'Yep. Come on then.'

Visiting my parents isn't all bad. The house is warm inside. All old wood. Soft rugs. Pictures of farm animals. The wooden floorboards and banisters and skirting-boards and everything else wooden seem to glow orange.

'Hi, Mum!' I shout through. I take my shoes off.

'Francis!' she says, coming through from the kitchen. She gives me a hug. 'You've lost weight. Dinner's ready. Come through. How are you? Are you OK? Is Manchester treating you well?'

'Yes thank you,' I say. She lets go and turns away immediately. 'Are you OK?'

'We're OK,' she says. She heads back into the kitchen. 'Of course we are.'

My mum is called Joan. She is less of an old hippy than Dad. She is quite tall and has long brown hair, usually tied up. In old photos she's wearing make-up but she doesn't wear it any more. But then she looks quite young for her age, I guess. Her and Dad should both be fat, the stuff they eat, but they're both quite thin. Mum loves books by Ian Rankin and Stephen King. She loves music by Seal and Joni Mitchell. She loves *Forrest Gump* and *Robin Hood, Prince of Thieves*. I don't think she's afraid of much. Apart from maybe something bad happening to Dad or me.

'Throat cancer,' Mum says, later.

'All the rollies, son,' Dad says, managing a feeble laugh.

'Cancer,' I say. 'Cancer.'

'Should be operable,' he says.

'Then why the fuck don't you stop smoking, Dad?'

'Language,' Mum says.

'Fuck off,' I say, and she starts to cry.

I go to the room that used to be my room.

I have to get home.

The next day, over a cooked breakfast, I apologise.

'I'm sorry,' I say. 'I was just shocked.'

'I know, Francis,' Mum says. Dad is outside. He sits in

a deckchair on the tiny patch of grass that is their back garden. Looking up at the sky.

'What's happening next?' I ask.

'He's waiting for the date of his operation. Should be getting a letter any day now. Then he'll go in, and you know. Get the thing cut out.'

'And that's the end of it?'

'All being well.' She smiles at me. A washed-out smile. All being well. 'Francis,' she says, sitting down. 'Your father and I know how you are about all this kind of thing, and—'

'What do you mean?'

'You think about it a lot. You know what I mean.'

'I don't know if I can help it, Mum,' I say. 'It's everywhere. You know, I circled the word cancer every time it appeared in the paper last week. Just to see how many times. Too many. It's not me thinking about it a lot, Mum, it's not me. I can't help worrying. The whole country is obsessed. It's natural, though. I just want to prevent it.'

'No, I know,' she says. 'But we don't want it to get in the way of your life. We don't want you to worry so much you can't, you know. Get on with your life. That's all I meant.'

'What? You want me to just forget about dad dying? Is—'

'He is *not* dying!'

'No, I'm sorry. I know.'

'This is what I mean, though. Always thinking the worst. Fear, Francis. It would be very easy now to be afraid forever.

18

Every little pain or illness. But you can't. Do you understand me? You can't.'

'OK, Mum,' I say, and smile at her. Another washed-out smile. As if it's not already too easy to be too afraid. I blink. 'Mum,' I say, 'I think I want to go back to see my friends.'

'What? Already?'

'I think so. I think it would help.'

'Oh, Francis. I don't know.' She starts shaking her head. 'I don't know about that.' She starts stacking the empty plates.

'As long as I stay here, Mum, I'm just going to be watching him. Waiting for him to start coughing again.'

'I know,' she says. 'That's what I do.'

'I'm sorry, Mum.'

'Don't say sorry. I guess I understand, Francis. I'll take you back to the train station this afternoon. Promise me, though. Promise me you'll be back soon. Come back for Christmas, hey?'

'Yeah, of course. Of course. Thank you, Mum.'

So I'm back on the small, rural train. Crawling through countryside, towns, villages. Watching the sky get deeper in colour. It's not that late: it's just the time of year. Late August. Warm, soft air rises up from the grimy heater running along the bottom of the side of the carriage. It smells dusty. The seats are grey with a pattern of small, green squares. Each is slightly obscured by a smaller, darker-green square. How anybody could be satisfied with the pattern is a mystery. It's horrible. As I look at it, I start to see cells; I start to see the cells that make up human bodies. I start to imagine them splitting, subdividing, mutating. I look away.

The plastic casing that covers the inside of the carriage sides – that is, the wall of the carriage – is beige. Sick beige. The train only has two carriages. They vibrate, rattle and shake. Outside it is dark now. Two girls – one with dark-brown hair and a square jaw and the other with light-brown hair and a big, sharp nose – share jellybeans. They laugh. On the opposite side of the aisle, over the textured, turquoise, plastic floor, a boy in his early teens sits in a seat facing backwards, so that he's looking in the opposite direction to the one we're travelling in. He has very dark – nearly black – hair, and pale skin. He wears a dark green hoodie and black wires snake from his ears. His backpack rests beside him. Portable music players generate an electromagnetic field. Electromagnetic fields, they think, may cause cancer. Behind the boy sits a tall man with a round, tanned, shiny head. He is wearing a suit and forces a mobile phone to his ear with a claw-like hand.

'Yeah,' he says, 'in Wakefield.'

It is quite dark inside the train now. Not dark, but dingy, dim. A woman in a pale blue parka-style coat coughs into her hands and blows her nose. We approach a stop and the boy in the green hoodie stands up to get off. Squares of orange light float across the interior of the train as we pull into the small station. Light that's made it through the windows. As we pull away, the squares of light are a strange whitish-yellow. Like the inside of a grapefruit. On either side of us now, industrial estates and car parks. Outside. But also, the reflections of the inside of the train are visible in the windows. They travel with us. Like ghosts, in that they disappear when the train passes a light source. But are at their most vivid in the deepest dark.

Suddenly, a large, brightly lit object appears in the windows on the left-hand side. Descending as if from the sky and approaching our train at incredible speed. My mouth drops open and a warmth spreads up from my stomach and I laugh. I start to laugh. Dad always says that space is so big that it's stupid not to believe in intelligent extraterrestrial life. I always thought he was just being a fantasist, but now. I press my face to the glass to get a better view of its approach. It's incredible. Beautiful.

'What's tha'?' asks a young boy with a Liverpudlian accent. 'It's gonna hit us!'

'A UFO!' I am about to say. To exclaim. To shout. But his father answers.

'It's another train, son. Another train on a higher line.'

The train runs alongside ours. I stare at all the people on it. I wonder what they think of me. A strange boy crying at them from the window across the space.

JACK

The local papers were full of the news of the remains found up that back alley, except they were all quite vague about it – they didn't say what, exactly, the remains were comprised of, or who had been killed, or who the suspects were, or even when they thought the person might have been killed. Which suggested to me that they *couldn't*, because obviously they would include all the gory details if they could.

Kenny, I thought, as I put the paper down, what were you doing down there? What was on your mouth? Could you be connected? I mean, that would have been ridiculous. But I couldn't let it go. I couldn't forget the bloody-looking stuff on his face. But what could I have told the police? I saw a man sicking up some tomato sauce? No. No, I didn't think so.

'I suppose I should go to work,' I said.

'I'm afraid so,' said Taylor, sitting across the dinner table. 'It's that time again.'

'Taylor,' I said. 'You have to tell Erin how you feel. You

22

have to. She told me so in Ice Bar on Friday. She said if you don't tell her how you feel then she's going to run off with Graham.'

'I know,' he said, 'I know.'

'That bit about Graham, I made that bit up. What's the hold-up, though? You know she likes you too. She's hardly going to say no.'

'I guess. I don't know, Jack; I don't know. I'm nervous. I've never asked a girl out before. She's just – I just want it all to go right and for it all to be alright and just – right, you know?'

'You sound stoned,' I said, standing up.

'I'm not.'

Our kitchen took up the whole basement of our house, and so was pretty big, and it was lit by one of those windows that looked out on to a kind of pit that let light down from the surface. The fridge was covered in magnetic words from the erotic-poetry fridge kit that had been arranged into sentences like TONGUE MY HOT, WET HEART and COME ON YOURSELF, DOG. Taylor would have been responsible for those, probably. There was a row of wall-mounted cupboards, along the top of which we proudly displayed empty bottles that had once contained unusual or unusually strong alcoholic drinks, and there were potted plants behind the sink.

'See you later,' Taylor said. 'Might see you in the canteen. I'll be in at three.'

'Maybe see you there, then,' I said.

*

From the road outside the house, I looked up at Francis' bedroom window and saw that his curtains were closed. They had been closed since he had returned the day before.

The sky was a milky-yellow wash, laced with poisonous-looking streaks of brown vapour. Despite the fact that I was walking, I found myself overtaking cars and buses, the traffic so slow it was more or less stationary. The city was clogging up. All the cities were, as far as I could see, with too many vehicles, too many shoppers, too many plastic bags, and the earth, too; I had read that there were only seven years of landfill left. We were filling it up. The closer I got to work, the thicker the crowds got, the denser the mass, the slower the circulation, the wider the mouths. What day was it? Monday. With working shifts, I lost track.

Looking around the city at everybody with their massive mouths and tiny mobiles and bags of early Christmas shopping, it was as if people traded part of themselves for the money with which to consume and then used that money to fill the vacuum. Especially then, at that time of year, just a couple of months before the desperate frenzy of November and December. Already people seemed laden and haggard, heavy bags stretching their arms. Those people would probably ring me up later, angry about something, no doubt. People liked being angry. They got frustrated, looking for something they'd lost.

Disillusionment was the primary shaping force of my mental landscape, I realised as I walked through the central business district towards the call centre which lurked like a demon totem somewhere in the middle. My feet carried me surely and inexorably towards the pestilential plug-in point of the desk. Disillusionment was the ice that formed the glaciers that carved out my world. Manchester – the city, any city – was grim, and adult life was rubbish. I missed the forests and rivers I grew up with. I wanted them back.

The building was one of those that looked quite clean and shiny and impressive until you got close up and saw the grime and graffiti and large, flat planes of dull colour. I swiped my employee card through the little black reader and the LED turned from red to green to indicate that the door was open.

That switch in the colour of the LED was the point at which the real numbness kicked in, and oh God, I thought, I'm in now, it's beginning. I pushed open the door and stepped through. I worked five storeys up, and so headed for the stairs.

There was something organic in the electronic buzz and hum and the complex interactions of the call centre, partly because the carpets and walls were green. It might have been a fresh green once upon a time, but now it was just kind of rotten. And I don't mean 'organic' in a positive sense, like the forests that I used to wander through when I was a child. I mean like we were a half-dead riot of maggots, blind and buried inside a rancid avocado.

I was sitting at my desk with my head resting on my

hand, my fingers holding the bridge of my nose and my eyes closed, trying not to see the CASH FOR CHRISTMAS posters pushing overtime, when I heard somebody running. I looked up and saw a girl dashing past the bank of desks, and my stomach suddenly seemed to be trying to crawl up through my chest cavity.

She was beautiful, but not the tawdry modern beautiful that was used to describe pop stars or actors or actresses, she was beautiful like I imagined Morgana le Fay to have been: delicate yet severe, wild yet self-possessed. She had long, flowing black hair that streamed out behind her, glossy and gorgeous, held back from her face by a deep red headscarf, and her pale skin was smooth across her even, well-defined features, and the light glinted from three adjacent lip-rings grouped together at the right-hand end of her full lower lip. Her ears were small and sharp and she had red eye make-up on that swept backwards to fill the spaces between her thin eyebrows and her big, green eyes. She wore a black shirt and a lacy, layered calf-length black skirt. She looked at me as I stood up, and then looked away. Was she upset about something? I watched as she disappeared into the girls' toilets.

'Jack,' said somebody from immediately behind me, and I turned around to see Artemis Black, the manager of this floor, a big, bald, well-dressed man, with a little black goatee. 'What the hell are you doing, you awkward dreamy bastard? Sit your arse right back down right now, get your headset on, and wrap your ears around some of our lovely customers. Any more funny business and I'll have to start

26

thinking about you, and that would be bad news.' He stopped to draw breath. 'This here is a job for life, and you'd be a fool not to realise that, Jack. My boy.'

'Yes sir,' I said, and sat back down, and he smiled, nodded and wandered off, evidently satisfied. I put my headset back on and looked back over at the toilet door, and then I looked back at Artemis and waited until Artemis had disappeared into the maze of desks and whiteboards and raised management platforms. Then I looked back at the toilet door to see the girl re-emerging, red-eyed and pale. She started making her way back through the room. I stood up and threw my headset down on the desk. It was not like me to ignore my boss so decisively, but I could sense that something important was happening. I hurried over to her, through the thick air and in between the over-flowing desks, and the closer I got the more nervous I became, until, by the time I reached her, I couldn't think of anything to say. Not just because of my nerves; close up, her eyes paralysed me.

'Hello?' she said, after a moment or two of us just looking at each other, and her voice was smoky, dark. I had Artemis' words running through my head – awkward, dreamy bastard.

'Hi,' I said. 'Um. Are you OK? Do you want a cup of tea?'

'Yes. Oh, yes please. That would be good. Are you on your break?'

'No,' I said. 'But it's OK. Let's go to the kitchen.'

The kitchen that adjoined the main space of the call centre

was a greyish, grimy little box lined with chipped tiles and lit by a strip-light that buzzed like a huge insect. We drank tea from other people's mugs that were heavily stained and had faded phrases printed on the side. Hers said something like 'I'll wake up sober, but you'll always be ugly', and mine said, simply, 'You underestimate the power of the Dark Side'. Some ancient *Star Wars* mug.

'I just had a sad call,' the girl said to me. 'Reminded me of my mum.'

'Why? Is she dea— I mean, is she, um, why did it remind you of your mum?'

'It was somebody ringing up to close their mother's account down, because she'd died. And yeah – my mum's dead too.'

'I'm sorry,' I said. It was hot there in the kitchen, and I felt red-faced and sweaty with the heat, with embarrassment, with nerves.

'Don't worry,' she said, smiling. 'It was a while ago. It's just sometimes you get a call that brings it all back. When they're crying and stuff, over the phone. I remember doing that too. I was probably speaking to somebody in this building at the time. It's weird to think about it like that.'

'What's your name?' I asked.

'Jennifer,' she said. 'Sorry. I should have started with that really.'

'Don't worry. I'm Jack.'

'Nice to meet you, Jack.' She shook my hand over the table and smiled a brilliant smile. Her teeth were small and bright.

'Nice to meet you too.'

'I'm not going to be here much longer,' she said. 'Handed my notice in a few days ago.'

'Lucky thing,' I said.

'Well, I've inherited a lot.'

'Oh,' I said, and looked down at the table. 'I'm sorry.'

'Stop saying sorry!' she said. 'I mean, I inherited the money and the house a while ago. I just kept on working because I thought it was what I should do. But then I started thinking, you know, may as well attempt to live the kind of life I want to live. Since I've got the opportunity. It's more than most people ever get.'

'I suppose,' I said. 'And what kind of life is that?'

'I studied design at university. And I'd love to have my own studio, you know, somewhere to study and think and draw.'

She fell silent.

'Yes,' I said.

'I never had time to keep it up, what with working and looking after mum. Although I did make my own clothes. I lived with her, see, and looked after her. We had a carer, but only for when I was at work. I didn't mind, but I'd like to get back into it. The drawing and things. And I'd like an interesting house. A project, you know. And to grow my own vegetables, to raise my own poultry and livestock.' She sipped from her mug. 'I don't have much faith in the systems that govern this country. Or this world. I want to be self-sufficient. Only then will I feel safe.'

'That sounds like a good plan,' I said. 'That sounds like

a really good plan.' We both went quiet for a moment and she looked at the table and I looked at her. 'Must have been hard,' I said, 'looking after your mother. What was it she had?'

'Brain tumour. Yeah, it was difficult. Distressing. I mean apart from the bodily stuff. She didn't understand how one day was different to the one that went before, or how time changes things. She would get me mixed up with the me I was years ago, when I was a little girl. Are you sure you don't mind me talking about this?'

'I don't mind, if you don't.'

'Thank you. I wouldn't mind, actually. I don't really have many friends is the truth. She wouldn't speak much, apart from tapping the side of her head and saying "There's something in here. Something in here with me. How am I ever going to look after you now?" She used to think I was a little girl. Didn't see that things had turned around.' She shook her head and drummed on the tatty table with her fingers as if to distract herself.

The door swung open and Kenny entered the room. My body tensed as those empty eyes of his rolled over me. Had he seen me in the alley?

'Well,' he said. 'What's all this? Having a meeting, are we? A nice little chat?' He spoke in a complete monotone. In the flat, colourless light, I saw that he was incredibly thin. The light gleamed from his flat, greasy hair. I could smell something rancid on his breath, even though he was still standing by the door.

'We're on our breaks,' I said.

'We all know that's not true. What's wrong this time, Jennifer?' He looked her up and down as he spoke, and the way his eyes roved so slowly across her body unnerved *me*, let alone Jennifer.

'Nothing,' she said. 'Nothing is wrong, thank you, Kenny.'

'You don't know what I'd do for a chance to take a nice girl like you out,' he said. 'You're a lovely-looking girl, you are, Jenny. Can I call you Jenny?'

'It's Jennifer,' she said.

'Lovely-looking, you are. Probably won't want to go on a date with old Kenny Hicks though, eh? Looks like it'll just be Kenny alone again tonight.' His gaze slid off her and across the table until it was resting on me and he licked his lips. 'Have a good time the other night, Jackie boy?'

'What?' I tried to say, but it was just a croak. 'What do you mean?'

'You know,' he said. 'The other night, out in town. We saw each other, didn't we?'

Blast. Blast blast blast. He *had* seen me there in that alley and he must have known that I'd seen him doing whatever he was doing; if he did have anything to hide, he'd try to—

'Across the bar,' he said, nodding slowly. 'That was you, wasn't it?'

'Oh! Oh, yeah. That was me. Ha ha. Yes. That was me, alright.'

Kenny sighed and shook his head. 'I'm just not that

31

memorable, am I? But anyway. It's nice to have a catch-up.' He looked back at Jennifer again. 'Nothing like a good chinwag with a couple of friends. If I were you, though, I'd be getting back to your desks before I have to report you for taking the piss.'

'We'll have to go out for a drink after work then, Jack,' Jennifer said. 'I'll email you my number, yeah?'

I looked at her blankly for a moment, amazed, as my brain spluttered and spat. 'That would be great,' I managed, eventually.

'Good,' she said. She smiled a beautiful smile at me and stood up. Kenny offered her one of his skin-splitting grins as she left the room, but the moment she'd gone it disappeared from his face as suddenly as if it had fallen off, and his blank gaze turned to me. He didn't say anything, just stared at me, and I felt like I was in a room with an inanimate – yet homicidal – mannequin.

I stood and walked over to the door, past him, and as I did so he said something very quietly. 'I saw you,' he said. 'I saw you.'

I turned to look at him, but his mouth had closed again and his small eyes gave nothing away. They might as well have just been painted on. I hurried out on to the call-centre floor.

FRANCIS

Somebody knocks at my bedroom door. I look at it blankly for a moment.

'Come in,' I say. It feels like I am just waking up. But I've been awake for hours.

'Hi, Francis,' Erin says. She opens the door and sticks her head round. 'You OK?'

'Yes, thank you,' I say.

'You're not, are you?'

'I'm OK,' I say.

'I brought you a cup of tea.'

'Thank you.'

She smiles. Her mouth a soft curve through the shock of red hair hanging over her face. Erin loves *Blade Runner*, *No Country For Old Men*, *The Virgin Suicides*. She reads a lot. She likes Thomas Pynchon and Dave Eggers and also Anne Rice. She listens to everything. Hundreds of bands and artists that I've never heard of. Sometimes I can make out Grandaddy or Björk. She is scared of not enjoying music when she's older. She is afraid of ghosts. She is also scared of her dreams of whales. In her dreams, all kinds of whales swim through dark murky water. Moaning. Erin is afraid of their sheer size and their sadness. And the chance that they might just swallow her by mistake.

'How are your parents?' she asks.

'My dad's ill,' I say. 'Throat cancer. That's why they wanted me to go back.'

'Francis,' she says, 'I'm sorry.'

'No,' I say. 'It's operable. I don't know why I'm being so miserable.'

'You don't have to justify it. It's understandable,' she says.

'It feels good to be back here, though. Surrounded by people again. Feels a bit more *alive*, you know. A bit further away from dying. It feels safer. I know that sounds stupid.'

'It does sound a bit stupid.'

'Are you working today?' I say.

'No, are you?' she says.

'No. Thank fuck. You want to play Mario Kart?'

'I think that would be amazing,' she says. 'In fact, I've got an unopened box of Jaffa Cakes in my cupboard. As long as Graham hasn't found them. The way that boy eats. I don't know.'

'Jaffa Cakes?'

'Jaffa Cakes.'

'Today's turning out, you know. It's getting better, anyway.'

'Too right.'

'Have you asked Taylor out yet?'

'Don't you start on that, Francis. Don't you start.'

'Before we go downstairs, Erin. Have you got any stories you could tell me?'

'Afraid not, Francis. Not at the moment.'

Erin writes small story-like things that she'll memorize and recite to her friends. She doesn't want to do anything with them. Jack tells her to try and get published. But she's not interested in that. She's interested in the oral tradition, she says. Camp-fire stuff. And then Graham makes some sort of joke about blow-jobs.

'Oh well,' I say. 'You can't force these things, I guess.'

'You're dead right,' she says.

Mario Kart – the racing video game – is probably the thing that unites the five of us. Me, Erin, Jack, Taylor and Graham. As a house. It's one thing we all enjoy. Have in common. I think that, really, the most accurate description of somebody is a list of what they like. The things they've chosen. People are just accumulations of likes and dislikes. So if you drew a Venn diagram of all the things that we – the five of us – like, the area in which all of our circles overlap would contain one thing: Mario Kart.

I turn the console on and flash through the menu screens. I select my character. Erin comes back into the room with the Jaffa Cakes. And fresh cups of tea.

Amazing.

Graham emerges from his bedroom about half an hour later and joins in. I don't know what he does in there.

35

Probably just watches pornography. Graham likes American remakes of Japanese horror films. He considers the originals to be boring. He likes *Scary Movie* a *lot*, and all of the sequels. He likes most films that are adaptations of other things or other films. He loves listening to the Kaiser Chiefs and other bands that make that kind of anthemic, fist-in-the-air pop-rock. He is afraid of ugliness and bird flu and any kind of physical deformity. I think that deep down he is intensely scared of women.

We are still playing Mario Kart later, when both Taylor and Jack are back from work. Pretty soon we are all playing. One person has to sit out because we only have four controllers. But they then replace whoever loses that particular race.

Nobody asks for any detail on my visit home. And I'm glad. I guess they can tell I'm distracting myself from something.

Graham ends up playing as Princess Peach. A character wearing a crown and a huge pink dress, and driving a pink car.

'It's like one of those cars you see covered in *Playboy* stickers,' he says, concentrating on the screen.

'It's not really like that,' I say. I'm in first place.

'It is a bit like that,' he says. 'You know those cars, though? I'm always disappointed when I see the drivers. They're never that attractive. I always expect them to be incredibly hot, but they're just not.'

'You know, Graham,' says Taylor, who is sitting out, 'there's this idea that you shouldn't just judge people on the way they look. The idea that personalities can be as attractive as faces or bodies. Have you ever thought about it?'

'I have heard such things said,' Graham says, 'but I'm not convinced.'

'Is that why you spend so much time on your own appearance?' asks Erin – in second place and accelerating – with a smile.

'I'm going for the rugged look,' Graham says. 'You know that. Yeah, but anyway. Appearances matter, Taylor, whether you like it or not. Just because you look like Nick Cave.'

'Nick Cave is *hot*,' Erin says.

Me, Jack and Graham just stay quiet. In an effort to keep the uncomfortable silence going for as long as possible. All five of us are staring at the screen now. Jack is in last place, as ever. Erin and I are neck and neck on the long bridge that precedes the finish line. Just as we're about to make the other side, though, she sideswipes me into the river below. I hang my head. Erin wins.

I look at Taylor. He is looking at Erin.

I guess appearances do matter more than anything if the world is full of people like Graham.

'Who wants a cup of tea?' I ask. 'Everybody? Jack and, um, Graham, can you give me a hand carrying them up please? Thank you.'

I try to give Taylor a meaningful look as we leave the room.

*

'I think I've met someone,' Jack says. In the kitchen. He leans against the washing machine. Above which a big *Barton Fink* poster has been stuck to the wall. 'I mean I really do.'

'Is she hot?' Graham asks.

'Yes, yes she is, actually,' Jack says. In the voice of Jemaine from *Flight of the Conchords*. Saying *yes* like *yis*. It's a good impression. It makes me laugh so much I spill the sugar all over the worktop.

'What's her name?' I ask.

'Jennifer,' Jack says.

'What's she into?' I say.

'Oh, I don't know,' he says.

'What if you find out that she likes the Foo Fighters and Woody Allen films?' I say. Jack hates the Foo Fighters and Woody Allen films.

'It won't matter,' he says. 'I really like her.'

He seems serious, so I let it drop. Even though really I wonder how he can think that he likes her so much when he doesn't even really know her. I put sugar in Graham's tea. And Taylor's.

'You put the sugar in before the milk?' Graham asks.

'Yeah,' I say.

'You're such a fucking freak,' he says.

'I know,' I say. 'But at least I'm not a dick. At least I'm not branded head to fucking toe. At least I haven't sold my skin to a thousand different corporations, like you.'

'What are you talking about?'

'Your clothes,' I say. 'Your label-hunting tendencies. Your brand loyalty.'

'Nothing wrong with buying quality,' he says, sniffing.

'There is if it's overpriced tat and unethically produced,' I say.

'If it's tat, why would it be overpriced?' he says. 'If it's sweatshop, why's it all so fucking expensive?'

'To trick gullible people into thinking it's good,' I say. 'Not to mention profit! You give them money in order to display their name. They fuck you over every which way.'

'Well, it's my money,' he says. 'I'll spend it how I want.'

'See,' I say. 'This is the great illusion. "I've worked all my life for this money and I'm going to spend it how I like", etc. That's the *myth*. That because you can afford something you are entitled to it. That's why there are so many fucking cars in the world. That's why there are so many nuclear weapons. That's why there are sweatshops, rising sea-levels, snuff movies.'

Graham sticks his middle finger up at me. 'Swivel,' he says.

'They own you,' I say. 'Body and soul.'

Graham unzips his flies and shows me his bollocks. I open his cupboard and put as much of his food onto the worktop as I can before he stops me. That is my revenge. He hates it when I do that.

'Anyway,' Jack says, glancing briefly at Graham's still-exposed testicles. 'Jennifer was upset. Her mum died recently. A few months ago, I think. And she had a call that reminded her of it.'

'It was cancer, was it?' I ask. 'I mean, it was probably cancer, wasn't it?'

39

'It was,' Jack says. 'Brain tumour. How did you know?'

'Always is,' I say. Toast can cause cancer. Plastic bottles. Red meat. Tissue damage. The sun. The situation is hopeless. It comes from nothing. Maybe I could talk to Jennifer about it. She might understand. Erin's good to talk to. And so are Jack and Taylor. But none of them know what it's like to think about it all the time.

'Kenny Hicks came in though,' Jack continues, 'and we had to get back on the phones. He's such a pervert, he is. One day somebody's going to knock seven bells out of him. You can see it coming.'

'Deserves everything he gets,' Graham says. He finally zips himself back up. 'There are some people in this world that I'd properly go to town on if it wouldn't land me in prison.'

'You know Morgana le Fay, from the King Arthur legends?' Jack says. 'Well, that was who I thought of when I saw Jennifer. And Morgana – she was supposed to be able to inspire profound change. And guide in times of intense emotion, like anger or lust. Also she was very good at sex, apparently.'

'Well, she wasn't though, was she?' Graham says. 'Because she wasn't real, was she? This Jennifer bird isn't Morgana le Fay, Jack. You're just getting excited.'

Jack comes over to the side to pick up a couple of mugs. 'I know,' he says. 'I know.'

Jack loves myths. And legends. And folklore. And all that kind of stuff. He reads a lot of history. Sometimes he talks like a book. He writes articles for local papers and magazines. About nearby haunted houses. Or the origin stories that gather around unusual features of the landscape. He's even had one or two short pieces published in the *Fortean Times*. He loves the Narnia books, especially the ones where some kid discovers another world – *The Magician's Nephew*, or *The Lion, the Witch and the Wardrobe*. But he doesn't like the film adaptations. As far as films go, he likes documentaries – *Grizzly Man, Touching the Void*. He listens to Fleetwood Mac, Sigur Rós, R.E.M. He is scared, above all things, of the world being no more than it appears to be.

I think that it's already too much.

He is a complete fantasist. He pays no attention to the war. To the economic situation. To the human-rights atrocities in the news. To climate change. To cancer, getting closer. To the things that stop me sleeping. He just retreats into this other world. That doesn't exist. He reminds me of Dad.

'You'll have to invite her round,' I say. 'This Jennifer.'

'I will,' he says.

We pause in the doorway of the living-room. Erin and Taylor are kissing. They're sitting side by side. Holding hands. Their heads turned towards each other. Like five-year-olds might kiss each other. I guess it's kind of sweet.

'What's happened?' Jack asks. 'Are the fires out in hell? Is it getting cold down there?'

'No,' Taylor says. 'It's quite simple. It's commonly believed amongst scientists that, given an infinite timespan – like the length of time it takes you reprobates to make the tea – then anything that can happen will happen.'

'Might not give you your tea now,' Graham says. 'Arsewipe. Talking science at us when our hands are full.'

'Don't you talk to my boyfriend like that,' Erin says. 'And give us our fucking tea.'

Taylor loves *Blade Runner* and *Jules et Jim*. He loves Truffaut. He loves weird instrumental music that I can't listen to, like Philip Glass and John Cage. When he's feeling poppy he listens to Godspeed You! Black Emperor, or Tom Waits. He is addicted to the *Resident Evil* series of video games. He knows every word Orwell ever wrote. And he reads a lot of science books too. He is terrified of growing old. Getting lonely. Becoming stupid.

We hand out the teas and I look behind me. Back through the open door. Opposite the doorway – on the hallway wall – there is a huge poster. We took it from a bus shelter. It advertises the remake of *Dawn of the Dead*. I glance at it. Again, the only way of working out the true personality of a person, their true soul, is by their taste. In films, music, books. Everything sprouts from the one root. The words across the bottom of the poster resonate with me every time I read them.

WHEN THERE'S NO MORE ROOM IN HELL,
THE DEAD WILL WALK THE EARTH.

JACK

I tried clothes on in front of a little mirror that was about five inches square. The smell of my rattan mat permeated the room and I felt sick at the thought of mine and Jennifer's first proper 'date'.

Sometimes Francis bothered me. Erin had told us all about Francis' dad after he went to bed the previous night, and it was awful, but still. His obsession with what people *liked*, and the implication that not knowing what Jennifer liked or didn't like meant that I didn't really know her at all, I mean, it boiled down to defining a person by what they *bought*, really, didn't it? It boiled down to a list of all the crap that people bought in order to fill the emptiness they felt inside themselves. What Francis thought of as the essence of a person was more accurately defined as the substitute for the essence of a person, as far as I could see.

I decided on an outfit – jeans and a shirt, which is all I ever really wore when not at work – and looked for my hair stuff. I looked on the windowsill, and found myself looking through the glass at the early September clouds.

'I don't believe in monogamy,' Jennifer said. 'I think it's important that you know that right from the start.'

'OK,' I said, something quivering inside of me. Morgana le Fay, I thought, Morgana le Fay would never have been monogamous either. 'OK.'

'I honestly believe you can love more than one person at any one time. And also that sex is something that should be enjoyed outside of love as well as inside of love.'

'OK,' I said.

'I know we're not together or anything, but I don't want you to get the wrong idea. Because I like you, and I think that something might happen between us.'

'OK,' I said. 'Yes. I think that too.'

She looked at me over the table and our empty cocktail glasses, her huge green eyes hypnotic.

'What bar are we in?' she asked. 'I can't even remember, they're all so similar. And I can't believe the Fidel Castro and Che Guevara posters!'

'It's probably called Cuba or Havana or something like that,' I said, but really I was still thinking about sex.

'Communist revolution consumed by capitalist enterprise, and then regurgitated. Idealism as a theme.' She shook her head. 'It's sad. I don't really like it in the city. All cities are basically the same and all the places within the cities are basically the same, so wherever you end up for a drink or a sandwich or whatever, it doesn't really

44

matter. It was inevitable that you would end up there. There was never anywhere else to go. Well, it's a generalisation. I know.'

'I suppose if you take the time to look, you can find all sorts of decent places,' I said. 'But you have less time in cities.' This is better, I thought. I'm finally engaging. But really, I was still thinking about sex.

'Sometimes I think I'm growing up in the wrong decade,' she said. 'I should be in the sixties.'

'I'm a bit like that. Sometimes I think I should have been alive at the beginning of the nineteenth century.'

'Why?' she asked, laughing.

I shrugged. 'Oh,' I said. 'You know.'

I was glad that she didn't like the city. I supposed I shouldn't really get involved with somebody who didn't believe in relationships, but I didn't know if I could help it. I looked at her. How could I not fall for her when she said the kind of things that I thought about saying? Although in truth I fell for her the moment I saw her.

Her hair was wavy tonight, held back by a rust-coloured headscarf, and she was wearing a brown dress that reminded me of old-fashioned Roma-style gypsies, like those in the *His Dark Materials* trilogy, and she told me that she made it herself. There was a story about an old gypsy fortune-teller who, apparently, spent so long hunched over, smoking a pipe, that she couldn't straighten her body out at all, and when she died she had to be buried in a cube-shaped coffin. I didn't mention it though. I was afraid that Jennifer would think me strange.

I became aware of a figure somewhere in the middle distance, over her left shoulder, standing absolutely stationary, and I looked up at the figure, but it was moving now, making its way towards the exit. Its identity was difficult to establish amongst the growing crowd, but I was pretty sure it was him. Kenny.

'Shall we go?' I said.

'Yeah,' she said. 'Shall we go to yours?'

'Yeah,' I said. 'OK. If that's alright with you.'

Outside, the street was nearly as bright as it was during the day, and it was as if we'd driven the natural night-time out of our cities with electricity, and replaced it with a darkness of our own invention, all muggings, murders, rapes. The Christmas lights were up but not yet turned on. Electricity meant we could work all kinds of shifts and stay out all night with our vision unimpaired, and it turned us into unnatural creatures, awake and ravenous all the time.

FRANCIS

Jennifer came home with Jack last night. She is like the sky at night. She is beautiful and crisp. She is like frost on a bare black tree. I love her lip-piercings. I love her body. Her skin is pale and her hair is black. She is like all those vampire women in all those black-and-white films. She is like Renée French in *Coffee and Cigarettes*. She is like a chessboard. From the moment I saw her I have been lusting for her. So badly that it has opened something up inside me. Something very much like a wound. She sat on the edge of the sofa. With her feet pointing at each other. And looked around at all the posters. And the shelves full of books and CDs and DVDs. I asked her what she likes.

Jennifer loves *Fear and Loathing in Las Vegas* and *Secretary*. She likes Patti Smith and Eastern European music. She likes books by Kerouac and Aldous Huxley.

When I went to bed, she and Jack were in the living-room drinking wine. And she was still here this morning. I saw her in the kitchen eating a bacon sandwich. Dressed for work. So I guess she stayed the night. I am confused, time-wise. I don't know what day it is. One of the problems with working shifts.

We are out in Manchester. Drinking. In celebration of the fact that none of us are working this evening. It's 9.57 by the clock on my phone. And we're in a bar called Sandbar. Just off Oxford Road. We sit around a dark wooden table in a corner lit by light from red bulbs.

I am drinking a strong, dark imported beer out of a strange, squat bottle. Graham is drinking lager. Taylor and Erin are drinking red wine. Jack is drinking a guest beer called Copper Dragon. Jennifer is drinking whisky and Coke. She finishes it and sets the glass down.

'Today was my last day,' she says. 'Thank fuck. No more scripts. No more cash incentives. No more sales. No more debt collection. No more Kenny!'

'Speak for yourself,' Graham says.

'God,' Jennifer says. 'I'm sorry. I just didn't – didn't think.'

'Ignore him,' Jack says. 'Nothing to stop him looking for another job if he's that miserable. Except he's too busy updating his profile on Facebook.'

'What are you going to do, Jennifer?' I ask.

'Start drawing again,' she says. 'Start designing. Try to find a house that I can afford to buy and start living like, you know, freely. Maybe even set up some sort of commune, or collective. I'm nostalgic for the sixties and I wasn't even alive then.' She laughs. 'We'd grow our own vegetables.'

48

'It should be Kenny who's leaving, really,' Taylor says. 'Should have been sacked a long time ago for harassment.'

'He should have been,' Erin says, 'but it's one of those places where you can be as vile, malicious and poisonous as you like and it won't count against you. You could be the sorriest excuse for a human being. You could be a thousand rats stacked up inside a suit and still do OK. Most workplaces are like that I guess. Kenny will always be there. Always be fine.'

'So what are you going to do for work?' I ask Jennifer.

'Oh,' she says. And falls silent. She looks a bit embarrassed. 'I don't know if I'll get another proper job. I'm going to sell the house, and – well, I was left a bit of money. I'm going to try and set up a studio, sell the clothes that I make, you know. Might be a while before that ever makes any money though. Wouldn't mind doing some sort of editing or proofreading if I got desperate, but I doubt that it's that easy to get into.' She laughs again. 'I'm just a bit of a pervert for grammar.'

I like the way she says *pervert*. Her lip-rings shine. I want to ask her about her mum. I want to tell her about Dad. She is wearing a tight, low-cut top.

'Who wants a drink?' Jack asks.

'Yes please,' I say. I down the one I've got.

'Tell us a story, Erin,' Graham says. He slurs his words.

'I need to think of one first,' she says. 'I had this dream a while ago. It was strange. Haven't been able to think of much else since.'

'Write about that, then,' I say.

49

'No,' she says. 'I didn't like it. It was about a giant. I can't. I don't know why, but I can't.'

'Make something up on the spot,' I say.

'Well,' she says. 'It won't be very good. OK. I'll just tell you something that happened. A few little things that happened.'

'OK,' I say.

'One day I went to the dentist after work. This was out of town. He was playing some Dire Straits album quietly in his room. I listened to 'Sultans of Swing' and he gave me a scale and a polish. Then, on the way to the train station, I saw an ex-boyfriend's mother and sister walking along. His sister nodded as if to say hello, but thankfully his mother didn't see me. At the train station, the guy in the ticket office was listening to Joy Division. 'Love Will Tear Us Apart' was the particular song. I bought my ticket and sat on a platform near the back of a nearby super-market. I could smell baking bread and nobody else was around and I couldn't hear any music.'

She falls silent and frowns.

'Go on,' I say.

'It was wonderful,' she says.

'Is that the end?' I ask.

'Yeah.'

'I didn't know people could listen to music in the ticket offices at Piccadilly,' I say.

'I don't think they can,' she says. 'I made that bit up.'

The table is dark and shiny with varnish. Various chips

in the surface reveal the bare, pale wood beneath. People fill the room up. The walls are red brick with tall, thin, black radiators plumbed in. Lights hang on long wires. Sandbar. This is Sandbar. My head is in my hands. There comes a point in every night like this. When you realize that understanding has just slipped out of reach. People around me are saying things but I can't put them together.

I get up and go to the toilet. I push open the door marked TOILETS and am confronted with a small, confusing space. All the walls are covered with pages of magazines. There are two doors, one on the right and one on the left. I don't know which to go through at first. It takes me an age to find the symbol for 'men'. It's hidden amongst the pictures and words that surround it. I push the door open. Behind it is a long, dented urinal that looks like it's full of thick piss. There's a cubicle at the end. That's where I go.

I push open the cubicle door and lift the seat. The toilet water is red and there's something opaque at the bottom of it. Probably shit. But I can't be certain because of the red water. Rusty-brown gobbets of something are splattered all over the bowl. Looks bloody. I leave the cubicle and use the urinal. Somebody has something wrong inside of them. Some part of their body is the wrong shape.

Back at the table, I can hear 'Jailhouse Rock' playing. Graham is arm-wrestling with Jack and winning. Crap photos adorn the red brick walls, printed on canvas. A girl in a woolly hat is dancing outside the window.

Amongst the reflections and the streetlamps. A song by Nina Simone starts up: 'Feeling Good'.

Dad loves Steven Spielberg films, especially *Close Encounters of the Third Kind*. He loves the Blue Oyster Cult and Ozric Tentacles and Joni Mitchell. And he sits in the car to listen to them. Because Mum isn't so keen, apart from the Joni Mitchell. Sometimes the car fills with smoke from his rolled-up cigarettes. I think sometimes he smokes cannabis. Judging by the smell of the car. He goes out on clear nights looking for UFOs. Looking for a sign of some other world. He is scared that we won't make contact with extraterrestrials in his lifetime. He is more scared – terrified – that we won't ever make contact at all. The idea of a lifeless universe stops him from sleeping, Mum told me. And it makes him deeply unhappy for days if he really thinks about it. He is also scared of his boss at the warehouse-sized computer shop that he works in. He works at the branch on the industrial estate up on the edge of town. He looks like Tony Robinson, with thicker glasses maybe. And slightly longer, whiter hair. And maybe a little bit taller. Wears a lot of open-necked shirts and beads. He looks basically like an old hippy. His name is Eric. I want to tell Jennifer about him. But not here, not in front of everybody else. I pick up my bottle. Dad is nostalgic for the sixties, like Jennifer. But he was really there.

'Francis,' Taylor says. 'Come on. We're leaving.'

*

Now we're at Trof. In the Northern Quarter. The seedier, more fashionable district of the city. We're outside in the smoking area because it's so full and hot indoors. Although I don't actually smoke. For fear of the damage. It must be a weekend, I think. Otherwise this place would be closed. Graham is taking something in the toilet. It's raining. There is a tarpaulin ceiling, but it's only half-rolled out. We huddle beneath it, but the rain drips off it and it drips down the drainpipes and it drips on to the low wooden stools and it spreads out towards us, making our bottoms wet. Graham comes back.

On the other side of the balcony, red brick walls and huge air-vents and dull metal chutes plunge downwards into darkness. There is a gap between two of the walls through which the bright, white horizontal bars of a multi-storey car park can be seen. Behind the car park, the squareish bulk of some giant shopping centre rears up into the sky. Bright red neon letters adorn the top. Light falls down it. It's a cathedral. We sit here for hours, drinking, talking.

Later. Taylor and Erin sit next to me. 'I didn't tell you the real ending to my story before,' Erin whispers.

'What really happened?' I say.

'That's not what I mean. I told you what happened, more or less. But there was an ending that came to me that I didn't tell you.'

'What was it?'

'Well I was sitting on the platform at the train station. My train was late. There were no announcements and nobody around to ask about it. By the time the train finally arrived, it had gone dark. It pulled up, but the doors didn't open. I stood by one of them, waiting. Nothing moved for ages. And then the doors opened, and a tall man in a long black coat got off, and he had hooves.'

'Ha,' I say. 'I like that ending.'

'I don't,' she says.

'But you made it up,' I say.

'I don't know,' she says. She looks confused. 'I don't think I did, not really. But at least I can say for certain that it didn't really happen.'

'It's that dream you had,' Taylor says. 'Resurfacing. At times of great communal anxiety more and more people report visions of strange creatures. People were seeing angels everywhere in 1999.'

'Are we in a state of great communal anxiety?' Erin says.

'I think maybe it has become constant,' Taylor says.

'I don't know,' I say. 'Maybe it's getting worse.'

Later. I'm staring at Jennifer. I drink her in. Absorb her. Like she is liquid. And I am soft, blank paper.

The six of us get back to the house. We are standing in the road. It is a quiet road: a cul-de-sac. The rain is heavier now. The sky is throwing it down like it doesn't want it any more. Go on, the sky is saying. Get down. Get out of me. Go. The sky is black.

'Come on, Graham!' Erin says. She is wearing Taylor's long coat. Shivering.

'Yeah, hang on,' Graham says. He is looking in his shoulder bag. 'It's just in here. Can't see it because of all these receipts. This whole bag is just full of fucking receipts. So many fucking receipts. Who'd think there are so many fucking receipts in the world? It's somewhere under all these receipts. Just a minute. So many fucking receipts. Hang on. Here it is.' He holds up the key. 'We're in.'

JACK

We woke to the sound of the alarm clock on Jennifer's phone, and it was wonderful, some sort of slow violin music that seemed to rise gently, lifting us out of sleep along with it.

The room was still dark, but that kind of darkness through which you can still see things, a darkness alleviated by dim light filtering in through the curtains. I sat up on the edge of the bed and looked for the glass of water that I had put on the floor the night before. Finding it seemed to take me an age. I took a drink to wake my mouth up.

My room was quite large and the walls were painted blue and the bed was low, snuggled into a corner, with a plain orange bedspread thrown over it. Against the opposite wall was a desk, above which I had a framed *The Lord of the Rings* poster from the sixties, which had been a present from an uncle. The wall to either side of the desk was given over to bookshelves, and I also had books stacked up against the wall all the way around the room.

'What day is it?' I asked.

'Sunday,' murmured Jennifer. She was lying on her front, the bedcovers gathered down around her waist. 'Fucking Sunday.' She pushed herself up, swung her legs over the side of the bed, and stood and groaned and sat back down. She was wearing plain white knickers and a small white vest. I battled the urge to reach over and touch her; bring her back into bed with me. She might have let me, but I wanted to save it – save the first experience of her nakedness for when we had time to enjoy it fully.

'I'll get up now as well,' I said.

'Why? You're not working, are you?'

'No. Just thought I'd make you something to eat. Give you a lift to work. Do some reading.'

'You just wait until you stand up and the hangover hits you. Won't be considering such gentlemanly behaviour then, I bet.'

I stood up and it was like something popped inside me. Suddenly I was weak and I wanted to be sick. My head was aching, and felt like a huge raw egg. The thought of raw egg worsened my nausea and I sat back down.

'You're right, of course,' I said, but the words came out thick and muffled.

'Yep,' she said. 'Sleep it off. Don't worry about me, I can just get some toast or something.' She got up again and moved over to the radiator with a grace that was remarkable considering the hangover she must have had, and picked up a towel and turned to me, the towel in one hand, and a strip of early morning light from in

57

between the curtains fell across her body, warping over her glorious curves and colouring her skin in such a way as to make me think of pale blue milk. She smiled.

'Come to my house tonight,' she said. 'It's my turn to host.'

'Will do.' I brought my knees up in order to hide my burgeoning erection. 'Will do. But no alcohol.'

'Have you got an erection?' she asked, still smiling.

'What? No! I mean, oh, not that you don't look nice. You do. But I haven't. Haven't got one. Nope.'

'I know you have,' she said. 'It's OK, you know. I want you to have one. I like that you haven't tried it on while I've been staying, though. Most men would have.'

I looked down at my hands and saw that I'd knotted them together while she'd been talking. 'I wanted to,' I said, still looking down. 'When we were kissing on the first night. Well, every time really. Every time we've been in here. All the time, Jennifer.' I laughed, nervously. 'All the time.'

'Good,' she said. 'I want you to want to.'

'You wear such tiny things at night,' I said.

'It's all part of the fun,' she said and stretched, extending her legs so that she was standing on her toes and lifting her arms up above her head. She leaned backwards and her little top rode up to reveal the undersides of her breasts and I saw, through the fabric, that her nipples were erect.

I realised that she was regarding me from the corner of her eyes as I was staring at her body. Immediately I looked away, at the wall, the curtains, the floor, my hands, and she laughed, her teeth flashing.

'It's OK,' she said. 'It's better than OK. It's a turn-on. Knowing that you're holding back. I like it.'

'I'm sorry,' I said, but I didn't know why.

'Don't you say sorry,' she said. 'Don't you say sorry at all. Just don't get carried away with that cock of yours. Wait for me.'

'I will,' I said. My face felt red. My whole body felt hot.

'Good,' she said. 'I'll see you tonight, then.'

'See you tonight,' I said.

She picked up the bag that contained her work clothes and slowly walked from the room, looking back over her shoulder, smiling that wonderful incendiary smile.

After she had gone I breathed out. How did I end up with a girl like her? But no. I had to remember, she didn't do monogamy. I was seeing her but she was not mine, even though she now owned and controlled every last drop of me, every last sweat-gland, synapse and skin cell, every bodily part of me that was physically real and every soulish part of me that was only hypothetical, owned and controlled them completely and utterly and eternally – she would never be mine.

I heard the shower start up in the bathroom, which was adjacent to my bedroom, and I imagined her rolling that vest up over her head and the steam from the hot water dampening her lips and every other part of her. But I wouldn't let myself get carried away, as she put it, so I gingerly rolled out of bed, the hangover still ugly inside me, and started to get dressed so that I could walk her to the bus stop. Better not drive in that state.

I enjoyed the walk back to the house after the bus had taken Jennifer away. The air was crisp, and my breath misted, but the sun was bright, and I felt my hangover shrinking, and the sky made me think of the Enid Blyton books I used to read when I was little. There was a simile she used in lots of her stories – something like 'the sky looked like the rain had washed it clean'. I couldn't see a clear sky without thinking of Enid Blyton, which would have bothered some people I guess, what with all the racist accusations.

I walked a short distance down a quiet street lined with big terraces – they were like our house, but they felt like they were owned by real adults, real people, and lived in by families, people with mortgages, and long-term plans, and gardens. The houses were well maintained and well defined and livened up with newly painted window-frames and greenery, whereas ours looked a little dilapidated in a minor, roguish sort of way.

I turned off this street on to another with similar houses lining one side of it, but a long fence of spiked, black railings on the other – cast iron – and beyond the fence was a huge expanse of neatly trimmed grass, punctured by the giant crossbars of a rugby pitch. And then beyond the playing field was the school that owned it – a long, low, old building that looked like it was a long way away. I remember one warm night a couple of summers ago when we had walked back from some club in town and stopped there.

'Ten pounds to the naked person who touches the school first,' Taylor had said.

Graham hadn't needed any encouragement, of course, and he'd stripped off drunkenly, left his clothes and shoes here on the pavement, struggled over the fence in such a way as to hang above us all with his legs wide open – Francis, Taylor, Erin and myself all laughing and not knowing where to look – fell down the other side, narrowly missing leaving his scrotum behind on a spike, and then dashed clumsily across the grass towards the shadowy building in the distance. Too shadowy to really even see. It seemed to take forever before we could discern him coming back to us, but I remember our conversation stopping as the pale shape of his body materialised from the darkness. With his long, messy hair, and his big wild beard, and his nakedness, there was some primal aspect to his appearance, something a little intimidating. We fell silent and watched his approach.

'Ten quid, then,' he had said, panting, after dropping back to the ground on our side of the railings.

'Sorry,' Taylor said. 'We can just about see the building, but it's too far away for us to be able to tell if you really touched it or not. In fact, we couldn't even tell if you ran all the way there. For all we know, you stopped somewhere in the middle and lay down to rest.'

'What bollocks!' Graham shouted. 'What absolute bollocks! I can't believe you bunch of fucking arseholes!

You lot are like a bunch of grapes, but made out of arse-holes instead of grapes!'

'Will you put your fucking clothes on, Graham?' Erin said, laughing.

'Also,' Francis said, quite seriously, 'a hole isn't a physical thing that you can join to another hole. It's just the absence of something else.'

'Oh, fuck off,' Graham said, and tripped over his jeans as he tried to put them on.

It was all quite funny at the time, but it felt like things had changed. Even though Taylor and Erin had only been together a few days, I doubted Taylor would be suggesting any naked games with the rest of us, and likewise, I didn't think I'd want Graham exposing his frankly massive manhood in front of Jennifer. Even though she was not all mine. I had to remember that.

I had never been a jealous person. I had never really had a proper relationship to get jealous about, but I thought I could feel it there now, inside me, even though I'd only been seeing Jennifer for a couple of days. I wanted her all – it was that simple. I wanted all her attention, all her mind, all her beauty, all her body.

Tonight, maybe, and I smiled again, and felt a lightness in my chest.

I never wanted to let Jennifer out of my sight and that was the truth. As soon as I realised it I knew it was wrong to want to possess another person so completely, but it was still the truth.

I turned away from the school. As I did so I saw a figure

dart behind a tree at the end of the street and I paused, momentarily, then walked briskly towards it. I turned off on to another side street before I got there. Then I picked up my pace and started to feel hot despite the cold air. I looked behind me and sure enough there was somebody there, a misshapen figure, wrapped up in a thick grey winter coat, loping after me, no longer trying to hide. My first thought was that it was Kenny, but they were a little too tall, and also, I realised, slightly hunchbacked. I started to run properly, trying to ignore the grotesque moaning that the person was making, like a man with no tongue trying to shout. When I got to the next corner, I risked another look behind me and saw that they seemed to be struggling to try and take their coat off, which made no sense to me in the cold. Maybe they were ill in some way, and maybe they weren't dangerous, but all the same I ran full pelt down the next couple of streets, stopping only when I reached our house and threw myself through the front door.

I hated living in this blasted city.

FRANCIS

When I look up, the sun is bright beyond the bay window. The outside world is washed-out and white, with nothing but vague patches of shadow to give shape to things. On this side of the glass the room is big and empty. Two brown sofas, and a glass coffee table. And a brown footrest. And a small TV, and shelves full of books and DVDs and games and even some old videos. There is an empty fireplace and various empty candleholders on the hearth. Used once but never refilled. Erin is sitting next to me and Jack is standing in the doorway. Erin smells like limes. Jack is red-faced and out of breath. He leans on the doorframe. 'You OK, Jack?' I say.

'Yeah,' he says. 'Well, kind of. I walked Jennifer to the bus stop and then, on my way back, I thought someone was following me. Well, they *were* following me. Chased me home.'

'Jesus, Jack,' Erin says. 'Do you know them? Do you need to call the police?'

'No,' he says. 'No. Just some weirdo.'

'You're not the type to make enemies, I guess,' I say.

'Not usually,' he says. 'I think I may have made one in Kenny Hicks, though.'

'Why's that?' I ask.

'Oh, erm, he seems to have a bit of a thing for Jennifer,' Jack says.

'Right,' I say, nodding. 'You don't want that.'

'Any decent person is naturally Kenny's enemy anyway,' Erin says. 'It wasn't him outside, though?'

'No,' Jack says. 'No. It wasn't him. Just be careful if you leave the house.'

There is an *Adbusters* calendar on the wall beside the doorway in which Jack stands. The photograph for this month – October – is of a blank billboard. The walls of the room are painted white. The floorboards are bare.

'Mum rang just now,' I say. 'Dad's got the date for his operation.'

'That's good then,' Erin says. 'It'll all be over before you know it.'

'I guess,' I say. 'Yeah. I hope so.'

I have a bottle of red wine in the kitchen, so I take it upstairs with me along with a glass and one of our many corkscrews. Once in my bedroom I push all the books and magazines off my bed and sit on the edge. I uncork the wine and throw the cork at the far wall. I pour some wine into the glass and look across at the bookcase that's full of books by Stephen King and Robert Rankin and Dean Koontz and Anne Rice. The Anne Rice books are

Erin's, really. Also, there is the big yellow brick of *The Shock Doctrine* by Naomi Klein. Standing out like a lit window at night. I drink some of the wine and inhale some of it in a cough.

My room is square with a desk. And a computer, and a CD player, and a chair and a bed and a TV. And a window and a bookcase and lots of posters and the floor is covered with CDs and DVDs. There is not much wall visible in my room. It is mostly covered in posters. I choose a CD to put on – *As the Roots Undo* by Circle Takes the Square – and press play. I turn the volume up and let the noise wash over me. Fast-moving bricks. Certain words snag in my consciousness but mostly it's just beautiful noise. I sit back down again and drink some more wine. I fill the glass up again. I down it. I fill the glass up again. I turn the TV on and choose a DVD to watch. I find the complete boxed set of *The Outer Limits* and pick a disc at random.

I'm about five minutes into an episode. I haven't seen it before. For some reason I can't tell what's going on. Then I realise that I've still got the music playing, so I turn the TV up louder so I can hear it. It's all too loud, though, so I turn the music off and then turn the TV volume back down again. I watch the bar on the screen shrinking as the sound gets quieter. I put the bottle of wine down. As I do so I see my notebook. I pick it up and let it fall open at any page. On the page that it falls open at, I've written a list entitled Fears.

Car accidents
Earthquakes
Tidal waves
Being stuck in love
Not getting in love
Making someone pregnant

The list goes on and on. For pages. I skip to the end.

Sharks

I don't even remember thinking sharks are that scary. I reach inside my boxer shorts and start checking my testicles for lumps. I flip to the beginning of the book and look in the inside cover. There it is.

To Francis, on your eighteenth birthday – Many Happy Returns! (For recording what you see!) Love Dad.

He gave me this book years ago. And I've only filled half of it. His handwriting is the same as mine. I guess maybe I could go watching for UFOs with him after all. Take this book. Show him that I use it. I mean, I still don't believe in UFOs, but just to spend some time with him. Except he's not going to die, so I shouldn't go acting all weird. That would almost be as if I'm wanting him to die. Acting like he's dying. No. I won't do that.

Blue static fills the TV screen. I'm on my side. The glass and the bottle are both empty too.

JACK

Erin and I remained in the living-room after Francis had gone upstairs.

'He was just sitting here when I got back from the shop,' she said. 'Completely still.'

'Poor Francis,' I said. 'It's not what he needs.'

'No,' Erin said. 'Not what anybody needs.'

'No, but you know what I mean. Francis is a bit low at the best of times.'

'He's just one of those types,' she agreed. 'Melancholic. Will you get in here, out of the doorway? You're making me nervous.'

'Sorry,' I said, shrugging off my coat and sitting down on the other sofa. 'Where are Taylor and Graham?'

'Taylor was on an early this morning. Left ages ago. Be back soon, actually. Graham's still in bed.'

'Taylor's on an early? God. I don't know how he does it.'

'He doesn't really get hangovers. It's magic.' She brushed some hair away from her face. 'Is that Graham I hear emerging?' She cupped her ear.

Graham's room was next door to the living-room, with a window that looked out of the back of the house. Sure enough, we heard the sound of his bedroom door opening accompanied by the blunt chords of some crap band's music. He shambled through to join us, wearing a blue T-shirt that bore the words 'I Facebooked your mum'.

'I like your T-shirt,' said Erin.

'Thank you,' he said. 'I spend fucking hours on Facebook. Thought I'd own up to it at last.'

Graham did indeed spend hours on Facebook, and MySpace, and Second Life, and all those social networking sites. He revealed a creative side online that wasn't that apparent anywhere else. He set up loads of email accounts, then used them to set up loads of different user profiles on the web, and each of these profiles was for a made-up person, more or less, except he gave them all his name – he didn't pretend to be other people in the conventional sense or, at least, not that I knew of. He built versions of himself, almost, and then used them to oversee a vast, labyrinthine network of 'friends' and acquaintances, with whom he communicated more than he did us.

I didn't like those websites – they were all a bit point-less as far as I could see, and somehow symptomatic of something.

'How's it going with Taylor, then, Erin?' I asked.

'Good, thank you,' she said, grinning. 'It's wonderful.'

That evening I stood by my clapped-out old hatchback in the cul-de-sac outside our house and tried to decide whether or not to drive to Jennifer's. Tempting as the car was, I tried not to use it inside Manchester any more than was necessary. Besides, it was not far to the bus stop and once I was on the bus I'd probably be safe from any strange, grey, hunchbacked figures.

About half-way between our house and the end of the short street I stopped because I saw, at my feet, a pool of congealing blood, peppered with dark slimy clots that seemed to swim in it, like bloated insects. Immediately the image of Kenny in the alley came back to me, and so did the panic that propelled me as that sorry, broken man chased me to this very street earlier today, moaning and staggering. I bent down and saw that one of the lumps was actually a solid knot of hair, casting individual strands out to wind through the grim mess, getting entangled with each other and the sinister coagulations that protruded above the liquid surface. They looked like more than just drying blood, and I quickly stood back up in order to prevent reawakening the nausea I had overcome already that morning.

I turned and hurried back to the car.

From Jennifer's address – a Didsbury address – I'd guessed that she lived in a nice part of town, but that didn't prepare me for just how wide and clean and leafy her street was, or how big and shiny the cars were. I didn't feel like I should be there in my little old hatchback; it was more of a crustacean than a vehicle by comparison.

I parked in her driveway and looked up at her house.

It was beautiful: detached, all old red brickwork with white window-frames and a well-maintained ivy plant that covered one wall. It was a proper house. I couldn't help comparing it with ours, which we'd just kind of settled in since university. None of us had ever got around to moving out. Time flies when you're working full time. Overhead, the sky was darkening. I reached over and picked up the carrier bag from the passenger seat – I'd stopped off at an off-licence on the way for some decent wine and crisps – and opened the door, climbed out of the car, and locked it. When I turned around I saw Jennifer standing in the doorway, wearing a black vest and soft-looking white trousers. She too was holding a bottle of wine in one hand, and in the other she held a DVD, and she was smiling. I smiled back.

The next day it was raining and my shift started at ten so I got ready to set off at about half nine to allow for traffic. As I was putting on my waterproof coat Jennifer came downstairs in a dark-green dressing-gown.

'Have a good day, Jennifer,' I said.

She yawned and stretched. 'Oh, I will,' she said. 'Here, Jack. You want to see a film tonight? They're showing *Easy Rider* as a one-off at the Cornerhouse. Some anniversary or something. Seven o'clock.'

'I've never seen *Easy Rider*,' I said.

'You go now,' she said, 'before I recover from the shock of hearing that and start to re-evaluate our relationship.'

'Is it good, then?' I asked.

'It's amazing,' she said. 'I've never seen it on the big screen though. Could be quite special.'

'Then yes,' I said. 'Though I would have come even if I had seen it and they were just showing it on a TV in the corner.'

'Seven o'clock,' she said, and put her arms around my neck and kissed me on the lips.

I sat in the car in some queue and listened to an old mix tape I'd made when I was about fourteen and the tape sounded stretched and warped and I thought that I should play it to Jennifer before it snaps, say here, this is the kind of music I used to like, can you believe it.

As I was logging into my phone and terminal in the huge, dirty room I heard somebody approach me from behind. I could tell from the flat footsteps and wet-mouth noises and sudden cloud of bad breath that it was Kenny.

'Jack,' he said. The room was full of people, but none of them were looking at Kenny or me.

'What?' I said. My voice felt slightly out of my control. 'Kenny, I'm logging in.'

'You're late,' he said. 'Jack. Jack Sprat could eat no fat. Jack. You're late. Supposed to be in at nine.' He picked his teeth with a filthy fingernail.

'No,' I said. 'Wait. I start at ten.'

'Check your shifts.'

'I've got them here.' It seemed to take me an age to find the print-out amongst the papers on my desk, and then I had to scrabble to pick it up, my hands felt like they weren't part of me. Eventually I got hold of it and showed it to him.

'This is wrong,' he said, handing it back after a quick scan. 'Jack Sprat could eat no fat, and his wife could eat no lean.'

'What are you going on about?' I said.

'Your shift has been changed. If you'd checked it at the end of your last shift, you know, like the bosses say you should. Instead of printing them out in advance.'

I turned back to my screen and checked the system and he was right – I was supposed to have started at nine.

'See,' he said, leaning in over my shoulder and breathing all over my face. 'Nine.'

'Yeah, OK,' I said. 'Well, I'll be finishing at six, so it's still eight hours, so that's OK, isn't it?'

'I'm sorry, Jack,' he said, and smiled faintly. 'If there was anything I could do to get you off the hook then I would, honest. But there's rules about this kind of thing, and I'm just Kenny, I'm just a nobody round these parts.' He sighed deeply. The weirdly strong smell of his breath clung to my nose and mouth like cobwebs.

'What are the rules, then?' I asked. Outside the rain was getting heavier, and I could see it pounding into the windows.

'You have to stay an extra hour, Jack,' he said. 'I'm sorry.'

'I've already said that I will,' I said.

'No, I mean an *extra* hour. You know. Until seven.'

'That's not true,' I said. 'Where does it say that?'

73

'It's in the contract,' he said. 'It's in the conduct book. If it wasn't, then I wouldn't have to be such an old stick in the mud, but it is, and I do.' His attempt at a smile disappeared and his flat eyes swivelled around.

'I can't,' I said. 'I have to be somewhere else at seven.'

'Well then, Jack,' he said. 'We'll just have to go and see Artemis, won't we? Just don't say I never do anything for you.'

'What?' I said.

'Come on then, Jack,' he said again. 'Little old me can't bend the rules but Artemis maybe can. Come on.'

'OK,' I said, and stood up. I'd never seen Artemis' office before. He was already drifting away and I headed after him.

We were walking along one of the seemingly endless halls when he stopped by a door, opened it and walked through. I walked in after him and the door slammed shut. The room was a small training room, full of rows of ancient dead computers, with a dusty data projector hanging haphazardly from the ceiling.

'Jack Sprat could eat no fat,' Kenny said. 'And his wife could eat no lean. And so between the two of them, they licked the platter clean.'

'This isn't Artemis' office,' I said. 'Why do you keep reciting that nursery rhyme?'

'You make me think of it,' Kenny said. 'And no, this isn't Artemis' office. You're very bright.'

'What is this about?'

'You know what it's about, Sprat,' he said, and took a

step towards me. The walls in here were white but covered in smudges and knocks. The sound of the call-centre floor was muted beyond the door, and there was an old, ghostly smell of sweat in the air. 'I saw you that night and you saw me, didn't you?'

'I don't know what you're talking about,' I said. 'What night? Where?'

'In the alley, Jack. In the alley when I was all not being very well and you were sneaking down to have a good laugh at me. You remember, don't you?'

'I don't remember,' I said.

'Well, I remember,' he said. 'And I'm worried that you're going to be thinking all kinds of crap up in that big old head of yours.' He walked around me and leant backwards against one of the desks, his baggy shirt coming untucked from his ill-fitting trousers. His greasy fringe flopped forward as he put his hands over his face.

'I hate it here, Jack,' he said. 'It does my fucking head in. I fucking hate it. Sometimes I'm all just ready to burst, like a balloon or something. I'm not very well see, I've got, like, a disease, and that's what you saw down that alley, OK? I was just not being very well. That's all it was, just like a little bit of sick.'

'OK,' I said.

'Sometimes I just don't know what I'm going to do,' he said, and his eyes were flat and his long lips were wet. 'I need a nice little girlfriend, that's what I need. Just to sort me out like. Make me a bit more normal. Take the edge off these places.'

'Which places?' I said.

'These fucking places,' he said, and lifted his arms up as if to gesture at all four walls at once, and by extension the whole building I suppose. 'Feels like I've worked fucking lifetimes in these shitholes and it's so hard to keep myself, like, all under control, Jack. I come in every day, little old me, just Kenny, for years and years and years trying to pretend I'm OK when I'm not, Jack, I'm not.'

'I know what you mean,' I said. 'You think you're better than a place.'

He looked directly at me and his mouth seemed to change shape somehow into an angry, uncomprehending hole. He shook his head. 'Nobody's any better than this place,' he said. 'Especially not little old Kenny. And anyway, if everyone was all too fucking good, who'd answer the phones? No, Sprat. You don't know the start of what I mean. I keep telling you. I'm not well.'

'I'm sorry to hear that,' I said, trying to keep my voice steady in the glare of his sad, furious, twisted face. 'What have you got? I mean, what's the disease? I mean, no – sorry – I didn't mean it to come out like that. I mean, what's wrong?'

There was a silence.

'I used to be a bit like you,' he said, and put his head in his hands again. 'I try so hard, I do, Jack. Where's Jenny at these days anyways?'

'Jennifer?' I said, uncertainly. 'She's left.'

'What?' he said, and his head snapped back up again. 'She's all gone away?'

'Yes,' I said.

'Oh now that's just the icing on the coffin, that is, Sprat. Oh no. Now I am sad.' He shook his head, his fringe flopping like a dead thing. 'I liked her so very much, I did. She's such a pretty girl is that Jenny. Kenny and Jenny, eh? Imagine that. Well I might just have to try and find her. Like I say, a nice little girlfriend might sort me out. There's something about girls, Sprat, something about girls that makes the illness seem not so bad. In all my life of being ill girls have been the tonic, Sprat. Something about the smell of them or the taste of them. Honest to God I can't explain it. Young Jenny might be just the thing to sort me out good and proper.'

'I'm sorry,' I said. 'Jennifer and I are together now. I'm sorry. I thought you knew.'

He didn't say anything to that at first – he didn't even move, he just froze, back to his mannequin self, not even breathing. Eventually he spoke.

'I heard her ask you out that time,' he said with a small, tense voice. 'But I thought that was just to put me off.'

'What?' I said. 'No, she meant it. Of course she meant it.'

'Like playing hard to get, is what I thought she was doing,' he said. 'But this just gets worse and worse. I'm not happy now, Sprat. Things like this is what breaks people up when they're already all tired and desperate.'

'I'm sorry,' I said.

'You're not sorry even a little bit,' he said. 'You don't think I deserve a nice little girl like her, do you? You're glad you've got her all to yourself, aren't you? All wrapped up and yours. Honest to fucking God, Sprat, you don't know how fucking close I am now to sorting you out all good and proper.' He looked up at me and there were tears crawling out of his flat eyes. 'If it weren't so fucking messy I'd do you right now.'

'I'm going now,' I said, and stumbled backwards to the door, swung it open, and left him there in the room, his sweaty hands gripping the desk edge like he was trying to occupy them, trying to stop them escaping and wreaking their havoc.

I found Artemis wandering the floor on the way back to my desk and told him of Kenny's threats.

'What exactly did he say?' he asked, frowning. He was wearing the blackest of black suits and his skin was tight, smooth and tanned.

'He said he'd do me right now if it wasn't so messy,' I said.

'What did he mean?' asked Artemis.

'I think – I think he meant he'd kill me.'

'I'm sorry, Jack,' he said, frowning, 'but I find that highly unlikely.'

'I wouldn't just say something like that,' I said.

'Where was this?'

'In that room over there,' I said, turning and pointing at the door to the old training room.

'Come on then,' he said. 'I'm sure Kenny will have a perfectly reasonable explanation for this. It all sounds a bit outlandish to me.' He marched purposefully off before I could refuse to accompany him, and so I followed him hesitantly, at a distance, afraid of what we might find.

Kenny was not there any more, but the window was broken. Artemis dashed to it and looked out over the edge. 'Fuck,' he said. 'He's jumped.'

I backed out of the room and could only look at the big yellow poster to the left of the doorway.

HELP OUR CUSTOMERS STAY OUT OF DEBT.
DEMAND PAYMENT IN FULL TODAY!

FRANCIS

I am plugged into a telephone. And sitting at a long straight row of desks. The room is busy with the low hum of a thousand computers and there are no windows. The room is strip-lit, and the air feels thick and green. My headset pushes my ears into the side of my head. The humming is an audible static – a kind of ethereal, intangible acid. People ring up to pay or query or dispute their water bills. Sometimes they just ring up to show us all how angry they are, and how good they are at putting people down. You get some sick, sad, rage-filled bastards. And some real senseless aggression.

That's not why Kenny jumped, though. He didn't answer the phones. Jack says Kenny jumped because of Jennifer. But I don't think there's any mystery as to why he jumped. Anybody could probably talk themselves into it. The interesting thing is where he went after he disappeared from the hospital.

There is a local TV news crew filming the call centre. The reporter is a tall blonde girl with small eyes and a smart blue suit. She and the cameraman walk down the central aisle. The cameraman sets the camera up not far from where I sit. He's going to film Artemis talking about Kenny. Then, no doubt, the cameraman will pan across the floor. I should remain just out of shot.

'He must have been very popular,' the cameraman says to me. 'Everybody looks so sad.'

'Mm,' I say.

And another thing that bothers me at work is this idea that electromagnetic fields might cause cancer. And here in this room there are I don't know how many computers. How many phones. And beneath my desk there are so many wires that they're like hair. I look at them and ask myself, can I feel my cells mutating? I don't know. I'm watching the liquid-crystal display on my desk phone at work. I'm finishing my shift at five, which is two minutes away. These last two minutes are horrible, because you can't turn your phone off; the managers look out for that. And if you get a call through, you'll be late finishing. And it's always the biggest idiots that you end up getting when you're supposed to be finishing. The most self-righteous, think-they're-clever, patronising dicks. And they always go on for ages and ages. Talking slowly because they think we're stupid.

The date of Dad's operation is more or less here, all of a sudden. And he's going into hospital the day after tomorrow.

Inside me a huge clock is ticking. My hands clench.

Fuck it.

I log off my phone a minute early and grab my coat and bag. I make for the door before anybody can stop me. Everybody will be too distracted to notice. Too distracted by the camera.

So they can put me on an overtime ban, or whatever. Give me a warning. Sack me.

Outside it's raining. People run around with their jackets pulled up, or struggle with umbrellas. Or shelter in the doorways of shops and office blocks. I was going to walk home as I don't have any change for the bus. But I don't really fancy it, given the weather.

I could duck into a shop or two until it's blown over.

I head for the record shop. Or what was a record shop and is now a kind of department store for all things media. CDs, DVDs, video games, posters, books. A few vinyl records. Not many. I love it in here. Love the loud music. The black carpets and shelving. The tricks they develop to make you spend more. The staff recommendations. The quiet studiousness of customers. I could spend hours and hours just browsing. Sometimes I find that I'm picking up more or less every item on the rack, looking at it, considering it and putting it down again. And I have to stop myself, otherwise I would be trapped like an ant in honey. Today though, I head straight upstairs to the DVDs.

I don't let myself stop at the boxed sets of TV series which are on sale. Or the world-cinema section. Or the new releases. I need to restrict myself to the bare necessities.

I start off in the horror section. And then move on to the feature films A–Z. I pick up *Rocketship X-M. Creature From the Haunted Sea. Earth vs. the Spider.* (Tag-line – 'Bullets . . . won't kill it! Flames . . . can't burn it! Nothing . . . can stop it!') *The Brain That Wouldn't Die.* (Tag-line – 'It's madness, not science!') I should have picked up a basket. I get *The Crawling Eye. The She Beast. The Woman Eater.* I look at *War of the Colossal Beast*, but it's a sequel to *The Amazing Colossal Man*, which really was just shit, in a bad way, so I put that one back. I also find a few I've never heard of before: *Dungeon of Harrow. Hercules Against the Moon Men. Dr. Goldfoot and the Bikini Machine.* Featuring Vincent Price! So that's ten. I should probably leave it at that. I carry them as a stack towards the counter.

Might have stopped raining too. If I'm lucky.

Back at the house, Graham, Taylor and Erin are playing Mario Kart. I sit down on the sofa and put the bag of DVDs on the floor next to me. The cartoony music and toy-like zooming sounds of the game make me feel kind of safe.

'What you got, Francis?' Graham says. Without taking his eyes off the screen. 'More shit films?'

'No,' I say. 'Well, yeah. But funny, probably. I don't know, do I? Haven't watched them yet. You should watch them with me, Graham. Could have a boys' night in.'

'I've made plans for tonight,' he says. 'Meeting someone later.'

'Graham's got a date,' Erin says.

'Online,' Taylor says.

'It's still a date!' Graham says. 'Christ almighty. You'd think I was planning to murder some children.'

'Who with?' I ask. 'I mean, who's the date with?'

'Some girl,' Graham says.

'Do you know her name?' I say.

'Yeah.'

'What is it?' I say.

'I know her name,' he says.

'What is it?' I say.

'See, now you're making me lose.' He gestures angrily towards the screen.

'You don't know, do you?' I say.

'Alright!' he says. 'I don't know her real name. Her avatar is called Miss Lynch, though, and no, before you ask, nothing kinky, she's just a David Lynch fan. OK?'

'*Avatar*?' Erin says. 'You mean, like, it's an actual *virtual* date?'

'Yes,' he says. 'Yes it is.'

'You're not going to be looking at porn while you're on this date are you, Graham?' Taylor asks.

'You know, I don't know why I even bother trying to be friends with all of you perverts,' Graham says. 'Erin and Taylor the Siamese twins and Francis the – the weirdo.'

'You're not supposed to say Siamese,' I say. 'You're supposed to say conjoined.'

'Fuck you,' he says. He points at the screen again. 'See! Straight into the fucking lava! I'm going to make a cup of tea – no, I'm going for a can – and you can all go piss up a rope if you think you're getting any.'

He storms from the room.

'What films did you get anyway, Francis?' Erin asks.

'Lots,' I say. I hand her the bag. 'Here. It's a bit sad but I can't even remember all of the titles.'

'Wow,' she says. She looks inside. 'It's a wonder you've got any money left for train tickets. "*The Woman Eater.*" "It devours only the most beautiful", apparently. Hey, Francis, we should watch some of these tonight. You're off tomorrow, aren't you?'

'What did you say?'

'We should watch—'

'No,' I say. 'No, sorry. I know what you said. I mean – train tickets?'

'Yeah,' she says. 'You're going home for the operation, aren't you? On the train?'

'Oh shit!' I stand up. 'Train tickets! Fuck! I completely forgot!'

'Well, these have still got the cellophane on. You could take them back.'

'No. Well, I could, I guess – but I could also ask Jack for a lift. What do you think? Then, afterwards, I could give him one of these as a thank-you present. Yes!' I sit back down. 'That's what I'll do.'

'The abominable Francis Wood,' Taylor says.

'I'm not abominable,' I say. 'So. Which one shall we watch?'

JACK

The girl who had been found dead in the alley that night had worked at the call centre, on one of the lower floors, working on a different contract to us, and none of us had known her. The local media seemed to pick the story up again once Kenny jumped from that window, and the following couple of weeks were busy with news or, rather, speculation. Nothing definite was in the *Manchester Evening News* or on the TV, unless we'd missed it, but I doubted that because Francis watched as much news as he did Hammer Horror films, and I was trying to follow the story on the web.

As for Kenny, I hadn't been able to stop thinking about him since it happened, and I hadn't said anything to anybody, but I knew there was something deeply wrong with him, something to do with the dead girl. I felt like I should ring the police and tell them what I'd seen, but now I'd look suspicious because I'd left it so long and the whole thing was a bit of a mess.

I was lying on my bed. I could hear the others playing Mario Kart downstairs, but I couldn't bring myself to go and join in.

If there was anybody in my entire life that I'd be surprised to see crying, it was Kenny. It was still possible that he'd died, although the general consensus was that he was still alive and he had walked out of the hospital himself.

I sat up.

The thoughts ran around inside my head like a toy train, as they'd been doing since it happened. He'd wanted to know where Jennifer had been in order to seduce her somehow, to ask her out, and found out that he was too late, and given his illness or whatever it was, this perceived rejection was too much to take and so he jumped . . . that was the only way I could see it. I wasn't responsible, was I? Soon after it had happened, I had to make a statement to the police. One of the policemen had looked like Christopher Lee – tall, with hollow cheeks and deep eyes and a white beard – and he'd looked bored. The other had been fat, tremendously fat, with an oversized tooth jutting out from his lower jaw and protruding out above his lip. He'd worn small gold studs in his ears.

'You were the last person to see him before he jumped,' Christopher Lee said.

'Yes,' I said. 'I think so.'

'You didn't like him much, did you?' the fat one said.

'Well,' I replied. 'No. Not really, no.'

Despite their best attempts to make out it was something more suspicious, Kenny's jump had been a suicide and they all knew it. Apparently it hadn't been the first time he'd tried to kill himself.

'Do you know of any places or people that were special to him?' Christopher Lee asked. 'Did he ever talk about any family or loved ones?'

'I don't know anything about him,' I'd said.

That had been before he'd woken up and left the hospital, otherwise I might have mentioned Jennifer. As it was, they had no reason to believe he was a danger to others... after all, I supposed, the police were just people like us. It was unreasonable to expect too much of them. Jennifer and I would just have to keep our eyes peeled.

I headed downstairs for some food, and as I passed through the downstairs hallway Francis stuck his head out of the living-room door.

'Jack,' he said.

'Hello,' I said. 'You OK?'

'Yes, thank you. I'm after a massive favour though. Like, really big.'

'I'll probably say yes.'

'My dad's going into hospital the day after tomorrow,' he said, 'and I was wondering if you could give me a lift up to Cumbria? I'm sorry to land it on you so short notice.'

'Actually, I'd like that. Yes. Definitely. I feel like I need to get away for a couple of days. I'll ask Jennifer too. I mean, we won't stay at yours, obviously – we'll find a bed-and-breakfast or something.'

'Thank you,' he said. 'Thank you very much.'

I would never have thought of it myself, but a couple of days away would be nice, as long as Jennifer could come too. I didn't want to leave her on her own.

FRANCIS

When I wake up it is dark outside the car. Some old R.E.M. song – 'I Remember California' – is low on the radio. The car smells like apples and the night is full of red and white lights. Jennifer is asleep in the passenger seat, and I'm in the back.

'I've been asleep,' I say.

'Yes,' Jack says.

'Are we on the motorway?'

'Yes.'

'That was quick.'

'It's not that far from where we live,' he says. 'Besides, you've been asleep. We might have been going for hours for all you know.'

'Have we?'

'No. Maybe an hour. Only another couple to go, if that.'

I look out of the window again. I see the orange lights of some distant town. But I don't know which.

'I appreciate this,' I say.

'Don't mention it. I might head off the motorway soon,

though. Go through the Dales. It's nicer, less busy. Fewer cars. And doesn't really take much longer, either.'

Dad tends to stick to the motorways this time of night. I listen to the faint music. The music makes me think of huge open spaces under a big, empty sky. I find myself thinking about UFOs. When I was a child, some nights I would go and sit on our neighbour's garage roof, and look up at the sky for hours. I would look up at the stars and I would be convinced that somewhere up there was another, better planet that I could live on, that I would find, one day. When I grew up. I always wanted to be an astronaut, and when people asked me what I wanted to be, I would say so. 'You'll have to work hard at school,' they would always say.

'Yeah,' I would say, smiling, 'I will. I'll work really, really hard.'

Some idiot on Radio 4 burbles on about nothing. We are crawling through a black valley somewhere in Yorkshire. I saw a sign saying something like Gardale or Garsdale or Graydale, but could not read it properly in the dark. The sky above us is thick with stars. Bare, crooked trees bend over the road from either side. Beyond them, hills rise up as solid silhouettes against the starscape. Every now and then we pass a farmhouse. The farmhouses have no lights on and have holes in their roofs. And sometimes the sooty signs of a fire around the windows. And sometimes a wall is missing.

'Why are we listening to Radio 4?' I say.

'I like Radio 4,' Jack says. 'I like the voices on it. I don't really know what they're talking about, though.'

'It's not even loud enough to hear. Can we put something good on?'

He looks like he's about to argue, but thinks better of it. 'OK then. There's some CDs in that wallet in the back.'

'It's OK. I've got some in my bag.'

'You carry CDs around in your bag?'

'Yeah. Why, don't you?'

'No.'

'What have you got, then?'

'Apart from my toothbrush and stuff, just a book. Have a look, if you like.'

I open up Jack's backpack. Looking into it, I can see the top side of a very big, thick, hardback book. I pull it out and see that the cover is a reproduction of part of an old map. It's heavy; it's huge. It's called *The Lore of the Land*.

'Looks big,' I say.

'It is. It's basically an encyclopaedia of folklore, myths and legends, from all around England.'

'Not the United Kingdom?'

'No,' Jack says. Trying to keep the exasperation from his voice. 'England. And it's very, very good. I started just dipping into it, but in the end decided to read it cover to cover. It's excellent.'

I put the book back. It looks like something my dad would like. He would read it. And believe half of it, if not more. Looking for signs of this other, better, more magical world. Well, there isn't one, Dad. Unfortunately. I shake my head. They take the piss out of me for watching films about these things. But Jack seems to really believe.

'I can't believe you carry CDs around with you,' Jack says.

'Well, I do. Here. Put Patti Smith on, please.'

'Good choice,' Jennifer murmurs.

'Thank you,' I say. 'Thought you were asleep?'

'I am asleep,' she says. 'Travelling makes me tired.'

'Here, Jack,' I say. 'Got a DVD or two in here as well. Look. *Creature From the Haunted Sea*. And *The Crawling Eye*. Oh, and *Rocketship X-M*.'

'I don't know how you sit through those films,' he says.

'The point is not how good something is,' I say. 'Or true, or honest, or believable. You know, like a lot of what's in the papers or on the Internet just isn't true, but it doesn't matter – you can still read them as texts, as sources that tell you about a time, or place, or culture. You shouldn't just dismiss these things out of hand as bollocks. These films work in the same way. You have to read them on a different level. That's all.' I look out of the window. 'Besides, I don't know how you can read a whole encyclopaedia of crap that's supposed to be real. Guess we're just different, hey?'

'I won't take offence,' he says, 'given everything.'

I don't say anything. The weird dark valley rolls by.

'Were we supposed to come this way?' I ask, eventually.

'Yes,' Jack says. 'I looked at a map before we set off. This is right.'

'Where are we?'

He doesn't reply. Just looks like he's concentrating. And then slightly panicked as the car seems to slide a little towards the other side of the narrow road.

'Black ice,' he says. After regaining control.

'Jack,' I say.

'Yeah?'

'I'm not going to talk any more if that's OK.'

'Of course it's OK. You don't have to ask.'

More bare trees. Empty farmhouses. Broken walls along the tops of the hills that rise up on either side. Shreds and smears of cloud starting to obscure the stars. Sheep in the road, with small electric eyes. Shadows between the trees. Cattle grids. Huge, silent barns. Road signs shot at, dented. No more cars. No more people. Black ice. A world that was all like this would have less cancer in it. But we would have less choice in who we are. Maybe that is the exchange we made.

I have to go to sleep.

JACK

The spare room was decorated with lots of floral patterns that, although mismatched, made it feel warm and comfortable and homely. Francis' parents obviously knew exactly what they were doing. Joan seemed like that kind of person, although of course it was hard to really be sure what someone was like when they were having such a horrible time. I sat on the deep, soft bed, and sank into it.

We'd arrived at Joan and Eric's house after I had gotten us completely lost somewhere between Garsdale and Kendal, which made the journey about two hours longer than it should have been. Once we had finally arrived, Joan insisted that Jennifer and I stay the night, which I was very glad of because neither Jennifer nor I could be bothered to look for a b. & b. I looked over at Jennifer, and she was already flat out in bed.

At the same time, I really didn't want to be there.

I could hear Francis and Joan talking in the room next door to ours – his old childhood room – and I could hear her crying. I didn't want to just sit there and listen, so I got out my laptop. As I set it up, the sounds from the room next door continued – muffled weeping and low talk, sometimes a startled laugh, but uneasy, like a flock of birds rising up in shock at a sudden movement nearby.

I stared at the blank screen. I wanted to plan out an article on the myths that gather around empty buildings, after seeing all those abandoned farms on the way up, but could not. All I could think about were my parents. I supposed that once they died, it would be as if there was one less thing standing between me and my own death, one generation removed, as if they were in front of me on the conveyor belt. As long as they were there I would know I had some time left before I reached the end myself, but once they'd dropped off, I would know it was my turn next. The screen remained blank.

Somebody knocked at the bedroom door.

'Come in,' I said.

'Hi,' Francis said, sticking his head round the corner. His eyes darted towards Jennifer. 'Can I just ask a quick question?'

'Go ahead.'

'Do you think I could talk to Jennifer? About, you know. About everything?'

'Yes,' I said. 'Of course. Because her mum was ill?'

'Yeah,' he said, looking down.

'Sorry. I didn't mean it to come out like that. So bluntly.'

'No, don't worry.' He paused. 'I'm going to go to bed now.'

'Yeah,' I said. 'Goodnight, Francis. Just give us a knock if you need anything.'

'Thank you,' he said. 'Thank you.' He closed the door. He must have been thinking about it. The cancer and everything. There must have been a lot happening beneath the surface.

I couldn't be bothered trying to write anything after that, and even if I had been able to squeeze anything out, it wouldn't have been worthwhile. I was about to turn the laptop off when I saw that they had a wireless Internet connection, and so I went to the Manchester news-sites to see if there was any information about Kenny's whereabouts. There wasn't.

FRANCIS

I close my old bedroom door. I lie down on the bed, fully clothed. The ceiling is covered in small glow-in-the-dark stars. They will spring out at me once I turn the light off. The room is full of my old stuff. Books and old console games and figurines of characters from films. Like the alien from *Alien* and Han Solo from *Star Wars* and Leatherface from *The Texas Chainsaw Massacre*. I turn on the TV. It's showing old footage from the train bombings in Madrid. I watch as a middle-aged man appears from the smoke and the rubble. He's covered in dust that looks like flour. Mouth wide open. Trickles of blood cutting through the floury dust. Eyes shut, screaming. I imagine hearing somebody walking up the stairs. I see more people. Injured and confused and bereaved. Stumbling around on the screen. They are all imploring me to help them find their lost loves and dead children. I grit my teeth and dig my fingernails into my palms. I imagine the bedroom door opening. Jennifer steps through into the room. Her skin is white and her clothes are black. She is like frost on a dead tree; like a chessboard.

'Have you seen this?' I point at the TV.

She slowly and deliberately sways over to the TV and turns it off. 'I don't care.'

'What are you doing?' I stand up. 'What the hell are you doing?'

'Watch me instead,' she says. And she starts to take her clothes off. She strips. She sheds her clothes slowly and gracefully. And I let the lust build within me. Until it hides the news-anger beneath it. I watch her unblinkingly. I have never seen anything like it. It is sexual, but there is also this sense of wonder. Seeing what is covered up. Underneath. I am witnessing something mystical. Almost mythical. She accentuates one panel of flesh with her movements, and then another. Shoulder-blade. Navel. Thigh. Hip.

We make love. Here, in the bedroom of my childhood. We make love in black and white. I turn the light off and the fake stars shine out. Better and brighter than the real ones out above. And then Jennifer is no longer with me. I mean that in my imagination, she has left the room. Smiling.

I wake up. I must have been sleeping. I am still fully dressed, and the light is off. But the TV is on. The room is filled by that ghostly TV blue, and it jumps around the edges of my film figurines. They cast strange shadows. They dance around and snap back and forth on the wall.

I stand up, agitated, open the curtains and look out of the window. The light from my TV spills into the outside world. It illuminates the road in front of the house. Jack's car looks so much like Dad's. They are both old Metros. Jack's is blue and Dad's is white, but apart from that – the rust, the moss, the mud, the bird-shit. The cars sit on the road, nose to nose, like old friends having a catch-up. Talking about UFOs and ghosts and whatever other crap it is that they believe in. I mean, there is so much here in this world to occupy your mind already. Too much to do as it is. They are similar in that way I guess. Delusional. Fantasists.

A music video starts up on the screen. It is made up of still images – photographs, rapidly switching, replacing each other. The light jumps and jerks and the shadows on my wall start leaping up and down, higher and higher. The music increases tempo and the images on screen alternate more rapidly. The shadows start to jump faster and faster, all around me, until they seem too joyful, almost. Too happy. Gleeful. And I can't take it any more and have to turn the TV off.

I know that Jennifer and Jack are an item. I *know* that. And he's a good friend and I want him to be with somebody. And I don't want to ruin that. I guess I just want that too. Somebody. Having somebody. And I want it to be her. Typically, I want it to be her.

She must get scared of it too. As regularly as looking at a photograph. As regularly as looking in the mirror. Every time you think about the future, it's there. Or every time I think about Dad, now. Every time I think about Dad.

*

In the morning, I'm sitting at the kitchen table when Jack and Jennifer come downstairs. Jack is talking excitedly about the old mines at Whitehaven.

'I read about it in *The Unseen World*,' he says. 'The manager of the mine was dismissed, and a new manager appointed, and the old manager took the new manager down the mine somewhere that he knew was unsafe, and they were both killed in an explosion. It was intentional, see. It was a drastic revenge. And it was said that you could hear their last angry conversation down there, long after they had died.'

The two of them sit down.

'It sounds interesting, Jack,' Jennifer says. 'But we're not going to have time. It would mean heading north-west, as opposed to south-east, which is the way home.'

'I know, I know,' he says. 'We can't go today. Maybe we could go up there one weekend though? It would give me some more time to read about it. There's another story, you know, recounted by Baring-Gould, about a miner who half-cut a rope that was lowering some colleagues whom he didn't like. The rope snapped, and they died, and forever after he was prone to shaking fits that would cause his eyes to wander around the room and see their ghosts.'

'Jack,' Jennifer says, firmly. 'I'm not sure this is appropriate breakfast-time conversation.'

'Oh,' Jack says, looking up at me. 'Oh right. Sorry.'

'Don't worry,' I say. 'Look. I'm going to stay up here for a few days. I know you need to get back though.'

'Yeah,' he says. 'We do, really. Might drive through the Lakes this time. Give Whitehaven a miss.'

'I'll worry about you getting lost again.'

'You don't need to worry about me,' he says.

I wouldn't if I could help it. Except it's nothing as little as getting lost that I worry about. I worry about all of you. Your flesh bubbling up into hard lumps. Meaty eruptions deep within your bodies. The programming of your cells being altered by some carcinogenic agent, or some other malevolent force. And getting carried away. Multiplying feverishly. Accumulating and becoming misshapen. I think about the shadows on my bedroom wall last night and shudder.

I do worry about you. I worry about all of you. All the time.

All the time.

'OK then,' I say. 'I won't worry.'

'Good,' he says.

'Where are your parents?' Jennifer says.

'Oh,' I say. I look at the clock. It's a long lie-in, for them. 'They're still in bed.'

'Oh right,' she says. Then looks a little awkward.

As soon as Jack leaves the room to go and look at the map, I touch Jennifer's hand. It jerks slightly, as if surprised. And then stays still, maintaining the contact.

'Jennifer,' I say. 'Is it all right if we – if I talk to you?'

'Yeah.' She frowns briefly. 'Of course. Everything OK?'

'Well, kind of. I – I wanted to ask you about your mum,

if that's OK. I mean, like – what it was like and every-thing. Before she – before she died, and afterwards.'

'That's fine with me. I don't think it was the same as what you're going through though, especially because – well, your dad's, you know. He's not—'

'He's still alive.'

'Hey!' she says. 'Not *still*. He is alive. End of story.'

'I suppose.'

'I got used to the idea of her dying a long time before she did. It felt like she'd been ill for a long time. Well, she had. Sometimes she would forget who I was. It was hard. Like, really hard. Sometimes she just wasn't my mother. Was somebody else. Something else.'

'You don't have to talk about it, you know,' I say. 'I know I asked, but I know it must be difficult. And it's good of you to come up at all.'

'It's good to get away. It's beautiful round here. And it's good to see where you're from. I think it's important to know where people are from.'

'I've never thought about it.'

'The truth is I was kind of relieved.' She looks me directly in the eyes. 'I know that sounds awful. But her life was just a big trap. A maze that she didn't really have the energy to find her way out of. Like a big elaborate cage. Life should be lived as, I don't know, as *freely* as possible, with as few restrictions and commitments as possible. And she had so many. I had so many.' She looks down at her empty mug. 'Don't judge me, hey? I know I sound bad. But I was upset. You know.'

'I know.' I put my arm out to hug her. And then stop. Awkward. But then she hugs me. 'There's something I want to talk to you about,' I say. 'I feel like I can talk to you about it, because you must be scared too.'

'What?' she says. 'What do you mean, scared?'

'You must be scared. Cancer. It was cancer, wasn't it? You must be scared.'

'Yeah, it was cancer. But I'm not scared. I mean, it was fucking awful. But you've got to die of something. Dying is dying is dying. There must be worse ways to go.'

I look at her for a moment. And then I try to kiss her. Just lean in and try to kiss her on the mouth. My lips make contact with hers before she pulls back. She could have pulled back sooner. But she didn't. I realise that my eyes are closed and open them. She is so close to me, still. Her eyes are huge and green like clouds in space. Nebulae. It is as if she half wants to kiss me back. We stay like that for a moment. Five seconds. I'm counting them out in my head. Ten seconds. She blinks. Neither of us is breathing.

The spare bedroom door opens upstairs. Jack's footsteps on the landing.

'Jack and I have an understanding,' Jennifer says. 'But there's a time and a place. And you have a lot on your mind at the moment.'

'Well,' I say. 'I don't know. Maybe. I'm sorry.'

I can hear Jack coming downstairs. I move backwards in my seat.

'You are gorgeous, though,' she says. Quietly.

Jack arrives in the hallway and comes back to the

kitchen. He dumps his backpack in the doorway. He smiles at us.

So they have an understanding.

I don't know what she means.

JACK

We were glad to leave Francis' house. Being there felt uncomfortable, like we were intruding on something very private, however hard they tried to make us feel welcome.

We were approaching a valley called Wasdale. It was somewhere in the western Lake District, a little south of where Joan and Eric lived. As I drove slowly up the narrow fell road that would take us there, Jennifer turned down the radio.

'We should stop in this valley,' she said. 'It would be good to get some fresh air.'

'Yes,' I said. 'I could take some photos and make some notes, maybe.'

'For the farmhouse thing?'

'Yeah. I thought we could go back to Garsdale, but it might be nice to find another way.'

'I don't know it up here at all. I like it though. You could probably buy quite cheap. Get some land too.'

We crested the low fell and were granted a view reminiscent of a scene from *The Hobbit* or one of the Narnia books. A patchwork blanket of green fields was draped across a valley floor, the middle of which cradled a still, clean-looking lake, and the fields were strange spaces inside irregular arrangements of drystone walls. There were small dense copses of deciduous trees that were turning yellow and brown, waterfalls leaping from the steep grey mountains that rose up on all sides, bright streams and rivers that wound, shimmering, through the landscape towards the Irish Sea which shone in the distance. White farmhouses were scattered around and stood out from the green backdrop, and as I looked more closely I saw other houses that were less obviously coloured. The mountainsides were dotted with sheep that I could hear bleating through the open window, the sky was high and blue. There was something magical about this place. It immediately seemed to be a simple, honest, natural, beautiful place where people could just be people.

'In cities,' I said, 'or just more modern places, people are so much more superficial.' The car rattled over a cattle grid. 'I mean, they seem so image-conscious. You can't move for people trying to be *individuals*. But somewhere like this it feels like things could be different. Here, you could strip all of that away. Like taking your clothes off and just being you.'

'Nothing wrong with clothes, Jack. I mean, nothing wrong with no clothes, but remember. I make them.'

'No, nothing wrong with clothes. But what matters is that you'd continue to make them up here, where nobody would know. And if they did know, they wouldn't think you're any cooler or more individual for it.'

We pulled over in a small lay-by beneath a vividly coloured hedgerow that towered up and hung over the car. The greenery smelled fresh and clean. We sat for a while, just breathing.

On the other side of the road was a small, whitewashed village shop. There we could get a paper and something to eat on the journey so that we didn't have to go to one of the grim, grey service stations that crouched next to the motorway like giant, broken-down machines. We got out of the car and crossed the road.

My eyes had to readjust as I pushed the old door open, because after the bright sunlight outside it seemed dim in here, dingy. The small room was lined on all four walls with shelves piled high with tins, jars and packets. In the corner opposite was a tiny counter behind which a large, grey-haired woman sat. There was also an island in the middle of the room, as equally laden as the walls. The shop sold a wide variety of things, considering that it was so small.

'Alreet,' said the old lady. 'Owz it gaan?'

'Hi,' I said. 'Hello. It's – it's going good, thank you.'

She didn't say anything else; just smiled and nodded, as if in time to some music that only she could hear. I picked up a copy of the *Independent* from the floor, and saw that there was actually a refrigerated cabinet buried between the racks of bags of sweets and a stack of toilet roll. The cabinet contained bottles of milk, bottles of juice, bottles of water and locally made sandwiches. I took one of the sandwiches – egg, bacon and sausage – and also a big packet of crisps, which I deposited on the counter alongside the newspaper.

'Have you got any ice-creams?' Jennifer said to the old woman.

'Sorry,' she said. 'Az wun't sellin' 'em.'

'Well,' Jennifer said, putting another sandwich and a big bottle of water on the counter next to my purchases. 'Who needs ice-cream, really?'

'Just those please, then,' I said to the shopkeeper.

'T'll be five-twenty then, ta,' she said. 'Just passin' through, are tha?' Her hair was curly and short, and she wore a floral dress that seemed muted in that yellowish gloom. Her big arms wobbled as she passed me the change from my ten-pound note.

'Yeah,' Jennifer said. 'Been visiting a friend and thought we'd take the scenic route back home.'

'Ah, weel!' she said, laughing goodnaturedly. 'Tha'll not be disappointed then!'

'No,' Jennifer said. 'No, it's lovely here. Wasdale, is it? What's the lake called?'

'Wastwater, the lake is. Aye. Wastwater.' She scratched her slightly hairy chin and nodded even more vigorously. 'Bottomless, 'tis.'

'I'm sorry?' I said.

'Bottomless.' She laughed again, and I found myself laughing too. 'Fancy that!' she chortled. 'Not having a bottom! Poor bugger.'

'Yes,' I said. 'Ha ha. I suppose it would be quite awkward not having a bottom.'

'Nivver looks the same twice,' she said.

'I'm sorry? I mean – I'm sorry?'

'The lake.' Her demeanour suddenly became serious. 'The, y'know, the top of it, the surface, nivver has the same look aboot it. 'S allus diffrint. Ivry single time.'

'Oh right,' I said. 'I might go and have a look at it after this.'

'Tha like it round here then, aye?' she asked.

'I think it's wonderful.'

'There's a yam gaan up yan o' them fells.' She nodded her head towards the window that I'd not noticed up until now. It was covered in curling scraps of paper that had been tacked to the inside, which was probably why it was so dark in there. Jennifer and I looked at each other.

'Pardon?' I asked.

'It's grand to meet a man wi' manners!' she exclaimed, and began to laugh again. 'Fellers round here divvent offer two wuds to rub togither.'

'Right,' I said, nodding, smiling.

'What Ah meant,' she said, speaking a little more slowly, 'is that theer's a house up theer. Fer sale. Y'know. Little notice in yon winder if tha's interested. God knows it's bin empty long enough, tha can tekk the notice. Bin theer yeers.'

Jennifer had gone to the window already.

'Well,' I said, walking backwards as I spoke. 'Thank you! We could drop by and have a look. We should probably

110

be getting off now, actually. Thanks very much though.'
I stopped by the door.

'Which notice is it?' Jennifer asked.

'Near the top. Left-hand side. No, futher down. Futher down. Next one in. That's t'yan.' She grinned broadly at Jennifer's back.

'Yep,' Jennifer said, looking at it. 'It's for a house.'

'That's t'yan,' the woman said again.

'Well, thanks again,' I said. 'Bye-bye.'

'Alreet,' she said. 'See tha soon.'

As we left she was nodding and smiling again, her bulky frame wedged in that back corner like she'd never moved from there, and like she never would.

The house was called Fell House. Jennifer put the advert on the dashboard. I liked the name of it, and I liked the way that the woman called the mountains *fells* because it sounded old and mystical. I looked again at the shoddy, torn-off yellowing bit of paper.

> Four-bedroomed farmhouse for sale!
> Structurally sound but needs a lick of paint!
> Address is:
> Fell House, Fell Road, Wasdale
> Cumbria
> Call 07842 220348 for details

The text had originally been written in pencil, and gone over in ballpoint pen (presumably by the woman in the shop) once it had started to fade. I looked over at Jennifer and saw that her eyes were closed, but she was not asleep, just thinking. I started the car up again and set off. The sun was bright; the windscreen looked filthy.

I kept my eyes peeled for Fell Road.

FRANCIS

Mum and Dad are sleeping in late today. They didn't even get up to say goodbye to Jack and Jennifer, which is unusual behaviour for them. I sit on one of the two cream-coloured reclining chairs in the living-room. I flick through the music channels on TV but they're all full of shit. All I want to find is a song that I like. It shouldn't be this hard, given the stupid number of channels. The choice is nice to have, I guess, or would be, if there was anything to choose between.

I notice that the other recliner is empty. The empty chair bothers me because the other one is occupied. By me. So I get up and sit on the sofa, leaving both chairs empty, which is better. I carry on flicking through the music channels. I'll stop when I find something worthwhile. But I don't. I don't find anything, I mean. I don't find anything.

By the time Mum comes downstairs, I am watching *Rocketship X-M*. It's a nineteen-fifties science-fiction film.

One of those that sometimes gets read as a Cold War paranoia film. My mum walks in at my favourite moment; the
trajectory of the eponymous spaceship is being drawn out.
It shows the spaceship heading straight up from the surface
of the earth and then, once it has emerged from our
atmosphere, turning a ninety-degree angle in order to
continue on to the moon.

'What are you watching, hey?' she says.

'An old film I brought up with me.' I look across at her.
'You slept in.'

'We didn't sleep.' She sits down on one of the recliners.
The same one that I sat in. 'Have your friends gone?'

'Yeah,' I say. 'Where's dad?'

'In the bathroom.'

I look away from her and back at the paused image on
the screen. I un-pause it.

'It's OK, you know,' she says. 'It's OK to sit in the quiet
sometimes. Just sit and think. It might help.'

'Mm.' I don't look at her. I bite my lip. I try to talk
without letting go of it. 'I can't—'

'Francis.' She gets up and sits next to me on the sofa.
'Francis.'

'Mm. I can't – I can't do that.'

'Here.' She turns the TV off. The house falls completely
silent. Apart from the white noise of Dad's shower, a
couple of rooms away. She holds me and I start to shake.
'It's OK,' she says. 'You can only distract yourself for so
long.'

JACK

We followed Fell Road up the mountainside – the *fell*side – as it twisted and turned and narrowed and bucked and buckled and burst open over the harder, older rocks beneath it. It hairpinned onwards and upwards, and dead-looking grass encroached upon it, stealthily obfuscating the hard edges over time, and breaking them up with the patient strength of all nature. Every now and again we had to stop because of sheep lying across the uneven way and refusing to move. They stared at me with their disquieting yellow eyes and I felt like they were judging me, each and every time, and only once they had found me worthy did they stand up and shamble off.

'These sheep look strange,' Jennifer said.

'They're Herdwick, apparently,' I said. 'They have their own sheep species up here. Descended from some that swam ashore after one of the galleons of the Spanish Armada was wrecked near here. A place called Drigg, or something.'

'Are you joking?' she said.

'No,' I said. 'I looked the area up in *The Lore of the Land*. It's not confirmed, necessarily, but it's one of the favourite theories. Beatrix Potter thought they were a lot older, though. Here before the Romans, according to her.'

'They look really wild. Dirty, too.'

'Maybe it's their long wool,' I said. 'I know what you mean though. Look at that one!'

A particularly big sheep stood on a rock to the side of the road, and its front end seemed especially bulky because the wool from its rear end had partly been shaved off and hung behind it like a sloughed skin. It must have dragged the coat around with it all the time. Its eyes were big and yellow and so were its visible teeth, and its head followed our movement as we passed by.

Eventually, we found the opening of an even narrower, bumpier road – just a dusty track, really – that had a ramshackle metal five-bar gate hung up across it, between two wonky stone gateposts. I pulled over and we got out of the car. The gate put me in mind of a hugely fat drunk man being supported by two slightly less drunk, skinnier men. The name Fell House was daubed across one of the bars of the gate in white paint, which was fading badly. The gateposts were unusual, though – they were each made up of huge shards of slate driven downwards into the ground, with the grain of the stone running from top to bottom. They were pretty vicious-looking things.

'Look,' Jennifer said, reaching her hand up and running her long fingers delicately over one of the stones. 'Look at this.'

Joining her, I saw that the slate gateposts had once been ornately carved, but now the carvings were too weathered – split and splintered – for me to be able to tell what they were, or had been.

'Can you see what they were carvings of?' I asked.

'No,' she said. 'Too damaged.'

Beyond the gate, we could see Fell House itself, low and dark grey and ancient and *available*, I unintentionally reminded myself, and we stood still and silent and I looked across at Jennifer and the sudden breeze picked her hair up and held it out backwards from her, like she was falling forwards.

It was hard to make out where the house ended and the fell began, partly because of the grey stone that it was made out of, which was the same as the stone around it, as if the house had been carved out of the ground, and partly because it was surrounded by smaller outhouses that were even more rock-like than the house itself. The whole thing just looked so at home there, nestled into the land in a way that it couldn't have been anywhere else; anywhere else it would have looked crude and ugly and awkward, but there, where it was, it just fited as if the fell had given birth to it.

Fell House seemed old and heavy with time, and strong, like it had weathered all kind of storms. Strong, but damaged – there was no doubt that the place needed work.

If I had a decent job, or some sort of financial security, then I would have been thinking of spending it, because the place drew me in.

Jennifer had money, of course.

Maybe every generation realises its age through the passing of its parents, and each generation reaches maturity through the death of that before it. I looked across at Jennifer again, but she was still entranced by the house, and her hair was vivid against the sky, which, behind her, was slowly darkening.

A huge black bird rose up from behind Fell House and flapped lazily around and around. It was followed by another, and another, and another, and another.

They just kept coming.

It felt good to be back in my own room, although less good to be back in Manchester. Jennifer had her eyes closed and was breathing regularly by the time I slipped into bed. I reached out and turned off the bedside lamp.

'Francis?' she murmured.

'What?' I turned the lamp back on. 'No, it's Jack. What do you mean?'

'Jack? Hell, I'm sorry.' She smiled sleepily and sat up a little. 'Must've been dreaming.'

'Well.' I didn't know what to say. I looked around and saw that her eyes were closing again. 'What were you dreaming about?'

'Francis, I think. I mean that would make sense, right? We did just come back from his parents' house today. Can't remember the details, I'm afraid.' She stretched. 'Nothing to get so uppity about, though. Nothing sexy.'

118

'I'm not getting uppity!'

'You are getting uppity.' She yawned. 'Hey, I've just remembered. He made a pass at me this morning, over breakfast. He wasn't with it though. He was upset, like, completely wide-eyed and confused.'

'*What?!*' I spluttered, sitting bolt upright. 'He did – what did he do? And you didn't tell me?'

'I forgot! Jesus, Jack. It's not a big deal. He just tried to kiss me. He was so upset. Like I said to him, he wasn't thinking straight.'

She was right, so I kept my mouth shut and tried to swallow the anger.

'All the same,' I said, 'he should have more self-control. Like me, right now. See? I'm exhibiting self-control right now.'

'Oh, Jack.' She was dropping off again. 'I guess he's just a bit more impulsive than you. It's not a good thing or a bad thing. Anyway, you're not always in control, hey? Look at Kenny.'

My stomach froze and I looked to the window, expecting to see his weird face looming through the glass before I realised that she was making a joke.

'I didn't push him,' I said.

'I know that. I was joking.'

After a short while, I turned the lamp back off and lay next to Jennifer. She shifted so that she was lying on her side, resting her head on my chest. I wanted to be impulsive right then, to kiss her. God knows I wanted to. But I didn't know if she wanted to sleep. Should I have been running my hands over her stomach, her thighs, trying to instigate something?

My erection stuck up like something not quite a part of me, and I could feel it too vividly, and it reminded me of something Taylor said sometimes. What was it? A battle with your body is a battle lost, or something like that. I wanted it to just go away.

I had to get up early as I was working at half eight, and Jennifer woke up with me, the slow violins of the alarm clock drawing us upwards together.

'Sorry about last night,' was the first thing she said.

'I'm sorry too,' I said, and squeezed her. 'I know things are hardly normal at the moment.'

We had breakfast in the basement kitchen, the two of us huddled together in the lowest part of the big, silent house. Everybody else was still in bed.

'She would see other people in the room,' Jennifer said. 'Mum would, I mean. She'd say "Look out, Jenny. There's a girlie behind you, trying to do your hair." I'd turn around, but there was never anyone there.'

'Was that one of the hallucinations?' I said, but really I was thinking about ghosts. Did imminent death mean you could see them? Maybe some part of the brain that normally inhibited the sense that perceived these spirits could be damaged. But I didn't voice the question in case it sounded a bit sick.

'I don't know about hallucinations,' Jennifer said. 'I think she could see souls. I never saw anybody there, but sometimes I did feel a gentle tug-tug-tug at the back of my head, or cold fingers, you know, pressing against – against here. The back of my neck.' She pointed.

'I didn't want to say it, but I've thought that too.'

'Do you believe in that sort of stuff then?'

'Well,' I said. 'Yeah, I do, really.'

'Yeah,' she said. 'And me.' She looked down at the remains of her breakfast: soggy orange flakes floating sadly around in a shallow bowl of milk. 'I still feel it sometimes. So I'm going to sell the house.'

'What?'

'I'm going to sell the house,' she said. 'Now. As soon as possible.'

'But – can you do that?'

'Of course. She left it to me. Dad paid the mortgage off a long time ago.' She looked up at me again. 'I know you probably think I'm some sort of money-grabbing monster. But I just think – it is full of her and the things she imagined. Things stick to places, don't they? I don't think I can really bear to stay here.'

'Jennifer. If there's anything I can do, you know, to help.'

'No,' she said. 'It wasn't as bad for me as it could have been for somebody else. No, that's wrong. I mean – I mean I'd been grieving for years. She'd died a million times in my head. I would think about it all the time. All the fucking time. Is it today, you know? Or is it tomorrow?' She wiped a tear from her eye before it fell. 'A million times in my head. Sometimes I killed her. Smothered her with a pillow. Honestly. I shouldn't be telling you this. When she died, it was just how I had imagined it would be. I don't feel that different to how I did before. Except I don't have to dread it happening any more.'

'Because I won't go to work today if it's getting to you.'

'No!' she laughed. 'Listen to me, Jack. Sure it makes me sad sometimes. But I'm fine. OK?'

'OK.' I stood up and rinsed the bowls and spoons in the sink. 'Jennifer,' I said, as I did so, 'what did your dad do?'

'Lots of things. I'm guessing you mean job-wise, though?'

'Yeah, sorry.'

'He was a high court judge.'

'Wow,' I said.

'I don't know, really. I don't know if I like the whole idea of judges. I mean, nobody can know everything, right? And I don't know what he would have made of me.'

'I'm sure he would have been proud, Jennifer,' I said. 'Well, I'm sure he was until, you know. Until he died.'

'I like the idea of the sixties, and Mum always says – said – that he didn't much like the sixties. I want them back, Jack. The soft drugs, the free love. No, I don't know what he would have made of me. But then I couldn't be me at all if it wasn't for the money he made. The freedom I want; I couldn't have it. You have to have a lot of money to be really free.' She stood up and stretched. 'And he was a churchgoer. I hate the church.'

I hate the church too, I wanted to shout. I wanted to dance naked around a fire and have an orgy beneath the trees. There was something in her that reminded me of a kind of freedom. The acknowledgement of the animal aspect. The kind of freedom that died when people started to wear clothes.

'Speaking of money,' I said. 'Well, of day jobs – I'd better be going. You stay here if that's what you want.'

'If that's OK.' She stretched again, and the slow ease with which she moved put me in mind of one of the birds that flapped so slowly through the air above Fell House. 'You know what I'm thinking, don't you?'

'I think so,' I said. I looked at her for a moment, then left the room and ascended through the house towards the front door.

Fell House. That had to be what she was thinking, didn't it? That would be perfect, or it would be if she asked me to go with her, but she wouldn't, she probably wouldn't, not with us being so casual and everything.

She might, though, mightn't she? I smiled as I headed for the bus stop. Daylight was starting to show, like something huge and pale slowly arriving out of space, just the other side of the still-dark sky.

PART TWO

Jack

We bought the place with Jennifer's inheritance. It was dark by the time we got there. Our first night and the rusty moon was low and swollen and we made frantic love in an empty room with peeling wallpaper and her screams scared the feral cats out there in the yard. They scratched and yowled around the loose old five-bar gate that banged and banged against the sandstone wall as the wind picked up and wrapped that full moon in thin sticky strands of black, black cloud.

Throughout the daytime, the sky above the house was full of large black birds, like splashes of ink after the nib has snapped. They shrieked like hungry babies or like old people struggling to hear themselves. When they were not flapping and wheeling through the air, they sat in the branches of the many dead trees of the old Fell House orchard which lay behind the buildings, but it was unrecognisable as an orchard any more; it was an unruly tangle of lifeless wood, hanging over the ground like wiry mist.

The place felt different now we'd bought it, even to the extent that it looked different; it looked hungrier, and colder, and at the same time less like a house and more like something living. The exposed, misshapen head of some buried giant. Almost as if, by virtue of owning it, we had changed it. I suppose that once we were responsible for it, we saw it differently – it was no longer a fantasy, but a series of duties, of jobs. Something to maintain, to defend and to keep.

Fell House was an old house, and it was like something that boiled out of the earth fully formed, rather than something built by human hands. A solid, slate, L-shaped building, three storeys high, including the attic, dark grey and squat against the fellside, side by side with a cavernous barn. The roof was made up of razor-sharp slates, poised to slip away down the slope and plummet over the guttering with enough speed and power to bury themselves almost completely in the mud of the yard. The windows were small and you could tell that the wooden frames had been painted white once upon a time, but now they were split open and rotten, brown streaks open to the elements. The front door, too, was a weird old thing – an uncompromising slab of hundreds of years' worth of layers of paint, with a dark heart of oak, so that it was an off-white colour with flashes of red and smears of grey, like an unhealthy mouth.

Inside, the walls were a patchwork of wallpaper and bare plaster, and in places you could see that areas of wallpaper had been peeled off by previous occupants, revealing other patterns beneath, and sometimes beneath those too, as if the wall was made up of layers like the earth and you could dig into it, travelling back in time, discovering fossils and artefacts buried between two different wallpapers. In other places, you could see evidence of damp. Stains like faces.

There were no carpets; the floors of the house were bare, unvarnished wooden floorboards, apart from in the kitchen, where the floor was hard, cold, evil-looking black slate. In places the skirting-boards and lower walls were broken and cracked, as if kicked repeatedly with steel toe-cap boots.

The windows were made of old, brittle glass which was thicker at the bottoms of the panes than at the tops, due to imperfections in the way it was made back in those days – not because it flowed, as many people thought. The house had an electricity supply, but the wiring was bad, installed by some inexpert resident. The light bulbs dangled too low, switches and plug sockets hung off the walls, and sometimes, for no apparent reason, the power flickered on and off – a loose connection, maybe.

And the attic – I had dreamed of a room like the attic when I was a child: a large room at the top of the house with an angled ceiling, skylights and beautiful wooden beams, and I'd always dreamed of filling it with wooden toys and old books. The attic at Fell House was already full, but of old cardboard boxes, broken furniture, a couple of bent and rusted bikes, empty picture frames.

There was an outhouse, a little lean-to with a padlocked

door stuck to the end of the barn, and inside there was a small, metal chair on which rested a hacksaw. Its walls were lined with whitewashed, rotting plaster, some of which had fallen off in places, exposing the raw stones beneath.

Draughts prowled the corridors and the walls whispered like they were full of creatures. Old cobwebby blankets or empty tins could be found in small, tucked-away cupboards, alongside coils of rope that were tied like nooses, and rusty hammers. Beneath the floorboards, the dust was a foot deep. Fell House was an old house.

I lay there, aching, as Jennifer slept. I looked across the room at the window and outside the night was dark. A draught was tickling my face and making my exposed torso uncomfortably cold. We didn't have any curtains yet. I slowly disengaged myself from Jennifer's arms and slid off the bed, and then walked quietly across the room, across the bare, splintery floorboards, to the window. I looked out eastwards over the old yard and beyond on to the fellside, so that my line of sight ran parallel to Wastwater. I could see the fell as a pitch-black shadow curved against the sky, and the sky was a solid dark grey cloud that moved southwards from somewhere up above towards somewhere down below the curve of the fell. As a result it looked like the fell was growing, getting even bigger, and in the darkness it all looked even steeper than I remembered. I felt vulnerable and naked and exposed out there, hanging on to the side of this wild stone colossus.

Somewhere below us was the lake, and I got the impression that we were all ready to just slide on down and drown. The chilly air was giving me goose-pimples.

I stepped back from the window, shaking my head slightly, when I heard Jennifer speak behind me.

'It's moving but it's not you,' she said.

'What?'

'I touched something and it moved but it wasn't you.'

I turned around.

'Jennifer?' I said.

She didn't say anything else. Her eyes were closed and she was talking in her sleep. I sat down on the mattress. The house had been empty for decades.

I woke up before Jennifer did, although I hadn't been properly asleep, just drifting in and out of a dream in which we spent the night arguing about not having any curtains. In the dream I'd wanted curtains because I was scared of seeing people at the window, but Jennifer didn't want any curtains because she said that she wanted people to watch her.

'Watch you do what?' I had said.

'Make love,' she had said.

'No. Let's not, not without any curtains.' Or something along those lines, but we did anyway, and in my dream I was shouting and trying to push her away, but I couldn't stop her and she took me, and behind it all loomed this square black hole of a window on to the fellside.

I lay there, sweating, awake. It was still dark outside. I

tried to swallow, but my mouth was too dry. The wind bellowed and fumed around the house like some steam-driven whale. I could understand, completely, why people used to personify high winds or thunderstorms as living beasts. For example, one Sunday, early in the seventeenth century, a dramatic storm swept through the village of Great Chart. People reported seeing a huge bull-like creature charge into the church, killing one villager, injuring another and knocking down part of one of the walls. They took it to be the Devil, of course, furious with the congregation for worshipping God.

I left the room and closed the door quietly after me, wishing that I could sleep as deeply and as easily as she did. The landing was long; our bedroom was at the end of it, opposite the bathroom. I stood there in between the two doors and looked down the landing, at the end of which was the stairs. There was something wrong, but I couldn't tell what it was. I counted the doors that opened off the landing: there were five, including the ones for our bedroom and the bathroom. The other three were bedroom doors. Suddenly I saw what was wrong – one of them was open, when I was sure they'd all been closed the night before.

Outside, the wind roared, and it probably had just been the wind, some draught, that had felt its way into our house and pushed the door open. I looked in on my way past, just to make sure that the room was empty – to make sure that no feral cat or big black bird had found its way in. It was indeed empty. I quite liked that room –

it had blue and white striped wallpaper that only reached half-way up. It looked as if it had been torn off above that, like somebody had started stripping it, but never got round to finishing. Where it had been torn off you could see a rich, postbox red colour beneath. And there was also an old, impressively solid-looking wooden beam running from corner to corner, with a hole in the middle like a big, dry, empty eye-socket.

I closed the door again, making sure it was firmly shut.

Just the wind.

When I got back, Jennifer was awake.

'Where did you go?'

'I went to get some water. I brought you some too.'

'Thank you.'

I passed the drink to her and she sat up to take it. She sipped at it, and then put the glass down on the floor.

'I was dreaming,' I said. 'And it woke me up.'

'Were you dreaming about me?'

'Yes.'

'Good.' She rolled over on to her side and stretched, curving her body backwards.

'We should get some curtains.'

'I like not having any curtains,' she said. 'I like feeling that little bit closer to the outside.'

'You were talking in your sleep last night.'

'Was I? Oh Jack, you've just reminded me. Yes. I had a horrible dream.' She rolled back over so that she was looking at me. 'I dreamt that I woke up needing the toilet and it was pitch-black and on my way past the bed I stumbled and put my hand out and touched something and it moved and I thought it was you but then I realised that it wasn't. And I ran out of the room and for some reason the bathroom was downstairs, and when I got to the bottom of the stairs some plaster, or some dust, or something, fell from above, and I knew that whatever or whoever had been in the bedroom was waiting for me at the top of the stairs, and I knew that you weren't there. I carried on to the bathroom and closed the door. And then I just knew, straight away, that whatever had been upstairs was now outside the bathroom door, waiting for me, and so I couldn't leave. I was trapped in there. This tiny little room.' There was a silence. 'It was horrible. And everything was dark.'

'Are you OK?' I put my hand out and stroked her beautifully sculpted shoulder. Everything about Jennifer was intentional.

'I am,' she said. 'But you know when you have a dream and the feeling stays with you.'

'Yes.'

'It's cold, isn't it?'

'Yes.'

We found breakfast in a farmyard down in the valley after following small, hand-made signs advertising fresh eggs and organic meats and local veg around the small lake road until we came to a gravel lane that wound through a beautiful patch of woodland and ended in a small, clean yard through which a clutter of fat chickens squawked. Jennifer squeezed my hand.

'This could be us one day,' she said. 'Wouldn't that be wonderful?'

'Yes,' I said. 'It really would be. Come on. Let's see what they've got.'

We got out of the car. The day was warm for November. We walked over to the white door that opened on to the yard and had a doorbell and a little 'Ring Here' notice. Jennifer pressed the button.

The door was answered by a little girl who looked up at us fearfully. She was blonde-haired and brown-eyed and was accompanied by a little boy of the same colouring and of about the same age.

'Hello,' Jennifer said, smiling at them.

They didn't say anything. They just stood and stared at us. They were joined shortly by an old bent-over woman who rested her gnarled hands on the children's shoulders. She looked at us with bright little eyes and said, 'Morning! Here fer eggs? Veg? Sausages?'

'Please,' Jennifer said. 'Some eggs would be good. And some sausages. And what vegetables do you have?'

'Well,' the old lady said, 'it's all in that little shed, ower theer.' She pointed over the yard at a wooden and weathered door. 'Shoo, you two,' she said to the kids, and pushed them gently outside. They ran around the corner of one of the farm buildings, chasing a chicken. 'Ooh,' said the old lady, shuffling out of the doorway and into the yard. She was obviously arthritic, and wore a misshapen blue cardigan and tatty slippers. We followed her. 'Always under me feet, them kids are. God love them though. Just so innocent, they are. And Jim always says, "If anybody ever does anything to hurt them two. And if anybody ever spoils their happiness . . ." You two got any kids?'

'No,' I said.

'Well, you know when you see kids and they're just beaming,' she said. 'And Jim always says, "If anybody ever hurts them two, I don't know what I'll do."'

'They are lovely kids,' Jennifer said.

'Oh, they are,' the old lady said, opening the door. 'Right, then.' She gestured inside at a couple of big fridges, and a wall against which tall racks were placed. The racks were full of carrots and potatoes and pumpkins and butternut squashes and apples and turnips and more. 'First fridge is eggs and milk,' said the old lady, 'and second fridge is meats. Theer's a bucket down here somewhere' – she waved downwards – 'and you can jist stick yer pennies in that. Me son normally does this and he weighs everything out like, but he's off out so don't wurrit too much about the cost. Just call it two pund and take what yer need. I'd best get back in t' house though. Just got the fire going. Yer should go and see t' lake after this, though, cos yer not far from it now.'

'Thank you very much,' Jennifer said.

'Oh, it's quite alright, dearie,' the old lady said to Jennifer, and then 'She's a pretty little thing, isn't she?' to me, bright eyes twinkling.

'She is.' I smiled.

'I'll see you again anyways, all being well,' said the old lady, and left us alone. I watched her shuffle slowly back across the yard.

'Look,' Jennifer said, quietly. 'There's a price list here on the wall. We'll use this. Isn't it all perfect?'

'It is,' I said. 'We'll have to make this our regular.'

'We'll have to get our fire going too once we get back in. Need to keep the house warm and dry it out a bit.'

'Definitely,' I said. 'It needs a bit of heat.'

We loaded up on fruit, veg, eggs and milk, and left a bit more than the price lists suggested, but even so it was still cheaper than the supermarket we lived near in Manchester. We carried it out into the car in a couple of cardboard boxes provided for the purpose, and set off to see the lake.

Later, we were sitting on a large rocky mound that looked like it had grown too much and burst out of the grassy skin that once covered it. The grass around us was bright green and the earth was iron-hard – the naturally crumbly soil bound by the cold that descends at that time of year. Jennifer cupped a spliff in her hands, sheltering it from the wind. Despite it being quite mild before, the wind was now bitter. It tugged at our scarves and the hair that stuck out beneath our hats. We looked out across the ruffled and restless surface of the lake and it was the colour of the sky on a stormy night, and on the other side of the lake the monstrously huge fells reared upwards and somewhere up there was our house.

'The deepest lake in the country, apparently,' I said. 'I looked it up on the Internet. Also, it was on the news a few years ago because they found a body in there. They only found it because when the body had been dumped, it had floated through the murk to land on a shelf that runs around the inside edge of the lake. If it had been dumped in the middle of the lake, it would have sunk all the way to the bottom and never ever would have been found.'

'No,' Jennifer said. 'I guess the centre isn't where you'd expect it to be. The surface doesn't accurately indicate what is beneath, it doesn't map, you know, doesn't correspond to the depths. You can't guess at the middle.'

'Also, Wasdale has the smallest church.' I held Jennifer to me and we sat there, staring at the deepest lake in the country. There was some gravity there that made natural things more significant and impossible things more believable, more possible. Something disturbed the surface of the water with a loud splashing and I jumped, but then saw that it was just a bird.

'They have the Jinny Greenteeth legend here, in the Lake District,' I said. 'You know. The freshwater mermaid that drowns children. Although mermaid as in maid of the mere, not as in half-fish half-woman. You know, like in the legend of *Beowulf*. How the monster's mother lived at the bottom of a bottomless lake. She was a mermaid, in that sense. The bottom of a bottomless lake.' I shook my head. 'How do you reckon that works? When people who believe in them talk about bottomless lakes, what are they imagining?'

'I don't know,' Jennifer said. 'I don't know.'

The cold penetrated. The sound of several vehicles approaching woke me up. I turned to see an old, rusty camper van rattling down the lakeside road. The van was a short, squat thing that had once been a nice cream colour, perhaps, but was now covered in green streaks, as if mossy. It raced past us and continued on down to the head of the lake, followed by an equally scrappy-looking motorbike, ridden by a huge man wearing full leathers and goggles. He had a grey beard and long grey hair. After him was another camper van, and at first I thought it was a classic Volkswagen, but it wasn't – it just looked a little similar. It had been painted purple with what looked like household matt paint, and, judging from the brushstrokes, by hand.

After we'd got the fire going and eaten lunch, I stacked the plates up next to the sink and looked out of the window. 'The barn,' I said.

'What about it?'

'We should have a look inside it!'

Jennifer looked over to the window from her seat. She was sitting on stacks of unopened boxes with her legs crossed, and resembled a stunning Buddha balanced on top of a little tower. I followed her gaze out the window to the barn, a hard dark shape against the boiling greys of the sky. 'I don't know,' she said. 'I think we should maybe – just maybe – start to unpack.'

'Yes,' I said. 'OK.' I stood there for a moment looking at

the boxes, and I reached for one, but then draw my hand back, suddenly deflated by Jennifer's words. 'Jennifer?'

She didn't answer. She stared vacantly out over the yard, eyes transfixed by the hulking great barn.

'Jennifer,' I repeated. 'Are you OK?'

'Yes,' she said. 'Yes I am. Sorry. I was just distracted. Sorry.' She gave me a smile, her lip-rings glinting. 'I was just thinking, maybe you're right, you know, about checking out the barn. I don't like not knowing what's inside.'

'No time like the present,' I said.

'Come on then.' She stood up. Her feet were bare, and she started hopping from one foot to the other. 'Jesus,' she said. 'Is the heating on? These floors are cold.'

'Yes,' I said. 'The heating's on. Just getting back into the swing of things, I imagine. It's the time of year. It's the stone.'

The barn was sandstone, and so was weathered and pitted. It had a covering of lichens and moss that colluded with the unevenness of the surface to create a sense of it having rough, scabrous skin, and at one end it had a mouth, a huge, ugly, corrugated steel mouth that was hinged like a door. The metal looked like it had been cut from an even larger sheet of metal, with its edges all bent and sharp, and it had been nailed to some sort of metal frame in order to cover the gaping hole that lurked behind it. It was nearly twice as high as I was tall, and about fifteen feet wide.

It was about four o'clock and getting dark, and the layers upon layers of cloud gave the sky a peculiar depth. Jennifer squeezed my hand.

'It looks like we're going to have a draughty month or two,' I said.

'It's good to get closer to the world, though, don't you think?'

'I guess,' I said, although I didn't know if I wanted the world sticking its million fingers in through my walls. 'OK. This barn, then.' I reached out to the fastening, which was an unlocked, rusted latch.

'It's a bit scary, hey?' Jennifer said, lightly.

'It's really scary,' I said. 'And I don't know why.'

'Don't worry, I'll protect you.'

I undid the latch. The door was heavy and, as I slipped it off the bracket of the fastening, its corner dropped to the ground. Looking down, I saw a huge scrape traced out across the cobbles where the bottom corner of the door had been dragged across the yard time and time again.

I pulled the door outwards. It screeched across the ground so loudly that I imagined all the sheep across the fellside jumping up and bolting, all the people in the valley below looking up at the fell and shuddering.

It's just a barn, I told myself. It's just a barn.

The mouth was open, and inside the darkness was absolute. It was so dark that the darkness gave the impression of spilling out into the yard, rather than being driven back by the ailing sunlight.

'There we go,' I said, my voice sounding very small. 'We should have brought a torch.'

'Never mind,' Jennifer said. 'Our eyes will get used to it.'

And so saying, she strode forward, disappearing from sight immediately. Jennifer strode through doorways without seeming to realise it, as if it were some happy chance that resulted in the portal and her pathway coinciding. My Morgana. I opened my hands and closed my hands and again told myself that it was only a barn, it was only a barn, it was only some space inside some walls. But there was something wrong with the light, unless there was something wrong with my eyes of course, or maybe my brain.

I followed her in and it was like going underwater, but sure enough my eyes adjusted and I could see her just in front of me, an ill-defined blur.

'Hi,' she said. 'You OK?'

'Yes thank you.' My vision was getting clearer and I could see her face in front of mine, and I could see that there was no floor, only bare earth. It was just a huge space.

'It's empty,' she said, smiling.

'Thank God.' I almost burst out laughing with relief. 'I thought for some reason that we were going to find something horrible.'

'Oh Jack,' she said. 'You would.'

She put her hand out and stroked my cheek and I smiled and looked around. It's amazing how quickly you can start to see in the dark. I could already see into even the furthest corners.

I saw that the barn wasn't empty after all.

'Oh,' I said, 'God. Jennifer.'

FRANCIS

And now I'm sitting here at this desk. Feeling pretty desperate actually. Pretty low. I find myself thinking about Dad. I wish I could believe in things like he does. But I just don't. He's started going out UFO-spotting again.

I'm scared of doing this forever. I might really end up doing this forever. I don't know what else I can do. Sweat on my forehead.

'Good afternoon, you're through to Francis. Could I please take your account number? Thank you. And how can I help you today? Certainly, that's no problem. I'll just have to put you through to a colleague in another department. It won't take a moment. Is that OK? OK. Thank you for calling.'

I press the button to make the transfer. Immediately another call filters through to me.

'Good afternoon, you're through to Francis. Could I please take your account number? Thank you. How can I help you today? OK. OK. I can do that, but I must advise you, if you keep talking to me like that then I will terminate the call. Mr Carter. Mr Carter. Please. Mr Carter. Do you want me to help you or not? OK then. That's a no, Mr Carter. The way you think you can speak to me like this is despicable. What? OK then. As if. Yeah, but I don't care about that. Goodbye.'

The way people talk to people they don't know makes me so angry. It makes me so, so angry. The way customers talk to me over the phone. Like they're cleverer. Or better. It makes me want to scream down the phone at them. People like you cause wars. But I don't. Obviously. I just cut them off. They don't deserve my help. If people can't manage good manners, then they can fuck off.

'Good afternoon, you're through to Francis. Could I please take your account number? Thank you. How can I help you today? Absolutely. No, don't worry. The reminder was sent out before the payment cleared. That's all. You don't owe anything. No, don't worry. Don't worry. It's OK. Everything's OK. Please don't worry. Don't worry. Don't worry. Thank you. Take care. Bye.'

A thick beep signifies another customer waiting. 'Good afternoon, you're through to Francis. Could I please take your account number? Thank you. How can I help you today? OK. OK. No, that's because – OK. I'm very sorry about that, but – I'm afraid that's not what's happened. Could I just try and explain why that is? No? I don't appreciate your tone, sir. No, if you talk to me like that I'm not going to help you at all. Well, do you *want* to go to court? I'm going to terminate the call now but before I do I want you to know that my colleague understood you perfectly and was deeply upset by your comments. No, he hung up because you became abusive. I've got all the notes right here. No, fuck *you*. Fuck you. Fuck you. I'll talk to you the same way you talk to me. I am but a mirror. You're just shouting at yourself now. Looks like you are your own worst nightmare. Jesus. Goodbye then.'

I don't know how in hell I'm ever going to be able to bear the rest of the day in here. How in hell I've managed to bear working here for nearly fifteen months. Thought it would have got better since Kenny disappeared. And it has, in a way. But it was so bad to start with that the improvement hasn't made much of a difference. I'm fantasising about burning the place down. Or stabbing myself in the eye with a pen. And running around the building screaming. Or battering somebody around the head with a keyboard. Somebody taps me on the shoulder. I jump.

'Don't worry, Francis,' says a voice behind me. 'I expect you were all ready and waiting for your next call, eh? I remember when I worked on the phones. In between calls, I would be so *tense*. So *primed*. The anticipation was *so* pleasurable. It was what I loved about the job so much. If anybody tried to – *talk* to me, or tapped me on the shoulder, in between calls, I would jump out of my skin. When I was in between, I was ready to just go *off*.'

The voice is rich, and clear. Like James Bond. Artemis Black. Role model for lowly customer advisers like me, apparently. Fascist. All-round English gent. In his imagination he sleeps with a different school-leaver every night.

Working his way through all those doe-eyed sixteen-year-old girls. Like he does ready meals. He loves his job.

'Hello, Artemis,' I say. I log back out of my phone and turn round warily to face him.

'Francis, Francis, Francis.' He sits on my desk. And lowers his head so that his face is close to mine.

'Yes,' I say.

'You've been cutting people off, haven't you?'

'No,' I say. Hoping the odd occasions that I have cut people off haven't been picked up by the RCRS – Random Call Recording System. Or Arsy-Arse, as Graham calls it. 'Why would I do a thing like that?'

'Pride,' he says. 'Or maybe some silly little sense of righteous anger. I would say laziness, but not in your case, Mr Wood. No. You're too sharp. But there is no room for idealism in the workplace, not when we have to get the money in. We're seven million behind our year-to-date target. Remember that. Cash. Cash. Cash. Do you understand me, Francis?'

'I think so,' I say.

'Now, I know that you've been cutting people off and abusing our customers, but I only know because I can *tell*, because I'm experienced in this line of work. Once we have proof, you're sacked. OK?'

'Yes,' I say, 'I understand. Thank you, Mr Black.'

He claps me on the back. He points up at a huge A0 poster that reads – PAYMENT IN FULL. EACH AND EVERY TIME. 'Don't mention it,' he says. 'I'll see you soon.'

'Any news on Kenny, Mr Black?' I ask.

147

'No,' he says. 'If he does turn up though, he can forget coming back here to work. Not having that kind of pathetic behaviour pardoned on my watch. One foot out of line is all it takes, Francis. OK?'

'OK,' I say.

He stands up and starts to walk away. My mobile starts ringing. He turns around. Grinning like a madman, like he's delighted to have an excuse for some serious disciplinary action.

'Now then,' he says, 'that wouldn't be the ringing of a mobile phone, would it? You do know that the use of mobile phones is strictly prohibited in this place?'

I pull the phone out of my pocket. I maintain eye contact. I answer it.

'Hello?' I say.

Black's face is turning red.

'It's me,' Graham says over the phone. 'I was just wondering if you were at work?'

'Yes,' I say. And then Black snatches the phone out of my hand. He twists it into two.

'Mr Black,' I say.

'You might think that you're clever,' Black says, 'but really you're just a smarmy little prick. A smart-arsed, arrogant bastard. You think you are entitled to the kind of life you want, but you're not. You fantasise about something bigger, about something important, about some sort of ideology that will give your life meaning. But there's nothing there, Wood. All there really is is the need to eat and drink. A hungry stomach. Each person is just a mouth,

Francis, and no better than whatever it takes to fill it. You'll find that out as you get older. Now get out. Get out!'

I open our front door and stumble through into the hallway of our house. Shivering like a dog in a thunderstorm. 'Taylor!' I shout. 'Taylor!'

'I'm here,' he says, quietly. He slowly emerges from the living-room. He's holding an unopened bottle of red wine in his hand. 'I'm here. What is it?'

'Keep me from that awful prick,' I say, 'or I'll beat his head against the wall. Until there's a hole in it.'

'You can only mean Graham.'

'Yes!' I say. 'Graham! Is he in?' I'm taking off my shoes and coat. A puddle grows beneath me as the rainwater trickles from my clothes.

'He is,' Taylor says.

'He got me sacked.'

'How?'

'He rang me up! To ask if I was at work. Right in front of Arty fucking Black.'

'And you answered it?'

'Yeah, of course I did.'

'It's not exactly his fault then, is it?' Taylor says. 'I mean, you could have ignored it. Pretended it wasn't yours. Even turned it off and apologised. I mean, you could have had it turned off in the first place like you're supposed to. But I bet you made a big deal out of it. And you know why.'

'Do I?'

'Because you *wanted* to get sacked. You know that, without a shadow of a doubt.'

'Taylor,' I say, 'you infuriating bastard. Why haven't you opened that wine yet?'

'I was waiting for you before I opened it, naturally,' he says. 'And I'll open it once you stop asking me questions. I have to go to the kitchen and get a bottle opener, see.'

'Go then. Hang on. Did you say that Graham is in? Is Erin in too? Taylor?'

'I'll see you in a moment, Francis. I'm going to open this wine.' He turns and heads downstairs into the basement kitchen. 'Set the console up. Mario Kart or Monkey Ball. But not Resident Evil. I've had too much.'

I head through the open door into the living-room and fall onto a beanbag.

'Evening, Francis,' Erin says, from the sofa.

'Erin,' I say. 'I didn't know you were there.'

'How are you?' she asks.

'Very well, thank you. I got fired. But it's no great loss. I was thinking of trying to be homeless for a while anyway.'

'You don't have to go homeless. We can cover you till you get another job.'

'No, I mean like an experiment. Like Orwell.'

'What would you eat?'

'Oh, I'd find something. I'd eat the bodily secretions of women. With my dirty unwashed mouth.'

'Ever the charmer.'

'Taylor didn't say you were here.'

'He was probably hoping I'd scare you.'

'Listen, Francis,' she says. 'It's Jack's birthday in a couple of weeks. We're thinking of organising a surprise party. It would be a house-warming too. And a Christmas party.'

'What?' I say. 'Up there?'

'Yeah,' she says. 'We'll go up in a week or so, say that we're going up for his birthday, you know. And then one night, the world and his dog turn up out of nowhere, armed with drink and fancy-dress costumes. It couldn't possibly go wrong. And it has to be one of the best parties. One of the best parties we've ever been to. It will be the first party since he moved out. We have to set a precedent. Because we should never stop seeing each other. It is too easy to get too busy. We have to make this clear.'

'That sounds like a good plan,' I say. Because it would mean seeing Jennifer again. Properly. If nothing else. Jack never said anything about my stupid attempt to kiss her. But the way he acted, and the way he never brought Jennifer around after that, makes me think she told him. 'But then,' I say, 'your beautiful, beautiful voice could make any plan sound good. I could listen to you all day.'

'Make your own tea, Francis,' she says.

'You know you're very beautiful,' I say.

'So you're complimenting a girl on her physical appearance in order to persuade her to cook you your evening meal?' she says. 'And in this day and age. You should be ashamed.'

'All I'm capable of feeling is hunger,' I say. 'Otherwise I'm sure I would feel guilt and remorse. I would have some sort of conscience.'

'Must we do this every night?' she says.

'Sometimes you say yes,' I say.

'Rarely, Francis,' she says. 'Get off your bum and go cook yourself.'

'I'm too hungry,' I say. 'Do you think Taylor would want to make me some tea?'

'Francis,' she says.

'Yes. I know. The party.' I run my tongue around my teeth. 'Have you spoken to Jennifer?'

'Yeah,' Erin says. 'Yeah, she was up for it.'

'That Jennifer girl is *hot*,' Graham says, as he bounds into the room.

'You got me sacked,' I say. 'Artemis Black saw me answer my mobile.'

'Fool,' Graham says. Slowly.

'No,' I say. 'I'm not a fool. I wanted to leave anyway.'

'Then stop whingeing,' Graham says.

'Yeah,' Erin says. A pause. 'But anyway. The party.'

'What party?' Graham asks. His head jerks up.

'We're arranging a surprise birthday party for Jack,' Erin says. 'Also it would be a house-warming. And a Christmas party. But mostly a surprise birthday party for Jack.'

'Amazing,' he says. 'I'm going to charm like there's no tomorrow. I mean, the girls there won't know what hit them. I'll be a bull in the china shop. I mean, like a kid in a sweet shop. A shark in the swimming pool. With no ladders.'

'Not a pretty picture, Graham,' Erin says. 'You don't paint a pretty picture.'

'I'm only speaking metaphorically.'

'Yeah,' she says. 'I'd gathered that.' She runs her fingers through her hair. 'Maybe you need to think about the way you present yourself.'

'Well,' he says, 'I might have a haircut.'

'That's not what I mean,' Erin says. 'I mean by the things that you say and do.'

'What?' Graham says.

'Graham,' I say. 'Graham, Graham, Graham. I'm really hungry. Could you make my tea, please?'

'OK. Wait. No! Make it yourself. You'd be the worst dictator ever.'

'Worst as in most evil or most incompetent?' Erin stretches as she asks the question. Her arms uncurling out from the end of the sofa.

Graham thinks for a moment. 'Both,' he says. 'Francis would just be crap. As dictators go. At any job, in fact. As proven just today.'

Taylor appears at the entrance to the room. He looks at the TV. 'Francis,' he says. 'Where's Mario Kart? Where's Monkey Ball?'

'I've been busy! And where have you been, anyway?'

'I was making Erin a sandwich. Here you are, Erin.' He hands over the plate.

'Too kind, Taylor!' she says. She grins.

'You make Erin a sandwich, but for me, nothing?' I say. 'That's, you know, I think that's probably sexist.'

'We have this deal where we're nice to each other,' Taylor says. 'Works well. Besides, she said she was hungry.

You just wanted me to open the wine. All you ever do is take. Erin gives something back.'

'Don't want to know!' Graham says. He never misses a trick. Or at least never an easy one.

'Not like that, knobhead,' Taylor says. 'Like, she took my books back to the library when she went earlier.' He sits down. 'Anyway, what kind of boyfriend would I be if I didn't make my girlfriend a sandwich?'

'So,' Erin says. 'The party. We have to make it special. We need loads of people. And it needs to be fun. A decent sound system. Enough fairy-lights to illuminate the whole house. Maybe fancy dress. Definitely fancy dress. What's the theme going to be?'

'Bad taste,' Graham says.

'Black and white,' I say.

'Christianity through the ages!' Taylor says.

'Let's ask Jennifer,' Erin says. 'She'll know best.'

I've been meaning to go shopping for days. Weeks. But never got round to it. I'm standing in the kitchen. Alone. Looking up at the *Terminator 2* poster that looms over the table. I turn to my cupboard, and open the cupboard door. There's nothing inside but a nearly empty packet of bread. I look inside and there's only one piece left. I take it out and start to nibble. Work my way around the mouldy bits. Once upon a time people would have eaten everything. Because they wouldn't have had anything else. But I read that mould can give you cancer. Once upon a time people wouldn't have worried about cancer. Because they were

154

too scared of the wolves. And the woods. And the dark. The bread comes apart in my hands and falls to the floor. I look at it for a moment and then pick it all up and throw it into the bin. A spider runs out from behind the bin. The thing is huge. It criss-crosses the floor around my feet. Then lurches off towards the shadows behind the washing machine. I turn the kitchen light off. I make my way out into the small hallway at the bottom of the stairs. I lean against the wall. The stairway walls are gold in the light from upstairs, but where I am it is dark. I could eat a horse. A hoss. A scabby hoss between two bread vans. I slip my hand down into my boxers and check my testicles for lumps. Whether my fear is genuine fear or media-inspired paranoia I don't know. It's just, you know. You read and hear so much. Probably there isn't any difference.

Upstairs, Taylor is pacing around the living-room with an anxious look on his face. I watch him from the doorway for a moment.

'What is it?' I ask. Eventually.

'Graham and Erin are getting ready,' he says.

'Ready for what?'

'To go out,' he says. 'And I am trying to make my mind up whether or not to join them.'

'I need to save my money.' I run my tongue around my teeth. 'Now, you know. I haven't got a job.' The truth is that I don't feel too much like going out. I want to stay in and play Resident Evil. Watch a film. Maybe *Attack of*

155

the 50 Foot Woman. Or *Barbarella*. Or maybe *Sympathy for Mr. Vengeance* or maybe *Fargo* or maybe *Rawhead Rex* or *The Fly* or *Night of the Living Dead* or *Metropolis*.

'I'm running low too,' he says. 'But.'

'But?'

'But. I've decided. I'm going with them.'

'OK.'

He sweeps past me and on up the stairs to the next floor. *Amélie* smiles down at me from her poster on the landing. I look up at her for a moment. Then, suddenly, I realise that Graham's face is present. In the corner of my field of vision. To my left. Motionless, like it's pinned to the wall. It's poking around the edge of his doorway. He shakes it.

'Francis,' he says. 'Francis, Francis, Francis.'

'I'm tired,' I say. 'I have no money. I'm getting up early. I just don't feel like it. I'm busy.'

'You know what I'm going to say.' He raises an eyebrow.

'Yes.'

'You're only young once, Francis.'

You're only young once. That's what Graham shouts through the house if he's trying to persuade me to join him in going out on a Friday night. Or Saturday night. Or Thursday night. Or Monday night. Or any night of the week for that matter. Come on, Francis. You're only young once. This is the only life you'll ever have. Have fun while you still can. Before you get some incurable disease. Before your fears rise up and gut you. Lock you up in some god-forsaken suburban flat. With no company.

I don't say anything.

'Francis?'

'OK.' I hang my head.

'OK?'

'I'm coming.'

He comes out of his bedroom and stands next to me. He looks like a Viking. He claps me on the back. 'Good man, Francis.' A wolfish smile. 'Good man.'

I smile back at him.

I am never sure of myself.

Fear is always there in my head. There is always the one big fear that lies over my life like soot: cancer. And then there are other fears that rise and fall like waves. Two fears in my head right now.

Cancer.

And – like a thick worm in the gut – Jennifer. Not Jennifer herself. But myself. Around her.

JACK

Something tall and thin was leaning against the wall, and it was hard to tell what it was because it was still just a hard edge to a patch of shadow but it looked like it was too thin and its head was too big. My throat closed up as I saw that its head was turned towards us, and the head was ugly and wedge-shaped against the wall.

'Jack?' Jennifer said. 'Jack, what's wrong?'

'What's that?' I tried to ask, but nothing escaped my lips other than a dry, throaty croak.

'What?'

I nodded over her shoulder towards the corner of the barn, and the thing stared back at us unblinkingly, unmoving, as if we'd shocked it into stillness. It was a cold hard face sticking out of the darkness, but as soon as she turned around I knew it would duck back into the corner, out of sight, and she'd start to doubt my sanity, and maybe that was how it would start. Small cracks between one person and another, slight differences in experience or perception, and then sooner or later one or the other would end up mad.

She turned around to look and the thing didn't move.

'Oh Jack,' she said. 'It's just an *axe*.'

'What?' I said. 'No. Oh. Wait . . . oh yeah.'

Giggling, she patted me on the chest and walked over to the wall with the axe resting against it. I followed her, and even though I knew what it was now and I was standing right next to it and could see that it was just an inanimate object, I was still not entirely comfortable, or even comfortable at all. It was huge and heavy-looking, and rainwater or something had dripped through the roof on to one particular patch for I didn't know how long and left a rusty spot, like a knot in wood, like a bloody eye. I hated it.

'I don't like it,' I said, not letting myself use the word *hate* out loud, for some reason even I didn't understand.

'You wouldn't.'

'What do you mean?'

'Nothing.'

'Jennifer.' I couldn't think of anything else to say. 'What do you mean?'

'Nothing. Just. Nothing.'

From the kitchen, I could see into the living-room through the open door, and I watched Jennifer without her knowing I was there. She was touching the back of her neck. She ran her fingers up through her hair, then turned around and looked behind her. She looked confused. She turned around again, so that she was facing the way she was facing originally, and she put her hand to the back of her neck again and I realised that she was feeling that presence behind her. That girl her mother used to see touching Jennifer's hair. And I watched her, alone in the room, turning around and around and around.

I sat behind my desk, in my new favourite chair, which was one that Jennifer had stolen from her design studios when she was a student. It was an old leather spinny one with no arms, just like a round stool with a back. I was wearing a coat because even with the fire and central heating on it was still pretty cold in there. I found myself looking at all of the boxes stacked up in my office, or what would be my office, once I started working in it. We were also using it as a storeroom for all of the boxes that we hadn't yet unpacked. I had three big framed pictures up, which were presents from Taylor – a beautiful photograph of Stonehenge, one of Brian Froud's faery paintings and a Kieslowski poster. This was the only room that I could put my pictures in, as Jennifer had plans for the other walls in the house: family photos here, empty spaces there, artwork by a friend in this other room. I didn't mind – it was her house, really, and I was lucky to be there. Besides, I liked having them with me, as it were, there in that one place, and she was right – they wouldn't fit with anything anywhere else. They didn't even fit with each other, really, but this room was my room, and it didn't matter if things fitted together or not. If I was only

160

going to have one little space in which to honestly show myself, then I'd have it however I wanted. I realised that I was shivering.

Even there, though, even surrounded by my pictures and books and objects (stones with holes through them, dream-catchers, little models of faeries in jars), I couldn't help thinking about that axe when I should have been thinking about work. About the lake, specifically, because that was what I wanted to write about. Only that was just going to be a starting-point, really, and then I was planning to move on to why the idea of the bottomless lake has persisted across the country despite the protestations of geography and physics. Really, the durability of folk tales was the point. If I ever finished the blasted thing – if I ever started it, even – then I could send it off to a few magazines, see how it went. But I couldn't shake that damned axe from my mind. I played with a lump of Blu-tack until it was a perfect sphere rolling around between my hands, a thinker's hands, Jennifer always said, and she said it like it was a compliment. I couldn't help taking offence though, although only internally, of course – I didn't show that it bothered me. I looked at my pale, soft fingers and squeezed the ball into a worm. That axe.

A thinker's hands, she'd sometimes say.

Thank you, I'd reply.

Would they carry on their Mario Kart league table without me, back in Manchester? Was I gradually going to move further and further down it, until I just fell off?

*

I walked downstairs to see the back door wide open, and the grey air and brown earth just lay flat outside like they were dead things. Why couldn't I stop thinking like that? I knew why – because there was something wrong, with me, with Jennifer, or with both of us, or with the house, or with all four, and I didn't know what.

I got to the bottom of the stairs and Jennifer appeared, framed by the doorway as she came in from outside. Behind her the sky was darkening. In her hands she held the axe. It was as long as she was tall.

'Jennifer,' I said. 'What are you doing?'

'I thought we could make a feature of it,' she grinned. 'Isn't it beautiful?' She hefted the thing up into my face. The head was bigger than I'd realised: sharp-edged, solid, heavy, totally uncompromising. Thin tears of rust ran down the metal and into the shaft, which was wholly carved from one dark-brown piece of wood, and the grain was a dark web of contours. There was an ingrained ring of dirt around the middle of the shaft where I imagined two thick-skinned muddy hands gripping the thing, lifting and swinging it, time and time again. I imagined it silhouetted against the white-grey sky, weighted with potential energy, as it hung stationary in that split-second before it fell.

'I was going to say we could throw it away,' I said. 'Could use the handle for firewood.'

'What? *Why?*'

I shrugged. 'We're not going to use it, are we?'

'No, but I thought we could varnish it and things, and

hang it up on the wall. Look at the grain. At the patterns in the rust.' She rested the axe on the floor and pointed at the spot that looked like an eye. 'Look at this.' She smiled. 'Come on, Jack.'

'I just don't like it, Jennifer. I'm not sure—'

'Oh for God's sake, Jack. What's wrong with you? You should free up a little. You're so – I guess scared is the word. A little bit uptight.'

'I'm not scared! I'm just – well. What's wrong with being scared? Why can't you just accept me being scared? Normal people would say, you know, so you're scared.'

'What?' she demanded. 'Is that it? Have you finished your sentence? Is that your argument? Normal people? What the fuck is that supposed to mean, Jack? Normal people. Fuck's sake.' She leant the axe against the wall and stormed into the kitchen and through from there into the living-room. The living-room light came on and the door slammed shut. Her raised voice carried back through the door. 'I know you're trying to say that I'm not normal, but I don't care, and if you don't like me this way then you can always leave!'

I stared at the axe for a moment, unthinkingly, and then grabbed it and threw it out the back door, but it was heavy and didn't go very far. It landed near some small white plants that looked pretty dead, actually, pretty withered, and they looked quite strange because they were so regularly spaced. I followed the axe outside to see what they were.

They were bones, not dead plants at all, but the ribs of

some animal sticking up out of the ground, like a cat, or maybe they were big enough to belong to a lamb if I were to dig them out, which I was not about to do. I picked the axe up again and hurled it further away.

FRANCIS

Graham is sitting on the living-room floor. He is planning the party. He has several A4 sheets of paper taped together. A handful of different-coloured ballpoint pens. He is mapping the thing out. He has lists of people all over the paper. Lists of names. He has connected up various names to indicate who has whose telephone numbers. To check that the invites will cascade as intended. The names are also grouped by association – those who know each other through school, or university, or work. And location, so that he can suggest car shares or railway routes. He indicates these groups by ticking those included with the coloured pens. He uses the pens to draw connecting lines as well. He connects lines between various people. Green for friendship. Blue for long-term couples. Red for broken relationships. Yellow for mutual dislike. Purple for unrequited love. Orange for casual sex. There are numbers in amongst the lines too. 'It's a recipe,' he says. 'You need the right number of people who have never met each other, the right number of old friends, the right number of single people. Old grudges, to bring in an edge. Some people need to have some things in common. Others, nothing.' There are digits that he's scribbled down as he's worked out how many people Jack and Jennifer can expect to arrive. 'You want people to experience as many different positive emotions as they can. They need to be amused, aroused, excited, stimulated, hopeful, made to think, infatuated. Also, sad and scared at the thought of the whole thing ending. That's how you keep a party going indefinitely. The idea that it is keeping a worse and more real world at bay.'

'Graham,' I say, looking at his work, 'we should hang this thing on our wall. It's a work of art.'

'Fuck off,' Graham says. 'It's not *art*. I don't know anything about art. Better things to think about.'

I sit back down.

'There is one problem,' Graham says. 'The same problem any good, proper party faces. There is no way of chav-proofing it.'

'Don't use that word around me,' I say. 'Please.'

'What?' he says. 'Chav?'

'Yeah.'

'Chav chav chav chav chav?'

'Yeah.'

'Why not?'

'It's classism,' I say. 'Snobbery. Bigotry.'

'What's wrong with classism? They're not called the lower classes for nothing.'

'You're such a prick,' I say. 'An utter dick. The whole

166

chav thing is just a weird backwards prejudice. Legiti-mised and perpetuated by, you know. Certain awful news-papers.'

'Get off your high fucking horse.'

The curtains are drawn against the winter dark. The standard lamp is lit, giving the room that orange warmth. I'm sitting on the sofa with my knees up. I'm wearing jeans and stripy socks. My jeans and stripy socks take up much of my attention. The socks are blue and yellow. The TV is on – it's some music channel, but I don't know which. There's a woman on screen. She wears a bikini, and squashes one end of a long cream éclair into her cleavage. The other into her mouth. She gyrates to the beat of whatever tinny dance track this is the video for. She is beautiful. With wavy brown hair down to the middle of her back. And thick lips. White teeth. A long tongue. How much of her is real I don't know. These videos are included on single CDs now along with the music. So young boys and maybe older boys buy them for the soft porn, not the tracks. Their sales go up. I mean, she is, you know. Beautiful. But she's not Jennifer. I don't even get an erection looking at her. Maybe there's something wrong with me. Maybe I should get checked out.

Graham is not transfixed by the screen like he normally is when semi-naked women appear on it. He's scribbling away at his plan.

'Graham,' I say. 'Have you seen what's on TV?'

'Yeah,' he says. 'This video's fucking amazing. But I'm getting into the zone now. See, if I get this plan right then I'm certain to pull and get at least a lap-dance. Probably more. Better than any ten-a-penny wank video, anyway.'

'I really don't know how you reach that conclusion.'

'That's because you're not the King, like I am.'

I turn the TV off. The room falls silent. The girl disappears. I feel a momentary sadness. Like she was the ghost of somebody important to me. Seen and then straight away lost.

It's about ten o'clock. The front door opens and closes. It must be Erin getting in. When I hear a knock at the living-room door I know it's her. When she opens the door slightly and sticks her head around it I see that it's her. 'Hi!' she says. 'You organising the party, Graham?'

'Yep,' he says. 'Sure am, Erinnio.'

'We need to talk about it,' she says. 'I'll just sort myself out and come back. Anybody want a drink?'

'I'll just have some milk, please,' I say.

'Any beer there is left,' Graham says. 'Please.'

Later. Graham, Erin, Taylor and I are huddled around the blue glowing screen of Erin's laptop, which Graham holds on his knees. Graham has the most Facebook friends. The past few days he has been systematically looking through the friends lists of all his friends. And sending out friend requests to any and everybody he might possibly know. And quite a lot that he doesn't.

'I just contact people based on what they look like,' he says. 'There's not much else to go on here.'

168

'You could look at their likes and dislikes,' I say. 'Favourite films. Books. Music. All that stuff.'

'Well,' he says, 'None of that necessarily means anything. Especially because people fill those details in when they first register, and then forget about it for months. Years.'

'But how do you know the photos are real?' Taylor says.

'I don't,' Graham says. 'But what people want you to think they look like is as important as anything. The right mix of indie kids, Goths, hardcore freaks, whatever – it's not as important as the mix of people who *want to be* indie kids, Goths, etc.'

'What about her?' Erin asks, pointing to a picture of Jodie Marsh. The glamour model. The name next to the photo is Quick Lips. 'What does it mean when they put a photo of someone they're not?'

'Depends,' Graham says. 'Hopefully, low self-esteem.' He looks up and grins. 'Easy pickings, maybe.'

'Oh you're disgusting,' Erin says, standing up. 'I knew you were going to say something like that.'

'Well,' Graham says, 'I'm a single man. What do you expect?'

'You're not a man,' she says. But leaves it at that.

'What about Miss Lynch?' Taylor says.

'Well, yeah, sure, I see her most nights,' Graham says. 'But I'm still single in essence.'

'Whatever that means,' Erin says.

'Anyway,' I say. 'Let's get the actual party invites out.'

'On it,' he says. 'Just setting it up as an event on here. We should give it a name. Like, how old is he?'

'Twenty-six,' Erin says.

'Cross the Threshold!' Graham says, immediately.

'I'm not sure I see the connection,' Taylor says.

'Nothing to do with his age,' Graham says. 'To do with moving in with your *love*. Like after a wedding. Also – penetration.'

'Then why did you ask how old he is?' Taylor asks.

'Just curious.' Graham sits up. Pulls away from the screen. 'I'm thinking,' he says. 'Won't Jack see this?'

'You know as well as all of us that Jack hates Facebook, Graham,' I say. 'He only uses the Internet for research and stuff.'

'Oh yeah,' Graham says. 'I forgot.' He pulls a face and attempts to change his voice – making it softer and putting on a posh accent. Doing an impression of Jack, I guess. 'Too much surface! Too modern! Buh-buh blah blah blah. Yeah. I remember now.'

'I'll ring Jennifer,' Erin says. 'See what she thinks about the name and the theme and everything.'

I have to try really hard not to shout out. I'll do it, I nearly shout. Let me ring her. But I know it's not a good idea. I wouldn't talk about the party at all. Just scramble my desperate words and fuck it up. Erin's dialling already. She leaves the room.

'There,' Graham says. 'Invites sent. I've made it an open event as well, so guests can invite other people.'

'You reckon Jack's going to go for this?' Taylor says. He looks at me and purses his lips.

'I'm not sure,' I say. 'Maybe it should be a closed event,

Graham. No viral invites. No legitimised gatecrashers.'

'Gatecrashers are important to a party,' Graham says. 'Everybody else pulls together, like antibodies in the face of cancer. Or something.'

'Not sure that's quite what happens when people get cancer, Graham,' I say.

'Oh yeah,' he says. 'Your dad. Dude. I'm sorry.'

'It's OK.'

'Maybe that's why I've got it on the brain, hey?' he says. 'Anyway. It might mean we get a few dicks turning up from work – I saw Kenny on somebody's friends list before – but that always happens. And this place of theirs is so out of the way that they probably won't bother. They'd need a real good reason. Which reminds me – transport. I need to do more work on the transport side of things.'

'I doubt Kenny will show up,' I say.

'Kenny wasn't so bad anyway,' Taylor says. 'Although I didn't know him that well, I suppose. He just seems a bit sad. A bit lonely. A bit fucked-up.'

'He was a dick,' Graham says. 'Come on. Just say it. Some people are just dicks. You don't have to justify it. That's what they are, through and through. Solid *dick*.'

'Anyway,' I say. 'He's missing, isn't he? Doubt he'll show up at some party for people he doesn't really know.'

'Hey,' Erin says, coming back into the room. 'Jennifer's going to come down to get some drink and decorations and stuff. She's going to drive down and tell Jack that she's visiting a friend.'

'What?' I say. 'She's coming here?'

171

'Yeah,' Erin says. 'I said she could stay here for one night. Jack's room is still spare, after all.'

'Yeah,' I say. 'Of course. That makes sense. Yeah. Oh right.' I nod in a way that's supposed to be thoughtful. 'When? When, um, when is she coming?'

'A week tomorrow. Next Thursday.'

'Cool,' I say. I nod again. I can't stop nodding. Stop nodding. Try to appear only mildly interested. 'Excuse me,' I say. 'Back in a moment.'

I leave the room and stand outside the door. Not sure where to go.

JACK

I knelt on the floor, looking at the skirting-boards that ran around the bottom of the living-room walls. It was Wednesday evening, and I was ashamed of myself for missing TV, just for the sound of some other voices in the house. I was glad that Jennifer had ordered a little portable one, and wished that it had arrived before she'd gone visiting Teresa.

Outside, the wind was high and strong, and every now and again something spattered against the windows, as if there were small pockets of rain caught up in the knot of gales and gusts that had settled over the fell.

'That was Teresa,' Jennifer said, re-entering the living-room and dropping her mobile phone on to the sofa. 'I've arranged to go and see her next Thursday. That's good, hey?' She smiled and stood over me. 'I'm dead excited. Haven't seen her in ages.'

'Teresa?' I said. 'Who's Teresa?'

'A friend!' she said. 'I must have mentioned her before. Maybe not. I don't know. Jack. What are you doing?'

'Look at this.' I ran my fingers along some grooves in the skirting-board. 'All these scratches.' There were deep gouges in the wood – scattered groups of three or four regularly spaced scratches, but the groups were all around the room, at frantic angles to each other. 'They must have had a dog here once.'

'Yeah,' Jennifer said. 'A big one. Jesus. They're really deep.'

'We used to have a dog,' I said. 'It would try and dig its way out of the room if it wanted to get out. They must have just kept it shut in here sometimes.' I stood up. 'Sorry, Jennifer. You're going to stay with Teresa?'

'Yeah.'

'On Thursday?'

'Not tomorrow, next week. Why? Do you have a problem with that?'

'No!' I said. 'Not at all. I think it's a good idea. She doesn't live in Manchester, though, does she?'

'No. Why?'

'Oh,' I said. 'You know. All that stuff with Kenny. I know he hasn't been in work, but he might still be lurking around.' And all that stuff with Francis, I thought.

'Teresa lives in Leeds.'

'Oh, right then.' As long as it was nowhere near Francis. Unless – no, she wouldn't have been going to see Francis and telling me she was going elsewhere, would she?

'I know what it is.' She smiled the smile that shot bolts through my body. 'I know what the problem is. You don't want to be up here on your own, do you?'

'Well.' I smiled sheepishly. 'That's kind of it.'

'Don't worry,' she said. 'It'll just be the one night. And you'll be safe as anything up here, with these big thick walls looking after you.' She stepped closer and wrapped her arms around me. 'You're a sweet thing.'

I didn't want to be a sweet thing, though, I wanted to be the thing that drew her hottest breath, coloured her cheeks, the thing that she found irresistible, that she clung to as she quivered and came, the thing that surprised her, the passionate thing. The thing that I wasn't. We held each other.

'What shall we do for my birthday?' I said.

'What would you like to do?'

'I don't know. We could see if there's anywhere good round here to go for a meal. I'm sure there is. Or we could maybe go camping!'

'That's a good idea,' she said. 'Or – what about if we ask Taylor and Erin and the others up? Your friends from Manchester? Would you like it if they came to visit?'

'Well,' I said. 'Yeah, that would be good.' And I did want to see Taylor and Erin and maybe even Graham, and I wanted to see Francis too, but not with Jennifer around. How could I say that?

'Good,' she said. 'Well, I can sort that out. And we can have a nice meal here maybe, and some drinks and stuff. How does that sound?'

'Good,' I said. 'Thank you. Yeah.'

'And what do you want for your birthday, anyway?' she asked.

'I don't know,' I said.

'Thought as much,' she said. 'Not to worry though. I've got some ideas. Some very good ideas.'

Jennifer fell asleep before me again. The wind had died down a little and, restless, I got up and went over to the window. The sky was clear tonight and full of stars in a way that you didn't see in the city, or even in any towns. A slim crescent moon hung up there too, indecently luminous, and the whole scene had an old kind of beauty, like Jennifer's, and like all those old kinds of beauty, it was intimidating, awesome, terrifying, irresistible.

From the horizon to directly above the house, the stars lay across the sky like granules of bright powder. Some of them were fatter and brighter than others and when you looked at the black in between, you just started to see more and more and more, further away, until you had to stop for fear of seeing the whole night sky as white light.

The valley was silent and blue-grey and seemed completely still. I wanted to open the window and breathe the air, but the windows were old and heavy and it would have woken Jennifer. I thought about going outside. I turned around and looked at her and she was almost completely motionless, like a wooden thing.

I got dressed as silently as possible and wrote out a small note on a page of my notebook, explaining that I was going for a walk, but rather than tearing the page out, which might have woken her, I left the notebook itself open on the pillow.

I put my parka on in the hallway, and also a thick scarf, hat and gloves set that my sister had knitted for me a couple of Christmases before, and my Wellingtons. It was only five weeks until Christmas. Should Jennifer and I see Christmas in in our new house, I wondered, maybe invite my family over? The thought of being there, Fell House, at Christmas, with the draughts and the damp and the feral cats outside . . . although it could be wonderful. We could get a big fire going, we could get a *huge* tree in that living-room, and besides, five weeks was plenty of time to get some builders in, or whoever it was that fixed draughts and damp and cold, naked stones. Was five weeks long enough? I didn't know anything about these things. The following year, we might even be able to have a fully home-reared Christmas dinner, with our own turkeys, our own vegetables.

The hallway was dark and I was sitting on the bottom step of the stairs. When I looked up and behind me, the top of the very steep-looking staircase and the landing seemed to be a very long way away. Each banister had one corner picked out in pale blue light, but they were otherwise just regimental shadows that marched on down. The wall to my left was covered in coats and in the dark they looked like weird, humanoid moss-things. I desperately wanted to turn the light on, but didn't dare risk some shard of it spiking through into the bedroom and waking Jennifer; I wanted to go outside on my own.

The cold was severe enough to have thickened the car windscreen with a layer of ice, and I was tempted to take the car for a moment, but decided against it, partly because I didn't have the keys on me, partly because I wanted the air, and partly because getting in the car would mean stepping into the shadow cast by the barn, which I really didn't want to do.

The barn was a great, hard-lined monolith against the sky.

I turned and walked away, lifted the gate gently, swung it open, and carried on towards the road, having to stop myself from running. I didn't know if it was my childish excitement that was driving me onwards or the fear of the barn, but something was picking my feet up faster and faster until I was actually running, and it was OK because nobody could see me, and the road was a wound in the skin of the fell and my feet pounded into it, again and again and again. On either side of the road, grassy banks looked like mounds of blue hair. The sky above was just black now that I was moving too fast to focus on it, and somewhere in the valley something that sounded like a cow bellowed and groaned, accompanied by the shaking and scraping of metal and the barking of dogs. Before me and below me, and getting slowly closer as the road curved towards it, was the great dark lake. Wastwater.

I stopped running, out of breath, and put my hands on

my knees. Parkas weren't made for running in. I looked at the lake again, and it didn't look like something made out of water, it looked like a hole in the surface of the earth, a surface which was thin and fragile. Wastwater looked like an absence; that's what it looked like, as if something important had been rubbed out, cut out, removed. Something important, or maybe something dangerous. There was this persistent idea that we existed, lived out our entire lives, on the surface of an empty, hollow earth. Looking down at the lake, it was almost impossible not to believe it.

I started walking again, but then stopped immediately and took a slow step backwards.

Just as I had moved, I had caught sight of something by the lake. I could see it again, now I had moved back a little; somebody had lit a fire down there, at the far end. I could see how it flickered and jumped, despite the fact that it was only really a tiny orange light to me. The air up there must have been incredibly clear. I smiled to myself and breathed deeply, hoping to catch a scent of wood-smoke, and it was there, just about, or maybe it was wishful thinking. I looked up at the stars again and listened, and could not hear much beyond the tender movements of small things through the world, and the docile wander-ings of nearby ancient sheep. The air was still, and there were no cars. I kept my eyes on the far flame, put my hands in my parka pockets and set off towards the nearest patch of woodland I could think of, which was a little further down the road. I became aware of sheep standing at the tops of the grassy banks, staring down at me with their glass eyes and sliding their lower jaws violently against their upper jaws.

I started to run again.

Beneath the trees the starlight did not penetrate, and I had to pick my way slowly through the fallen branches and head-height mounds of moss and evergreen needles that were swaddled around rocks and tree-stumps.

The trees were close to each other and the spaces between them were dark and all appeared to be still, although I could hear more movement there than I could from the road. I could also hear the mournful calling of the sheep, although what they were trying to communicate to each other I didn't know. Every now and again something, some night-bird, rustled through the foliage above and stopped me dead.

I couldn't help thinking of the Robert Frost poem, 'Stopping by Woods on a Snowy Evening', and the last stanza ran round and around in my head.

The woods are lovely, dark, and deep,
But I have promises to keep,
And miles to go before I sleep.
And miles to go before I sleep.

Except those woods were not deep; the depth was an illusion, created by the density and the darkness. Maybe once upon a time they had been extensive, but judging from the fresh tree-stumps I was starting to find, and the orange crosses spray-painted on to the bark, the trees were being felled.

I found a high stack of tree-trunks on the outskirts of the copse, piled up so that if you stood facing their ends the pale circles appeared to form a kind of huge triangle pointing upwards. Not one hewn-down tree, but several. There were a few single trunks lying about as well. I rested my hand on the exposed flesh of the end of one of them, probing in between two of its inner rings. It felt slightly rotten. Those trunks must have been cut down and forgotten about, and I felt a wave of anger, nausea almost, at the waste. In the future, our era would be defined by how much we threw away.

On the way back, I turned around and looked at the lake again to see if I could still see the fire. I could, but it seemed to keep blinking in and out of existence, as if somebody kept moving in front of it, maybe walking around it, again and again.

I wanted to be these mountains at night, for Jennifer. I wanted to be the strength and the wilderness. Rocks and snow and wind.

FRANCIS

Jennifer's visit comes round in no time at all. Job-hunting swallows up the days. As if they were never yours to start with. And before you know it, it's next week.

It's another dry day, but windy. We wait for her to arrive. I imagine my nerves as long strings, all knotted up. Each nerve sparks something off in those with which it's in contact. I'm full of excited chain reactions.

I give her a hug when she arrives and so does everyone else. Everybody's hair is blowing around. We all smile like idiots. Jennifer is wearing a layered dark-green skirt and a brown shirt. And that red bandana. She says hello to everybody, locks Jack's car up. We go inside.

'Francis,' Erin says, quietly. We are the last to go in. 'You're staring at her.'

'What?' I say. 'No, I . . . I'm sorry. I mean, I wasn't.' I make eye contact with Erin. 'I wasn't,' I say, again.

'Hey,' Graham says, later. In the kitchen. We're making

White Russians. Jennifer, Erin and Taylor are upstairs in the living-room. The strip-light flickers and buzzes. 'You know what Erin told me a couple of days ago? That that Jennifer bird is well into free love, all that kind of crap.'

'Oh really?' I go to the fridge for more milk so that he can't see my face. 'Then why has she bought a house with Jack?'

'She hasn't, has she?' Graham wraps some ice cubes up in a tea-towel. He starts opening and closing drawers. Looking for the rolling-pin. 'She's just bought it on her own, straight from whoever owned it before. Not even a fucking mortgage or anything! And she just happened to be with Jack at the time, maybe. Maybe she wants to start a big hippy commune or something.' He finds the rolling-pin and brings it down. Hard. On the ice cubes. 'Imagine that,' he says. 'Imagine fucking *her*. Jennifer. What would you give for that?' The worktop judders under the blows of the pin. I can hear the ice cracking. So Jennifer and Jack have an arrangement. That makes a little more sense now. I close the fridge.

Imagine it. I turn around and watch Graham. I put the four-pint bottle on the worktop. It jumps and skitters. Imagine it. I'd give everything. But I want more than her body. I want her mind. I want her fearlessness. I want her freedom. I want her time. I want her all.

Upstairs now we are all two or three White Russians to the wind. Taylor and Erin are sitting together in one armchair. Jennifer is sitting in the other.

183

We are listening to *Hot Fuss*, the album by The Killers. Graham's party plan is spread out on the floor.

'When did this album come out?' I ask.

'It was our first year at university,' Taylor says. 'Three or four years ago, maybe.'

'No,' Erin says. Laughing. 'Try six or seven years ago.'

'I don't believe that,' I say.

'It's not as if we're old, though,' Jennifer says. 'How's your dad now, anyway, Francis?'

'He's OK, thank you,' I say. Grateful for the opportunity to look at her openly. 'Well. He's been better. But he's not, um, he's not dying, anyway. The operation went well. He's still having treatment.' Her eyes invite me to be honest. 'I should give him a ring, but he'll just go on and on about UFOs.'

'Ha,' Jennifer says. 'Jack's like that with his folklore. He loves it up there, though. It's like he's found another world. That's what he keeps saying. Like he's found another world where his stories might be true.'

'I miss him, actually,' Taylor says.

'Gay,' Graham says.

'Fuckwit,' Erin says. Without too much affection. She prods Graham with her foot. He puts on a hurt face.

'Last week sometime, I woke up in the middle of the night and he was gone,' Jennifer says. 'He'd left a note saying he'd gone out for a walk. This was, what, two in the morning. He really seems to have fallen for it. I mean the landscape and everything. I didn't like it, though. Being on my own in that house at night, when I didn't expect it.'

'What was he doing?' I ask.

'Just walking,' she says. 'Don't think he'll be doing it again though! Not without telling me first, anyway. Do you mind if I light up?'

'No,' I say. 'I don't.'

'Go ahead,' Erin says. 'As long as you share it with us.'

'No worries,' Jennifer says. She takes a small tin out of her woollen handbag. She opens it to reveal three neatly rolled joints. She removes one.

'What are we doing for food?' Graham asks. 'Shall I order some pizzas or something? Well, I'm going to anyway. You lot can just tell me if you want something. You've got five minutes to decide.'

'I like the theme,' Jennifer says, later still. 'Black and white. It's a good one. Whose idea was that?'

She's looking at me, as if she already knows the answer.

'Me,' I say. 'Mine.'

'Yeah,' she says. 'I like it. And I like the name – Cross the Threshold.'

'That was mine,' Graham says. He is sprawled across the sofa. Lying on his back with a pizza box open on his chest. From where I'm sitting, on the floor, it looks like he's taking the slices of pizza out of his ribcage and eating them. 'You don't have to give me anything,' he says. 'But if you're, like, you know, a proper free-love hippy and everything and you wanted to say thank you, then a blow-job would do.'

Jennifer laughs. 'I'd rather try and chew out my own eyes.'

'How's your virtual girlfriend, anyway, Graham?' I say.

'Yeah, it's going well,' he says. 'We've been seeing each other most nights. Usually have sex, too.'

'Really?' Taylor says. 'How?'

'Well, it's a bit like masturbation at the moment,' he says. 'But with someone else telling me what to do. Got video and everything though. I've ordered some tele-dildonic bits and bobs to make it a bit more, you know. A bit more like proper sex.' He drinks from his glass. 'She's wicked, though. Really like her.'

'You're a one-off, Graham,' Erin says, 'and no mistake.'

'I am,' he says. 'I'm fucking brilliant. Anyway. Let's get back to this party, because if it goes well then I can show my brilliance off to lots of new women.'

'Well, I'll get all of the balloons and stuff in town tomorrow,' Jennifer says. 'And the drink. And Jack's birthday present. You know, there aren't any off-licences or supermarkets near where we live.'

'We'll bring some food when we come up,' Erin says.

'You'll be on the train though,' Jennifer says. 'Are you sure that's OK?'

'We'll bring what we can,' Erin says.

'Have many people responded to the Facebook invites?' Jennifer asks. 'We haven't got the Internet at the house so I haven't been able to check.'

'Loads,' Graham says. With his mouth full. 'What are you getting Jack for his birthday?'

'Oh,' she says. 'You'll see. What about you?'

'God knows,' Graham says. 'I was going to give Francis or Erin some money and ask them to get it.'

'Well you can piss off,' Erin says, 'if you think I'm running errands for you.'

'Alright!' Graham says. 'Jesus.'

'We always used to get him the same things,' Erin says. 'Like, I would always get him a shirt. Taylor would always get him a CD and a poster. Francis would always get him a couple of DVDs.'

'A good one and a bad one,' I say. 'Like, a really good film in a special edition case or something, and then some weird three-films-for-a-pound DVD from the tat bucket at the record shop.'

'Graham normally got him some sweets, from what I remember,' Taylor says. 'Because they sell them at the corner shop.'

'That's it!' Graham says. 'I couldn't remember. Well, that's what I'll do this year too.'

My bedroom is next to Jack's old room. Now the spare room. Now occupied by Jennifer. I lie in bed and think about her. Just a wall's thickness away. I have a headache. I want to go and knock on her door. I want her to tell me that she isn't scared. My head aches like it's too big for itself. Like there is something trying to get out. Like a moth from a cocoon.

If there was a way to be with her.

If there was a way to cut the anxiety out of me. Take all the fear and throw it away. If there was a part of me that I could just remove. I would.

I imagine that I can hear her breathing. I close my eyes. If there was a way. I would.

JACK

I watched as the little Metro beetled off down the track, into the mist of low cloud, and I was thinking that there was something too sudden about this trip to Leeds, something that didn't make sense. I'd never even heard Jennifer mention Leeds before.

I let out a little shout and kicked at a cobble which clattered against the far barn and was immediately insignificant against the bulky building. The sound scared a bird or something, and the bitter, gnarled croak of it echoed sorrowfully around the yard. I looked up to see nothing; I couldn't see anything up there, it was just a disembodied voice coming out of the thick white air.

She was going to see him. Francis. I knew it.

Back indoors I turned all the lights on and closed the curtains even though it was only midday. Having said that, the low cloud cover made the landscape dark and the rooms of the house seem dim so it was not entirely unjustified. I moved from the front door through the hallway to the front room, and the only sound, apart from the sounds of my own body, was the heavy cawing of the big black birds outside. I looked at all of the walls and the few unpacked boxes and the furniture and those things we had unpacked, like books and crockery and electronics and ornaments, and I looked at the stack of empty, flattened boxes in the corner of the room.

Something tapped at the front-room window, a slight rat-a-tat-tat like a fingernail or coin or tooth. I looked at the curtains for a moment and realised that from outside the lit windows would be quite visible across the mountain due to the dark skies. I imagined seeing the thin edges of lights from a distance. I imagined looking in through the window at the curtains from the point of view of somebody standing out there. I felt my pulse speed up. Who or what could the electric light have drawn across the far reaches of the fell?

It couldn't have been Kenny, could it? No. Why would he look for us? How would he have found us? I could just picture it, though, however unlikely it might have been, I could just picture him slouching across the barren slopes, too absent from himself to even notice the time and distance elapsing around him. I could picture him standing at the window, tapping, his huge mouth hanging open and his eyes all wooden and his body bearing the injuries from his jump. He would have come to see Jennifer.

I moved quickly over to the side of the window and looked for some sort of gap that I could peer out of without moving the curtains and drawing attention to myself, but

I couldn't, so I gripped the edge of the curtain firmly between finger and thumb and moved it ever so slightly.

There was nobody there, or at least if anybody had been there, they were not there any more. It must have been something held in the wind, like a clutch of leaves or small insects.

The thought of Kenny getting his hands on Jennifer made me go cold, but then she wasn't going back to Manchester, was she? So there was nothing to worry about, nothing to worry about at all. And also the house was as draughty as ever.

I started laying a fire in the empty fireplace, bunching up newspaper and pushing it tight into the grate. I went to stack some kindling on top of the paper but there wasn't enough really, just a few sticks. There were no logs either. Which meant I'd have to go outside.

I sighed and put my shoes and coat on. I made my way to the front door and struggled to open it against the wind. The first fat drops of a heavy rain were falling, so I double-checked that the house keys were in my pocket and let the wind slam the door shut. I hurried round the corner of the house to a couple of outhouses that leant against the end of the barn before the rain started leaking in through the patchy roofs. One outhouse just had that chair and hacksaw in it, while the other held a pile of old wood. Some of it looked like driftwood from the beach, and some of it was sawn-up fence-posts, and there were a few sawn-up tree-trunks in there too. I gathered up a rotten armful and staggered back to the house, dumped them on the doorstep, and then went back to the outhouse for more – I wanted enough to see tonight and tomorrow through. The rain was heavier now, and forceful.

The second time, on the way back, I noticed something in one of the few uncobbled spots of earth, one of the places where the stones had sunk beneath mud or had been lifted completely. I stopped, despite the weight I was carrying and the precipitation, to look more closely, to double-check that I wasn't being tricked into seeing things by my jumpy mind. But no, it was real.

A footprint. Not immediately recent, necessarily, because it must have been made the last time the ground had been wet, but also it couldn't have been very old. A foot-print itself wouldn't have been that strange, it could have been mine, or Jennifer's, except this one had been made by a naked foot with no shoes or socks, and an unusually shaped foot at that. It was very narrow, and the pads of the toes seemed just a little too far away from the heel.

I stood back up and looked about me, and both the outhouse doors looked guilty, as if they could have been hiding something, as would the barn door if I could have seen it. I turned all of the way around, scanning the near, middle and far distances for non-meteorological move-ment, but all I could see was the ever-worsening rain and the speeding clouds and scrubby grass being buffeted by the wind. Some animals were groaning down in the valley and the wind made a hollow sound as it fluted between the buildings of our home.

Back to the house, as quickly as I could go. I dropped

the wood on the step on top of the last load, unlocked the front door and spilled inside, dragging some wood in with my feet and shovelling the rest of it in with both hands so that I could get the door closed as soon as possible. This meant that the more rotten pieces started to break up, spreading black flecks across the floor, along with tiny spiders and gluttonous orange slugs covered in thick mucous. Once the door was shut I locked it from the inside and leant against it, panting.

FRANCIS

Two weeks since Jennifer's visit. Two weeks of trying to figure out the unemployment-benefits system. Looking for another job. Wasting money. We're on our way up to Jennifer's. And Jack's, of course. But a small, rickety train carriage is no place for a hangover. The four of us sit on two pairs of seats that face each other. We all have our heads in our hands. I want to protect mine from the bouncing of the train. It hurts enough without being bounced around like this. The four of us would probably look quite funny to some sober local. But the carriage is empty.

I listen to some music on my MP3 player. But quietly. Again, I think about the stories that appear all the time, in certain newspapers. About the electromagnetic fields given out by electronic devices. Like personal MP3 players. Mobiles or laptops. Computers, TVs, telephones, games consoles, hi-fis. About how they somehow corrupt the body. Twist and warp cells into ravenous cancers. You don't know what to believe. I tell myself it is just another attempt by the lunatic mainstream to scare us. To shepherd us away from the future. To make us so scared to live and look forward that we subscribe to their miserable, backwards world-view. And become fearful, bitter and pliant. Ready to lay the blame for all of our made-up problems on whoever they point their bloody fingers at. All the while shrivelling up and shaking our heads and wondering why we're not happy. This is what I tell myself. Even so, I start to imagine that I have a headache. I find that I'm cradling my testicles through the pocket of my jeans. Checking them for lumps. In public. I stop.

I see Taylor stand. I turn my MP3 player off and rise, shakily, to my feet.

'We're here,' he says.

'Where?' I whisper.

Graham and Erin stand up too. We all move into the aisle. Taylor signals to the conductor, who's further down the train, that we want to get off.

'Request-only stops,' Graham says. 'Amazing.'

I don't like trains. I don't like being on my way. Or in between one place and another. It's like being unanchored. As if, not being either here or there, there is nothing to prevent me from floating away. Just disappearing. Trains are strange things. And aeroplanes. But they pretend to be normal and perfectly ordinary. Trains and railways are at the edges of the world.

We get off the train. But I'm still slightly nervous. The wires and the rails are humming. The track is straight in both directions. The station is near a beach. I can see the

195

sea down a long straight road. I look the other way. Shadowy purple mountains rise upwards. The grey sky thickens into darker clouds around their peaks. I feel like I'm in a desert. A cold one. The tracks are polished silver. The sky is pale grey. Everything is touched by sand. As if the whole place has just suddenly been revealed by some freak wind in the Gobi. As if ancient dunes have just been swept away to reveal the concrete platforms. The shining tracks.

I look down the tracks one way. Then down the other way. There is something moving on the tracks. A cat. Or maybe it's a little bigger than a cat. It looks like it's playing with something. A little bird or a mouse. But I can't see exactly what it is, or what it's doing, because it's too far away. It jumps on to the tracks. And then it jumps off the other side. Good luck or bad luck, for an awful lot of people. Whichever. I can't remember. Taylor is holding a big shopping bag full of birthday presents for Jack.

We head across a tiny car park. Over a small humped bridge. Jack is approaching in his Metro. He waves at us through the windscreen.

'Have you got satellite TV set up yet?' Graham says. He sits in the front passenger seat. He drinks from a can of Guinness. It looks tiny in his huge hands. Erin, Taylor and I get in the back. We are moving slowly. Trapped behind a caravan. The caravan is low and looks heavy. It looks like it's full of people. Every now and again their faces press outwards from the caravan windows.

'Do you think they're immigrants?' Graham says.

'What?' I say. 'Like Erin?'

'No, dickhead,' he says. 'Like, illegal immigrants.'

'Then say that. And what if they were?'

'I'd report them,' he says. 'Might be terrorists.'

'Are you trying to piss me off?' I say.

'Yeah,' he says. 'Fuck, yeah. Pissing you off is so easy.'

'There have been loads of caravans and stuff,' Jack says. 'Seems to be a bit of a gathering going on, down by the lake. Or something. See, that car behind us with the roof-rack – bet they're going too. Car's full of tents.'

'New Age travellers,' Graham says. 'Scum.'

'Anyway!' Jack says, before I can react. 'It's good to see you. It's really good of you to come. I know it's a difficult place to get to.'

'It's not a problem, Jack,' Taylor says.

The grey, brown and green landscape rolls by. We slowly creep up the side of a mountain. The sky is grey and getting darker.

'It's mostly cloudy here,' Jack says. 'Sometimes the clouds are all bright white, with the sun behind them. But sometimes at night the sky is clear. It's funny. Jennifer went to visit a friend last week, she took the car to Leeds, and looking at the mileometer, it was exactly as far as going to Manchester and back! Who would have thought it?'

Erin and I look at each other. He suspects something.

The house is big. Really fucking big. Old, grey and big.

We see it from a distance first, and then turn off the road on to a bumpy, muddy track. We carry on for a minute or so before creaking to a stop in front of a metal five-bar gate. The bars are dented and bent. The words Fell House are painted across the top bar. Jack gets out of the car and opens the gate.

'We're going to get a proper sign,' he says, getting back into the car. 'Made out of some sort of stone.' We drive through into the yard. I get out of the car and stand in front of the door, which is huge and ancient-looking. The paint is peeling off. Underneath there is more paint, and under that there is more, and more, and more. And more beneath that too. I am staring at it when it swings inwards. And there, right in front of me, is Jennifer.

'Francis,' she says.

'Jennifer.'

There is a smile playing around her mouth. She steps forward with her arms open. She hugs me, tightly. 'Jennifer,' I say, 'do you think this is a good—'

She lets me go and moves away. She throws her arms around Erin, Graham, Taylor. I relax. Every muscle in my body had been tensed. It's not as if we've done anything other than kiss before, anyway. Big black birds squawk and shriek from the bare branches of a couple of trees over behind the barn. Jack invites us inside.

'There were four bedrooms in this house,' Jennifer explains, 'but Jack had to turn one into a study, so now there are only three. Do you mind sharing?'

Jack looks thoroughly uncomfortable.

'Or course not!' Erin says. 'We just thought we'd sleep in the living-room or something. But having *bedrooms* . . . it's a luxury.'

'I'm really sorry,' Jack says. 'It's just that working from home, I needed somewhere a bit separate.'

'Jack,' Taylor says. 'Seriously. Don't worry.'

'I thought maybe we could share, Erin?' Jennifer asks. 'Jack has to endure me every night, normally – might make a nice change for him!'

'I'll share with Jack then,' Taylor says.

'And that leaves us,' Graham says, looking at me. 'Francis. Will you be the sugar or the spoon?'

'I don't know what you mean,' I say.

The room has a sofa-bed in it. And some rugs and bean-bags. And a TV, a CD player. I put my bags down on the floor and look around. In one corner a wooden beam sprouts from the wall. It disappears into another room. The wallpaper is striped, vertically, blue and white. It only reaches about half-way up the walls though. And above that it is torn off, revealing red. I lie down on the sofa-bed. Half-hoping that I might be able to sleep away the last of the hangover. But then the door opens and Jennifer slips in.

'Francis,' she says.

'Jennifer. Hi.'

'I'm glad you're here, Francis.'

I don't know if she means me, or all of us. Sometimes when she visited Jack in our old house I would think that she was trying to communicate something to me through her eyes. She's looking at me in a way now that may be friendly warmth or it may be desire. I just don't know. I feel my mouth drying up. She is heart-stopping. I imagine her naked. Her three lip-rings catch the light from the window and for a moment I see them as three teeth curving down over her lower lip. Her long, artfully messy black hair is held back from her face by the blood-red bandana. Her deep green eyes are wide. Her full lips are parted ever so slightly. She wears a tight black jumper and white jeans.

'What are you wearing for the party?' I ask.

'Black dress. Black wings.'

I imagine her walking towards me from the door. Putting her hands on my shoulders. Closing her eyes. Kissing me.

'Jack's making his famous lasagne,' she says. 'Come down and get a drink.'

'I will. I'll be down in a moment.'

Fell House stands naked against a bloody sky. Tall thin figures like stretched men are blown against it by the bitter wind. They accumulate around the building like dead leaves, whispering and crackling. There's something about them. Something awful. But I'm too far away to make out the detail. The sky is cold, red, still, blank and dying. Dying slowly. I'm holding on to the ground like it's unstable. My fingers are muddy and raw. I'm forcing my forehead into the hard earth. My mouth is full of soil.

Somebody is shaking my shoulder. I roll over. Jack's wide eyes are staring down at me. 'Jack?' I say.

'Hey, Francis. Francis. What's wrong?'

'Jack?' I say. 'Oh. I'm sorry.'

'It's OK,' he says. 'I have bad dreams in this house too. But try to forget about it. The lasagne's ready, and it deserves your full attention.'

Jack and Jennifer have a big old wooden table that they've put in the living-room. There's a big coal fire blazing. Taylor's leant the big carrier bag of birthday presents against the wall. The room is bathed in orange light. Erin's plugged her MP3 player into the stereo and is playing something relaxing, with extraordinary female vocals. I feel like I'm in an advert or a lifestyle magazine. But I like it. Jennifer and I are on opposite sides of the table, but not actually facing each other. We don't talk to each other much. Which I'm glad about. Because it means I can relax a little. I look at her, though, when she's talking to the others. When I'm not looking at her, I can feel her eyes on me. She is beautiful. I look at her face. Her arms. Her hair. The curve of her breasts as they rest against the table edge.

'This room,' Taylor says. 'It's lovely.'

Jennifer's skin glows. I smile and nod. 'So is the lasagne,' I say.

'Francis had a bad dream,' Jack says, to Jennifer. 'I was telling him that we get them in this house.'

'Yes,' Jennifer says. 'It might just be new surroundings

and stuff though. You know. Doesn't have to be anything sinister!'

'No,' Jack says. 'Interesting phenomenon though. New-house dreams.'

'Your presents are over there,' Graham says, pointing with his head towards the carrier bag. 'You going to open them?'

'He's not opening them,' Erin says, 'until his birthday. End of story.'

Despite all the red wine, I can't sleep. Graham is snoring away next to me. I keep thinking about the dream of the red sky. I try counting. Usually, if I have trouble sleeping, I start to count to try and clear my head. But tonight, I get to the number 666 and then start to panic. I don't remember ever getting that far. I am too hot. I'm sweating. I think about the Devil. And, you know. When you think of the Devil. The Devil thinks of you. I stop counting and turn the lamp on. Graham snorts, but doesn't wake up. I dig a Paddington Bear book out of my backpack. Start reading. I keep one on me at all times. I read it and reread it. After two hours, I put the TV on. There is an advert for some rolled-up pizza or something. In the advert, the police can't catch these criminals. Because they – the police – are all eating these rolled-up pizzas. And they can't talk to each other because their mouths are full because the pizzas, being rolled up, are perfect for, you know, eating on the move. And then there is this advert for a mobile-phone company. In which nobody speaks to each other.

Even when they're standing next to each other. Because text messages are so fucking cheap. And then there is an advert for bathroom air freshener. With a talking toilet. And then a repeat of some circus of a singing-contest-talent-show thing comes on. And by this point I am thoroughly pissed off. I turn off the TV without checking the other channels. Because I have a feeling that every channel will be identical. I turn the lamp off too, and close my eyes. I should have just watched *Dr. Goldfoot and the Bikini Machine*.

We are sitting in the living-room. This morning we went for a walk. We headed uphill so that we could see across the mountains opposite us. We could see another lake in the distance. Bright white and flat. Something metal in the middle of all the green. Then we came back and started playing Scrabble. But at some point we stopped. Jennifer, stoned, is swaying to the music like she's underwater. The board is laid out on the floor. There are cushions and Scrabble tiles scattered around.

'What are your plans for the next few years, now you're sacked?' Taylor asks me.

'I'm going to travel,' I say. 'Well, once I get some money together and stuff.'

'I'm going back to Ireland, maybe in a year or two,' Erin says. 'But I think I'm going to have to work in this country for a while first. I'll probably go to live with my dad in London and get a job there, and then – yeah – move back to Ireland.'

'What about you, Taylor?' I say.

'I don't really know,' he says, looking at Erin. He bites his lip. 'I might go to America. Live there for a while.' He shrugs. 'But I'll need some money first. And it all depends, I guess.'

Outside, it is only just turning dark and the sky is clear.

I didn't sleep again last night. In the paper today I saw that evidence has been uncovered of further atrocities in Iraq. I have said little since then. We are all sitting in the living-room again. It's approaching ten o'clock. There is an advert on the TV for some top-end supermarket Christmas food. Except, it's not just Christmas food. It's ridiculously expensive Christmas food. It does make me hungry though. And the bread sauce being poured over the turkey in slow motion, well. Kind of turns me on.

'Can I watch the news?' I say. 'I need to watch the news.'

'Why?' Jack says.

'What do you mean, why? It's about the war. It's important.'

'It's always about the war,' he says.

'It's always important,' I say.

'*Eurotrash* is on, Francis,' Graham says.

'And anyway,' Jack says. 'There's more to life than the war. I was reading about the Coffin Trail over Burnmoor Fell, where they took coffins on horseback to the church over in—'

'Everything,' I say, 'is to do with the war.' But I say it quietly. I keep a tight hold on my third bottle of Copper Dragon. My little finger pulling at the corner of the label.

'What did you say?' Jack asks.

'Nothing,' I say. It didn't really make much sense. 'I didn't say anything.'

'You've got a right cob on,' Graham says, as *Newsnight* starts. I notice Jack, Erin and Taylor looking at each other. And then away. Jennifer is watching me like a cat watches a mouse.

'I'm fine,' I say. 'OK? I'm just watching the television. And maybe you should watch it too. You know. If you think I'm in a bad mood, and you want to know why.'

'But I thought you just said that you weren't in a bad mood,' Jennifer says. She's smiling.

'Let's just all watch the TV,' Graham says.

At that moment, the screen fills with a video recording of some of the abuse that was taking place in Abu Ghraib. Certain areas of the screen are blurred out. My arms are shaking. I don't understand. I genuinely don't understand how Jack can ask me what's wrong. How they avoid feeling the anger and disgust and shame that I feel. And I can feel my face turning red. I'm filling up with hot water. I'm chewing my lower lip so viciously that I can taste blood. But I don't feel any pain. Each and every time new videos or photographs of these abuses are released, the images are burned into my brain. I never forget them. And times like this they all come flooding back. They're followed by the execution videos. The hostages that get decapitated. The videos they never show on the news. But that inevitably turn up on some dickhead's mobile phone which gets shoved in front of your eyes at a friend's birthday party and you can't look away. You can't. And there are people that swarm round and giggle. Who find these videos funny, or interesting. And others that collect them. These videos of beheadings and torture and abuse and rape. They're all there like so much pornography. Because that's what it is to people now. Porn. My legs are trembling and my eyes are filling up. And how can Jack just bang on about some coffin trail over Burnmoor or whatever? I could justify it and say that I feel like it's my duty to make them see. To make them understand the deep toxic depths of the terror that surrounds the planet and is yet apparently invisible to the vast majority of people. I could say it's that which makes me want to roar and shriek and smash my teeth together until they shatter. But in reality my anger is just anger and I can't claim to understand it.

I take a deep breath. Control.

I look back at the TV. Somebody's talking about how Saddam used to torture his opponents in the prisons where his followers are now held. He used to dissolve people in vats of acid. Rape women with dogs. Somebody is talking to the camera about a specific prison. Their face is pixel-lated out.

'The place is haunted. Haunted. It is an evil place and the shadows make people do evil things. There is a spirit there. The memories of the women and the dogs are still there. You can still hear the noises when you're on guard duty. You can still see—'

*

Later. We are all sitting in the living-room. My eyes are closing. Opening. Closing again. I open them again. Try to keep them open. But every battle against your body is a battle lost, like Taylor says. Somebody suggests a film but Erin says 'No!' and insists that we turn the TV off. Because the TV is responsible for the death of the art of conversation. And if we lose the art of conversation then we've had it. She suggests that we play some kind of game. Everybody sits around talking about what we should play. The conversation is warm. I don't open my mouth. Chess, I think. Hey, Jennifer. Want a game of chess?

I keep my thoughts to myself. I am the first to fall asleep.

JACK

Outside it was snowing. It was accumulating across the fells, each layer providing a softer, more comfortable landing for that which followed.

'I was thinking about tomorrow,' Graham said. Graham was always there, just *there*, at the periphery of my perception. 'I was thinking we should all dress up because it's your birthday. Make an effort. Maybe we should all put our suits on.'

'You brought your suits?' I said.

'Yeah,' Francis said, as he entered the room. Francis always went through doors slightly nervously, head first, as if there would be something dangerous on the other side, and the habit probably came from watching too many second-rate horror films. ''Course we did.' He clapped me on the back and grinned. 'Like Graham says, we want to make an effort.'

'Is Taylor wearing his too?' I said.

'Yeah,' Graham said. 'And Erin brought a dress.'

'OK then!' I said. 'Thank you! I'm starting to look forward to it a little bit now, actually. It's really good of you all to come up like this and bring your suits and everything, just for this. Feel like I should have organised a party or something!'

'Who needs all the hassle of a party and all those people you don't really know,' Graham said, smiling widely, 'when you've got all your best friends with you?'

'I know,' I said. 'Yeah, you're right. Not like you to say a thing like that, Graham.'

'No,' he said, and scratched his belly, and then his chin. 'I know.'

Francis turned on the TV. Seventeen people had been killed by a roadside bomb in the Gaza Strip. It sometimes felt like the bad news happened because Francis was around to hear about it – genocide, environmental disasters, global panic, hellish war crimes – they were all very much a part of him. Or maybe it would be more true to say that he was very much a part of this world, a product of it, inextricably linked. The Prime Minister was giving a press conference.

'We will stop at nothing' – he said – '*nothing* – to find and bring to justice those who persist in committing these dreadful atrocities. These attacks are tearing the fabric of our global society apart, and the time has come—'

'Lunch'll be ready in a couple of minutes,' I said. 'Beef sandwiches, and the beef up here is really good.'

Francis just stared at the TV, as if he hadn't heard. I saw that his knuckles were turning white.

'Food,' Graham said, standing up. 'Wicked. I'm always hungry. Always, always hungry. Come on. Let's eat.'

'What are you wearing for tomorrow night?' I asked Jennifer, over lunch.

'What?' she said, looking up sharply. 'What's tomorrow night?'

'Well,' I said, 'it's my birthday.'

'We, um, we all said that we'd wear our suits,' Francis said.

'*Oh*,' Jennifer said. 'Oh, right. What are you wearing, Erin?'

'A dress.'

'Think I'll wear a dress too,' Jennifer said. 'Yeah. Simple but effective.'

Later, alone, I walked to the river and wandered under the trees, where the sun had not yet penetrated and the earth was still snowy and hard with frost. The river had escaped the freeze and ran on between the white and frozen banks, overhung by boughs and branches that were laden with ice and crystal drops. Everything looked like it had grown a deep coat of fur in a futile effort to keep out the cold.

I didn't know if Francis and Jennifer thought they were being subtle when they had been looking at each other the night before. I should have been thinking about my article – it was never going to get written, the way things were going. What was happening with the two of them, really?

The sky was pale grey. I looked at the patch of cloud sheltering the sun, and it was beautiful, and bright around the edges. I liked it down there; I would try to go more often. Sometimes it felt like I could get things in order, sort things out, if I had a moment to think and a clear brain to do it with, like that was all I needed to make everything OK.

I stepped on to the grass that protruded from the snow and snapped it. I picked up handfuls of the little crystals that it had broken into and scattered them about, along with the cold fluff of the snow itself. I could see Fell House up on the fellside back above the lake and the windows were squares of bright silver. Why didn't I think of it as *our* house, really?

Crossing a field, I found a wide hollow filled with water that had frozen solid. Had it rained yesterday? Last night? I stepped on to the ice, warily at first, but with more confidence as I saw that it was thick and would not break beneath me. I stepped back on to the grass, and then ran and jumped back on to the ice. I flew right across to the other side of the hollow, then I turned around and did it again, only the other way. There was grass sticking up out of the ice, long grass that grew in wet places, and when I slid over the ice the grass snapped off and the cold breeze scattered the fragments. I slid and I spun and I jumped. The ice in the hollow caught the bright autumn-yellow light that filtered through the clouds. I ran and I slipped and I nearly fell and I *did* fall, and when I fell the ice cracked, not much, but enough to make that creaky ice noise. The cracks spread as I skated and I saw the cracks get deeper and spread and lengthen until they covered the ice, but the ice didn't actually break, not once. The surface remained intact. It was like a disguise, like it was disguising something deeper and more true, but at the same time it *was* the thing that was deep and true. The disguise of the thing was the thing itself. Ice. I fell on my knees but it didn't hurt and I fell on my hands but they didn't get wet and I fell on my face but I didn't bruise and I didn't bleed. And I was alone and I didn't care if I *did* hurt myself, really, not right then.

The blood would only have frozen anyway. Once it came out.

I flew towards the edge of the ice, and I couldn't stop, and my foot hit the hard grassy earth, and I tumbled towards the ground, face first, and burst my nose and the blood poured out on to the white grass and all over my hands.

Jennifer. I loved her but I didn't think that she loved me, and I didn't know what to do.

On the way back, I had to wait at the road as two girls and a boy riding bicycles passed by in the direction of the far end of Wastwater. The boy was fair-haired with husky-blue eyes, while both the girls had jet-black hair and huge brown eyes. All three were lean and tanned and laughing. As they whipped away, I heard one of the girls shout out something in a language I didn't know. Her voice was high and sharp and clear, and I could hear their laughter all the way home.

It was getting dark by the time I got back, but when I saw Fell House through the dim blue twilight I saw that none of the lights were on. I stopped by the gate and felt reluctant to go any further because the lights should have been on, they should have, they really should have at this time of night. What if something had happened? I mean, it was probably just a power-cut but the house looked strangely smug and self-satisfied, like an intelligent animal that had helped itself to something it knew it shouldn't have eaten.

I rushed to open the gate and scramble across the yard to the house, because if it had Jennifer, then as far as I was concerned it could have me too. Then I saw something, somebody, standing in the path between the barn and the house, and stopped. There were two of them. Two children. They didn't move. I walked closer to them, lifting my hand to wave. I could see them a little more clearly now – their tousled blonde hair and their fingers in their mouths. They were the kids from the farm shop. I smiled at them, but it was a forced smile. The house remained unlit and quiet.

'Hello!' I said. But they just turned and ran. Their bare feet flashed pale in the dark.

Their bare feet.

I thought back to the footprint I had found. Then I threw open the front door and all the lights came on at once, all the lights and all the sound, strings of lights like sparks all over the wall and music so loud that I didn't recognise it at first as 'Shiny Happy People' by R.E.M.

'What?' I said. 'What's going on?'

'Fuck what I said before!' shouted a big shaggy thing that I realised was Graham. 'We're having a big fuck-off party and it's all for you!'

'What?' I said.

'We're having a kind of surprise birthday party,' Erin said. 'This isn't it though. The party's going to be tomorrow. We just had to decorate tonight because people are going to be turning up all day tomorrow, so we had to do the surprise bit tonight!'

Everybody was laughing. The light was bright and the hallway was decked with black and white crêpe-paper streamers. The walls were covered in fairy-lights and music was spilling out of the living-room.

'Well.' I smiled. 'Thank you.'

FRANCIS

I'm reading the paper. An eleven-year-old girl knifed her twelve-year-old classmate to death in Japan. The murder was the latest in a series of killings by children that stunned the adults of the nation. The knife used was small. With a retractable blade. Usually used to cut paper. The victim was stabbed in the neck and arms. The article also mentioned two other, previous killings. Last July, a boy of fourteen was arrested for beating a classmate to death in Okinawa. And in the same month a twelve-year-old boy kidnapped, molested and killed a four-year-old. In Nagasaki. We bombed another wedding in Iraq. 'It is true that we bombed a wedding,' said a US Army spokesman. 'But don't forget. Terrorists have weddings too.' There is a full-page advert for a new robotic-dog pet-toy thing. I think it's an advert. It looks like an article about this year's top Christmas toy, but I think that's a trick. I can't really tell what's what any more. Everything is made to look like something else.

'Where's your costume?' Graham says. From the doorway.

'What?' I say.

'Why are you not dressed up?'

I am slumped on the sofa. It is the morning of the party. It is raining outside. Jack came back from his walk last night with bloody hands. A bloody face. Said he fell over.

'What time is it?' I ask.

'Twelve,' Graham says. He is dressed in a black suit with a black shirt and a white tie.

'What's the theme?'

'Black and white.'

'Black and white?'

'Black and white. Look – just look at the walls. You *know* it's black and white. Stop being a prick.'

'OK,' I say. I grin. 'I did know really.'

'I know you knew.' He smiles his Nordic-warrior smile. 'Get your fucking suit on. People will be here soon.'

Me and Erin and Taylor are making some punch. Something poppy and danceable is playing loudly throughout the house. It is mid-afternoon. A few guests are outside, looking at the view and being introduced to Jennifer by Jack. We're using alcohol that Jennifer brought from the little shed where she hid it.

'How much of this should I put in?' Taylor asks. He holds up a bottle of whisky.

'All of it,' Erin says.

'You sure?' he says.

'Yep.'

216

'I have this feeling,' Taylor says. He pours the whisky into the brown, murky liquid sloshing around in the punch bowl. 'I have this feeling, rising in me. We could start a magazine. Make a book or film. Write a sitcom. We could start a band, us three, and Jennifer and Jack, and maybe even Graham, and we might not be technically proficient but we'd have this energy and creativity, or, at least, we *could*, if we put the time in, and we'd be completely original and powerful. We'd be a balloon inside people's heads, expanding their minds while they dance 'till they want to die. Honestly. What do you think?'

'As long as we inspired a kind of fear,' I say. 'A kind of scary – but exciting – amorality.'

'I'm sure that, between us, we couldn't help it,' Erin says.

'Good people though,' Taylor says.

'Of course,' I say.

I scoop a cupful of punch from the bowl. Take a mouthful.

'How is it?' he asks.

'It needs some ginger beer. Have we got any?'

'Of course.' He pulls a bottle from nowhere. From his sleeve or something. Taylor can be like that. Tall, mysterious. A subtle master of understated showmanship. He pours some into the bowl. 'It's going to be beautiful,' he says. Then he lifts a bottle of some cream liqueur from the pile of drink that we've amassed. He unscrews the cap and empties the whole bottle into the punch.

'I'm not sure about that,' I say. 'Not sure that will work. Won't it curdle?'

'I don't know.' He fills his glass from the punch bowl. 'The Irish used to have a grading system for sour milk. The curdled, thicker stuff was something of a delicacy.'

'You know too much,' I say. There is a heavy pounding at the front door.

Taylor smiles. 'Come on, Francis. Get it down your neck. The guests are arriving, and soon there won't be any left.'

'Has Jack opened his presents yet?' Erin says.

'No,' Taylor says. 'He said he'd open them later.'

'I don't know what he's playing at,' I say.

Later. People have been arriving constantly. I stand outside, beneath the clouding sky. I look out over the yard and the recently appeared cars. I shake my head. I have a near pint of punch in my hand. I feel tingly and warm all over. There must be nearly a hundred people here so far. And I can see another car snaking its way up the mountain road. Graham obviously knew what he was doing.

Except, of all those who have arrived so far, nobody seems to have heard about the black and white theme. Just that it's fancy dress. People are dressed as animals. Monsters. Robots. Soldiers. Rock stars. Nuns, monks. Doctors, nurses. Priests, kings, queens, dolls. Presidents. Faery-tale heroes and villains. Pirates. Belly-dancers. Scarecrows. Serial killers. Gods. Characters from films. From books. From computer games. Ghosts. And more. Only me, Taylor, Graham and Jack are wearing suits.

Jennifer and Erin look beautiful in thin, floating dresses and huge pairs of bat-like wings. Jennifer in black and Erin in white.

I hear giggling behind me and see the pair of them. Erin and Jennifer. They're falling out of the house. 'Look!' Erin whispers, loudly. 'A car! They're nearly here!' They're unrolling a banner that looks as if it's been made out of a sheet or something. Both ends are attached to ladders which they lean either side of the door. They've sprayed the words 'Cross the Threshold' on to it. Once the banner is up, they each stand in front of a ladder. And hold one hand up towards the top of the door. Like they've been carved from the wall. Like gatekeepers.

The car pulls up and some girls get out. I don't recognise any of them. 'Happy birthday!' they shout. 'Happy house-warming! Happy Christmas!'

'It's not my birthday!' I shout back, but they don't seem to hear me. 'It's not my house!' They pile in through the open front door. One of them turns around and smiles. 'It's not even Christmas yet,' I say, but they're all too far away.

'Where are all these people from?' I ask Graham. He turns away from a girl wearing a fantastic unicorn horn and tail. I think she's called Chloe. Recognise her from work. She has neatly bobbed black hair. A tiny, glittering piercing in her small, delicate nose. She slaps Graham on the arse and canters off. Graham is grinning wildly.

'Did you see her?' he asks. 'I mean, did you really see her? I've got her number. I'm in love. There are some amazing drugs here tonight, Francis. I'm tempted to really test my body. How far can I go? I believe my body to be completely foolproof, but I need to know for sure.'

'What do you mean?' I laugh. The ceiling is webbed with fairy-lights. 'Your body is foolproof?'

'I don't know.' He is laughing too. 'I really don't know.'

'Graham. Where are these lights from? All the people? I hardly know anybody here.'

'Some things we give birth to and then they take on a life of their own,' he says. 'This is one of those things. Don't worry about the details, or how, or why. That's how I live my life. And I have a fucking good life. All these people' – he waves his glass around – 'are here with us. And that's all we need to know.'

'Maybe we should start a fight club,' Taylor says. His big eyes drift over to rest on the projector screen. It's showing back-to-back episodes of *Flash Gordon*, the cartoon series. I think about one New Year's Eve a long time ago. When there was a fight in The Crook, the pub I used to work in. Before university. Two men, both quite big, in white shirts, just punching each other in the face. Again and again. My face was flecked with their blood, and their shirts were dripping with the stuff.

'I don't think I'd want to do it all the time,' I say. 'I'd be too scared of brain damage.'

'I guess,' he says. We watch some more of *Flash Gordon*. Ming the Merciless has a massive super-computer in his ice fortress. The computer has legs. It looks like a huge, mechanical spider.

'That computer looks like Shelob,' Taylor says.

'Another drink?'

'I'll come with you.'

We're nearly at the door when we both stop dead. It's Kenny. Floating through the hallway. And then swinging to face us. As if he's hinged to the door-frame. He's wearing a baggy navy-blue shirt and black jeans that are too small. He stands there in the doorway and smiles at us. 'Boys,' he says. 'Fancy seeing you here. Like the suits. Very swish.'

'Kenny?' I say.

'Yeah,' he says. 'It's me alright.'

'How are you?' Taylor asks. 'Are you alright?'

'As alright as I'll ever be.'

'But you've been missing,' I say.

'Have I?'

'Yeah,' Taylor says. 'Since you left the hospital.'

'I just went to see some friends,' Kenny says. 'Didn't think anybody would miss me much. Who would have gone to the police about me, eh?'

'They were looking into it because, um, oh,' Taylor says. 'You know.'

Kenny doesn't say anything. He just looks at Taylor.

'Not dressed up?' I say.

'No,' he says slowly. 'No, I'm not.' His flat eyes swivel around the room. They linger on the projector screen. 'I just didn't see the point.'

'It's just, you know. A bit of fun,' I say.

'Can't tell who people are though, when they're all wearing these stupid costumes.' His eyes return to rest on me. 'I just like to know who I'm talking to and everything. Communication skills are very important if you're a manager.' He licks his lips. 'I get so hungry sometimes.' His eyes return to the screen.

'Doing anything for Christmas?' Taylor asks.

'What?' Kenny says. He looks confused.

'Christmas,' Taylor says. 'You know. Any plans?'

'That time again already, is it? No. No plans. Oh, I'm hungry.'

Taylor and I look at each other.

'Um,' Kenny says, after a moment. He doesn't move his eyes. 'Is that Jenny girl about?'

'Who?' I say.

'You mean Jennifer?' Taylor says.

'Yeah,' Kenny says. His eyes flicker on to Taylor and then off again. 'Jenny.'

'No,' I say. 'Jennifer's visiting family.'

'Oh really?' Kenny says. 'That's a shame. I was looking forward to having a little catch-up with my favourite employee. Oh, that is a shame. I'm disappointed now. Well, I might as well just leave.'

'Yeah,' I say. 'You might as well.'

'I heard there's another party happening around here tonight anyway. Might go and check it out. Heard it's better than this one. Heard it's more *real*.'

'Charming,' Taylor says.

Kenny's eyes just drift away. His body follows. He turns

222

slowly around. 'Kenny and Jenny,' he murmurs, as he does so. 'Kenny and Jenny.'

Taylor and I look at each other again. We stay there, in the doorway. We watch him worm his way through the mass of people until he reaches the front door and leaves.

'That Kenny,' Taylor says. He looks back towards the front door. 'I don't know. Kenny and Jenny. Kenny and Jenny.' He shakes his head.

The kitchen table is covered with empty vodka bottles. 'Fill your boots, boys!' shouts Jennifer. She's standing at the CD player. She turns to face us. Something erupts from the speakers, too loud for me to identify at first. Unnervingly loud. A sleazy wall of sound. All the empty bottles have a picture of Lenin on the front.

'Protocol vodka!' Taylor roars. A slightly manic grin on his face. He waggles a bottle at me.

'It's the cheapest, nastiest vodka I could find!' Jennifer screams. I can only just hear them. Taylor pours each of us a large glass. We down them. My stomach contracts as soon as I swallow the stuff. My eyes close involuntarily. Tears stream down my face. I bend over. Sure that I'm going to be sick. But the feeling passes. I open my eyes and stand back up. Jennifer is in front of me. Biting her lip. Taylor is leaning against the fridge.

'Have you taken some clothes off?' I shout to Jennifer. So that she can hear me above the music.

'I kind of like you!' she shouts back.

'Jennifer,' I say. 'Put your dress back on.'

'Francis,' Taylor mouths. He staggers forward and puts his hand on my shoulder. 'Francis. Help me.'

'I have to help Taylor,' I say to Jennifer. 'You have a kind and loving boyfriend. You don't want me ruining that.'

Taylor and I turn. We leave Jennifer in the kitchen.

'Do you really need help?' I ask.

'I'm not sure,' Taylor says. 'I feel violent.'

'Don't do anything you'll regret,' I say. 'Hey. You know what I read in the paper on my way up here?'

'What?'

'Condoms,' I say. 'Even condoms are a cancer risk. Most condoms contain a cancer-causing chemical, apparently. Tests showed twenty-nine out of thirty-two different types contained the carcinogen N-Nitrosamine. The chemical is used to improve elasticity but is released when the condom comes in contact with bodily fluids.'

'How do you remember all of those details?' he says. 'The numbers?'

I shrug.

A boy dressed as a Templar Knight runs past. He is being chased by a girl in a skintight lycra catsuit and a long-nosed masquerade mask. 'But I'm chaste!' he screams. 'I'm chaste!'

I feel a sweat break out on my forehead and under my arms. A sharp pain lances through my brain. I close my eyes.

JACK

I put the bag of birthday presents – including the one from Jennifer – down in the safe room with the other breakables. I had been about to open them before, but Jennifer was busy putting streamers up and then all the guests arrived, so I thought I might as well leave it overnight. It would stretch the whole thing out a bit anyway, make it last longer.

The one from Jennifer looked exciting. A thick, heavy rectangle, wrapped in thick rough purple paper and tied with a golden ribbon. Like a present in the Shire, Middle Earth, might have looked. I picked it up again and marvelled at the neat wrapping, the intriguing weight of it. I put it back down again and locked the door.

I stepped through the kitchen doorway and saw Jennifer shrug off the straps of her dress in front of Francis and Taylor. Both of them were staggering, eyes shut, so didn't see the act itself, but Jennifer – she looked so lovely, and so happy. I backed out of the kitchen immediately, and maybe she'd noticed me, maybe she hadn't, I didn't know.

I went upstairs and walked into the bedroom where Graham and Francis were staying, the one with blue and white wallpaper. Graham was sitting on the sofa-bed with Simon and Chris, a couple of friends from uni, and seemed quite upset.

Graham always exploded through doors, banging them against the wall as if he didn't know his own strength. Time and time again he left small round marks on the wallpaper or the paint, indentations made by the door handles. Often he walked into rooms by mistake, drawn in by voices; he'd throw open the door and then stand there, looking confused.

'What's wrong?' I asked.

'This sounds stupid,' he said. 'But it's only just kind of hit me. I mean, the full impact.'

'What?'

'I won't ever actually sleep with Rihanna, Angelina Jolie, Avril Lavigne, Jessica Alba or even PJ Harvey.' There was a silence, and he looked genuinely distraught. 'I mean, *never.*'

'No,' I said.

'It's awful,' Simon said, whose speech was slowed down due to the huge spliff he was smoking. He was dressed as Ziggy Stardust. He looked suitably emaciated. Chris was dressed as Willy Wonka, with a long purple coat, purple gloves and a top hat, and his cane was resting against the wall. Golden paper spilled from his pockets and he had chocolate smeared around his mouth.

'Just think about that for a second, Jack,' Graham continued. 'It's an awful truth to come to terms with if you *think* about it.'

I thought about it, but no; I couldn't get past Jennifer.

'No,' I said. 'I'm happy with Jennifer.'

'Honestly?' Simon asked.

'Yeah. Honestly.'

He looked down at the rug. 'I'll have to meet her,' he said.

'She is gorgeous,' Graham said. 'She is incredibly hot.'

'You might meet somebody tonight,' I said. 'Those celebrities probably aren't all that pretty in the flesh.'

'I might,' he said. 'I guess I'm just being morbid. Hey. I had a dream last night. It was fucked up. I dreamed that I rented out a video of a film with me in it. It was called *Dances in Wolves*. And I was watching it, and in it I was in a car, and I was driving, and my ex-girlfriend was in the passenger seat, and my ex-girlfriend's mum and somebody in a wolf costume were in the back. And this – this *wolf* bites my ex-girlfriend's mum's arm off, and then her head, and then my ex-girlfriend's head, and then he starts biting my shoulder, and then he bites *my* head off, and the car's still going, straight – we were driving across somewhere, wide, open, flat, hot – and the wolf takes his head off, the, like' – Graham mimed taking off a helmet or something – '*costume* head thing, and it's *me*.'

There was a silence.

'Shit, man,' Chris said eventually, smiling, nodding. 'A *video*? Not a DVD? That *is* fucked up.'

'*Dances in Wolves*,' I said, laughing, but really I was uneasy – the dream seemed somehow more unpleasant than it should have, and also strangely fitting, as if something inside me recognised certain elements.

'So, you're in your own dream, like – three times, but' – Chris tried to work out how to phrase it – 'at the same time?'

'Yep,' Graham said, nodding vigorously.

MTV2 was on the TV and showing a video in which two big spiders were fighting, and a woman with artfully smudged make-up was running, clambering, staggering through these dark, misty woods in some reference to Little Red Riding Hood, maybe, but she was not wearing red, so probably not.

The spiders reminded me of Taylor. He walked through doors like he was a spider, his long legs appearing first, and then the rest of him, and he would do it slowly and methodically, like he did everything. Erin never walked through a door without knocking on it. Then she'd stick her head round the corner and smile a radiant smile and as she entered, the room would light up.

I twisted my head around, and I saw them kissing in a doorway.

I left the upstairs bathroom after expelling an impressively vast volume of urine and looking, confused, into the mirror for a while. I saw Jennifer on the landing, standing in front of the *American Beauty* film poster – depicting a naked girl surrounded by roses – that had appeared at some point since the party started. She was talking to a boy called Aidan, at least I *thought* he was called Aidan, and whoever he was, he was dressed as the Tin Man. They were both looking intently at the screen of Aidan's mobile phone, which he was holding up in front of him like it was a torch or something.

'That's amazing,' she said. 'I like the bit with the cat.'

'I like the fuck-up with all the bottles around him,' Aidan said.

'Hi,' I said, after deciding to approach. 'What are you looking at?'

'Oh, hey, Jack,' Jennifer said. 'It's a music video. A good one. Excuse me. I need the bathroom. Been waiting.'

She pushed past.

Aidan just stood there grinning, his mouth visible through a slit in the box. Every now and again he shifted his feet as if to maintain balance.

All around me, all throughout the house, strange people surged and merged and fell back, like waves.

I waited for her outside the bathroom.

When she came back out, I said, 'Jennifer.'

'Jack.' She smiled, and put her arms around me. 'It's a good party, hey?'

'It is. Thank you. It's really good. Jennifer, I want to talk to you. Can we go to our room?'

'Yeah,' she said. 'Sure we can. Everything OK?'

'Let's – let's just go in here.' I pushed open our bedroom door and there were two people wearing huge cardboard boxes standing in the corner. An unusually long hairy arm was coming out of a hole in one of the boxes and going into a hole in the other one, although I could not tell which it was coming out of and which it was going into, and it was moving vigorously, getting faster.

'Excuse us,' I said. 'Please. Get out.'

The arm stopped moving and the boxes shuffled silently out. One of them got stuck in the door, but I gave it a little push and it popped through. I closed the door after it. The room felt quite empty after the crush of everywhere else, and because the window was a single blank eye looking at us, I felt exposed. We really should have bought some curtains, some basic things that make a house a home. There was a full-length mirror propped up against the wall, next to the door.

'Jennifer,' I said, 'I want to know what we are.'

'What do you mean?'

'Are we a couple? Are we together, properly? Or am I just here with you?'

She held my shoulders. 'Jack, being a couple, being together – they don't really mean anything important. Those are just things people do because it's what they think they're supposed to do. They're constructs – very human constructs – and they, you know, they go against the grain. Of what *is* important, which is our natural instinct.'

'No,' I said. 'That's not true. I want to be with you and I want you to be with me, and basically, Jennifer, I don't want you to be with anybody else. I mean, that's my natural instinct. And I'm scared that you might end up with somebody else, like – like Francis.'

She took her hands off me and her face turned hard. 'You mean you want me to be yours and in return you give me yourself.'

'Yes!' I said. 'Exactly that!'

'No,' she said. 'No, Jack. I don't *want* you to be mine. I don't ever want to *have* anybody. And I am not yours and never will be, do you understand? I am mine and mine only and I will continue to be mine only forever and ever. The idea, the whole idea of couples and *being* together is based on this thing of mutual ownership, Jack, and it's *creepy*.'

'I thought there was some biology in it. Like, pheromones or something. Nesting. Mating, I mean, having children. That kind of thing. Isn't that why people stay together?'

'No,' she said. 'People stay together for two reasons. Because they're too scared to break up and risk being alone, or because they are manipulative and possessive and like owning another soul. Having kids, having sex, having a laugh, *love*, you don't need to be in a couple for that.'

'I don't know if I agree with you.'

'So I have to subscribe to your way of thinking because I asked you if you want to live with me, to sleep with me? I'm sorry if I've given you the wrong idea, Jack. I thought you understood.'

'But – but – what about if we try to be, I mean, just us? I really like you Jennifer, and I – I saw you flirting with Francis, and—'

'Jack!' she shouted, stepping back. 'Please! You do not own me! This is what I'm trying to say! This is the conceit that people have, the trap they fall into. Whether or not I flirt with Francis is up to me! I haven't ever committed myself to you, Jack, but because we live in a way that mirrors a conventional relationship you think that I'm *yours*?'

'But—'

'Stop trying to make me into something I'm not, Jack.' She lowered her voice and looked down. 'I'm sorry. I really am. But you're trying to bend me into something I'm not, just to suit yourself. And I won't have it.'

'Jennifer,' I said.

'I'm sorry we had this fall-out on your birthday. I'm sorry. I really am.'

She left the room.

I went to the bathroom.

FRANCIS

The smoke in here is thick, despite the high ceiling. Cigarettes and weed and roll-ups rolled with cherry or vanilla tobacco. All knitting together in the air and floating upwards. Hanging there like something fibrous. I peer through it to try and work out who's in here. I see this girl in the corner. Lying on the floor. She's wearing black bin-bags cut like a cape. She looks like she had her skin painted green at the start of the night. Now it's mostly worn off. Her witch's hat lies beside her on the ground. She looks dead. I recognise her as a girl Graham used to go out with. Mary.

'Hey.' I put my hand on her arm. 'You OK? Mary?'

She doesn't answer. She's completely unconscious. The smoke can't be doing her any good. I pick her up and carry her upstairs. I push open the door of the first bedroom that I come to. It's the room Taylor and Jack are sharing. It looks like it's also some sort of cloakroom for the party. There is a pile of bags and coats stacked so high against one wall that it's like a lost-property department.

Or a small model of the mountains that surround us up here. I lay Mary on the bed and she just flops down without so much as a flicker of her eyelids. I bite my lip. I wonder if there are any tests you can do to detect alcohol poisoning. I see that the bin-bags are tied quite tightly around her neck. I start untying them. As I loosen them I see that she's not wearing anything underneath.

'Oh aye?' says a voice from behind me.

I turn around. Somebody dressed in tinfoil and kitchen things is standing in the doorway, leering. The Tin Man. Aidan. He has a box that is covering his head. On top of this, a colander. There is a hole through which I can see a wet mouth. And a slit masked with gauze that hides his eyes. 'What's this?' he slurs. 'Secret party?'

'What?' I say.

'Secret party?'

'No. Look. Mary's passed out. It was the bin-bags round her neck. And they're plastic. Hot.'

'I know exactly what you were doing, Francisco,' he says, advancing. 'But don't worry.' He leans forward. Conspiratorially. 'I won't tell a soul. Not me.'

'You're wrong,' I say. 'I'm helping her. And don't call me Francisco.'

'Maybe we could have a secret party. You and – and – Mary and me.'

He lowers himself on to the end of the bed. The colander tips forward as he sits. 'I've got my camera.' He licks his lips.

'Aidan,' I say. 'How are things? Haven't seen you in what. I don't know how long. Since uni.'

'Time flies, eh? I'm good. I'm in sales. What about – what about you? What do you get up to when you're not molesting pretty girls?'

'I don't – look, Aidan, I wasn't touching her.'

'Yeah, right. We're all the same, Francis. You may as well admit it. All – all men. Nothing more than a load of big, fat cocks.' He lifts the box off his head. His hair is matted across his forehead with sweat. His eyes are beady and bright.

'Aidan. She's not even conscious. I don't care how sleazy, ill or sad you are; you're not touching her. Come on. Get out.'

'You want her all for yourself,' he says.

'Just – just fuck off.'

'Hey,' he says. Completely ignoring my anger. Drunkenly digging his mobile out of his pocket. 'Francis. I got something for you.'

'What?'

'Just – just wait. I'm looking for it.' He has his mobile phone out. Is gazing intently at the screen. I pick up the colander and absent-mindedly spin it around and around in my hands. 'Here it is. Feast your eyes.'

He hands the phone over. The video is already playing. A man is pinned to the ground by somebody kneeling on his back. The person kneeling on the man's back is holding the man's head up by his hair. So that he's looking straight into the camera. Blood is running down his nose and his eyes are swollen. Suddenly somebody out of shot kicks him in the face with heavy-looking boots. And again, and again. And again. Then they step back and the camera zooms in. I drop the phone.

'Francisco,' Aidan says, 'you missed the best bit. His jaw's come half off so that he can't close it and then—'

'Stop.' I stamp on the phone and hear it crunch beneath my heel.

'Jesus, Francis!' he says. 'That's my phone, you wanker! I've only got one!'

'What was that? Where do you get it from? Does it entertain you?'

'It's footage,' he says. 'You know, San Francisco. From the war.'

I slam the colander into his face. His head bounces off the wall behind and then back into the colander again. He's bleeding already. I haul him up to his feet. I go to punch him in the stomach. But he digs his thumbs into my wrists. I have to pull away. He punches me in the stomach but I don't really feel it. I hit him back. My fist makes a hole in the tinfoil over his belly. I punch him again, this time in the face. He falls to his knees. I feel cool hands grasp my waist from behind. I turn to find that I'm staring into a pair of deep green eyes.

'Jennifer?'

'Calm down,' she says. 'Calm down.'

'Jennifer. I'm sorry.'

'Shh. Don't worry. He's OK. Look.'

I look back to see Aidan standing up, slowly. He staggers past, shooting me a murderous look. 'Prick,' he mutters.

'He just wound me up,' I say.

'I know,' she says. 'Come and sit down, somewhere out of the way.'

She takes me by the hand. Leads me to her room.

'Lock the door,' I say.

'Yeah,' she says, 'I will.' She kisses me. I kiss her back. Too tired now to resist. I could say no. But I don't want to. I don't want to make the decision at all. I want her to take me. Her mouth is hot, red and hungry. Her lip-rings roll over my mouth and tongue. They send delicate tremors radiating out across the whole surface of my body. I can hear music from downstairs. And the wind shrieking through the attic above us. But in here there are only the sounds that we make. She pushes me down so that I'm sitting on the bed. She smoothes my jacket from my shoulders. She kneels over me. Then she's working busily at my tie. I run the straps of her dress down her arms. She leans forwards so that I can kiss her now-exposed breasts and they tremble, rising and falling with her quickening breath. I start unbuttoning my shirt, but struggle, the buttons being slippery with Aidan's blood. So she finishes it. Her hands carry on down to my belt buckle while I dig my nails into the small of her back. I bite her shoulder. She pulls my trousers down but they snag on my shoes. She crouches down and unlaces them deftly with one hand. The other creeps up my thigh and under my boxer shorts. I kick my shoes off and shrug off my shirt. She lifts her dress up over her shoulders and her wings. She is wearing black knickers beneath. I lie back on the bed.

She sits astride me. I look up at her. She's smiling the beautiful smile from my fantasies. Her eyes are half closed as she leans back down again to kiss me. Her wings spread outwards. They obscure the light bulb that dangles nakedly on the end of its sad, cobwebbed wire.

I drop the used condom into a wooden waste-paper bin on my way out of the room. It lands greasily amongst the other rubbish. Carcinogens coating my penis. Nausea bubbles in my gut. Guilt, maybe. I look back at Jennifer. She's sitting on the bed.

'Go,' she whispers. 'I'll be out in five.'

I look briefly in the full-length mirror that's propped up against the wall. I have dried blood smeared around my face and on my hands. My white shirt is splattered with it. There are several dark stains on my black jacket. I look back at Jennifer.

'Go!' she says.

I go.

The house is full of people that I don't recognise. They are mostly young. They have an unhealthy air about them. They are thin and pale. Their hair is lank. In contrast to their stretched, manic mouths, their eyes convey a boredom so absolute that they might be dead. Girls and boys. They eat, drink and touch each other casually. Yet intimately. They drift through the party like stray dogs. Scattered amongst them are people that I do know. I am startled to see how similar they are to the strangers. Their apparent hunger. Their frantic, tired energy.

I head for the kitchen. Once there, I pour myself another large glass of Protocol vodka. The table has been pushed against the side. Lots of people are dancing. Erin is dancing with Taylor between surfaces laden with drink. And food. They wriggle and twist around. The floor beneath them is slick with spilled liquid. They slide effortlessly across it. The night is still going strong. There's plenty of time to get drunk. Forget about everything for a few hours. Lose myself in the noise and the shifting planes of a good party. Mess around like a dickhead on the wet edge of abyssal nihilism. I've finished the vodka already. I pour myself another.

'Annihilation!' Graham roars, directly into my ear. I jump. The glass slips from my fingers. Shatters on the floor.

'Jesus!' I say. 'Jesus, Graham. Jesus Christ. Look at this glass!' I try to point at the glass I just dropped. But there is so much broken glass on the stone floor that I can't tell which was mine. Graham shakes with laughter. 'What do you want, anyway?'

'You and me,' he says, 'are going to play the annihilation game. It's where we both drink until we can barely move, and then we have to drink *through* it, to the *other side* of drunkenness.'

'Is this a real game?'

'Yes,' he says. 'Of my own invention, too. Well, it's a lot more than just a game. It's a deeply spiritual experience.

The idea is that we learn a lot about ourselves on the way, maybe have a few adventures. Fall in and out of love, test our friendship, solve age-old mysteries, push ourselves to the outer limits of our endurance.'

'Well then,' I say. 'Get me another drink.'

Graham pours me another vodka. 'Why have you got so much blood on you, anyway?'

'I had a fight,' I say. 'With Aidan.'

'Aidan?' he says. 'Ha. What a bastard. I'm sure he deserved it. I thought he'd wind a few people up. Here.' He hands me the vodka. 'Right,' he says. 'First off; we go outside.'

'Who are all these people?' I point at a group dressed as bikers. Beards and everything. We push through the hallway. 'Did you invite them?'

'No,' he says. 'But good parties always get gatecrashers and the gatecrashers are part of what makes a good party good.'

We push open the back door. The cold air sweeps in over us. The wind is fierce. The sky low with cloud. There is a muddy, rocky stretch of ground before us that disappears into the darkness beneath the scraggy excuse for an orchard.

'Why did we have to come outside?' I say.

'To explore,' he says.

'Jack's already shown us around.'

'That's not what I mean,' he says. 'I don't know what I mean. It's weird, to be honest, Francis. I just felt like we should come outside.'

I hear the door slam shut behind us. The light vanishes. We move forward, slowly, towards the low trees.

'I don't like those trees,' I say. 'They're a bit warped.'

'No,' Graham says. 'Hey! Shit.'

'What?'

'I just tripped over something.' He's crouched down now. Feeling around on the ground. He moves on all fours. He crawls towards me. 'Look at this.' He stands back up.

'What is it?' I say. 'I can't see.'

'I think it's an axe,' he says. 'A big one too. Imagine Aidan's face if we went back in swinging this around!'

The wind tears the clouds open for a moment. Beyond them the sky is thick with stars. The faint light illuminates Graham holding a huge woodcutting axe. He's laughing. It's like the axe was made for him, despite the suit he wears. If you didn't know him, he'd be terrifying. Beyond him, the gnarled skin of the mountainside is momentarily visible. My stomach clenches as I see what looks like a person, tall and awkward, tottering across the bleak expanse towards us.

'Graham,' I say. The clouds close up again.

He stands the axe on the ground. He leans on it. 'Are there any girls here tonight?' he says. 'I mean, any that might sleep with me? It's been too long. I mean, three months.'

'Graham.'

'Don't worry,' he says. 'I'll be quick with them; I won't let sex get in the way. I mean, I'll fit it in around everything else. The game.'

'There's somebody out there,' I say. 'Past the orchard.'

'What?' He turns around. 'Some wayward guest, probably. Hello? Hello, who's there?'

They're close enough for us to see despite the darkness, now. They stop walking about ten feet away from us.

'Hey,' she says. 'Just here for the party, man. What are you? Like, bouncers?'

'No,' Graham says. 'Just getting the air.'

'Cool, man.' She carries on past us. Her huge eyes flashing. She opens the back door. She disappears inside.

'What was she doing out there?' I ask. My heartbeat still racing.

'Dunno,' he says. 'Maybe a local. Or maybe she's been here all night, and she's just been outside for whatever. A piss or something.'

'I haven't told anybody this,' I say. 'But there's something about this place that I don't like."

But he's not listening. He's looking back at the house. 'Maybe *she'd* sleep with me,' he says.

JACK

I heard it before I saw it. I heard it from the kitchen and made my way through the rush and pushed towards the sound because I liked it, because it was lively and hopeful and brought to mind folk music from another time, a wilder happier time, maybe in another country where music and love were more important than money, where a night spent dancing and laughing was the pinnacle – the ultimate aim – of human endeavour.

I saw people grouped in the living-room, crowded round the musician. I pushed through and there he was, standing on one leg, with the other resting on a chair. He was wearing tight black trousers and a loose white shirt and a tatty old black waistcoat. He was playing so fast his arm was a blur, and his eyes were closed, his face a mask of concentration, and many of the hairs of the bow had snapped, and whipped through the air around him. There was something about him that resonated deep inside me and I didn't know what it was, but it was hypnotic. It was like he had entered me, penetrated me, in some non-sexual way, but just as intimately, and I felt like I shouldn't have wanted to feel it, but I did want to, and we all seemed to – we were all standing and watching him as if we'd been waiting a long time for the opportunity, as if he was important to us all. He was a bit intimidating, because of his obvious talent and his somewhat forbidding demeanour – he was tall and strong-looking and his eyes were rolling – but that added to the excitement. Maybe he was some sort of celebrity, because there was something unnervingly familiar about him – but no. It wasn't that kind of familiarity, it was something altogether deeper, like the recognition that I imagine you'd feel if you met the ghost of your great-grandfather without ever having seen a photograph. We all felt it. And, all that aside, the music had this transcendental quality that took you out of your world momentarily, cutting through everything you chose, and opened up the part of you that was really you, the part of you that you never shaped or manipulated or dressed up for public consumption. I often thought that was what the soul might be. The part of you that was completely you. Whatever was left when you took away all of the CDs, books, films, friends.

Whatever that part of you was, his music revealed it, laid it open, as if he was peeling open our skins and looking inside.

A girl in a red skirt and a white shirt danced and danced and danced, whirled and stamped and shouted. I recognised her as one of the girls that I'd seen on their bikes the day before, and with her was a tall boy with long hair smashing a tambourine against his thigh. They must have been from the gathering at the end of Wastwater. I was glad they'd come actually, I liked their music and their dancing. But there was a story from Norfolk about two girls who danced to the music of a strange fiddler until they died. It was a variant on one of the explanations for stone circles – the stories in which girls dance and dance and dance to the fiddle music until they break the Sabbath and so get turned to stone.

I backed away.

I was looking for Jennifer but I couldn't find her, so I sat on the bottom step whilst all around me people span and drank, kissed and argued. A boy called Paul, who I knew from university, tumbled down the stairs and hit his head on the floor in front of me and lay there motionless. I half thought about calling an ambulance, but then he got to his feet, dizzily, and grinned at me before walking unsteadily away down the corridor.

The party raged like a caged animal on heat. I was still looking for Jennifer. I went up to the room that she was sharing with Erin and stood outside. I'd already tried it, but I supposed that it was entirely possible that she had wound up in there since I'd last looked.

I opened the door and quickly glanced around the edge. There she was, naked, with Francis, on the bed, and she was on top of him, rocking back and forth, his head hanging over the edge of the bed. Neither of them noticed my intrusion so I closed the door quietly and nodded to myself. So that was that, then.

There weren't any empty rooms for me to be alone in so I made my way outside. It was bitterly cold and there were still a few stars visible towards the horizon, although most of the sky was obscured by cloud.

FRANCIS

Graham and I stand before the barn. A tall, stooped figure lopes quietly across the yard to join us. Taylor. Three mice before a sleeping cat.

'Is the barn a part of our journey?' I ask.

'Part of your journey maybe,' Graham says, 'but I'm not going inside that fucking thing.'

I can almost feel the alcohol running through their veins.

'I will,' Taylor says. 'I've been thinking about Erin. I love her, I realize. I fucking love that girl. She's perfect.'

'Congratulations,' I say. 'So that means you're going into the barn?'

He turns and looks at me, smiling. 'I'm not sure the two things are related. Is Jack OK?'

'I don't know,' I say. 'I thought he was OK. Why?'

'He seems quiet,' he says. 'He should be out here, with us.'

'You know Jack,' I say. 'He's always been quiet.'

He just looks at me. Then strides off towards the barn

door. It is unlocked. He pulls it open and the sound is horrific. Metal on stone. A train grinding along the rails. An injured dragon. To say that it is dark inside the barn would be an understatement. Taylor disappears inside. Graham holds the axe in both hands, rotating it. Maybe Jennifer told Erin about us. Maybe Erin told Taylor.

'What do you think?' he says. 'What's he hoping to find?'

'I don't know,' I say. 'This is your stupid game.'

'Jesus. Somebody's suddenly turned into a miserable twat. What's wrong with you?'

'Nothing.' Jack, I think. Poor Jack. You invite us into your house. And I sleep with your girlfriend.

'Cheer up,' Graham says. 'Or I'm going to chop you into pieces. You're so covered in blood nobody would notice. Ha! What do you reckon – shall we hide while Taylor's in there?'

'Ha ha, yes!' I nod manically.

'Come on!' Graham is giggling. We start running towards the corner of the barn so that we can hide round the side.

'He's going to be terrified!' Graham says.

'Hey!' Taylor shouts. He emerges from the mouth of the barn. 'Where are you going?'

'Oh,' I say. I look and see that we're only half-way to being out of sight. 'Nowhere. We were going to come in with you.'

'Oh well,' he says. 'I wouldn't bother. It's just empty. Nothing there.'

*

As we re-enter the house it starts to snow. I register it dimly. Like when you hear somebody talking in another room as you wake up.

I'm sitting on a beanbag in the living-room. Slowly zoning out. Graham is next to me. Gazing meditatively at the joint in his hand. Simon dances slowly to an Avril Lavigne video that's playing on the TV. A girl called Lucy is lying along the sofa. I know her from before. Before what? Before we lost touch. Before work. I don't know. Some other people are here too. People I don't know. A boy with the clearest blue eyes. A man dressed up as a Hell's Angel. Sunglasses and all.

'Our journey of self-discovery didn't come to much,' I say eventually.

'Nothing ever does,' Graham says. He looks up at Avril Lavigne on the TV. 'I would give my right arm to sleep with her.'

'She looks like a little girl,' Lucy says. 'She looks like a kid.'

There is a silence.

'Don't say that,' Graham says. He watches the video for a moment longer. 'It's not true, anyway.'

'It is,' Lucy says. 'Look at her.'

'It's not!' Graham says. 'She wouldn't be so fit if she looked like a kid.'

'Unless you're a paedo,' I say. Graham elbows me in the ribs. I topple slowly to the floor.

*

The door bursts open. I wake up suddenly and sprawl across the floorboards in a panic. I am hot and have the impression that somebody is running away from me. But it fades quickly. 'Jack?' I say. 'What is it?'

'I don't know where Jack is,' Erin says, leaning over me. 'But we have to find him. It's snowing! We're going to build a snowman. Who's coming?'

'Me!' I stumble to my feet. 'I want to build a snowman!'

'Yes!' Graham says, standing up. Lucy and Simon are entwined on the floor. They don't say anything. Neither do the blue-eyed boy or the biker.

We follow Erin out of the room and are joined in the hallway by Jack, Jennifer and Taylor. Jack looks absent-minded, as usual. Jennifer smiles at me, flushed. Erin and Taylor grin at each other. I reach out to grab hold of the wall. 'Coats!' I say. 'It's going to be cold. Very cold. We should probably all get our coats on.'

'I'll get them,' Jack says. He slopes off upstairs. Frowning.

'Good thinking, Francis,' Taylor says. 'Good man. Good thinking.' He nods sagely.

Jack returns after a moment. His arms are laden with jackets and coats. He distributes them without speaking.

An unopened can of lager is lying on the floor by the wall. I pick it up on the way out.

There is a light on the other side of the clouds. I am not sure what it means. It is confusing. It just makes the clouds look thicker and stronger and blacker. They move slowly past like they will never stop. Either that, or the

250

light is floating gently through a static sky. And all around the snow comes down. Heavy and fast. It all starts to make my head spin. The cold air keeps me from feeling sick. The yard and the mountainside and the house and the barn are blanketed with deep fresh snow.

'What time is it?' I say.

'What day is it?' Erin asks.

'Ha ha,' Graham says. 'I don't know. It's like before I ever started school and keeping track of that kind of thing.'

I can't help but notice Jack's silence.

We start piling the snow on the bare patch between the back door and what used to be the orchard. We gather it from the ground. From the tops of cars parked near the house. And the drifts piled up against the walls. And the windowsills. And *everywhere*. It continues to fall from the sky and fill the holes we have made with our hands and feet.

'I haven't made a snowman in years,' Erin says. 'And I just looked out of the window and saw all this snow and knew that we should. It's perfect. Jack. Thank you so much for inviting us up here. This is amazing. You're lucky, you know.'

'Yes, I am,' Jack says. He flashes a lifeless smile at me. I smile back. Maybe he knows.

Soon we have a column of snow nearly six feet tall. It is still snowing. Taylor throws a snowball at me. It hits me in the eye, hard. It hurts. I laugh because it reminds me of being a kid. I roll some snow up in my hands. My fingers are mottling white and red. I hurl the snowball at Taylor. But he ducks and it whizzes off into the trees. I am so cold. I don't have any gloves. My hands are numb. I laugh to myself. The column thrusts out of the ground proudly. It's a growth. A phallic tumour.

Graham has leant the axe against the wall of the house, just next to the back door. He makes his way back and forth between the snow pile and the wall. Shovelling armfuls of snow up out of the drifts and striding back through the driving snow. He dumps it next to the snowman-to-be. His beard is full of snowflakes.

Erin starts work on the detail. She starts at the bottom, shoving snow into two foot-like mounds. She carves long, dextrous toes, slowly and carefully. She keeps on touching her earrings. They must be cold.

Taylor is building a snow-dog.

I am starting on the head. I roll a ball around and around, marvelling at the way it grows. I imagine a bunch of cells tumbling around inside my body, growing in the same way.

Jennifer takes the snow that Graham deposits. She smoothes it on to the body of the thing. She keeps looking at me and smiling. I smile back, but I'm nervous. I don't want anybody to see it.

And Jack just drifts around. Sometimes he helps one of us. Sometimes he just looks out over the mountainside. Almost as if there's something out there.

When we have finished, the snowman is over six feet tall. He has legs, arms, a scarf, a mohawk, a penis, a pipe, a dog, eyes, nose, mouth and a *28 Days Later* badge, courtesy of Erin. The badge reads 'THE END IS EXTREMELY FUCKING NIGH' and is pinned to the scarf.

'What are we going to call him?' Taylor asks.

'Tim Burton,' Erin says.

'I don't think we should name him after anybody,' I say. 'It should just be a good name.'

'Oak Man,' Jack says. His sudden excitement is surprising. But pleasant. And confusing. Everybody just looks at him. 'You know,' he says. 'Faery folks live in old oaks.'

There is a silence.

'Gandhi,' Erin says.

'Frankenstein,' Graham says. 'Santa Claus.'

'Oppenheimer,' Taylor says.

'Lucifer.'

'Jumanji.'

'Kilroy.'

'Homer.'

'Troy.'

'Brad.'

'Spacey.'

'Stipe.'

'Johnny 5.'

'Bush.'

'Spongebob.'

'Hitler.'

'What?' I say.

Taylor shrugs.

'I was only joking,' he says.

'I'm very cold,' I say.

'Balthazar,' Erin says. 'Out of *Romeo and Juliet*.'

'He was out of the Bible first,' Jack says.

'I like Balthazar,' I say.

'So do I,' Taylor says.

'And me,' Jack says.

'Does he have to have that badge?' I say.

'Well,' Erin says. 'I don't want it.'

His face looks like the face of a long-dead body. Uncovered at Pompeii, or somewhere equally tragic. We tried to make him smile, with stones for teeth. But his mouth just looks like a big rotten mess. I'm touched. He's kind of sad.

'He can be our guardian,' Taylor says, 'against those gatecrashers.'

'What about a name for his dog?' Jennifer asks. 'What's his dog called?'

'Withnail,' Taylor says.

'Do you just say the first thing that comes into your head?' I ask him.

He shrugs. 'Does the trick.'

'I like Withnail,' Jennifer says.

'It's alright with me,' Erin says.

'Withnail it is,' Taylor says.

Balthazar's scarf flaps and snaps in the wind. It flies out from the back of his neck, giving the impression that he is perpetually tumbling forward. The ground and the trees and the clouds all tilt. I look at his penis; the end of it seems swollen. Slightly tumescent. I squint.

Carcinogens in condoms. I have this image in my head of a big tumour on the end of my cock. I stare at Balthazar. My head is at right angles to my body. Everybody else is standing and looking at him too. Taylor breaks the silence.

'Makes you think about having children,' he says.

Graham laughs so hard he bends over.

'You'll be lucky, Taylor,' I say. 'We're all going to be infertile because of hormones in tap water and the radiation from mobile phones.' I pause. 'And the chemicals in plastic.'

'Not true,' Graham says, still laughing. 'That girl over the road had to have an abortion. You know. The one that dressed like Gwen Stefani. Come on. Think positive.'

I hear one of the monster birds shouting something. Up above us. A shape gliding through the night sky. For the duration of the time Jennifer and I spent inside each other, we were alone in the world. It's no excuse. But it's true.

A snowball hits me in the temple. I fall over. I burst out laughing again. The ground eats up my naked hands. The cold, like teeth. I laugh some more. I scoop some up and hurl it at somebody. I can't see who they are through the snow and the descending mist. It's starting to feel less like it's snowing and more like we're inside a snow cloud. It is being born all around us. I think it's Erin. The music emanating from the house is suddenly louder. As if somebody's turned it up. The lyrics are too sinister for party music. Balthazar stands above me like a totem. I feel more than drunk. Everything seems to be taking on more significance than it should. The whole landscape is spinning around my head. The people are blurring. The only thing that doesn't move is him. Our beautiful, beautiful snowman. Tall and proud and clever and handsome. I plunge my hand into his side to steady myself. The lyrics of the song inside the house flow outwards, above the dying wind. Balthazar is taller than me. I hang on to him. Cling to the side of the mountain as it bucks and rolls like the sea. The same fears come back. Like shipwrecks at low tide. Maybe they're irrational. But if they are – that doesn't make any difference. Once upon a time, there was a world in which people weren't scared of their own bodies. They were scared of other things. They were scared of things that moved out there. Just beyond the edge of their vision. Just beyond the fringe of trees that masked a deeper darkness. They were scared of things that they could fight off with swords and knives and spears and axes and shovels.

The water froze and the wolves came over the river. That was always the story. The pack. Thin and desperate. Lock the doors and board up the windows.

I am jealous of the fears that people used to have.

Erin giggles and hugs me. The presence of her warm body is like a smell that I remember from years ago. It cuts through the fog in my mind. It brings me back to the present. To the snowball fight. The friends. The party.

'Are you OK?' she asks. 'You've got your hand inside Balthazar and I'm sure he's enjoying it but you're going to get very cold fingers. You've gone really quiet. Are you OK?'

'Yes, thank you.' I bring my hand out of the snowman. My skin is blue. I don't feel the cold in it.

'Good,' she says. And then all of a sudden it feels like someone's run a knife down my spine and split me open. I fall over and writhe around on the ground. I can hear people roaring with laughter. After a moment or two of abject squirming, I realise. It's just a handful of snow dumped down my back.

Jennifer. Her eyes are red and teary with laughter. I stand and look at her. I cannot summon enough concentration to work out what expression I should put on my face. I just look at her.

'Jesus,' she says. 'What's wrong with you? Where's your fire? Where's your sense of fun gone?'

'What's wrong with me?' I say. 'What's wrong with *you*?'

'What?' she says. 'What do you mean?'

'You know what I mean.' I glance meaningfully in Jack's direction, but stop short of moving my head. The mist is thickening.

'What? What do you mean?' Erin asks. Taylor is listening now as well.

'Nothing,' I say. 'I'm sorry.' I walk away from Jennifer. I walk across to the other side of the small space that we're playing in.

'What's going on?' Graham asks.

'Nothing!' I say.

'It's nothing,' Jack says. I look across at him. He is close enough for me to see his eyes. His face is grim.

'But—' Graham starts.

'I want to believe in this whole other world,' Jack says, raising his voice to interrupt Graham. Shouting and whooping come from inside the house. I think he is crying. 'This whole other world from which the stories and the myths and the ideas come. I want it to be a world that we can go to. Sometimes, at night, I do believe. That we can reach it from some of the places round here. The forests and rivers. The mountains and lakes. But I've never had any real reason to believe. Nothing.' He starts to cry.

'Yes, Jack,' Jennifer says. 'OK. But stop now, hey? We're all here to have a good time.'

'Hey,' Graham says, 'Let him be.' He is leaning on the axe again.

'Don't tell me what to do, Graham,' Jennifer says. 'Don't you tell me what to do.'

I look over at Jennifer. I can barely see her now. The cloud is lowering still, and the visibility diminishing. The snow is getting wetter. I look over at Jack. No, I think. You don't need another world. There's more than enough going on in this one.

'Jennifer's right,' Jack says. 'I'm getting upset over nothing. You don't see how supportive of me Jennifer is. None of you have seen that. Not even you, Francis.'

The way he drops my name in confuses me. Maybe he *does* know. But then, he is defending her. Which would be strange, if he does know. Maybe his love is unconditional. She is freedom. He has faith.

'It's cold,' Taylor says. The momentary silence is broken. 'Maybe we should go back inside.'

Jack is standing with his arms around himself. His head hangs down dejectedly.

'Well, I don't know,' Graham says. 'Relationships! I'd never have one.'

I can make out Jennifer's outline. She stands with her arms folded. Her weight on one leg. She wears a long coat. Her face is indistinct. I can't help but feel desire.

I see somebody appear behind her. Somebody from the house come to examine our beast of a snowman, no doubt. But as I watch they put their arms around her. She starts screaming like nothing I've ever heard. The sound is shrill and terrified, almost inhuman. I imagine the back of her throat being peeled away by the force of it. The figure drags her backwards into the mist. I start to run after them. Despite the discomfort those arms inspired in me. They were weirdly long, and knotty. And the head was faintly bulbous. A little too large for the spindly body that supported it. Some people put too much effort into fancy dress. Jennifer. I don't know what I want from you. Or if I want anything from you. But you can't disappear. Not now. You can't disappear. Jack is running beside me.

'I know what you did,' he says. The words sound weirdly squeezed by the wet air. 'I know what you did.'

I don't say anything. I don't fully know where Jack is. I can't see anything through this mist other than the grey-green ground meeting my every footfall.

'Francis?' he says. 'Francis? Is that you?' His words sound distorted, unreal. He sounds further away than he did a moment ago.

'Yeah,' I say.

'Jack? Francis?' Erin shouts from somewhere else. I can't tell where though. Graham too. Their voices are faint. They seem to come from directly beside my ears. Like quiet whispers. But there's nobody there.

'Jack?' I say. No answer. I'm out of breath and have a stitch. I can't see anything. I stop running and bend over. I put my hand to my stomach. As I recover, I start to imagine other people running around me.

'Taylor? Hey, Taylor? Erin? Graham?' No answer. Instead, this sense of other people running. Scarily fast, all around. I can't see them or hear them. I just have this sense of them all rushing downwards. Like they're falling into the lake. But running, not falling. Maybe the blood in my brain is coursing around the wrong channels as the result of some growth deep within. I'm starting to lose it. There's nobody here. Just me in the fog. There's nobody around, running or otherwise. I tremble. My hands and arms jerk about like I'm a puppet. I start walking, not knowing what else to do. But then realise that I don't know where I'm going, so I stop again. 'Oh God,' I say, to nobody. 'Oh God.' I feel like things are creeping up behind me. So I turn around. I can't see anybody there. Just a grey blank. It would be black if not for the moonlight. I can just about hear the music of the party in the distance. A dull thumping. But I can't contemplate going back without Jennifer. The direction that the music comes from is not obvious at first. But then I hear a shriek in the distance. A thin wail that sounds like Jennifer screaming. The two sounds each give a context to the other, so I can make a guess at the direction I should be heading. Her scream is accompanied by a high-pitched whooping, and I tense every muscle in my body. 'Oh God,' I say again. I start walking.

After a few minutes I see a shape looming up in front of me. I shake a little. Shudder. I stop walking and just look. I half expect something impossible. Some troll or ogre or something. I don't know what. This thing is tall, and it has arms, and it's all twisted and fucked up. It is covered in hard-looking brown skin. I gather that it is looking the other way, because it hasn't shown any sign of noticing me yet. I look up at its head, thinking that if I can back away slowly enough, then I might escape. But what if this is what took Jennifer? No. It's too big.

It's a tree. The relief almost makes me laugh. I move closer to it. I am so cold. I am so cold that this dead tree actually looks like warmth and shelter to me. My clothes are soaked. But I have to find Jennifer. I am standing next to the tree now. I look closely at it. It still looks a bit like a creature. Or a weird person. It looks like the monster from *The Woman Eater*. I see there are two trunks, growing against each other. Just above my head height, there are faces in both of them, twisting, almost, as if to look at each other. Each trunk has two branches where arms would be. They stretch up into the sky like the arms of preachers with broken wrists. I start to get the fear again. I look lower down and am almost sick at the sight of what is there. A pale, thick, smooth branch protrudes from the trunk on the left. It lies flat against the body of the tree,

261

but it bends into the other trunk, and disappears into a fold of bark that is a perfect vulva. I put my hand over my mouth. Every hair in my body is trying to escape, is pulling out, like they are parasites and are independent of me. Oh God. I turn away, and start to walk, but I don't know where to. I go uphill. But we started running downhill when we left the house, so I should be going downhill. I turn again and make myself walk past the trees but I don't look at them. I don't want to go downhill, but I do want to get away. Fuck. Fuck. Fuck. There is something walking with me, I'm sure of it. I'm imagining it. No, it's here. It's there. It is just beside me, walking with me, just hiding in the mist. It's in my head. It lashes out and claps me on the back. My spine is suddenly a stack of slates, shattered by nerves. My knees bend. Hot jaws close on the back of my neck. A long, scalding tongue slithers into the wound and my legs fold. The pain is too great for me to retain control of anything. All of my strings snap. Heavy, hairy things are astride me. I bite at the ground and the black soil fills up my eyes.

I am moving through a deep grey fog, but I don't know how. All my limbs are flailing uncontrollably. My head rolls across from one side to the other, dragged by my desperate eyes. The fog slides past as I move forward. But still my body does not connect with anything. I am not lying down, or walking, or being carried. I'm just slowly writhing, wailing, floating through the fog.

PART THREE

JACK

I jumped and ran, the ground pounding into my feet like a hammer, in the direction of the screaming and the strange whooping and laughing. Francis wasn't far away; he was there, an unfocused smudge, rushing down the mountain beside me, and we ran side by side without speaking. At least, I thought it was him, although with the mist and the silence, it could have been anybody. Was it him?

'Francis?' I said. 'Francis, is that you?'

'Yeah,' I heard him say, or thought I heard him say, but I wasn't sure. I looked over to where he was, where the *shape* of him was, and my foot suddenly slipped on the snow and the whole blasted fell tipped up and over my head as I spun around, falling and falling and falling and it didn't stop until I was on my back, lying there, looking at the solid grey air above me. The thought swept into my head that I had to save her, I had to find her first, before Francis, and that was how she would know that I was the right one for her and he was not. I stood up.

The mist pressed in against my face like a blanket some-body was trying to smother me with. What took her? Of course, it could have just been some cretin from the party but that struck me as fanciful.

I didn't know where I was, but I kept on going.

I found myself standing over a dead body, and I held my breath in case it was her. I knelt down, every atom of my body fit to shoot off, and I saw that it was Francis. I breathed out and first of all I felt relief, and then panic.

'Francis?' I said, although I didn't think he was breathing. I could see my own breath misting in the air in front of me every time I exhaled, but there was no such sign of life from him. 'Francis?' My heart was beating against the drum of my chest and I felt hot, despite the cold air and the snow on the ground. The snow on the ground.

It was red; blood was seeping out from his prone body and all over my hands and my knees, pressed down into the wet ground beside him, and it was all over his face, drying into brown patches over his mouth and chin, and all over his *whole damned body*, I realised, numbly. What could have done this? And what were they doing to Jennifer?

I remembered Francis' face as it hung over the edge of the bed while Jennifer gyrated on top of him, his neck taut and his mouth open and his eyes closed. Some prac-tical voice was thrashing around beneath the memory, like maybe we needed mountain rescue, or an air ambulance, or something. My mobile. Where was it? I tried to get it from my pocket, my fingers cold and inflexible, and I dropped it a couple of times and only then did I see how badly I was shaking.

Eventually I brought the phone up to my face, only to see that the screen was blank. I fumbled with the buttons, but couldn't turn the thing on, however hard I pressed. It was dead. I kept opening my mouth to speak with him, with Francis, but then closing it again, and I wanted to play Mario Kart with him, beat him at last, knock him off the top spot, the git. That DVD collection he had, all the B-movies, more than I would ever have thought could have been made.

I wanted to cry, but Jennifer might miraculously have appeared and seen me, so I stopped myself. The energy that tears would have released built within me until I felt that I was vibrating, slowly lifting from the face of the earth, and I shouted and screamed as loud as I could. Maybe the others would hear me and be able to find me. He had a hole in his neck, a rupture. I didn't dare leave him, leave his body, in case I couldn't find it again and it disappeared along with the mist.

I shouted and screamed until I felt that I was vomiting gravel and then I found that I couldn't shout any more. I heard people running towards me, and then I heard Taylor's voice.

'Jack?' he said. 'Where are you? Did you shout? Are you OK?'

'Taylor!' I shouted, and it hurt like hell but sounded

no louder than a crow with its lung punctured by one of the cats that tumbled and yowled around Fell House, the dying bird jerking around like a leaf in a gale. 'Taylor!'

What would Taylor think? Taylor was like a role model to all of us, like in the same way that Christians asked themselves: What would Jesus do? We asked ourselves: What would Taylor do? WWTD? Francis used to hide behind the sofa when Taylor got in from work, and then jump up and scare the shit out of him, and Taylor would lean the ironing-board up against Francis' bedroom door, which opened inwards, so that when Francis opened the door to leave his room the ironing-board would fall on top of him. Now, though, one of Francis' ribs was poking straight up out of his chest, at almost ninety degrees to the position it should have been in.

'Jack,' Taylor said, from directly behind me. He put his hand on my shoulder. Erin was there too, and Graham, and I saw that the mist was clearing. 'Jesus. Francis.' Taylor leaned over beside me and threw up. The bile in it ate through the snow, leaving a patterned hole like the trail of a firework.

'We need an ambulance,' Erin said. She pulled her phone from her pocket and fiddled with it angrily before putting it back. 'My battery's gone. Taylor? Have you got yours?'

'No,' he said. 'Left it inside.'

'He's already dead,' I said. 'It doesn't matter.'

'He's not dead,' Erin said.

'He is,' I said. 'He's dead.'

'He's not,' Graham said. 'You can see his breath.'

268

'No you can't,' I said, 'I found him a few minutes ago. I've been watching him.'

'You can,' Taylor said. 'You can see his breath.'

'Look,' Erin said.

I looked, and saw breath clouding above his mouth.

'Maybe you couldn't see it in the mist,' Erin said. 'Come on. We need to get him back to the house.'

We tried to lift him, but I expected his spine to be rigid and it wasn't, so I dropped him. He landed on his side and settled on to his front. The back of his shirt was ripped open, and the skin was torn, and his splintered vertebrae were visible.

'Jack,' Graham said quietly. 'Who did this? Could he have just fallen, and – and – I don't know. Could he have fallen?'

'I don't know,' I said, thinking no, you idiot, of course not. 'No. I don't think he fell. Has anybody seen Jennifer?'

They all shook their heads.

We tried to lift him again when screaming started in the distance and we dropped him again, the shock of the sound having tensed our frozen muscles so that they contracted and let him slip from our hands. This time I saw the breath forcefully pushed from his lungs. It hung in front of his lips for a brief moment, then dispersed. We stared at his body, slumped and curved unhealthily, and those awful, ghostly sounds floated down to us from the direction of Fell House. Roaring and howling and screaming and hollering. I heard a boy shouting something that sounded like 'Lucy! Lucy!' but I didn't say

269

anything because I didn't know what to say and we all just looked at Francis and shook. Graham slowly turned the axe around in his hands. It looked wet with some unidentifiable substance.

'What is it?' Taylor said. 'What's that noise?'

'It could be the cats,' I said.

'Really?' he said.

'No,' I said. 'I don't suppose it couldn't be the cats, not really.'

'We need to go up there,' Graham said, and of course he was right. We gently picked Francis up again, his body heavier than it looked. Taylor took his battered shoulders and head and I took his twisted feet and Erin held his waist and torso tenderly, like she was carrying a baby, and Graham carried the axe.

'There's something coming out of his neck,' Taylor said. 'Something grey. There is a crack in his face that starts with the corner of his mouth and I can see the broken edges of skull through it. How can he still be alive?'

'I don't know how he's still alive,' Erin said. 'We have to be careful we don't spill anything.'

I knew the noise was coming from Fell House because I could hear the fiddle – it was still there, being played by somebody who was somehow not distracted by all the other violent noise, the thread of the music tied up with all of the other, more frightening sounds.

'I'm going to go on ahead,' Graham said.

'No,' Erin said. 'Don't.'

'I am,' he said. 'I can't not. How can I not?' He glared at us, and then he turned and started jogging.

'Graham!' Taylor shouted, but he didn't look back, and almost straight away he was hard to see against the fell-side in his black suit. He must have been moving quite fast.

A hoarse, rhythmic shrieking reached us from the hard shape that we could see silhouetted against the sky.

'What's that shape?' I said.

'It's your house, Jack,' Erin said. 'You don't know your own house?'

'My house?' I said, confused. It was Fell House, of course, it just didn't have any lights on. I'd never seen it like that before, from that angle, and besides, it wasn't really my house, not if I thought about it, because it had never felt like it and I didn't think it ever would.

It was still quite a distance away, and from it came that shrieking sound followed by a frantic yelping and a squeal that felt like a thin wire being pulled from my ear.

Carrying Francis was difficult because the ground was slippery. One or two or all of us kept slipping and nearly dropping him, but he carried on breathing. Taylor unexpectedly fell and the sudden weight was a surprise to Erin. Francis' head dropped and hit a rock, bouncing off.

'Be careful, Taylor,' I said, as he tried to stand but slipped again. 'This is a steep bit.'

'Francis,' Erin said. 'He's stopped breathing. He's stopped breathing! Look. Oh, he's started again. Thank God.'

Taylor didn't say anything. He didn't even look at me.

'What are we going to do about Jennifer?' I asked.

Nobody answered.

The sounds from Fell House stopped suddenly. We were still a little way away. Maybe Graham and the axe had fixed it, sorted it all out, but somehow I doubted it.

We reached the small space between the orchard and the back door, which was where we built the snowman. The house was dark and the wind was back, having chased the low clouds away. Everything was slightly luminous because of the snow reflecting the starlight, although there was something about the snow, something unpleasant. It was churned up, roughened, textured and corrupted by dark shadowy patches, and I couldn't help but feel that it had somehow been violated, and Balthazar was gone. Withnail the snow-dog had survived somehow.

I accidentally knocked it over as we scuffed past, and felt something crunch slightly beneath my foot. It was a skull. My first thought was that it was Withnail's skull, but no, that was ridiculous. It was a cat's skull. And next to where it had lain were those small bones I had seen that time I'd thrown the axe out. Cat ribs.

'Graham!' Taylor yelled.

There was no answer but the back door was open, so we manoeuvred Francis inside and Erin flicked the light switches, but they didn't work. We stretched out Francis on the kitchen table.

'Do you have any matches?' Erin asked. 'Candles?'

'In the cutlery drawer,' I said. 'And tea-lights. In case of power-cuts.'

'Where are all the people?' Taylor asked.

Nobody answered. What had a short time ago been a house too full to move around in was now just an empty box. Erin lit two tea-lights, and carried them over, her hands wrapped in dishcloths so that she didn't burn herself. Her face was drawn, and wet, and softly lit from below.

'I need to find Jennifer,' I said.

'You can't go back out there,' Erin said. 'We don't know what happened to Francis.'

'We don't know what happened here,' I said.

'Whatever happened here, it's over,' Taylor said, whose face was reduced to a single edge in the candlelight.

I shook my head. 'We don't know that. Besides. You could come with me.'

'We can't leave him!' Erin exclaimed, shocked.

'I have to go and look for her,' I said.

'Not on your own, then,' Erin said. 'Taylor. You go with him.'

'I can't leave you, Erin,' Taylor said.

'Somebody has to look after Francis as best we can. And it may as well be me. And I know what you're going to say,' she said, as Taylor opened his mouth. 'About me being a girl and all, but we all know that that's just offensive. So go on. Get.'

'I want to be chivalrous,' Taylor said quietly. I didn't

think he was talking just about the situation at hand, but his whole life, like he wanted to be some sort of Knight of the Round Table or something, and he felt like a sorry modern excuse for a good person.

'You are chivalrous,' Erin said, and kissed him quickly on the lips.

'I love you,' he said to her, genuinely, and they both seemed surprised.

'I love you too,' Erin said.

'We should lay him down on one of the beds,' I said, gesturing at Francis. 'Erin. Could you lead the way with the candles?'

On the way to the bedroom we saw streaks and splashes and smears and gobbets of dark red all over the walls, and the stone steps were slippery, but Erin didn't lower the candles to see why, and none of us spoke a word about it. Upstairs Taylor and Erin kissed again, more deeply this time, and we left her with Francis in the room with the blue and white striped wallpaper, him lying on the bed, the bed surrounded by little candles, the candles dipping and swaying and lowering before springing up again. Fragile in the draughts.

I stopped dead in the doorway to the kitchen, before realising that the pale figure hunched at the table was Graham.

'Jack?' he whispered, quietly.

'Yes,' I said. 'And Taylor.'

'Thank God,' he said.

'What's wrong?' Taylor said.

'I don't know,' he said, and I could tell he was shaking his head. 'I don't know where to start. Just. Don't go into the barn, Jack. Taylor. Don't go into the barn.'

FRANCIS

I'm itchy. Like I've been sleeping in a bed infested with fleas. There is a blanket or something lying over me. And it's heavy and rough. And I'm hot. Too hot. I'm lying on my back and scratching my shoulders. I grit my teeth and move my hands into a blur. My nails leave lines in my skin. I move my digging, stabbing nails down over my chest. Twisting and turning in this pit I find myself in. I reach my lower ribs and stop. I've found something. Soft and fleshy, protruding from my body. Another one. I can't move my hands over my stomach because it's covered in huge, lolling growths. A forest of flat, wide skin tags is covering my belly. It stretches from the bottom of my chest to my groin. They feel so dead. I try and pull one off. But the skin that connects the lump to my body is strong. It really hurts. I feel the rest of the skin around it tent up. I'm sweating. All these horrible things are so itchy. And the skin in between is itchy. And the skin underneath and all around and all over my whole body is so itchy that I'm drawing blood and tearing strips out of it.

'Francis?' The voice is gentle.

'FUCK OFF! FUCK OFF!' I scream. 'FUCK OFF!'

'Francis, it's just me! It's just Erin. Hey. Francis. Calm down. Are you awake?'

Suddenly my skin is coming off in great swathes. I feel like there is something inside me. Growing bigger and bigger. Or maybe just getting nearer and nearer from a great depth. Casting a shadow upwards on to my brain. I'm screaming. I open my eyes. Erin is looking down at me. She smiles. I stop screaming.

'I don't know how you're still alive,' she says, and shakes her head.

'I feel like there's something wrong with me,' I say. 'I had a dream.'

'You've been unconscious for hours. Something happened to you, out there on the mountain.'

'What?' I say. 'What happened?'

'We don't know.' She shrugs. 'But you're badly hurt. We thought you were dead. We tried to call an ambulance. We thought you were dead. I didn't know, Francis. I didn't know if you would wake up. You're so badly hurt. That's probably why you feel like shite.'

'There's something wrong with me. Something growing inside me. I can feel it, Erin. I have a lump. In my consciousness. There is something different in my body.'

'Francis,' she says.

'It's cancer,' I say. 'I know it.'

'Francis,' she says. 'You don't have cancer. You've got a fuck-off hole in your neck. That's what you've got.'

'Where is everybody?'

'Jack and Taylor are looking for Jennifer. Still don't know where she is. We don't know about Graham. And everyone that came to the party – we don't know about them either. It looks like something awful has happened. We're on our own in here.'

I look up and around. The room is full of tea-lights and other candles. The wallpaper looks black and white in this light. I see a rope – a noose – hanging from the beam. It is moving, as if somebody is hanging from it. But the noose is empty. I frown and shake my head.

'What?' Erin looks up behind her. Following the direction of my eyes. 'There's nothing there.'

'Erin,' I say. 'There's something wrong with me.'

We are silent for a length of time. Gradually the light from the candles diminishes. I prod the hole at the back of my neck. The flesh feels dry. Hard. Like fresh meat that's drying up.

I close my eyes. I think of a Radiohead poster that I have on the wall of my bedroom. I remember the words printed across the bottom:

I AM AWAKE AT 4 A.M. TO THE TERRIFYING UNDEN-IABLE TRUTH THAT THERE IS NOTHING I CAN DO TO STOP THE MONSTER

The terrifying undeniable truth. I can feel a presence inside my brain. Something inside my brain is slowly getting bigger. It mutates the cells around it and they clump together, all in one place, and have a big fucking party. I keep my eyes closed. I know that, ultimately, nothing is going to be OK.

'Erin,' I say. 'Tell me some stories. I need you to make me think of other things.'

Erin looks at me. Her eyes are dark and difficult to read. But she nods.

'OK,' she says. 'OK. Well, this is it. The End of the Party. Francis, Jack, Jennifer, Erin, Taylor and Graham arrived back at the house wet, cold, laughing, exhausted. The sky was deep black, the stars a bright white dust. Below them the mountain stretched down to the lake at the bottom of the valley, and the lake shone like the moon that hung above it. Several thin plumes of smoke rose from chimneys across the valley floor and the six of them looked out over what would normally be a patchwork of dark woodland and pale fields criss-crossed by hedgerows. Tonight, however, everything was blanketed by a layer of fresh white snow. The mountains were friendly guardians standing watch over the people that lived beneath them. Scattered across the valley floor were warm orange lights that signified where those people were – the places that they had found and settled in and come to rest at.

'"Where is everybody?" Jack asked. "All the music's stopped. There doesn't seem to be anybody around."

'"Let's go and have a look," Jennifer replied. "I'm sure everything is OK."

'She took Jack by the hand and squeezed it gently in hers before leading the others inside.

'"This is a beautiful place to live," Francis said, casting one last glance over the magical landscape. "You two are very lucky."

'The lights were still on inside the house, but it was empty of people. There was leftover food scattered across the brightly striped tablecloth and Graham picked at it.

'"We can't let all this fodder go to waste," he muttered.

'"Where *is* everybody?" Jack asked, again. "It's like they've all just disappeared!"

'"Hey!" Graham exclaimed, stopping in his slow hoovering-up of the crumbs. "There's a note. Here, Taylor. Read it out. I'm going to get some ginger beer."

'"OK," Taylor agreed, and took the note from Graham's hand. "Dear Jennifer and Jack, Sorry if our sudden departure has alarmed you – it's just that everybody's parents all arrived to pick us up at the same time!" Taylor looked up and grinned, the relief evident in his face. Everybody looked around and smiled at each other. "We just left this note to explain what's happened and to say thank you for such a wonderful party. We're sure you'll both be very happy here at Fell House and wish you all the best. Enjoy the rest of the night! From all your friends."

'"That's nice," Jennifer said. "It's a shame we missed them but I'm glad that they had a good night."

'"Fancy that," Francis said. "All the parents turning up at once!"

'"You know what we should do?" Graham said. "Gather up all these helium balloons, tie them to a tin can, put

280

a message in the can and let the balloons go and take the message with them. It could end up *anywhere*!"

'Erin wrote the message. She wrote:

> Yesterday, upon the stair
> I met a man who wasn't there.
> He wasn't there again today;
> I WISH TO GOD HE'D GO AWAY.

'"I know those aren't the original words," she said, "I know."

'The six of them emerged from Fell House as the sun was coming up, and let the balloons go. They stood there watching until the balloons had disappeared into the sky. By that time everything was sparkling in the rays of the newly risen sun.

'The air was cold, so the friends, smiling, turned and went back into the house for breakfast.

'The sun rose higher and higher, and when it hit the windows of Fell House, they shone out like beacons across the mountains.'

Erin's voice is rich. Her eyes are half closed as she finishes the story.

'That was nice,' I say.

'Thank you,' she says.

Behind her, hanging from the noose, the body of a man sputters into existence. Like a candle going out, but backwards. My eyes widen. Erin turns at the expression on my face.

'Why do you keep on looking up there?' she asks, looking back.

'It's nothing,' I say. The dead man spins slowly around. He was maybe in his sixties or seventies when he died. He has thick grey hair. He wears a checked shirt, and heavy-looking dark jeans. His hands are huge and gnarled. Strong-looking and weather-beaten. I touch my temple with the fingers of my right hand. Close my eyes. Shake my head. 'It's nothing, Erin.'

'Another story?'

'Please.'

'This is about Taylor,' she says. 'Or somebody like Taylor. Wanting to drive across America. Maybe I'm with him.'

'Maybe?'

'I don't feel like it's up to me.'

'OK,' I say.

'They picked up a four-wheel drive in Minneapolis and drove for days until they reached the point that they had worked out was the very centre of America. A boy and a girl, using maps, rulers and money that they'd earned serving chips and sandwiches to climbers in a country pub called The Shepherd Sleeps. They were both twenty-five and by the time they reached their destination they were thin and tanned and more pale-haired than they had been in England. They turned the engine off and the sun washed over them like hot thick water. They closed their eyes and fell asleep. After they woke up, they took a pair of shovels out of the boot and started digging. They were looking for some sort of energy source, or explanation, or massive pivot. They dug and dug and dug. They took their clothes off because they were so hot the sweat was running into their eyes and they hadn't stopped for water since they had started. The sun went down and the desert got cold, but they carried on digging. They were still hot. They were naked and covered in red sand. They dug and they dug and they dug until the hole was ten feet deep and ten feet wide.

'"I don't think there's anything here," declared the boy. "But maybe we knew that there was nothing here all along."

'"You're right," she said, and nodded. "Maybe the fixed point that everything revolves around is just a kind of empty space." She gestured carelessly at the world with her empty hand.

'They threw the shovels up on to the desert floor and climbed out of the hole. They were exhausted and their arms were on fire. Their skin was stinging because of the radiation from the sun. Their hands were stained red. The sky seemed bigger than ever before and they both felt incredibly small, incredibly unimportant. The boy was filled with a kind of ultimate peace and the girl was filled with a savage despair. She picked up her shovel and swung it at the boy's head with such force that it chipped the top of his skull right off so that the inside of his head was exposed to the elements. He remained standing and slowly raised his hand so that he could feel the texture of his brain with his long, dextrous fingers. The girl hit him again and this time she knocked his hand into his brain and he died and fell into the hole. She spent the rest of the night and the following morning burying him. She then got back into the four-wheel drive and fell asleep. Next time, she thought. Next time somebody comes looking they'll find something here.'

'Erin,' I say. 'That was a horrible story.'

'What?' She refocuses on me. She is incredibly pale in the gathering dark. 'What did you say?'

'I said, that was a horrible story. Where did you get it?'

'Oh, I don't know. I just made it up. Did you like it?' Her smile is wan as she asks the question. Behind her the dead farmer swivels around in mid-air. I know he is a farmer because I imagined him. This is my logic. He is some sort of hallucination brought on by the thing in my head. And because he has come from me and only from me, I can tell you that he is a farmer. Also, he killed his wife. And then he killed himself. In my mind's eye, he rows out into the lake and dumps her body.

'Did I like it?' I repeat, absently. But I don't answer the question. My pain suddenly diminishes. Then I feel movement inside me. It can't really be movement inside me. But it doesn't feel like anything else. It feels like my bones are realigning and clicking back together. The pain flows out of me. Erin starts again.

'This one's called "Depth Perception". It's about a woman. I never knew her, but I always imagine her reading; curled up in an armchair under a standard lamp, the room bathed in a lovely warm light, and she is very pretty, with thick, curly brown hair and the vestiges of a healthy tan. Without thinking, she puts her hand to her mouth every time the story gets tense, or some mystery is about to be resolved. She doesn't realise she's doing it – it's a reflex thing, like blinking. She's wearing heavy gold jewellery and it suits her.

'This is an image that I have in my head as vividly as if I'd seen her only yesterday.

'I don't know his name, and I never knew what he looked like. But he did it at night, and so it would have been dark (very dark – it was cloudy, the way I imagine it, and there are no streetlights in Wasdale) and so what he looked like doesn't matter. We can't see his face.

'It's possible that there were a lot of rowing boats moored around the edges of the lake in the sixties. So either he found one of those, if they were there at all, or he had his own. The only boats there now are a few rotten old shells in the boathouse at the western end, but the boathouse is too far away from the road. Too far to carry the body.

'He is parked on the road on the northern shore. To avoid being seen, all of his car lights have been turned off. For the sake of this story, he has brought his own boat. He has taken it from the trailer and dragged it to the little pebbly beach. At this time of night, in this weather, the lake is difficult to see. There is no light for the surface to catch. It's windy; it sounds as if the lake is whispering. He's scared. He's scared that at any minute a car might approach, and slow down, and stop, and that somebody might wind down their window and ask him exactly what it is that he's doing out here, in the dark, in the cold, all alone . . . he's scared that, after coming all this way, he'll be found out. He's scared that all his planning might amount to nothing. He looks out at the invisible, whispering water. He's scared that he might capsize. He's scared that he might drown. He's scared, suddenly, of the deep, dark cold . . . he is scared of forgetting how to swim. He is scared of whatever might be hiding at the bottom. He wonders how many people have had the same idea as him. He is reassured by the fact that he has never heard of any of them. By the fact that they have never been found out. He opens the boot. He lifts his dead wife, wrapped in the dirty bed-sheets, easily. She had always been quite light; slim. He carries her over to the boat, lays her down gently, her head towards the stern. He takes off his shoes and socks, rolls up his trousers. He pushes the boat out and, once it's freed from the ground and he can feel it floating, pulls himself in. He is sitting with his back to the prow, facing the body of his wife. He loses himself in his thoughts for a moment, looking at the corpse. Am I going to sell the jewellery? Am I going to pretend that all of her books are mine? Oh God, he thinks. I always envied the way she could lose herself in a book like that. Oh God. How much she loved reading. I would come in from the farm and lean in the doorway and watch her just reading. And I loved the way that she would express so much through her face and her body, even when she thought she was on her own. If the people she was reading about were happy, she would actually smile. If they were in danger, she would look worried. Oh God. These are his thoughts.

'He realises that he is drifting in the wind. He takes the oars from the bottom of the boat, places them in their brackets, and begins to row out into the middle of the lake. As he does so, he notices that there is water in the bottom of the boat. He panics; he asks himself, how long has it been since I used it? Did I check it for leaks? Am I sinking?

'He keeps on rowing. He reassures himself that this is the way with rowing boats. He is not sinking.

'He wonders what he will do with the boat. He cannot tolerate the idea of waiting for it to dry out so that he can burn it. Besides, somebody might see the flames and ask questions.

'He thinks that he has rowed far enough. We can't blame him for this; he doesn't know the lake, he doesn't know where the shelf ends. He doesn't even know how far he is from the shore. It's all a question of depth perception, and let's not forget – it's very dark out here. He takes the corpse in both arms and lifts it over the edge and drops it into the black, and the white of the bed-sheets disappears immediately. The boat rocks alarmingly, and suddenly he feels very alone. He realises that now he can't get caught, he was expecting the worry and tension to run out of him, like water, and into the lake. But it hasn't happened. Instead, the lake is draining into him, the night-water creeping in through cracks in his mind and filling him with a lake's worth of fear.

'Oh God, he thinks. She's gone.'

Erin rolls her shoulders as she finishes. Her eyes change. It is as if she is waking up. I am sitting up. I am staring at her.

'Francis,' Erin says. 'My God. You're sitting up.'

'Where did you get that story?'

'Francis.' She looks amazed. 'How on earth are you sitting up?'

'Where the fuck did you get that story?' I ask again. I climb out of bed. I am naked. I am whole.

'What do you mean?' she says. 'Francis, you're standing up. Here, put some trousers on.' She throws me my jeans. 'What – how are you standing up?'

'Never mind that. Where the fuck did you get that story? I had that story in my head. It was in here.' I point at my skull. 'It was in there.' I am salivating uncontrollably. 'Erin. Erin. Tell me.'

'I don't know,' she shrugs. She leans back just a tiny amount. Enough to show me that she's uncomfortable. Her white dress is torn and muddy and bloody. I sit back down. I put my head in my hands. A moment's silence.

'Erin,' I say. 'Imagine the clothes that the man in your story was wearing. But don't say anything. Imagine what he looks like. You got a picture in your head?'

She nods, hesitantly.

'Checked shirt,' I say. 'Dark jeans. Grey hair, in his sixties or seventies. Big hands.'

She nods, eyes wide. Around the house, the wind cracks like thunder. But the skies are clear now. We know that it's not thunder. I can smell sweat. It's mine. The scent of it rises in waves from the damp bedding. I am hot. Energy courses through me. Or maybe I can just feel the blood in my body. 'He's here,' I say. 'I can see him. Hanging from the beam. After he dumped his wife's body, he hung himself here in this room. I can see him, Erin. Look up there. Behind you.'

Erin turns and looks up at the beam. Slowly. She turns back. She opens her mouth to speak. She croaks something before clearing her throat and shaking her head. 'I can't see anything.'

'There's something wrong with this house,' I say. 'There is something here. Some history. Something getting into our heads.'

'Maybe that's what's wrong with Jack and Jennifer. They don't seem so happy.'

I stand up and make for my clothes. They're piled up on the floor by the door. But I don't manage it. Something in my back shifts and I fall to the floor. Suddenly I can't move my legs any more.

Erin starts talking. That voice. The voice. I don't even think it is completely hers. 'This one's called "Bearpit".'

'What?' I say, from the floor. 'What?'

'The sun beat down relentlessly, bleaching the grass and the stone and turning the whole fellside yellowish-brown. The house wavered in the heat. It was this house. Fell House. Where the barn stands now, there was nothing but a hole.

'The boy had been a shepherd. His long black hair was

greasy and kept falling into his eyes. Tiredly, he swept it back. And again. And again. He wore black trousers held up with string, and nothing else. The sun had turned his skin the colour of iron ore. His wrists and ankles bore the raw marks of recent captivity and his legs were weak. He stumbled. The mountains were steep. But he was less likely to get caught up there.

'Fell House lay somewhere behind him, and he knew that it would not be long before somehow it tried to find him. Despite the heat, despite his burning back, despite his bleeding wrists and ankles, despite the pain in his head and the heaviness of his feet and of his eyelids, he continued to lift one foot up and put it down again in front of the other. And again. And again. And again.

'He woke up and found grass in his mouth. The day had cooled, although the sun was still up. He could see that he was lying in shadow.

'"They know that you've escaped," somebody advised him. "They're sending out the dogs as we speak. You don't have long. You should not have slept."

'The boy got to his feet and shaded his eyes in order to look up at the man in front of him. The man sat atop a huge black horse with beautiful big eyes and wore a black cloak. Beneath the cloak, the boy could make out a strangely shaped black leather boot. It didn't seem to have much room for the foot – it was almost a ball. A flat-bottomed ball. In the distance, the sun was approaching the ocean. "Who are you?" asked the boy.

'The man dismounted, but even without the horse he stood a good two feet higher than the boy. The boy saw that both boots were the same unusual shape. His face was lean and lined, and his mouth was thin and flat, and his eyes were black and his hair was short and white. "I am the Lord of hereabouts," said the man. "And I know what happens at Fell House. And I want to help you because I know what they have in store for you." His eyes searched those of the boy for a moment, finding confirmation. "They will find you, boy. And they will take you back."

'The boy shook his head a little and, despite the shame of it, started to cry. "They want me to fight," he said. "Although really they just want to see me die." There was a silence. And then, "Have you any water, Lord?"

'"Water? Here." The man unhooked a black leather water carrier from the black tack of the horse and handed it to the boy. The boy drank deeply, and wiped his lips, and handed the carrier back.

'"Thank you," he said. The man smiled broadly, and the boy saw that his teeth were small and pointed. His ears too. The man put his head back and drank also. The boy heard a hissing sound as the water disappeared into the man's mouth, as if it had been poured on to hot metal.

'"So then," the man said. "Let me help you."

'"What can you do? Will you take me away? Take me to the town? Will you arrest them that live there? That man and his wife? The things they do, Lord. Them's not people, Lord, not real people like you an' me. Help me. Please."

"'I won't do any of those things." The man took the boy's throat in his black leather glove. "That man and his wife, boy, are indeed people. They are as human as anybody can be. And as for me – well, no, I'm not. And as for you – that's your choice."

'The man looked at the ground. They heard the rough, wet barking of savage dogs. The boy looked at the man and didn't really understand. The man looked back up. "I could take you away. I could destroy that house, and the people inside it. But I won't, because I built that house, and it is my house, and it will always be my house. And besides, it would be of far greater value to give you everything you need in order for you to do it yourself. Not just this time. But any time. Boy. I can give you power and strength beyond your imagining. All you need to do is pledge your allegiance to me. To me and my name. To me and my standard. When the time comes, your body and your soul are mine to command. Do you understand me?"

'The boy nodded, his throat still held in the iron grip of the Lord.

"'Good. In return, then. If ever you feel the need, or the desire, you can change yourself into something far greater. Something older and purer. Simpler. Stronger. Something like the wolves that haunt the forests and the moors. I have put much of the wolf into you now. And your soul is mine. Do you still understand me?"

'The boy nodded. The man took his hand from the boy's throat and blood sprang from the marks that it left and ran down the boy's neck. The man smiled again, teeth glinting in the fading light, and mounted his horse. A black fiddle was slung across his back, like a sword.'

'He let the men from the farm beat him and whip him and tie him up. He let them carry him back to Fell House. He thought about the bodies of the dogs; he thought about the earthy, fatty taste of the dogs' blood. He let the men untie him in the yard of Fell House, and he let them kick him, and he let them beat him some more. He let them throw him into the pit in front of the three-deep crowd that stood around the edge of it, whooping and jeering. He stood up in the bottom of the pit, illuminated by the the flaming torches, and looked up at the faces of the spectators. He let them spit on him, piss on him, worse. He looked at the wooden barricade – the trunks of three trees lashed together – that covered the hole in the floor of the pit that led to deeper holes, and he wondered who – or what – would be hidden down there tonight. He somehow knew the kind of games that had been played there before. The people that stood up above roared and laughed and placed bets. People. The boy smiled.

'A voice rang out. A depraved, cracked, creaky wheeze of a voice that reeked of decades of cruelty. "Bets in! Wiv git ready 'n's all set t'gor. On't three!"

'The boy tensed. He closed his eyes and willed the change upon himself.

'"One!" the crowd bellowed, a broken chorus. The ropes tied to the wooden barricade tensed. The boy fell over and his body jerked about like it was on strings being pulled viciously, randomly. The crowd laughed. "Two!" they shouted, and the boy found himself on all fours, coughing up blood and hair. He felt something rising up from his stomach and up his throat. The pain was so great he could hear it tearing through his muscles and nerves. He could not shake the feeling that he was dying. Everything inside him was rushing towards his face. The tree-trunks shifted slightly, maybe because of the people pulling the ropes, maybe because something underneath was trying to get out.

'"Three!"

'The word rose up from their hopeless, misguided mouths, insignificant in itself, but significant in that it was the signal for the raising of the wooden barrier. Significant in that it immediately preceded the transformation from boy into something else, not man, not animal, but something else entirely, something completely other, and outside their understanding. They watched, and their eyes – eyes that had seen the vilest things – watered as they conveyed visions to their brains that would induce such horror that, had these people survived, they would never have been able to escape the memory of it.

'Above the pit, the house and the fells, the stars hung in their empty spaces.

'The boy died and was reborn as something evil, monstrous. The boy's blood coloured the walls and the floor of the pit. The crowd stood stock-still, rooted partly through their own morbid fascination and partly through some other magic.

'Slowly, carefully, a huge animal emerged from behind the barrier: dark brown, bulky, hungry-looking and noble, in a sense. The bear revealed itself. It could smell the blood, and despite being able to sense the deeply unnatural nature of its companion in the pit, it had to eat. It approached the thing that had been a boy slowly at first, and then with a suddenness that shocked the onlookers, launched itself at the wolf-thing.

'The fight – not that it was much of a fight – was over before it had begun. The bear died painfully and messily. Its opponent leapt from the pit and killed every last man and woman that had been there; those that tried to run, it hunted and found and savaged. It ate some of them. It found that it preferred the taste of women.

'The day dawned on a young-looking boy with ancient eyes licking bear blood off his skin by the side of a pit half full of broken bodies. The boy who would henceforth be named Bearpit looked over the yard, the house, the fellside, the lake reflecting the glory of the newly risen sun, and he could not deny the joy inside him.'

Erin finishes the story. I watch a small grey scrap of spirit detach itself from the wall and zoom around the room a couple of times. It flutters to and from the dead man like a moth with a candle. Then it floats up to the ceiling, where it dissipates into a thousand smaller pieces. They fall like a kind of rain. But every single drop fades away before landing on my pale skin. Erin seems unaware.

'Francis?' she says.

'Yeah?' I try moving my legs. I find that I can. They are part of me once more. Part of my body. I stand. I lower myself back on to the bed.

'Francis? Have I been asleep?'

'No,' I say. 'You've been telling me a story. About the house. About a boy called Bearpit.'

'I don't know anything about the house.'

'You don't even remember telling me the story,' I say. 'I don't think you need to know anything about the house to tell the stories.'

'Francis, I'm tired. And I'm starting to freak out a bit. I can hear things outside.'

'It's the wind,' I say.

'It's not the wind,' she says. 'You know it's not the wind.'

'It's the gate.'

'It's not.'

'It's the cats.'

'No, Francis, it's not, you know it's not. Francis, I don't understand why you're not dead.'

'Thank you,' I say, after a pause.

'Francis, it's not *funny*!' Her voice is trembling.

'I'm sorry,' I say. Although I'm not sure what I said that she thought was supposed to be funny.

'You know it's all fucked up,' she says. 'Francis, what's that *noise*?'

I look over and she's crying. I can hear distant music from out on the mountain. I can hear a fiddle. I can hear laughter, of a sort. Warped and throaty. I can hear shouting and howling and yelping and a rough shrieking. The sounds are distant. They touch something inside me. I know that wherever the sound is coming from is where I'll find Jennifer. It's where I'll go.

'The noise,' I say. 'What can you hear?'

'Just that shrieking.' She wipes her face. 'It's freaking me out.'

I don't say anything. Because I'm suddenly aware of somebody else in the room. Somebody is sitting on the end of the bed. It's Balthazar the snowman. I feel the ice-cold water soaking into the bedclothes and numbing my feet. He turns to look at me. His back is crooked and blue. His head is overly large, and misshapen. His eye-sockets are big enough to have been gouged out by hands. His nose is long, bulbous and dripping. He doesn't really have a mouth. It's like the bottom half of his head has fallen away. He has brittle-looking arms and his body is thin. Thinner than we built it. He looks unhealthy.

'Turn,' he says. His voice is old, low. You can hear melt water in it. Snow falling from trees. Glaciers splintering. Falling into the sea. I look at Erin. She is looking at me.

'What is it, Francis?' she asks. 'What's wrong?'

I look back at Balthazar. 'Turn now,' he says. 'Before it's too late. You need to turn now if you want to find her. Francis. Turn.'

I think about that something that I sensed rushing up towards the surface as I woke. The shadow on my brain. Jennifer. I think about Jennifer.

'You won't regret it,' Balthazar says. 'It's what you've always wanted. Your fantasies, this idea you have of

297

Jennifer. You can find her with this gift. This gift is just waiting for you to take it. Waiting for you to discover it, take it, make it yours. And with it, you can change the world. This world that makes you sick. This world that makes you angry. The news that leaks into you. You can take this gift out into your world and spread it like freedom and never have to think about cancer or money again. Look at me. Change.'

My eyes absorb his image. His cold wraps around me. I realise his strangeness. It sinks into me. Strength floods my limbs. His head slips forward. A tiny movement like a nod of approval.

I close my eyes. I know it now. Beyond the shadow of a doubt. There is something deeply wrong with me. Hallucinating Balthazar. I focus inwards and I can feel something in there. Something hard and dark at the centre of me. Something growing. Ever-hungry. Swallowing up all of my healthy body for sustenance.

As I think about it, it wakes up. I feel it growing inside my head. Some sort of cluster of mutant cells expanding. Spreading. Corrupting the cells around them. I can feel them breaking off and flowing around the body. Lodging in joints and ligaments and building up in extremities. They're accumulating. Clinging to the insides and inside sides of me. Growing, growing, growing. Growing.

Taking over.

JACK

The sky was clearing when we got back outside, the inky black spattered with a thick spill of stars, the clouds rushing away over the sea like crows from a sudden, barking dog, and the cold air rushed into our mouths and throats and lungs. There was some sort of feeling in the air; Francis was not dead, we could see again, and the sky was beautiful.

The barn was behind us.

Graham was deathly silent, and against the settled snow I could see his silhouette tremble. It was that bright, beneath the stars, that we all stood out sharply against the ground, like cut-outs.

'Can you hear that?' Taylor asked.

'Yeah,' I said. 'The fiddle.'

'Yeah.'

'But there was a fiddle player at the party,' I said. 'Maybe it's not that bad. Maybe everybody got away from, um, whatever happened. Whatever it was.'

'No,' Graham said. 'They didn't.'

'Graham,' I said. 'What was in the barn?'

He just shook his head and stumbled on, not even turning round to look at me. Taylor and I made eye contact, Taylor raising his eyebrows ludicrously high, as high as only Taylor could raise them.

'Graham,' Taylor said. 'Come on. We need to know what's happening.'

Graham stopped walking and slumped his shoulders. The head of the axe slumped to the ground. After a long moment's silence, he turned to face us. 'They're all in there,' he said. 'The guests.'

Everyone we know was in the barn, he said, but that didn't mean everyone, that is, the people we didn't know, the people we hadn't known, the fiddler and his wild dancers, the aloof, preoccupied gatecrashers – they might have escaped.

Or maybe the gatecrashers had been the perpetrators, because they had been gatecrashers, hadn't they? After all, that girl, that dancing girl, she had been one of those headed for the gathering at the end of Wastwater. Maybe the fiddler was one of them too.

The sound of the fiddle sawed across my brain. It was coming from a distance, echoing around the mountains easily now that the mist had lifted. From down the slope of the fellside.

From the lake.

'Everyone we know?' I asked.

Graham nodded. 'There were none of those – people – that we didn't know. But everyone we know. Is in that barn. They're all dead, Jack.'

300

At least we were still there. At least Francis and Erin were still alive. But Graham's words sank into me like stones into the lake.

And Jennifer. Jennifer *had* to be still out there somewhere, but if all those people had been killed, then Jennifer, too, was surely dead?

I started walking, just struck out, and Graham and Taylor followed.

I noticed that there were no electric lights on in the valley.

'There are no lights on in the valley,' I said.

Taylor and Graham looked down, looked all around, from the overbearing fells at the head of the valley, down across the lake and the woodland that surrounded it, over the foothills at the mouth of the valley, along all of the roads that stretched out towards the sea, towards the places where the coastal villages normally twinkled with hundreds of orange lights, and everything was dark. Everything.

There were no ships out on the sea.

There were no cars on the roads.

There were no lights on in any of the houses that I knew dotted the fellside.

I looked up.

There were no satellites blinking their lonely paths through space.

The fiddler played.

There are stories of lost or missing fiddlers from all over

the country. The fiddler would become obsessed by some hole or tunnel entrance that led nobody knew where, and, despite the urgings of his family and friends and lover, would embark on an underground journey of discovery.

'I will find out where it goes,' he would say, or 'I will find out what is down there,' or 'I will find out what is beneath our town.'

'But how will we know where you are?' his lover, or friends, or family would ask. 'How will we know that you are not dead?'

'I will play my fiddle,' he would say. 'And by the sound of it you will be able to discern my presence, my location. My very existence.'

There would be nothing that the friends, family, lover, could do, and the fiddler would set off, and the sound of the fiddle would fade, but then remain constant. In some stories, those above ground trace its movement. In others, they don't. In some stories, the music of the fiddle suddenly stops, indicating that some tragedy has befallen the fiddler; in other stories, the music of the fiddle gradually fades away, indicating that the fiddler is descending yet further.

In no version is the fiddler ever seen again.

Sometimes the fiddler is accompanied by a dog which later reappears from the tunnel entrance, or the hole in the ground, or some other earthly opening (suggesting that they link, connect, beneath the surface), and the dog comes back completely hairless, mad with fear and tainted somehow with the smell of burning. This was generally taken to mean that the fiddler had met his fate at the hands of the Devil.

And the Devil! There is another story, recorded in the 1930s, that in Bushey, on the Middlesex border, on moonlit nights, the Devil sat on a stile and played the fiddle. If you stayed and watched, then after a while you would see the Devil leave his post and walk towards the woods, still playing the fiddle, until he disappeared. In English folklore there is this association between stiles and the Devil – maybe something to do with crossing over, as if being in between places you were more susceptible to something, or more likely to just step out of the world completely.

A sensory stimulus intruded on my chaining together of stories – a flaring up of lights, many and flickering, down at the eastern end of Wastwater, and the moment I noticed them, they stood out like beacons. The music was coming from that direction, and the other sounds.

'There,' I said, pointing. 'That's where they are.'

'Who?' Taylor asked.

'The others,' I said. 'Those others from the party. The fiddler.'

'Right,' Taylor said. 'Hey. Maybe that's the other party Kenny was talking about.'

'What?' I said.

'Kenny. Kenny said that—'

'What?' I said. 'When? Has he been here tonight?'

'Yeah,' Taylor said. 'Did you not see him?'

'No,' I said. 'Jesus, Taylor. I wish you'd told me.'

'Why?'

'That's where we have to go,' I said, and pointed down to the fires. 'That's where she'll be. Jennifer.'

The fellside was clear before us. It was a beautiful night, aside from the strangeness that gnawed at the back of my head, my mind. The stars were bright. The lake shone beneath them. We trudged onwards in silence.

We were approaching something, something black and hulking, unidentifiable by the starlight. We slowed down as we got closer because everything we could not immediately identify was threatening; we were at the bottom of the sea, or on an as-yet-undiscovered planet. Life could look like anything.

'What's that?' Taylor asked.

'I don't know,' I said, shaking my head.

'I don't like it,' Taylor said.

'It's just a fucking tree,' Graham said. 'For fuck's sake.' He walked on before us and put his hand against it. 'It's just a fucking' – he raised the axe – '*fucking* tree.' He swung the axe into the trunk of it, and the snow shivered off to the ground, and the bark came off in hand-sized splinters. He hit it again, and again.

'Graham,' I said. 'Come on. We haven't got time for this.' Graham looked like I didn't know what in his suit, stark against the snow on the ground, hammering the twisted naked tree with the axe, his face a mask. I noticed with a shock that the tree – or the two trees – looked like two people having sex, and Graham was cutting into what

304

would have been the man's stomach. Why had I not found this place before? I could have taken notes, drawn it for an article. People turning into trees is something that happens in stories up and down the land, all over the world, something to do with falling in love and putting down roots, or stagnating, becoming entrenched, bored, I couldn't quite remember…I shook my head. As if it mattered.

'GRAHAM!' Taylor shouted. 'Stop it!' He turned to me. 'Jack. That tree. Jesus.'

'I know,' I said. 'Graham! Will you – will you just stop it! Put that thing *down*!'

He did, eventually, and then he fell to the ground, and started to cry. I almost physically jumped as I noticed that, on the other side of the tree, there was a huge red stain in the snow. 'This is where we found Francis,' I said.

'I can't believe he wasn't dead,' Taylor said. 'Look at all that blood.'

'What's wrong, Graham?' I crouched down and put my hand on his shoulder.

'I think I killed somebody,' he said. 'In the barn. I think I killed somebody and I don't know who.' He put his head in his hands and, hunched over like that, sobbing, looked like some sort of shivering rock. The axe was solid and static beside him, as were the humanoid trees. They were like two damaged giants standing there, making love, curving up and over his hunched body.

'What do you mean,' Taylor whispered, 'killed somebody?'

Graham shook his head. I had that feeling again, like I was a body of water with cold, heavy metal things floating down through me, like hammers, or axes.

'Graham,' Taylor whispered again, 'what do you mean – *killed* somebody?'

Graham fired up off the ground like a jack-in-the-box, spitting and screaming.

'What the fucking fuck do you think I mean?' Taylor and I jumped backwards as Graham flew at us, his eyes red-rimmed and wild, his hands bunched into pale fists. 'You pair of numb fucking *imbeciles*!' he roared. 'What the *hell* is wrong with you? I hit them with the axe until they stopped *fucking* moving. What were you doing? Where were you? Where are you now? Are you in there? Eh? Soulless fucking – fucking – wankers!'

He spat on the ground and then sat back down.

There was a long silence.

'Graham,' I said, slowly, trying not to let the fear or the anger creep through. 'What do you mean – you don't know who it was?'

'It was dark,' he muttered. 'I couldn't see them. And they were – they weren't looking – at me. They were on the floor, eating one of the, uh, one of the bodies. I could hear them, and I couldn't – just couldn't – stop myself from, uh, hitting them.'

Taylor and I looked at each other. Taylor was pale, tired-looking, and I thought that I must have looked similar. In that light, in our current state, even Graham probably struggled to tell the difference between us. Sometimes I looked at other people and wondered if I looked like them. People used to get Francis and me mixed up all the time. Occasionally I just picked up attributes of the people that I spent time with. I think a lot of people did that; they were composites of people they knew. Still, people wouldn't have any trouble telling Francis and me apart any more. He'd be the one that couldn't walk.

'Fuck's sake,' Taylor said. 'For fuck's sake, Graham. What the hell is wrong with you? Eating a *body*? Are you on drugs?'

Graham just shook his head, returned to his trembling, deathly silence. After a while he answered, briefly. 'I know what I saw.'

'You can't really be sure, though,' Taylor said.

Graham didn't reply.

'Did you see their face?' I asked.

He shook his head again.

'You didn't see their face,' I said. 'Male or female?'

He shrugged.

'Graham,' I said. 'Male or female?'

'I don't know,' he said.

'What do you mean, you don't know? Male or female?'

'I don't know.'

'Long hair or short hair?'

'I don't—'

'You say you don't know one more time,' I said. 'You say it just one more time. Now I'm asking you. Graham. Was it Jennifer? Did you kill Jennifer?'

'What?' he said, looking up at me, confused. 'Look, Jack.

Taylor. You weren't there. You don't get it. It was dark. I was scared. And they were – there was something about them that just wasn't – wasn't right. They were too tall.'

'What?' I said. 'Too tall? Is that some sort of – what does that even mean? You couldn't make out their gender because they were too tall?'

'Why the fuck would Jennifer be on the barn floor eating some poor dead fucker?' Graham said.

'I, um, well,' I said.

'We're not – there's something wrong,' Graham said. 'Can you not see? Don't give me any shit, Jack. Can you not see that the normal ways of looking at things, the normal ways of acting, thinking, aren't making sense? The things we know that define one thing from another are gone. It's like the boundaries between things have been lifted away, suspended. Do you ever think of there being a grid or – or a system of some sort that lies over the land and wraps around the edges of things? Connects things together? Makes a tree something different to a person?'

'You want the honest answer?' I said, 'I don't know what you're talking about. I'm worried about Jennifer. OK? That's what I'm thinking about. Not one of your hallucinations. Your weird grid.'

'I need to get through to you, Jack,' he said. 'I think it's to do with Jennifer. That thing in the barn, Jack. Please. You saw those people at the party that we didn't know. You saw the look of whatever took her. Whatever was in the barn – whatever I killed – I mean, it was dark, but I *know* that it wasn't just a person. Please. At least try to believe me. And what's that fucking music?'

'It's a fiddle,' I said. 'He was playing at the party. And now he's playing down there.' I pointed down to the small orange glows that trembled and shook amongst the trees down by the lake.

'Apart from that thing in the barn,' Graham said, 'they were all gone by the time that I got up to the house. Nobody there.'

'They didn't pass us on their way down,' Taylor said.

'How can we really trust anything you're saying?' I asked. 'You've been taking God knows what all night, you're talking nonsense, you're basically telling us you've *killed* somebody – how do we know you haven't lost it completely?'

'Think whatever you want,' Graham said.

'Jack,' Taylor warned. 'Come on. Let's not lose it ourselves.'

I glared at him, at Taylor, and he held my gaze, his eyes calm and his brow slightly creased. He shook his head slightly. I didn't say it, but I still thought that if anybody out here was dangerous then it was probably Graham. 'There are hundreds of paths up and down this thing,' I said after a moment, stamping my feet in order to indicate the ground beneath us, the fellside, but instead coming across as petulant, or maybe just cold. 'They could have taken any one of them. They could have just run straight down to the valley and then along the valley road. They could have headed over the other side and then circled round. They could have hiked up the crest and then dropped down further along. They could have—'

'OK!' Taylor snapped. 'Jesus! Are we going down there then? Or what? I don't know. I'm worried about Erin. I'm worried that we've left Erin.'

'Come on, Taylor,' Graham said. 'All the trouble is in front of us now, down by the lake. Erin's with Francis. We need you with us. It sounds like there are a lot of them down there. Having a big fucking party. Come on.'

I didn't say anything, but looked down towards the flickering flames by the lake. We were standing at the place where I found Francis, the bloodstains looking black in this light, black on the white, and two black, bloody trails led away from it, and one of them led back to Fell House. We followed the other one.

It led us to the beginning of the scree slopes – a skin of broken bits of stone, grey shards that slid and rolled over each other, no easier to walk on than ice. The gradient too was unhelpful – it was steep enough for you to slip and fall and roll helplessly into the valley if you were lucky, or, if you were unlucky, straight into some ravine, or, worse still, some immovable piece of rock that would snap your neck.

Taylor fell. He was in front, concentrating on the trail of blood rather than on his feet, no doubt, and it was as if we all became aware at the same time of how his feet were sliding, and they slid down, and he landed heavily on his right side. The rock moved beneath him and started to carry him away, but he plunged his hand into it, in between the moving stones, slate knives, and grasped hold of something more solid beneath, like bigger rocks, maybe. Slower-moving. Graham and I just stood and watched as his hands helped him decelerate until he was completely stationary.

'I'm coming back up,' he said, at length.

The pale darkness around us seemed to elongate the time between him speaking and me speaking.

'OK,' I said.

He gradually crept back up, like an injured spider, and every movement was wary because he knew that the ground beneath his feet was unstable enough to tip him off again, to throw him. It seemed an age before he reached us, and when he did he held up his hands. They were shredded. His shiny red knuckles were surrounded with white skin that had been grated away from the bone. His fingernails were cracked vertically, with various nails fully or partially missing. The soft flesh of his palms was lacerated with snags and gashes, and all over his hands and wrists blood sprang from raised points and ridges that looked like they'd been created by the skin getting caught between two equally unyielding pieces of stone pressing together.

I remember reading that people came from all over the world to climb these mountains, they came to climb and walk and scramble and test themselves against something bigger than they were. They came with horrendously expensive clothing and equipment and years of experience and knowledge and maps and compasses, and still some of them died.

'We need to go higher up,' I said. 'If we stay on this scree, one of us is only going to fall again.'

'Also,' Taylor said, 'the trail is gone now all of this stupid rock has moved.'

'Shouldn't it be getting light by now?' Graham asked. 'What day is it, anyway?'

Neither Taylor nor I answered. We turned so that we were facing the hard ground that reared up to the right of the route we'd been trying to take, and headed on up.

FRANCIS

Everything is black. I'm rising, at speed. I'm falling upwards. Or maybe just falling. I'm travelling at a terrifying speed now. Falling. There can be no doubt that I'm falling.

My back hits something hard, too hard. My eyes open – again – and I'm looking up at the ceiling. The beam. The dead body of the hanging farmer. Every part of my body is full of blades and vinegar. My body is shuddering across the surface of the floor with the pain of the impact. I have no control over it. It twists and jerks like a kitten with a pin in it. I don't know why that image comes to mind.

It is a minute or two before my body stops moving.

I lie still for a while longer. Then I sit up. I'm sick. This time all over myself. I realise that I'm still naked. The vomit is dark brown. I start to shake again. I start to cry. Now all I can feel is the cold. The biting cold of the snow. And the bitterly cold wind that worms its way in from outside. And the clammy cold emanating from the body

313

above me. And the shameful cold of being naked and wet. And some other, deeper cold, radiating from somewhere in the back of my head. Like fear. Like the tendrils of some disease. *The* disease. The big one.

'Do you know what has happened?' Balthazar asks. He's still sitting on the bed. 'Have you any memory of it?'

'No.' I shake my head. 'I need her, Balthazar. What happened? I need her here. I don't want to talk to you. You remind me that I'm ill.'

'You emerged, Francis,' he says. 'We are all very proud.'

The way the candlelight is moving sickens me. The constant flicker and flux. The regular creaking of the body hanging from the beam above sickens me as well. I look at the walls. The contrast between the white stripes and the blue stripes makes me vomit again. I roll over. I try to push myself up with my arms, but they fold beneath me. I fall on to my chest. I see that the floorboards are slick with blood. I see it pooling in between them. I cannot tell what is blood and what is vomit. Maybe the cancer has spread. Maybe it is in my throat or stomach. I should speak to Dad. I should ring him up. The pain within me is focusing. Narrowing. Breaking down so that I can tell that it is specific to certain internal wounds. Great rips and tears. I have come apart inside. The evidence is streaming from my mouth. Overflowing. Relentless. Unstopping. Unstoppable. There is nothing I can do to stop the. There is nothing I can do. To stop it. There is nothing I can do to stop the. To stop the. My face is pressed into the stinking floor by the weight of my head.

I find myself on my back again. I'm looking up at the dead farmer. The pain has gone away.

'Have I got cancer?'

'The story of the farmer who hangs up there serves as a warning to those like you.'

'Like me? What do you mean? Balthazar? Have I got cancer? I don't understand.' I try to sit up. But don't have the strength.

'Let me tell you the story.'

'I don't want to hear the story. I don't want a story. Fuck you, Balthazar. What's happened to me? Where's Erin?'

'They were very much in love. The farmer and his wife. Until one day a young man came back to Fell House and claimed it to be his. A young man who went by the name of Bearpit. Still does, actually, and he's grown a little older now, but they age slowly, these lycanthropes. Anyway. The farmer closed the door in Bearpit's face. But he came back after dark and waited for the beautiful woman to put the cats out for the night. He grasped her wrist and pulled her out of the house, into the outside world, and the woman screamed. By the time the farmer had picked up the wood-axe that had been resting against the door-frame and arrived at the scene, she appeared dead. The farmer struck Bearpit with such force, Francis. Such force.' Balthazar shakes his head with an icy crackle.

'If he had been able to kill bears,' I say, shivering, 'why was she not dead?'

'He wasn't trying to kill her. Just . . . you know. Bite her,

315

maybe. Turn her. Anyway. He had his spine severed for his efforts.'

The body above spins. Swings. Hangs.

'As the farmer carried his wife inside, he saw that she was breathing, despite the damage that Bearpit had done to her body. She was alive. But she was different. Different in a way that you fully understand, Francis.'

'I don't understand anything.'

'You will. She was like you, you see. And one night, aroused by the animal keenings of the bastard cats that haunt this place, she became something other than human herself. Wild and free and dangerous. And here we come upon the real tragedy of the piece, Francis. The farmer, transformed by fear from a brave and decent man into a weak-minded fool – he killed her. He swung the axe with all his might as she approached him, and found himself in the morning, a husk, prostrate over her all-too-human body, her dead human body, and he was broken with guilt and with grief, and he was alone. And you know the rest.'

I do know the rest. How he took her body out to the lake. How he watched her fade into the depths. And then he hanged himself. I see it now. At some point, some-where along the way, the young man that had come knocking at the door was mended. And he walked away. Bearpit.

I see it now.

'Where's Erin?'

'Francis,' Balthazar says. 'Look around you.'

I try to sit up again. This time my elbows remain locked as I prop myself up on them. Erin's not here. I start to feel sick again as I see how much of myself I've coughed up and spat out. Balthazar sits on the end of the bed. He slowly turns red as the snow absorbs my vomit from the floor and blood from the bed. From the bed. I look again at the bed. There is something hanging over the edge of it. It's like a thin sheet. But looking closely I see that it's not. It's too wet. Too limp.

I raise myself higher. So that I'm actually sitting up now. And can see on to the bed properly. I see a long, white knotted rope lying down the centre of this pale and bloody sheet-thing. It doesn't mean anything to me. It doesn't look like anything I've ever seen.

It's a spine. It's a spine and some skin. I smash a hand into my mouth to stop the rising tide. But it is futile. Blood falls from my mouth again like it's a wound. And there's something else forcing its way up. I am choking. Choking. Coughing up something long and dry. It just doesn't stop. I am aware of something hanging out of my mouth like a tail. So I start to pull on it with my hands. I see that it is a mass of hair that was once beautiful and curly and red. The hair catches and clogs in the back of my mouth. In my throat. And everything starts to come out of me. Out of my mouth. I can feel it all rising from my stomach. Even more. Inevitable. Unstoppable. Hot fluid courses down my chin. Down the matted cord of Erin's hair. Over my hands. I try to curl up. My body starts to convulse. I close my eyes.

Take me away from this. Help me forget.

The thing inside me wakes up. Whatever it is. The cancer. The darkness. A doctor pointing at an X-ray would call it a shadow. This shadow over your brain. Frontal lobe. Neocortex. Whatever. I don't know science. But the shadow responds. Like it is sentient. Like it hears my thoughts. Like it wants to help me. The thing starts to breathe. Starts to help me forget. Come on. Ignorance is bliss. Help me. It widens somewhere in my body. It swells inside me. Help me. Please. And it's coming. It's working. A horrendous shock courses down my spine. My face smashing into the floor. I feel my cheeks tearing as my jaws open and open and open. They just won't stop. The overwhelming fear is reduction. Being reduced to nothing but a bottomless mouth. Ever-hungry. All-devouring. Endless. Indiscriminate. Widening. Widening. Widening. Bloody. Hot. Wet. Huge. Torn out. And my jaws are widening still. Growing. Opening so widely that they're folding back over me. And my own jaws clap together behind me, having somehow cut me out of space. Having replaced me. Changed me. Erased me and remade me. I test myself and find myself an absence. Not here, but all too real. Hard. Solid. Strong. Fast. Four feet on the floor. A mouth. The front of me. A mouth. Ravenous. And inside, a growing blankness. It's eclipsing me. Pushing me out. I'm nearly completely gone. Yes. And the echo of words that are fast becoming alien.

Oblivion.

Ignorance.

Bliss.

JACK

'It should be getting light by now,' Graham said. 'It should be dawn.'

'Well it's not,' I said.

The fellside was steep. We were looking for a way up a particularly difficult series of crags which jutted out into the starry sky above us, silhouettes of hard-edged fingers, sharp and empty.

'We should try and climb them,' I said.

'I don't think I could,' Taylor said. 'Not with these hands.'

'We have to find her,' I said. 'We have to.'

'Don't you think that there's a chance that we're too late?'

I didn't say anything at first, I just looked up at the rock-faces and the rock-faces looked back.

'Taylor,' I said, eventually. 'What do you mean? Too late for what?'

'You know what I mean, Jack,' he said.

'No,' I said. 'No, I don't. What do you mean?'

'We all know there's something going on,' he said. 'Don't

319

you think – don't you think that if she was in danger from – from something, then that – dangerous something – will already have presented itself?'

'I have to try and find her,' I said. 'And either you come with me, or you don't. You must understand, Taylor. Just imagine that it was Erin that had been taken, not Jennifer.'

I turned and slowly levered myself up a steep grassy ladder between two slippery stone walls.

And, God help them, they followed, Taylor unable to really bend his fingers, just wedging his hands into cracks so they got stuck and held his weight.

'There's somebody down there,' Graham said. 'Look. Back down the way we've come. They're watching us.'

We were at the top of the crags, resting on the spine of the fell, Taylor nursing his ruined hands. I looked down over the edge, and Graham was right – there was a figure down there, looking up at us, and it *was* a person, but disproportionate in a way that I couldn't make out. They were about fifty feet down. Behind them, the fellside dropped away. The figure raised its long arms and screamed. All the blood in my body suddenly seemed to reverse the direction of its flow, and I turned from the cliff edge and stumbled away, up the ridge.

'It's one of them,' I heard Graham say, behind me.

'Run,' I said. 'Come on. Just run.'

'Wait,' Taylor said. 'Look. It's gone.'

'We need to carry on,' I said. 'It – he might be coming after us.'

'I hope Erin's OK,' Taylor said. 'And Francis. Jesus. How did it come to this?' He laughed. 'Look at us.'

I turned back down to see him gesturing at the fellside and the valley, laughing, and he wouldn't stop laughing. Graham was smiling too.

'Come on,' I said. 'We have to carry on. Stop laughing. Stop laughing, the pair of you! Come on.'

'Jesus,' Taylor said again, and then stopped laughing completely. 'I just hope Erin's OK.'

'She'll be fine,' I said. 'She's inside the house. It's an old farmhouse. They're like castles. Don't worry about Erin,' I said. 'It's Francis and Jennifer that we need to worry about.'

I turned back to the ascending ridge, which fell away sharply on either side and then levelled out, so it was like a fin, or the visible spine of a thin person, bent over. The effect was enhanced by the regularly spaced hummocks and lesser summits that protruded along its length, like vertebrae.

And there it was.

The first one I'd seen clearly, standing a little further up the ridge in front of us, on two legs, like a person, but with the knees bent the wrong way, like Mr Tumnus from *The Lion, the Witch and the Wardrobe*. Its arms were long and hung low, and its hands were also long, with stretched-out bony fingers and vicious-looking fingernails, and they hung limply, like they were dead, and above its tiny waist its torso was bulky and strong-looking. Its head was shaped like a human head, but the features were wrong, as if it was mid-flux – the eyes were unevenly sized and at different heights, pushed up into the forehead along with the flattened nose by the vast opening that was the thing's mouth, which stretched from where the eyebrows should have been down to the chin and was edged with fraying skin. It seemed to gape open naturally, like the muscles were at rest, and it was bristling with sharp, yellow teeth that were cutting into the bloody lips. They were all at different angles, as if the gums were slowly liquefying. The whole of the creature was covered in thin grey hair, and it was naked.

It took a step towards us.

FRANCIS

The house is difficult to escape from, but for the weakness of the doors. I leave marks, scratches, spittle. And I can smell her scent. Jennifer's. All over the house. My mouth is open. I am howling the howl. Outside it is cold. There are stars, the sky, white snow, a white moon. Everything is wild and bright and bleak. There is another scent entwined with hers. That of rotten teeth.

I am heading for some distant laughter. And the bright light of real fire. Many of the scents are of things that have died. The endless reaches of bracken. The rot. All of the plants that I sense are dead. The scents are of things that are turning to soil. Birds-eye primrose. Butterwort. Purple saxifrage. Spring gentian. Yellowmarsh. Carniverous sundew. I remember these names from my mother's books.

Creatures like me, down by the lake. Inside out. Bent over. Half-split. Full wolf. Four-legged, human head. Cracked open. Long tongues. Full human. Humans, covered in hair.

Humans, long tongues, licking their own necks. Bald wolves. Dead eyes. Closer. Slowly. I mean, I thought I was ill. I just thought I was ill. But these, here. They are inside-out. Hunched wolves. Foetal people. Naked and newborn ancients. Other things twisted backwards. Stretched open, self-regurgitated. Shattered skulls. Soulless bodies. They are dancing, fucking, bruising, whooping, bleeding, laughing, singing, howling, swimming, playing, screaming, eating, drinking, burning, stripping, fighting, living. Wild. I know it now. I know I'm one of them. Not human. Not animal. There are fiery pits, burning pigs, gutted sheep. Shrieking lunatics. Spilling whisky. Nakedness. Riotous joy in every movement, every feeding frenzy, every sacred blasphemous fuck. There are made-up things. Above us all, there are lights in the sky. They are other creatures. Little ghosts, or fairies, or something. I don't fucking know. Dad would be happy to see these lights in the sky. But they are all just symptoms of something rotten. Something that isn't right. Isn't right at all.

I find myself in the middle of the happy wolves. But I am safe. I am one of them. I know it now. We are all dancing round in circles. Going around and around. The music is led by the fiddle-player. Perched atop a huge worm-eaten log. Eyes like mad stars all sucked together. In human form but His tongue flapping around His chest as He hops. There is power, here. There is power in Him. The music and the howling echoes across the black lake. Jennifer must be here somewhere. But I am slipping under. I am writhing in the press of them all. I am falling for the ease of it. Sometimes the wolves are women like goddesses. Sometimes I see other wolves appearing at the edge of the firelight. Tall with pride. They join us.

Jack

The thing took another step, unsteadily, as if weak or newborn, and then just stood watching us. We were deathly silent, not breathing, not moving, not speaking. It moved a little closer, shaking, but not with fear – more with a kind of suppressed energy, or excitement – and it held its arms out before it and as it got closer, we saw that it was changing – constantly changing – and something was emerging from its mouth, like another head, this one longer and more pointed. More like a wolf's head, and its old head kind of stretched open and fell backwards, a pouch slack at the back of the neck, leaving its new head all slick and wet and grinning at us.

I just stood there.

It leapt – it jumped so high and so far, and it landed on Taylor. Its claws were blurred, swooping down and gouging handfuls of black specks out of Taylor and throwing them backwards, scattering them on the snow. It only had time for that one blow before Graham, wailing, threw himself at it, the axe leaping like it had a mind of its own, and the heavy metal head punched a hole in the stomach of the thing, the thin waist. It howled like an injured dog and fell. Graham raised the axe and brought it down on the thing's arm. It whined and keened, writhed and morphed, wriggled and shrank.

Taylor was lying on his back, breathing quickly. His shirt was ripped open at the front and his breath hung over him, shapeless, visible. A large black patch shone unhealthily on his chest.

The creature squirmed and squealed like it was in tremendous pain and incapable of standing back up. Graham raised the axe again.

'No!' I shouted, and grabbed his arm. 'No. Look – it's changing – human. It might be her. It might be her.'

'We should kill it,' Graham said, panting.

'No. It's a werewolf. I mean – it could be her. Jennifer. Let it change. Just – keep it there.'

Graham kept the axe pressed down on its throat and stood by its head so that its flailing legs didn't catch him.

'Werewolf,' he said, and spat. 'As if.'

'Unless you can explain it otherwise,' I said, slightly sickened by the ease of his violence.

'Jack,' I heard Taylor gasp from behind me.

'Taylor,' I said. 'How badly are you hurt?'

'It hurts like hell,' he said. 'I don't know. It hurts. It could have been worse though. Just its fucking finger-nails.'

'It didn't bite you?'

'No. I don't think so.'

'You don't think so?'

'It didn't bite me,' he said, and struggled to raise himself on his elbows. 'It's so cold out here. What the hell are we doing? What are we playing at? What the fuck is happening? Where's Erin? Where's Francis? Where's Jennifer? I want to see Erin. Where is she? What's happened to us out here? What's happening, Jack?' He looked over to Graham. 'What's that *thing*? Oh God. What is it? What's Graham doing? Where's—'

'Shh,' I said. 'Quiet. We can't think about it. We won't get anywhere if we stop to think.'

'Where's—'

'Erin's safe,' I said. 'You know that. She's safe. Back at the house. She's looking after Francis. Don't worry. She's safe. You know that she's safe.'

He shook his head. 'I don't know that at all. We don't know anything.'

'We have to believe it, then,' I said. 'Or we'll all fall apart. We just have to keep on going. The only other options are to go backwards or stand still. And neither will help us now.'

'I don't know what to think.'

'Don't think,' I said. 'Stand up. Come on. Tie your scarf around your chest. Keep your jacket closed. Here.' He took my hand and I pulled him up.

'Werewolves,' I said, as we turned back to Graham and the thing. 'That's what they are.'

Graham's face was grim. We all looked down at the creature, although it was not so much a creature really, not any more, it was actually an old man – naked and weak, thin-limbed and brittle, with the same hollowed-out stray-dog look of the younger specimens that gate-crashed the party. Tears ran down his face.

'You lads,' he said. 'You've no idea how lucky you are to be young. Wait until you're my age, and you'll see. You'll pay any price, lads. Any price at all to be able to run again. To live a little. To feel strong. To dance. To fuck all night.' He paused. 'You might think you are good people. And maybe you are. You just don't know, is what I'm saying.' He paused again. 'Impotence is a terrible thing. And hunger too. Any price, lads. Any price.'

'We should kill him,' Graham said.

'What?' Taylor said. 'Why?'

'He might turn back if we don't.'

'Ha!' The old man laughed a sad, wheezy laugh beneath the axe-head. '*Might?*'

'We should keep him with us,' I said. 'We need to know more about this. More about them.'

'Werewolves?' Graham said.

'Yeah.' I shook my head. 'Werewolves.'

I was not proud of what we did. Trying to retain control of something with nothing to lose, something that could regenerate any wound, something that, once healed, could summon incredible strength, was not easy, and I'd like to say that we had some honourable motive. I thought we did. I wanted – needed – to find Jennifer, but even if that were possible, did it justify what we were doing? And Graham and Taylor – what was driving them forward, other than me? Maybe I was all it took, given the fear they felt. Maybe I was solely responsible.

We were confused and we didn't know what we were doing, but we knew that we had to do something. The world had turned into something huge and terrifying and strange that we didn't understand, but we wanted to make it better. That is all I can tell you about our motives.

Maybe we should just have stayed inside.

'Here,' Graham said. 'Hold his hand. There. Against the rock.'

'Just don't hit *me*,' I said.

'Of course I won't,' he said.

I took the old man's hand and pressed it firmly against the rock. I could feel some sort of resistance in his fingers, but against the whole of my body weight it wasn't quite enough.

The axe powered through the air, the blunt back of the head smashed the old man's wrist, and he screamed.

'Now,' Graham said. 'The other one.'

I took his other hand and pressed it down.

The crunch. The scream.

'This is wrong,' Taylor said.

'Oh yeah?' Graham said. 'How many people have you killed, old man? How many kids, across the decades? How many old couples in their little cottages out in the country? How many?'

'You really don't get it,' the man said. 'I don't know. A few, yeah, alright, but I didn't always know what I was doing. You get something growing inside you and all else goes flying out your head. But you don't do it for the killing. That's the price you pay. Not the reward. Unless you're one of the sick ones. And yeah. Fair enough. There's a few of them about.'

'This is wrong,' Taylor said again.

'It's either this,' Graham said, 'or we let him change back. And I for one don't trust him.'

'Well,' Taylor said, 'not now, not after everything we've done to him, eh, Graham?'

'What's happening here?' I asked the man. 'Why are you all here in Wasdale?'

He looked at me with his watery eyes.

'It's the Leaping, isn't it?' he said. 'The Leaping. And may it all be over soon.'

'Now,' Graham said. 'The legs.'

'Wait,' I said. 'The Leaping? What's the Leaping?'

'It's like a party. A real big party. Lasts for days. A traditional thing. And there's a contest at the end. The Leaping. Who jumps the furthest.'

'Why are there no lights in the valley?' I said. 'No satellites?'

'Because, it's the *Leaping*, boy,' he said. 'The Lord Himself is here tonight. Takes us all out of the natural way of things. The time and place as you know it is gone for the time being. Everything goes dark. Like we could be hundreds of years ago. Or hundreds of years into the future.

You all just kind of got caught up in it, because you were in His house. The Lord's house. Ha. Some of your friends might've got eaten. The rest just killed.' He wheezed a laugh. 'I would say it's very stupid of you all to be living in His house. But there's no way of knowing, I guess. What would the world be like if you knew something was a mistake before you did it?'

'The Lord?' I said.

'Yeah,' he said. 'The Lord.'

'You mean like God?' Graham said. He shattered the old man's ankle with the axe before he could answer. He screamed and screamed.

'Like God?' he wheezed, eventually. 'I don't even know what you mean.'

We stumbled across the fellside for what felt like hours. The size of the mountains was deceptive – their various features always appeared closer than they were, because they were so big.

Of course, in the dark, when we couldn't see much apart from the silhouette of the land against the sky, it was difficult to get any kind of handle on the scale of it at all.

Hours later. It had to have been hours. We stood by a stile over an old drystone wall, looking down at the flickering firelight bouncing off all of the trees below us, by the lake. 'You really don't want to go down there,' the old man said. 'I don't know what you're looking for, but if it's down there, you won't want it no more.'

'So,' I said. 'That's the Leaping?'

'Yeah,' he said. 'It is. Well, it's the gathering beforehand. Can go on for days before it really starts.'

Taylor was shaking uncontrollably. The fronts of his shirt and jacket were stained black with blood and gleamed wetly. He was standing with a forward stoop, so the skin of his stomach hung loose and relaxed.

'Why is it not getting light yet?' he muttered. 'Why is it not getting light yet?'

'Because that Lord of theirs is down there too,' Graham said. 'That's why.'

I was worried about Taylor, and not for his health – not in the normal sense – because he seemed OK or, at least, capable of moving. I was worried that he'd been bitten and he'd turn into one of them while Graham and I weren't looking, and that'd be it, then.

'What are we going to do?' Graham said.

'I don't know,' I said.

'I don't see that we need to keep him any more.' Graham tossed his head towards the old man.

'He's just an old man,' Taylor said.

'We should kill him,' Graham said. 'We're not going to be able to keep an eye on him once we're down there.'

'You won't be able to do anything if you're going down there,' the old man said. 'Not ever.'

'Shut the fuck up,' Graham said.

'He's just an old man,' Taylor said.

'He's not just an old man,' I said.

'Jesus,' Graham said. 'What the hell are we going to do?'

333

I thought back to when we'd found Graham in the Fell House kitchen – alone, sitting in the middle of the aftermath of a terrible slaughter. I took a few steps back, so that he was no longer behind me.

FRANCIS

Drumming fucking carnival. I start walking on two legs. Eat some meat from a pit, let the fat run down my chin and blister my skin. I realise that I am becoming humanoid again, and it's painless, effortless. All around me these creatures are in flux. Some of them, you wouldn't know they weren't human at all. I am naked. The women here are beautiful, vicious. Dancing with sticks, torches, claw-hammers. But they all put Jennifer in my head, thrust her forcefully into my mind. As clearly as if they were shouting her name with every movement, every word of every song, every fang, every item of clothing falling to the floor, every strand of hair, every fucking one of them, every fucking thing. Every torch. Every flame. Every hammer. Every guitar. Every van. Every tent. Every bodhrán. Every bloody transformation. Every orgiastic pile-up. Every torn-up ghost. Every giggling hobgoblin. The music is a whirlwind. Whipping weird things about and around the shore, the beach. The water is alive. Bubbling up with formless animals as they change shape. Their solid bodies churning around like the liquid they flop in. Squealing like the pigs they've been eating.

But she's not here.

'She's not here,' Balthazar says, who has crept up beside me.

'I know,' I say. 'I would be able to tell if she was here. What about you? What are you doing?'

'You're one of us now,' he says. 'You enter into our world, you can see us all.'

'One of you?' I say. 'What are you? I thought I was brain-damaged. So what does that make us?'

'You can see us, can't you?'

'The – the things? Like you?'

'Yes.'

'The faeries?' I say. 'Goblins? Spirits? The abominable snowmen?'

'Yes.'

'Will I see them all the time?'

'Well.' Balthazar pauses. 'Tonight's a special night.' He turns to look at me. His eye-sockets are overflowing with icy, tumescent lumps. I shiver. 'He's here, tonight. You've seen Him leaping. Hopping up there on that rotten log.'

'Who?'

'You know who,' he says.

'What are you?'

'I am just something that came to you,' he says. 'This world doesn't work like it used to. Erin told you a story before you ate her. About the boy and the bear. About the Lord on the horse. Swearing allegiance. The soul.'

'But we built you,' I say.

'It's strange the way things turn around. In honesty, this body is just a body. I am something else that inhabits it.'

'So – fuck's sake, Balthazar. You haven't explained anything.'

'I chose to come to you,' he says. 'To guide you into this existence.'

I look over at the frantic mad thing on the log. He has strangely shaped boots. Short grey hair. His tongue is slobbery and loose. His grin is impossibly wide. Stretching from below one eye to below the other.

I don't know what to say. It feels like a joke that I don't fully understand.

'Balthazar,' I say. 'Who's that on the log?'

'That's Him,' Balthazar says. 'That's the Lord. Of course He doesn't always look like that. He is a changeable sort.'

I shake my head.

'Francis,' he says. 'How do you really feel about Jennifer?'

'She's everything.'

'What about everything else?'

'It devours me. I look in the mirror and all the world devours me.'

'Then let us help you forget.'

'Fuck you, Balthazar. All this crap is no help at all.'

'Don't think for a moment that I have any answers, Francis,' he says. 'Besides, fucking is somewhat beyond me. Look at the state of this.' He gestures downwards, to his penis. It is massive, misshapen. Grotesque with tumours.

337

'I'm sorry,' I say. 'Have you got cancer?'

'Don't be such a fool. I'm a snowman. It's just the way you built me. Your fear is in everything you touch.'

'Have I got it?'

'I wouldn't know,' he says. 'But it doesn't matter now. It can't kill you. Nothing can. That's the joy of it.'

A woman with long black hair and a red dress runs past, shouting. She is being chased by a hairless wolf-thing with a human head. It scampers past on all fours. It hoots with laughter.

'I can't die?' I say.

'Complete dismemberment might kill you,' he says. 'Certainly for a while. Maybe you would retain some level of consciousness. And you can return, if you so choose; you could be a human again. And then you would be able to die. You would be prey. Cancers would stalk you through the woods. Through every waking moment. Various fears would make up the tune that you dance to. There are so many things to be scared of. The BNP. Terrorists. Paedophiles. Traffic accidents. Earthquakes. AIDS. Your conscience. Loving somebody. Nuclear war. Christianity. Topshop. Fast food. The *Daily Mail*. Used needles. Global warming. Tidal waves. Rape. America. Imagine subsidence – the ground beneath your feet opening up. Imagine infertility. Inexplicable headaches. Various pressures can materialise in the brain – they come from nowhere and nobody understands them. And then of course, there are the wolves. They never went away.'

I don't say anything.

338

'Being human,' he says. 'I wouldn't recommend it.'

'I'm not scared of dying.'

'No,' he says. 'But other people dying? As a human, you can become vulnerable to such things.'

'I'm not human.'

'No, you're not. You're not fully one of them though, either.' He gestures towards a small group of large, sleek wolves that gaze serenely up into the wintry sky. My breath catches at their tranquillity and quiet power. If I look around, there are others like them.

'What? Why not?'

'There is a deal you have to make,' Balthazar says. 'You have to give something up. Otherwise you are just a human being struggling with something you can't really control. You can turn into a wolf, but afterwards you will still be human, with a human consciousness, with all of the guilt and the worry about what you've done. The conflict between the two states can ruin people, Francis, if they're not strong enough.' As he finishes speaking, he looks mournfully down at a clump of snow that's just dropped from his waist. 'Bloody campfires,' he says.

'Why would anybody not make the deal?'

'Giving up your soul has this negative stigma,' Balthazar says. 'I don't understand it myself.'

'What does that even mean?'

'It means real nihilism,' Balthazar says. 'It means really, truly, not giving a fuck about anything except your own life. It means no chance, ever, of doing anything good for the world ever again.'

I open my mouth to reply, but don't.

'Like I say,' Balthazar says, 'I don't understand it myself.'

The choice is one that I never expected to be so clear. All around me the dancing and the flaming slows down; the music and the yelling fades. I am surprised, and pleased, that really there is no choice to make at all. And excited. Genuinely excited for the first time in years.

'What if I do want to be fully human again?' I ask. 'How do you go back?'

He creaks over and whispers in my ear. The sound of ice cracking. As he leans back, I see a look on his face that could almost be pride. I nod. First, though, I need to find Jennifer.

The fires are behind me. My shadow is cast forward, a long thin thing. Dark against the orange flickering light that illuminates the ground. I am facing the mountain. I try to taste the air. Looking for her scent. Jennifer. I need to find her. She is the thing that brought me here. Put me here. Led me here. Without her, none of this means a thing.

And then. Her scent drifts across from the air above. A thin, floating strand of spiderweb. It is accompanied by another. A strong odour of rotten teeth. Instantly I am fully alive. Every sense jumps up, thirsty for more. I take a step forward. Then another. I move away from the dancing, fighting, feasting. I move upwards. Towards

Jennifer. And the rotten teeth. I bend to touch the soil with the palms of my hands. I start to run. The mountain starts to speed past. Black earth. White snow. Points of light. Above. Blurring.

JACK

We were resting, trying again to formulate some kind of plan, when sharp bones sprouted from the old man's wrists, with smaller wiggling bones on the end of them, all roped in red flesh like seaweed. They were replacing the mangled, flattened hands that hung on to the ends of his arms by skin alone, and he started lashing out, flapping them about, evidently convinced that he had regenerated sufficiently to fight back. But Graham ploughed the axe handle into his face and he fell over.

The old man squirmed and twisted as Graham tried to hold him down, and I jumped in and struggled with him too. Graham was kneeling on his arms, forcing his head down by holding the axe handle lengthways across his neck and I was trying to hold the legs. Taylor was standing somewhere behind us, shivering and talking to himself.

'Where's Erin?' he was saying. 'Where's Erin?'

The old man snarled and hissed, and his mouth started to stretch open. Graham lifted the axe from the man's – or the thing's – neck and smashed it down again, with a strength and savagery that should have been shocking but wasn't, it was perfectly OK, and we all heard the bones crack. Although the thing kept moving, its head hung limply to one side, so that when it tried to stand it couldn't see straight, and fell over again.

'Right,' Graham said. He hefted the axe and chopped at the broken neck until the head came away and both the head and the body carried on changing until they were entirely, pitifully, human.

'Graham,' I said.

'What?' he said. 'He couldn't help us any more.'

'I don't know if that's what it's all about,' I said.

'Where's Taylor?' Graham asked.

I looked around but couldn't see him.

'He's gone,' I said.

'Yeah, I know.' Graham wiped his forehead. 'I know *that*. But where?'

'I don't know.'

But I could hear low voices, I thought, a conversation, just above the noise from the monsters by the lake, above the screaming and laughing and music. I crept forward, towards the low rise behind which the voices were coming from. I could see steam rising from beyond it, the physical presence of voices in the cold, and I ducked down so that I could approach without being silhouetted against the sky. One of the voices sounded like Taylor's, but the other – I didn't know. I couldn't even be sure that there was another voice, or if it was Taylor talking to himself. There were definitely questions followed by answers, responses, although I couldn't make out the words. Perhaps in fact they were the same voice, the sad voice of a person torn in two by confusion, pure and simple, calling out for help on the fellside and only being answered by himself, broken and useless. Holding on to the ground because it's the only solid, unchanging thing.

I didn't know what I was thinking. We were all coming apart in our own ways.

I crept forward a little further, lying on the ground, until I reached the top of the low rise. I peered over and saw two figures – Taylor standing, head bowed, before another, taller man, who was dressed in a soft black tricorne hat and a black cape that reached the ground. He was accompanied by two huge dogs that faded in and out of the shadows around his cloak.

'Dead?' Taylor said.

'Eaten alive,' the other man said. 'And she's here to tell you so herself. I wouldn't expect you to just take the word of a stranger like me on a night like this. Here, Erin.'

Taylor looked up and shuddered and seemed to dissolve onto his knees. 'Erin?' he said. 'Erin?'

He seemed to be talking to a point in space between himself and the stranger, but I couldn't see anybody there.

'Erin?' he said. 'Oh, God.' He stood up and opened his arms as if he was holding somebody to his wounded chest. 'What happened?' he said. 'What happened to you?' He was holding this empty space, kissing it, talking to it, asking it questions. I wanted to jump up and shout out –

'There's nobody there, Taylor, there's nobody there. Nothing.'

All the while, the stranger looked on, his face in shadow.

'Francis?' Taylor said. 'Francis?'

There was a silence, and more and more I was convinced that Taylor was delirious, hypothermic.

Taylor stared at the space that he seemed to think Erin was occupying, and his eyes were bright, like those of a lunatic drunk, and there was a furious energy to his taut, trembling frame. 'Francis did this to you?' he asked.

There was something occurring to me, slowly, and as I realised it fully I drove my face into the earth. Why hadn't I got it before? Eaten alive, the stranger said, Erin was eaten alive, and Taylor's words – Francis did this to you? I bit at the cold, wet soil. Why hadn't I seen it? That Francis' wounds had been inflicted by one of those horrors? That we had left Erin alone with him?

I looked up again, and Taylor was somehow going wild without moving. I could see it in every line of his body, and every one of his edges was shaking, his big dark eyes turning mostly white.

'Yes,' he said. 'I swear it. I'm yours. Whatever. Just give it to me.'

'Gladly,' the stranger said, then stepped forward and put his hand round Taylor's throat. He held it there for a moment, and then let go.

'It's done,' he said. 'C'mere.' He gave Taylor a big hug and slapped his back. 'It'll take a while before it's completely gone. It's got to untangle itself from all of your physical bits. But once it has, you'll feel better than ever before. Come and find me later and we'll have a drink.'

'Maybe,' Taylor said.

'Well,' the stranger said, and breathed deeply. 'You'll be seeing me later one way or another. You're one of us now.' Then he turned and strode away and Taylor was left, apparently alone.

'Erin,' he said. 'I'm sorry. We shouldn't have left you. We didn't know. We had no idea.'

I had an idea, I thought – however hard I had denied it, on some level I knew. I pressed my face down into the ground, rubbing it and grubbing it and crying and biting, covering it in mud.

Looking back up I saw Taylor stretch his arms out, his hands shaped as if they were holding Erin's face, and his thumbs moved like he was wiping away her tears. 'Can you stay?' he said. 'I don't understand. How does it work?'

I watched him as he received his response. I couldn't hear anything, but Taylor seemed to, something that caused him to start crying: thick silent sobs that made his chest swell until it looked like it might explode. He lifted his hands away from where Erin might have been, and brought them to his face to cover his eyes. I wondered what the stranger had meant when he'd said, 'You're one of us now.' A werewolf? Was that what he'd meant?

Taylor was standing alone in a hollow, a small dent in the body of the fell and he bared his teeth, pulling his lips back like he was in intense pain. His teeth shone bright white in the starlight. He let his arms fall to his side and dropped his head and jerked backwards suddenly, as if touched.

'No,' he said. 'No.' He looked back up and his eyes moved slowly as if tracking movement. He started to walk towards me.

I scrambled to my feet.

'Jack,' he said. 'What are you doing?'

'Taylor.' I stood up. 'Are you OK? We didn't know where you were. I thought that I could hear you talking to somebody.'

'No,' he said. 'I just had to pee.'

'You weren't talking to anybody?' I asked.

He seemed much more together than he had before the encounter, but at the same time everything about him was strained, tired. Maybe I looked the same. I didn't know.

'Like I said,' he said. 'I just had to pee.' He carried on walking past me, back towards where Graham sat with the dead man. Graham didn't even look up at his approach. I followed, slowly, and the three of us congregated and looked down at the old man's head, face down in the snow.

We were approaching a drystone wall which ran across our path, heading up the mountain in one direction and down the mountain in the other. We stopped as we reached it.

'We'll head downhill now,' I said.

We started to descend. The wall narrowed into a line in the lowering distance, a mark made on the land for us to follow.

It had been I didn't know how long, and I started to feel like my kneecaps were coming loose with the downhill strain, when Graham held his hand up.

'A voice,' he said. He pointed up ahead. 'Behind the wall.'

We stopped walking and then I could hear it too.

'Jenny,' it said. 'Fuck!'

The voice was wet, hairy, rising in pitch, approaching orgasm, nearby, close. It was accompanied by a series of moans, definitely her, I knew it, but somehow obscured, muffled, like she was trying to shout out for help. We looked at each other then ran towards it. We heard them on the other side of the drystone wall and we scrambled over, tumbling rocks and stones behind us, and there they were, we'd found her. At last. She was on her front, her face and arms splayed forward amongst snow and grass and soil and dead bracken. Her dress was around her waist and her wings were hanging to one side.

Something inhuman – one of *them* – was on top of her, thrusting, hips popping jerkily, snoutish face raised in some grimace. Its body was cracking back and forth, as if every bone was breaking and reforming. It was talking in that deep, snarly voice. 'Jenny,' it said. 'Jenny. For so long have I wanted you. For so long have I wanted you. A nice little – a nice little – oh, God and Jesus. Fuck.'

It didn't seem to have noticed us.

She was pinned against the ground, unable to defend herself against the attacker.

Everything rose up in me at once. I jumped forward and kicked at the side of the thing's head, hard, and the impact made a dull sound, but it didn't seem to have any effect other than causing it to turn its face in my direction. Despite the distorted, misshapen features, I recognised it.

Kenny.

FRANCIS

Rotten teeth. And sounds. Wolf grunts. Cat shrieks. Wet rhythm. Bones. Scratching stones. Reaching inside. Penetrative growth. Voices rising in pleasure.

She is there. I see her. Rotten-toothed Kenny on top. Fucking. Her smile. She smiles. Moans. Shoulder scabs. Bloody bite. Kenny speaks. Jennifer stretches. Her edges flicker with hair. I crouch, to pounce. To kill. But – Jack! He jumps in and kicks Kenny in the head. Kenny stops and looks and smiles. I pause. Jack stares down at him, unaware of my approach.

I howl and leap.

Jack

Kenny just smiled a slow smile at me, that terrifying mouth of his making more sense on that face. His dripping tongue rolled around uneven rows of long, yellow teeth. I stopped all movement, my eyes drawn to the pit of his mouth, as I grappled with the illusion that it – his mouth – was big enough to swallow me whole.

He smiled and drove his body down in one last, powerful thrust, and Jennifer squirmed beneath him. I brought my foot back in order to kick him again when something – another werewolf – hurled itself towards me out of the dark at my side, and everything was moving at the speed of continents, gracefully. Devastatingly slowly. Heavy with inevitability. Cities were sprouting and withering towards the other side of the world and this thing, this wolf, hung in mid-air, beautiful. A huge, noble, ferocious wolf, with four paws the size of my head raised, their claws fully extended, each claw nearly as long as my finger, with dark blue-grey fur along its flanks and a pale underbelly. Its face was a wolf's face, but it was elevated by a transcendental anger and its tail swept across the sky behind it, wiping the world away, and its teeth were bright and hopeful points of light against this dark night, and its mouth was a regal, snarling hole, like a window to the outside.

Its eyes were his.

It was Francis.

And I knew then that I wanted to be what he was.

FRANCIS

Falling towards them all. I am falling towards Jack. He looks up at me. Sad eyes. I roar.

Pain. Something rips open my side. I am thrown sideways. Away from Jack. On to my back. The pain tears through me. I flail around. I am thinking again. Conscious. Thin and weak. I am bleeding from a wound in my side. Taylor is on the ground next to me. It was he who did this. I roll over. I try to ignore the pain so that I can turn back. But he jumps on my back and flattens me.

'You killed her,' he says.

'I didn't know I was doing it,' I say. 'I don't want to be the way I am. You must understand. I'm not well. I'm imagining things.'

'No, you're not.'

'Then you and me,' I say. 'We're the same.'

'No,' he says. 'I know what I'm doing. Everything I'm doing, every change I make, I do it through choice.' He is talking into my ear. His mouth pressed against me. 'You

353

killed her, Francis,' he says. There are tears in his voice. 'You killed her.'

'I didn't know I was doing it,' I say. 'There are lots of things that I don't understand. Taylor. There's something I need to tell you.'

Taylor pulls his claws across my face. He rips my cheek so that it hangs off. I feel cold air on my tongue. My naked teeth.

'I don't think there's anything you need to tell me,' he says. 'There's nothing left that I need to know. The only thing left that I want to do is kill you. And then all I want to do is turn into an animal, Francis, an animal like you. Like you always were. And forget it all. Forget everything.'

'I haven't forgotten anything,' I say. 'Taylor, get the fuck off me. Get the fuck off me. Get off!' I spring up. I twist round. I knock him off my back. I grab him and dig my fingers into his arms. Literally into his arms, forcing them beneath the skin. He screams.

We are both too strong.

'Taylor,' I say. 'Jennifer is one of us too.'

'I don't care.'

'I know,' I say. 'But we both need to know. So whichever of us survives can tell Jack. Taylor. We have to tell Jack how to turn her back. There is a way. Do you understand me? If you kill me, you have to tell Jack how to save her. You might not care, Taylor, but do it for him. One of us is going to die now. Once I let you up. One of us is going to die.'

I lean down and whisper the secret into his ear.

354

He looks up at me. His face transfigured by either hatred or the thing, the I-don't-know-what, the wolf.

He takes advantage of my momentary hesitation. Two tooth-studded gums sprout out of his mouth. They fasten around my face like a hand. I can hear the fiddle like it's inside my head. Some abnormally powerful muscles force Taylor's jaws together. They clamp my head. I feel movement inside me. Unintentional movement. You know. Like my skull is slowly being squashed. Something wet squeaks against the inside walls of my cranium as it is pushed, flattened. My own jaws are being twisted diagonally. I try to transform but I can't, you know, I can't focus. I can't turn my mind away from the pain. The slowly shifting panels of bone. Like tectonic plates. One continent slowly shelves beneath another. And the tremors. The shaking. The shivering. The shuddering. It gets worse and worse. Dad, coughing in his hospital bed. Every fleshy lump inside quivering. Mum crying, her body tense and flickering with the strain of it. The ground beneath me and the sky above falling together, getting mixed up. My body is not quite right. I thought I was able to change and get better but I am not quite right. My body weakens and I am not entirely, you know, all together any more. And it's a shame because I was thinking we could maybe change things, Jennifer. Not even that. I just want to leave something valuable behind. I remember shivering at the beautiful manifestoes hidden in the sleeve-notes of incredible albums. Hands pressed over my ears to block out the sound of the big black birds beating their broken beaks and their tattered wings against the glass. And the sound of modern pop covers of sad old songs layering up on the radio. One on top of the other. Building to static. And out of the window if I had the energy to stand and look I would see all the way over to the war. To the war. The breakdown at the edges of everything. But I'm not quite right any more. Teeth are breaking through into my brain. Little hard nubs. Every body fails in the end.

JACK

I just stood there, gaping, as Francis fell towards me, his whole body evolved to kill, and then – then Taylor was there too, and Taylor barrelled into Francis' side. They plummeted to the ground in front of me, and rolled apart. I thought I saw blood.

'Graham,' I said. 'The axe. Give it to me.' Taylor had turned now. Graham would not hesitate before using the axe, I knew it.

Kenny and Jennifer had separated as well, and Jennifer was scrambling for the wall while Kenny was getting to his feet. In one movement I took the axe from Graham and swung it – it was heavier than I expected – at Kenny's head and he fell forward again. I stood on his back and brought the blade down in between his shoulder-blades. I dug it in until I could see his spine. He was trembling.

'Kenny,' I said. 'What are you doing?'

'I told you, didn't I, Jack?' he said. 'I knew she'd come over to good old Kenny in the end. Kenny and Jenny. It rhymes, see. That's how I knew. It's about time I got myself a nice little girlfriend, anyway. My mum always said it's about time I got a girlfriend. You'll struggle, she'd say to me, with that funny face of yours, but you could do with a nice little lass.'

Francis and Taylor were rolling tangled in the snow, wearing a hot melted patch into the earth. Graham remained on the sidelines.

'She didn't come over to you,' I said. 'That's not what happened.'

'You don't have to believe old Kenny here,' he said. 'Just tell me what you want me to tell you and I'll tell you it.'

'You took her.'

'Sure,' he said. 'It was me who grabbed her away back up there, my arms around her little tummy and all, holding her dead close like. I carried her across the mountain like we'd just got married, Jack, you should have seen us. Was dead romantic.'

'You abducted her,' I said. 'She didn't come to you.'

'Oh, she came around pretty quick after seeing our party, Jack. Was dead good it was, much better than yours. Still going on actually, even after yours has kind of stopped.' He sniggered. 'She joined right in.'

Graham was turning away from the bleeding wolves, turning away from their thrusting mouths and stained paws. He walked away and knelt in the wet.

'No,' I said, to Kenny. 'I don't believe you.'

'Oh,' he said, 'I wouldn't expect a good proper man like you to believe old Kenny here. Not a weird old creep like Kenny. Oh no. Don't believe me, Jack. I'm telling all lies.'

He didn't seem able to move, apart from his mouth. I looked over to where Jennifer was, and she was watching, horrified, as Francis sunk his fingers into Taylor's arms. I had this impression that everybody was quickly changing from one thing into another and back again, their skins reversing so that the hair was outside one moment, inside the next, their joints bending one way and then the opposite.

Up there on the fell the night was snow-muffled, colourless, starlit and cold, although fires still danced down by the lake and we could still hear the fiddle, now slow and moaning, like a huge, dying animal.

'She's a hot one, Jenny is,' Kenny said. 'Can do all sorts of things with her insides. You want to keep hold of her. Ha ha. Some advice is better never than late, eh?'

'What are you doing here?' I said.

'Why wouldn't I be here?' he said, one cheek pressed into the snow. 'Anybody with any sense would be here.'

'Did you offer something?' I said. 'Did you – were you approached?'

'Mm,' he said. 'I got bit by something that had been a girl, a dead fit girl, in her bedsit. She was fucking gorgeous, Jack, dead fit. Not as fit as Jenny, though. Anyways. Some feller came to see me afterwards, bit weird he was, and said he could make it easier. But I told him where to go.' He coughed. 'You know what mothers say about trusting strange men. Told him to fuck right off. Stupidest thing I ever did cos it's not like I had anything to lose.' He seemed to think for a moment. 'That was I don't know how long ago. Maybe I closed down eventually anyway. Not everyone does, like. Most get all dead sad and mad and fucked up. I just locked my self away deep down and tried to forget about it. It still comes back though sometimes, Jack, and it's like God when it does, huge and angry. Wish I'd got rid of the fucker when I had the chance. Had no plans for it.'

I stood there, one foot in the small of his back, the other holding the axe down in the hole I'd made. Every now and then a tremor ran through his spine. It sounded like Francis and Taylor were talking and snarling but I didn't look over.

'So you were a werewolf at work?' I asked.

'What, back at the call centre?' He laughed. "Course I fucking was. You're only ever a step away from us, Jack. We're, like, everywhere.' He coughed. 'Jack, let me see Jenny one more time before you, like, finish me off.'

'No,' I said. 'You're sick. Dangerous.'

'Nothing I don't already know,' he said. 'Don't you want to be?'

'No. I don't ever want to be anything like you.'

'OK.' He closed his eyes, and shivered. I felt another tremor and I thought he was trying to change, but the axe was still buried in his spine and he could not close over it. 'I'll believe you. Thousands wouldn't.' He coughed again and spat something black out into the snow. 'But what about Jenny?'

I lifted the axe quickly and brought it down hard on the back of his head which seemed soft and rotten and split open easily. He stopped talking, and wriggled a little more, then stopped moving completely.

Somebody put their hand on my shoulder and I turned to see Graham. He looked concerned.

'You OK?'

'Yeah,' I said.

'You did the right thing.'

'I know.' I'd not doubted myself for a second. 'Jennifer!' I said. I stumbled towards her, and her towards me, and I held her tight to me and she was covered in blood, her black dress torn and ruined. 'We need to get you back to the house. Oh God. I'm so so sorry.'

'No,' she said. 'No! Francis!'

I turned and saw Taylor standing, licking the blood from his mouth. Francis' dead body lay at his feet, the face torn off, the front of his skull visible – his teeth, the hole behind his nose, and the eyes in their sockets, coming out of their sockets, the skull crushed into a peak at the front. And yet the skin was still intact around the rest of his head, his hair was still there on the top. The window on his skull made me feel sick and I felt like a pervert, looking at something that I was not supposed to see.

Taylor stood there, his clothes, ripped and torn and falling off, piling up around his feet. He was walking towards us – me, Jennifer on my right, Graham on my left – and his body was lean and wiry, his eyes were spilling black light, his hands and mouth stained red, his hair a dark shock surrounding his pale face. He had the glamour that folklore and story often attributed to those imbued

361

with some sort of dark power – not glamour in the modern sense, but in the old sense, the charm, the aura, the beauty. He seemed to have drawn it from the mountain, the snow, the blood. He pointed at Jennifer.

'Jack,' he said. 'Listen to me.' His voice was deeper, more commanding. 'Francis told me that—'

The axe arced through the air towards him. Taylor's eyes shifted from me to the axe, and he jumped backwards, but it still caught him, the heavy, rusty blade slicing into his leg, and he fell. Graham stepped forwards.

'No,' I said, 'Graham—'

'You saw him!' Graham shouted. 'You saw him!' He swung the axe downwards as Taylor grew up from the ground like the primal thing he was, like the beast from beyond the firelight. The wolf that crossed the frozen river, born in the space beneath the world we knew.

'He was trying to tell me something,' I said. 'Graham. He was trying to tell me something.'

'I don't suppose it really matters,' Jennifer said. 'I don't think anything can matter that much after all of this.'

'You do,' I said. 'You are all that matters now. You were all that ever mattered really, Jennifer. I'm so sorry.'

'Don't say sorry,' she said. 'Jack. Thank you. Thank you so much.'

Yet more blood was flowing from the bodies of Graham and Taylor as they writhed across the fell, but I couldn't work out who was who, or who was doing what, or who was what. Darkness seemed to be closing in on me, and the music from the lake was increasing in tempo and pitch, and either Graham or Taylor managed to stand and start making his way towards us, but the other one pulled him back. Their faces were masks, their bodies a tangle of hair and skin and bone that couldn't be untied.

'Jennifer,' I said. 'We have to get back to the house.'

'Graham is going to become one of them,' she said.

I nodded.

As we made our way, slowly, across the fell, the music seemed to fade. The sounds of orgiastic revelry, too, faltered away – not completely, just enough for us to feel like we had put some distance between them and us. The way was hard and steep, and we were tired. We looked at each other, and at ourselves – at our far-away-feeling limbs. I was blue with cold, and Jennifer was wide-eyed and bloody. Our bodies ached but we carried on walking. I imagined Graham and Taylor straying too close to the edge of the crags and both of them falling off, bouncing down the fellside and finishing their fight somewhere on the valley floor.

Every now and then I slipped and stuck out my hand, looking for something to grab hold of.

As I saw the dark, hard-edged shape of the barn emerge out of the sky up ahead Jennifer pointed backwards, eastwards, and said, 'Look!'

I turned.

'It's getting light,' she said. The row of mountain peaks stood out sharply against the yellowy-blue glow emanating

363

from the out-of-sight sun, and they looked like teeth. We were inside a mouth and the light was coming in from outside, silhouetting the row of ugly, sharkish teeth. A mouth full of stars, but dark despite them.

'So it is.' I struggled with the sudden conviction that we had to turn around and head towards the light, away from the house. The house was in the wrong direction, being in the direction of the remaining darkness. I struggled with the idea for too long, and stood there, torn, until a sickening wail rose up from where we'd just come, agonised and hopeless.

'Was that Graham?' Jennifer asked. 'Or Taylor?'

'I don't know,' I said. 'I can't tell.'

We passed the trees. In the half-light of dawn they looked ill, misshapen, like they had been damaged as they'd grown, or maybe been planted wrongly, somehow, and I didn't look at the bloody, muddy ground – we just kept on walking.

We reached the house and stood before it. The truth was that it terrified me, and I didn't want to go inside. I really didn't want to go inside.

'What happened to you?' I asked.

'We had that fight,' she said. 'I'm sorry about that. The fight. I'm sorry."

'It's OK,' I said. 'What happened afterwards?'

'He grabbed me. I didn't know what was happening. I didn't know who he was. I felt his arms around my stomach

364

and I tried to pull them off and they were covered in hair. I looked down and saw that he had about five knuckles on each finger. That was what it looked like. I might have been wrong. I must have been wrong. And all the while he was dragging me backwards, pulling me backwards, and I was trying to hook my heels into the ground but they just kept bouncing off. I don't know how he was moving so fast. Then he lifted me up so that I was lying across his arms. He didn't speak. I was screaming because I didn't know what he was. I was just seeing these hairy arms and all those knuckles. He kept laughing. I was watching his feet, he was barefoot, and his feet were an animal's feet. His legs bent the wrong way and they were strange-looking, well, obviously they were strange-looking. He took me across the fell down towards the lake. It seemed to take forever even though he was moving so fast. My shoes came off and my feet turned blue and he put me down at one point and I cut my feet up on the scree. He was taking me to where the noise was coming from, I thought. The next thing I knew we were on the road that leads to the lake and I could hear them all closer. We were nearly there and I was crying and screaming because I thought, like, if they're all like him. What are they going to do to me? And then we were there, in the middle of them all, and it was awful, Jack, awful, they were all screaming and laughing and fighting and fucking each other and eating people and I thought they were going to do that to me, and they were all strange, like swollen in strange places or some of them had other creatures erupting out of them, that's what it looked like, or they were half-human, half-dog. And then he started dancing with me, spinning me round and around and around and I was still crying and I saw his face and he had a wolf's head, but at that point his body was completely human. He spun me round and around. It was like being inside a burning, rolling car. He had an erection. He just kept spinning me round and around and the fiddle-player from the party was there. And then another one jumped on to the one that took me, and they were fighting and howling like wolves and then another one grabbed me, the fat woman from the shop, and she held me down and tried to—'

'Did any of them bite you?'

'No. No, she tried to – tried to kiss me and pour this drink into my mouth, but he – Kenny – suddenly jumped up and pushed her away and he must have fought the other one off, I don't know, and he said, "We're going somewhere else," or something, and he started pulling me along again, but I said, "It's OK, I don't want to stay here," and he let me walk and I thought once we're away from this place I'll just hit him with a rock. That was what I thought.' She paused.

'The fat woman from the shop?' I asked. 'One of them?'

'Yeah,' she said. 'I know.'

A scratching metal sound drew our attention to the barn and we saw that the barn door was open. The wind was pushing it gently and the door moved slowly across the yard, creaking forlornly.

'Did you?' I asked.

'What?'

'Did you hit him with a rock?'

'Oh,' she said. 'No, I didn't. I picked one up but he saw it and knocked it out of my hand. Then he hit me. I kicked him and he hit me again. I started hitting him properly, punching him in the face, but it didn't do anything. Then he threw me face first on to the ground and pulled my dress up. You saw – you saw what he was doing.'

'Here,' I said, and held her slim, trembling body close to me, the house looking down at us, staring down at us, and gradually the day dawned. I tried to think of something else to say.

The first thing I did once we were inside was try all the light switches, and on finding that they were working again I danced an unhinged little dance there in the kitchen, hopping from one foot to the other, completely unmoved by the thick opaque globs of liver-coloured something that were smeared across the dark slate.

'Ha ha!' I shouted. 'Light!'

Jennifer sat down at the kitchen table, which was covered in the empty tin cups of burnt out tea-lights and empty bottles and paper plates and broken crisps. She looked around fearfully, as if the room was full of things that I couldn't see.

'Part of me thinks that I shouldn't say this,' I said, 'but another part of me thinks that it's a perfectly OK thing to say.'

'Just say it,' she said, tiredly.

'The kettle works.'

She did not reply – just looked at me.

'I'm making a cup of tea anyway,' I said. 'I'm going to make you one too, and you can decide whether or not you want to drink it.'

I turned and opened a blood-spattered cupboard door. Inside the cupboard, it was as if the whole night hadn't happened – everything was clean and undamaged. I took out two mugs and put them down on the worktop, on the edge of which there were marks and a nastily shaped bloodstain that suggested somebody's head had been smashed down on to it, their upper jaw bearing the brunt, the teeth shooting forwards and underneath the toaster. It looked as if the teeth were nesting beneath the toaster.

I opened the fridge door. The interior of the fridge too was refreshingly pristine, and it almost started to make me feel better. 'There's not that much milk left,' I said, 'but there's enough for this morning. It'll see us through most of the clean-up effort, I imagine.' I swung the milk out of the fridge as the kettle boiled.

'What the hell is wrong with you?' Jennifer asked.

'*Nothing!*' I screamed, throwing the bottle of milk at the wall. It burst spectacularly, and mingled with the stuff on the floor, pooling in puddles marbled red and white. 'There is nothing *fucking* wrong with me, alright?' I kicked the bin over. 'Now we've got no milk.'

'How can you care about *that*?' she spat. 'Everything's

covered in blood. I've been sexually assaulted. Your friends have all just killed each other. They're all dead.'

'They're not all dead,' I said, looking out of the window.

'We've seen monsters, Jack. We've seen that these things are real. You don't seem to get it. It doesn't seem to have gone in. I'll say it again. I've been sexually assaulted. You hear me?' Her voice was shaking. 'He raped me. That bastard.'

I looked at her but couldn't process anything – thinking was like trying to look through misted-up windows. There was a long, long silence.

I don't believe he assaulted you, I thought. I think you might just be one of them too. How could he have been fucking you and not have bitten you? That threat he had made all those months ago. I'm going to make her mine, or something.

I found myself looking at myself and thinking, how callous, how cold, as if I was splitting partly into an object that could be judged and partly into a consciousness that could do the judging and the two parts were drifting apart, losing touch.

'What did Taylor want to tell me, do you think, before Graham went for him?' I said. 'Why would he want to tell me anything?'

'I don't know,' Jennifer whispered. 'I don't fucking know.'

Maybe I should have tried to find him, but no, they were outside and we were inside and there was no good reason to interfere with that arrangement. I had everything that I had left the house to get in the first place – that was, Jennifer.

'Jennifer,' I said. 'You know the only reason I was out there was to find you. There was nothing else. No other reason for it. You do love me, don't you?'

She looked at me blankly.

'Jennifer,' I said.

'Yes!' she said. 'Of course I do.'

'Good.' I sat down. I felt that the seat was wet and stood up again.

We drank our tea black.

'We have to start upstairs,' Jennifer said, suddenly calm. 'If we clean up the downstairs, it'll just get all mucky again once we start bringing all the bits down from upstairs.'

'Upstairs,' I said. 'OK.'

Jennifer was doing the bathroom and I was doing our bedroom in theory, although really I was just standing in the doorway, neither in nor out, looking at the mess. It looked like somebody had filled about ten buckets with blood and then set off a firework in each one, covering everything in a fine mist, although in places there were streaks and splashes where denser things had landed. The landing was the same. Our whole blasted house. Our house.

'Jennifer,' I shouted through to the bathroom. 'We're going to have to burn everything. Everything.'

'What?' she shouted.

'We're going to have to burn everything!'

'OK!'

The bed was still dripping and one of the bedposts was covered in hair, as if the hair had been ripped from somebody's head and painstakingly stuck on to the bedpost with blood. There were huge gouges in the floorboards, the walls. Everything was coming home to me and everything that I had managed to push down, ignore, was floating close to me then, like a ghost, ready to seize me and shake me and force itself to the forefront of my mind. I vomited on to the floor directly in front of me and stepped backwards onto the landing.

I heard Jennifer singing.

I sidled along the landing so that I was outside the bathroom door and she was definitely humming something that sounded familiar. I knew it, I knew it now, it was like something the fiddler had been playing. I shook my head and narrowed my eyes. She had gone mental when I had tried to make a cup of tea and yet now she was cleaning up the stains and leftovers of our friends and *singing*? There was something wrong. Maybe she was pretending to be more upset about all of this than she really was – maybe when I had tried to make a cup of tea she had only been *pretending* to get angry. In front of me, she was damaged, distraught, but once I wasn't looking, she was fine.

Was she one of them?

I went to open the bathroom door and then stopped, my hand hovering, and retreated quietly to the bedroom, our master bedroom, as Jennifer had once referred to it.

She had to be one of them, but no, she couldn't be, because if she was, she would have killed me.

That was my thinking.

The window was broken. I had noticed it earlier but had not thought about it. I went over and looked out and then I went back and opened the wardrobe, which must have remained closed all through the night judging by the cleanliness of its insides, and gathered up an armful of clothes. Realising that there was nowhere to drop them without their getting covered in the fluids that coated everything, I put them back inside the wardrobe and closed the doors again. The wardrobe was to the left of the window. I moved to the left of the wardrobe and pushed it so that it blocked the open hole.

It left a strange space – a rectangle on the floor that had been spared the fine spray of blood, but was slowly being eaten into by spreading pools of the stuff. In between the drying puddles, the rectangle on the floorboards was clean and clear, the varnish shining brightly. On the wall, it was slightly different. We had painted the walls in this room pale green. There was a much larger rectangle on the wall. The pale-green wall. There was a much larger rectangle on the pale-green wall. This too had escaped the cloud of gore that seemed to have settled across everything else, and the rectangle of pale green was beautifully obvious and hard-edged and pure. Except that blood was running down into it from the wall above, blood-red blood, streams and trickles of it that gathered together and dribbled downwards at the behest of gravity, that ran together and dissected that pale pure space, the rectangle, that pale green pure green clean green square-edged space, invading it. I put my hand to my mouth. The thin lines of blood didn't make the space any less visible, in any way. It was still clearly there. A beautiful even green against the mottled red of the wall surrounding it.

The two opposed rectangles somehow created an object that wasn't there. That absence – the physical space that something should have been occupying but wasn't – drew tears, and I started to cry. I fell to my knees and my head hit the floor and I carried on crying, like a newborn.

Eventually some kind of sensory perception came back to me, but all I was aware of was lying with my cheek to the floor, fascinated by the way that perspective narrowed the discoloured floorboards the further away from me they were.

I woke up, disorientated. I had been dreaming that we were still at the party, Francis shoving CDs into my hands. 'You have to listen to this. And this. Oh, and these. Have you seen this?' In my dream, he wandered off into another room and returned with a DVD that he wedged under my arm and I went upstairs and put all of the CDs on at once and watched the DVD. It was *Postman Pat*, but all of the characters had strangely shaped noses – like long, wiggly worms – and stumbled around in the fog, accidentally groping each other. Then I was in a stone space underground, some sort of hallway, with archways regularly spaced and Postman Pat and the others wouldn't let me out, and they were all getting closer, their wormy noses wriggling furiously. It was bad, scary, because they were still like Plasticine. And then Taylor appeared from nowhere, and just held out his hand, and I took it, and there was a staircase just there, just in front of me, and he led me up it until we were outside, in the bright sunlight, the bright blue sky, a cool spring breeze, daffodils lively along the walls of a kindly-looking old church, and Erin approached from between the gravestones, her red hair a crown, and she said, 'We have to find them.' I knew she meant Francis and Graham. We followed her out of the churchyard and the whole world was just a long, wide, grassy path, and the grass was so soft, and the sides of the path curved upwards into space so we couldn't fall out, and space was illuminated by purple clouds like at the beginning of *Star Trek: The Next Generation* and in the distance, at the end, was an infinitely tall castle. I knew that was where they were, safe and warm, and we got there and listened to Francis' CDs all night and played chess and ate walnut bread and drank mulled wine and looked out at the sky and we knew that all the world was there, we could see it all and it all made sense and Erin took each of us to bed in turn, and it was not cheap or meaningless but the ultimate in tender, loving friendship, and she was a beautiful girl, such a beautiful, beautiful girl, and in my dream she wanted to free us all in every way imaginable and she did and she wanted to in real life too, she wanted to, I believe that. But what about her?

What about Erin? I lay there in her arms in the biggest bed and she was so warm and so perfect. The castle was infinitely tall. Towers springing from towers.

The dream made me sad. As a child I had loved *Postman Pat* more than anything. I stood up, put my hand to my head and stumbled out of the room. 'Jennifer?' I said.

'Yes?' she said, sweetly, making her way up the stairs towards me.

'I'm sorry. I fell asleep.' I cannot even begin to work you out, I thought.

'Jack,' she said.

I walked towards her and slipped on the stairs and landed on my coccyx. 'Ow,' I said.

'You're tired,' she said.

Back in our bedroom, Jennifer threw all the bloody bedclothes on the floor and turned the mattress over and said, 'Sleep on that.' The underside of the mattress was spotted with small red dots that signified columns of blood between one side of the thing and the other. I lay down all the same and fell asleep pretty quickly. Even when I woke up, periodically, I felt like I was still asleep, and the house at that point in time was not a good place to sleep and maybe it never had been.

For a short period of time I was standing over the bed in the other room, the one with the blue and white wallpaper, and there was a human spine there, and a skull, and a spread-out skin, and a tangled-up matted cord of red hair on the floor, covered in slime. I saw the white dress that Erin had been wearing and then I knew the spine, the skull, the skin, the hair – they were all hers. Thank God Taylor didn't have to see this, I thought, but then, Taylor was one of *them* now and of course, that was why. Her dress looked so, so small, the way clothes do once they've been discarded.

Then I was somewhere else.

In my dream – if it was a dream – Taylor and Erin made love in that room, and her spine was there too, underneath them, between them, beside them, and a man hung from a rope, his legs kicking, and the wallpaper tore itself from the walls, curling into bone-white scraps that accumulated around the edges of the room, piling into drifts that blurred boundaries, making it hard to tell the door from the wall, the wall from the floor, the floor from the bed, the bed from the bodies, the bodies from the bones, Taylor from Erin, Erin from Taylor. The man kicking on the rope spun around and I saw that he had my face, my face was his and I was the man kicking, dancing, spinning on the rope. Kicking kicking kicking on the rope.

I drifted in and out for I didn't know how long. Jennifer was there sometimes and sometimes she wasn't. Sometimes looking out of the window and sometimes holding my hand.

'Are you sleeping?' I asked. 'You've had a longer, harder night than I have.'

'I'm asleep when you're asleep,' she said. 'That's why you never see me sleeping.'

'Where do you sleep?' I asked. 'You're not here on this mattress with me. Where do you sleep?' But I must have asked that question in a dream, or half in and half out of sleep, because I was sitting upright all of a sudden, looking round for an answer, and she wasn't there. I shook my head, on the one hand amazed by her mental strength, but on the other not surprised, because she was incredibly strong, she had to have been, ever since her mother had started falling over, thinking their house changed shape just to trip her, confuse her, thinking her dreams were real, slapping Jennifer across the face if Jennifer suggested that it had only been a dream. Mum, *please*.

'Jennifer,' I mumbled occasionally. 'Don't go outside. We don't know what's happening out there.'

'Don't worry,' she said. 'I'm not going anywhere.'

At other times, I sincerely believed that I was being held captive. Was she drugging me? How was it that she stayed upright, smiling and making sense? She *had* to be one of them. She *had* to be. When I was thinking like this, I stood up, my legs feeling heavy and weak at the same time, like breezeblocks on the ends of elastic bands. I would show her that I was capable. I would show her that I would not be held there like a sick child. I walked over to the window and looked out on another world. The fellside was black, blasted free of all grass or earth, and the sky was pink along the horizon, deepening to a dark red straight above, and the features of the valley were lost in shadow, but there were fires down there, lots and lots of fires. I would not be kept like a sick child, I thought, and then was at an utter loss when it came to working out what to do next. Always, the next thing I knew was that I was waking up again.

Sometimes she was there and sometimes she wasn't.

I was quite prepared to believe that most of what I thought was happening was only happening in dreams.

I did not believe that dreams meant anything. I did not believe that they meant anything at all.

'Why don't you sleep?' I said.

'Where do you sleep?' I said.

'Don't go outside,' I said.

How could she have been keeping me captive? Not how, but why? Why would she be doing that to me after I had risked everything for her? There was something colossal that I was missing, something fundamental to the story, the situation we were in. Sometimes I woke up and heard her talking, but not to me.

'So when you hang still, that's just because you're tired of kicking?' she said in the next room, the one with Erin's spine in it. I heard her clearly and it struck me as strange at first, and then when I remembered the dream of myself hanging, kicking, on the rope, I made the connection and it froze me all up.

'So when you hang still, that's just because you're tired of kicking?'

I rolled around on the mattress, on the forever-stained floor, and my mind rolled around in my head like a globe, always coming back to the same point. This is where you live. Why was she keeping me captive?

I remembered Graham, leering out of the dark on some night earlier on in time.

'The thing with women,' he had said, 'is that they're all basically split down the middle.'

I rolled around and around the house, my mind rolling around and around inside my body, Graham and his poison slopping around inside my mind. It was a haunted house and I was haunting it as much as anything.

Eventually I came back to myself and I could walk around the room without verging on a breakdown. It looked to me like it would be possible to clean the room after all, and if I could clean the room, then why not the whole house?

I listened at the top of the stairs. I could hear Jennifer's movement in the kitchen so she was still there then, thankfully. 'I'm OK now, everything is OK!' I shouted down to her. Not that she had been as overwhelmed as I had, of course. 'I'm going to have a shower and get clean and get changed if that's alright?'

'Of course that's alright!' she shouted back up. 'Why wouldn't it be?'

In the shower – which was spotlessly clean – I started to wonder if I had actually been ill and, if so, why Jennifer had not called a doctor. Maybe the phones still weren't working, or maybe I had appeared more stable than I had felt, or maybe the whole period just had not lasted as long as it had seemed. Whatever had happened, she had been nothing but caring, dealing with her own trauma silently and internally. Really, I should have been stronger for her.

Those were the things that I told myself, but still I couldn't shake the impression of some emptiness right there at the centre of it all, in the house. A vacuum that we were circling around. The reason for everything that had happened, and the meaning behind it all, if there was one, just faded in and out around the edges, around the outside, around the fell.

The hot water coursed down my body and I started to feel more awake.

I remembered Jennifer squeezing my hand while I had been delirious. Her lips against my ear. 'Jack, my darling. My kitten. My lover. My Jack.'

Had ringing the police ever really been an option? I thought about this as I approached the barn. I mean, we hadn't had any working phones, but at no point had any of us thought of running down the fellside to find some other house in order to make a telephone call, because it just hadn't seemed feasible somehow, or realistic. And it wasn't feasible at this point, either, because how many people had died before our eyes, without us preventing it? I had killed Kenny myself. Did he have a family?

How old was he?

The sky was a dark pink colour.

I reached the barn door, which was still slightly open,

and braced myself. Graham's warning not to enter the barn resurfaced in my brain. Don't go into the barn. Don't go into the barn. His wavering voice circled round and round. The bodies I would see in there were the bodies of people – not lycanthropes, not monsters of any sort, just guests, visitors, people who had found themselves in the way. I could have set fire to the whole building, but that might have led to a well-meaning valley-dweller ringing 999 for a fire engine. No. I had a shovel with me, and that would have to do.

The things we become.

However far we thought we had come, we were only ever balancing on the edge. The world we knew was just the thin slippery spine of a high fell, and surviving with your mind intact was just a case of absorbing impacts, welcoming them into your body and dispersing the damage throughout yourself in order to prevent it being a force that knocked you from your feet and into the abyss. Sometimes I thought the best thing to be was something like an empty box, some sort of shell, designed only to hold. Either that or something completely shapeless, neither one thing nor another, able to adjust to anything at a moment's notice, not true to anything or anybody, but accommodating to everything and everybody.

Or both. Just being nothing in particular.

I opened the barn door and despite the holes in the roof the smell of a butcher's shop hung in the air like smog, and it took a moment for my eyes to adjust, but when they did I saw a small fell in the corner, an actual fell, with ridges and peaks and crags and gullies. A fell in miniature. I knew that it was made of bodies, though, and so I approached the mound apprehensively, half hoping that one of the bodies would move, crawl out of the mass and be OK. I realised that I was desperate for another face, a friendly face, somebody to talk to that wasn't Jennifer. But, in reality, if anything had moved, I would have split its head with the shovel.

The bodies remained motionless. There were lots of them. Lots and lots of them. I nearly tripped over one that was stretched out on the floor and was evidently the one that Graham had killed with the axe. It looked just as human as the rest. And there was that element of tragedy in everything, that idea of only being human at the end, a body like any other. Was that the case? Or was there some spirit in these lycanthropes that found somewhere else to go once their physical human shells had been broken up? I didn't know, and I didn't know which was worse. That body was going in with the others though. I was only digging one hole.

I didn't get too close to the pile of things that had been my friends – I moved into the opposite corner and started to dig.

Inside, Jennifer was continuing with the clean-up of the house. I had left her mopping the ceiling of the living-room. She was displaying single-mindedness and stoicism that unnerved me. I was split – most of me was trying to maintain that she was an angel, swallowing her grief and distress in order to push through this period of readjustment intact and pull me through with her, to keep it all together for both our sakes, as I had demonstrated that I was woefully incapable of doing so myself. The rest of me – only a small part – was convinced that Jennifer was a lycanthrope, a monster, and that was the only way she was managing to get through it all without a breakdown of the kind that I had had. That way of thinking was deeply arrogant, assuming as it did that she could be no stronger than I was. But even though the fear was only a whisper at the back of my mind, it worked its way right through every thought, every working of my brain. There was the proverb – a barrel of wine, a barrel of sewage. Put a teaspoon of the wine in the sewage, and it wouldn't make the sewage any more palatable. But put a teaspoon of sewage in the wine, and the wine would immediately be toxic. The world was weighted in this way. The quiet voice that insisted that Jennifer was one of them, a monster, that voice was the sewage inside me. Despite most of me believing in her virtue, that quiet voice slowly ruined everything.

I dug into the hard earth. The smells of meat and piss and shit clogged my nostrils and I imagined ruptured bowels leaking into the open air. I kept looking towards the door and being hypnotised by the movements of the blue-grey clouds across the archway. In there, in the barn, it felt unnaturally dark. I scrambled from the hole I was digging and surveyed my progress. The hole was maybe three feet wide, four feet long, a couple deep. I was sweating and I needed a torch, so I dropped the shovel and headed out of the barn, headed into the yard. It didn't have to be a torch, it could be a lantern – anything that would shed some light. From the yard, I saw Jennifer through the kitchen window. The room was warm-looking from out there, and she was beautiful. The air was a deepening blue. She was washing something in the sink and I paused to watch her. From where I was standing there was no sign of all of the violence, the gore, the fear, the hellish creatures that had broken into our lives. All that was locked away inside my head as recent memory, together with apprehension. I knew that it wasn't over.

Hesitantly, I put one foot in front of the other and made my way back to the house.

'I've just come for a torch, or a lantern or something,' I shouted through, pushing the front door open and wiping my feet on the mat. Just out of habit.

'OK!' Jennifer shouted. I could hear music coming from the kitchen. It was fast and lively and there was a fiddle in there somewhere. It put cold rods up my back. I saw that the living-room was clean now, more or less, apart from very faint pink stains on the walls. The upholstery had been taken off the furniture and washed and was hanging on a clothes-horse in front of the fireplace, in which Jennifer had stacked and lit a tight bundle of bunched newspaper, thin sticks and dusty coal. The flames licked up the back of the fireplace, hot and cheerful, and the room felt nice, or it would have felt nice if things had been otherwise. You could have walked into this room

384

and believed that everything was normal. The room *was* normal, almost. The valley could have been a wonderful place to raise a child. We could have cleaned the house right up and tried to start a family, and turned a spare room into a nursery and given the hypothetical child a fantastic attic bedroom with skylights, everything. I turned around in the living-room and looked at all of the walls and yes, everything was kind of normal, but that music – I couldn't bear to hear that music. And I had work to do, anyway.

I went through to the kitchen, and gave Jennifer a quick hug and laughed at something nice she said, I didn't know what, and moved away as she tried to kiss me. I pretended that I was just looking elsewhere, pretended I was not seeing her face getting closer with her eyes half-closed and her lips beautiful and hungry. I floated through into the utility room at the back. I found two torches – a big chunky red plastic one and a small metal one that I could slip into my pocket – and an old oil lantern that we always meant to take camping.

I picked the lantern up with one hand, then rushed back out through the kitchen so that Jennifer didn't see me and ask what was wrong. I picked up the box of matches from the mantelpiece above the now roaring fire, and went out through the front door.

I stopped in the yard and looked back over into the kitchen window. If I had a gun would I be able to stand there and shoot her? I could have got one, I could have got one from some Tony-Martin-esque local farmer, and it would have been easier to do, more palatable, than attacking and killing her at close quarters. It would have been easier to do it in a split second, before changing my mind, almost by accident. Thinking about it would almost be the same as doing it, once I was standing there with my finger on the trigger.

I turned and made my way back to the barn. Of course, I didn't have a gun and besides, if I had it in me to kill her with a gun, I had it in me to kill her without. But I was not going to kill her. She was just a person, just a human, only human, like me, and I could never have done that, not to Jennifer, my Morgana le Fay, my love, not you.

If only I was one of them and I could banish all doubt and worry, just like that, because rationalising did nothing for me. If she was one of them she would surely have tried to kill me by this point, but the idea was still there, a black thing polluting every thought.

Inside the barn, I lit the lantern. The flickering light warped the shape of the whole place, made it appear as if the walls and the ground and the bodies were bouncing to and fro, stretching, snapping back, bending one way, then the other, wavering like insubstantial things, films of water, flames, holograms, sheets of rain. It was as if things were jumping into my field of vision and then out again, whereas really I supposed it was my field of vision that was shifting. I put the lantern down between the hole and the bodies – I didn't want them where I couldn't see them – and I turned both of the torches on and laid them on the ground so that they illuminated the area in which I was working, and I picked up the shovel and started digging again.

I dug and dug and dug. I got too warm and took my jacket off, and then my jumper and then my T-shirt and still I was too hot. Sweat ran down my body in streams, cascading down from beneath my hair, under my arms, between my shoulder-blades, my forehead, and soil stuck to the sweat and slowly I became covered in mud. I dug and dug, and the torches shone their light horizontally across the top of the hole, so as it grew deeper the bottom descended into darkness and became invisible. Every now and again I stopped and looked across at the bodies and I recognised some of the visible faces but could not attach names to them, even though three days previously I would have counted most of them as friends, people that I could have talked to. I carried on digging.

I thought more about Jennifer's words of consolation. Jack. My darling. My kitten. My Jack. But there was so much blood in the air. I stopped digging. I wanted us to be OK, but how? How could we keep ourselves safe? We could leave, of course. Yes. We would leave, move to somewhere well away from there and that godforsaken house, but – what if Jennifer *was* a werewolf? How would we stop her from changing? How could I live with her? Was keeping myself safe possible? No. We couldn't ever leave, not as long as there was a chance that Jennifer was one of them, because there – Fell House – was the perfect place for keeping something like that hidden.

And I supposed we could never have children. Not as long as I didn't know.

I threw down my shovel.

I climbed out of the hole, more slowly this time because it was deeper than before. I left the barn and went around the back.

At the other end of the barn there was the small outhouse, not visible from any of the windows of the main house. I flicked the large, outdoor light switch and the low dangling bulb flickered on. The small metal chair and hacksaw gleamed dully in the dim glow. I looked at the door and it was heavy, sturdy wood, much like the front door of the house. I checked the padlock, which was slightly rusty, but looked like it would still work. The key was lodged inside. I worked it free and slipped it into my pocket.

The space would do, if it came to it.

I returned to the hole. The light from the lantern still trembled. The two torches caught the pit in their crossfire and it looked blacker than black. I climbed back inside. It was big now, but still nowhere big enough.

It grew darker outside. I was lost in the digging. When the barn door suddenly squealed like something alive, my skin tightened so much that it might have broken open. I poked my head up over the edge and saw that the noise had been made by Jennifer entering. She knelt down at the edge of the hole and put down a tray with a cup of tea and some sandwiches on it. She lowered herself down on to all fours and brought her head down to kiss me.

'Thank you for doing this,' she said. 'It must be awful.'

'I forget they're there,' I said, nodding towards the bodies. I looked back at her, and her huge eyes bored into mine. Resting on her elbows, she brought her hands in towards her chest and started unbuttoning her shirt.

'Jennifer,' I said. 'I don't know if now's the time.'

'I've been thinking,' she said. 'There is something to be said, maybe, for the way they live. We only have so long. This is something that we know, everybody knows it all the time, but with so much death happening all at once. Makes you think. I saw them dancing and I saw them fucking. It was like we could be, Jack. People could live that way. We could be like them. Without the killing. Just the pure joy. The passions.'

'You don't really want to be like them,' I said. I knew she did, though, and I knew I did too. 'We couldn't all be like them, anyway. Nothing would ever get done.'

'I wouldn't want to miss an opportunity to love you, Jack,' she said. 'And besides. You stand there with your shirt off, covered in sweat and dirt, looking at me with eyes like that and tell me you don't want me?'

'That's not what I said.' I pulled myself up over the side. Jennifer moved backwards so that she was resting on her knees. Beneath her shirt, her nipples were visible above the cups of her bra, hard in the cold, and she carried on unbuttoning and then shrugged the shirt off. She unhooked her bra and removed that too. She stood up and undid her butterfly-buckled belt and rolled down her jeans, bending over towards me as she did so, and

389

everything was either blue in the light of the moon or orange in the light of the lantern or black, silhouetted. She stayed in that position for a moment, leaning forward. Her back was smooth and almost horizontal, lit blue. I was at an angle to her, and saw her slightly from the side. Her hip, like her back and the side of her buttock, was also blue. Her hip marked the end of her straight back and the start of her curved buttock and was marked itself by the plain white fabric of her knickers. Her legs were straight. Her breasts hung and swayed gently, orange and flickering in the uneven lantern light, and her face was open, her mouth was open, her eyes were wide open, her tongue delicately probing her blushing lips. Her hair was long and flowed over her face, down her shoulders. She raised one arm and steadied herself on me before stepping out of her rumpled jeans, first with one leg and then the other. She stood back up again, slowly, because she knew I was watching her.

I *was* watching her, all of her, but my eyes kept returning to her mouth. If she bit me ... if she bit me, would I try to resist?

I took my shoes and socks off and then started to undo my belt, but she took over; I had thought my hands were moving at normal speed, but her hands were much quicker than mine. Next to her, it was like I was moving in slow motion. I lay back and lifted my behind from the earth so that she could take my jeans and boxers off, and I lay there naked, and against my skin the earth felt wet. I hoped it was just the sweat that had flooded from my body as I had been digging. I lay there and watched as she slowly walked back over to the barn door, her skin pale, and pushed it wide open. The light from the stars and the slim crescent of a moon poured into the space. She was a silhouetted shape under the archway, a beautiful shape. She walked back over, slowly, swaying, and my already swollen penis grew as she approached. I stood up and when she reached me she put her hands on my shoulders and pushed herself against me. She lifted her mouth to kiss mine, and I jerked my head back, thinking what if? But I didn't have the willpower to walk away as she took hold of my erection with her muddy hands. Mud, I thought, dimly. Mud. She gripped me firmly, and looking into her eyes, I thought I just don't know. It was a simple fact that my body was overpowering my mind by this point, although no part of me – body or mind – was left untainted by the fear of her, the fear that she was one of them. It didn't matter what I thought, what my mind was doing – when she went to kiss me my head pulled backwards instinctively.

'Kiss me,' she said.

'No,' I said, more brusquely than I had intended, although I wanted to, I wanted to feel her teeth sinking in. She pushed down on my shoulders and I knelt before her. She parted her legs slightly and I touched her between them and felt that she wanted this too. I took off the brief scrap of white cloth that covered her. We were both naked now. My knees were wet and I looked down to see that the ground was turning sloppy, and it must be blood, I thought. Blood. I looked over to the pile of bodies and saw that they were bleeding profusely. They had not bled at all when I was alone. It was as if some rule or some natural law had been suspended. Had all of their dead hearts just started beating in order to pump that sudden blood from their mouths, from the holes in their chests, stomachs? I remembered Graham talking about the grid, his science, his earnest concern, his panic.

I pulled Jennifer to the ground and pushed her on to her back. She leant up to kiss me again, but I forced her down and held her arms and slid inside her easily. Her arms and my hands were half submerged in that bloody mud and still the stuff cascaded down from the little fell, waterfalls of blood running from a hundred mouths, spilling over the other bodies and creating that ooze for us to writhe in. I held her down so that she couldn't raise her head to kiss me or bite me and she arched her back.

'Get behind me,' she whispered.

I withdrew and she rolled over on to her front, supporting herself on all fours. Her breasts and flat stomach were covered in mud, mud that I knew would be rusty in colour if the light was true and full, and the stuff dripped from her budding nipples as we juddered forwards and back, making them look bigger, longer. She lowered her head and threw it backwards, her hair streaming across my face. I reached underneath to find her clitoris.

Between her fingers the weird earth slimed up. I looked at the back of her head and wondered if her face had changed shape, if her mouth was stretching open like it was giving birth.

Every beat of my heart sent a jerky pulse through my penis and simultaneously seemed to bring fresh gouts of blood from the openings in the bodies in the corner. I watched them and I saw this, saw this connection, and they had become part of our sex. Everything was collapsing together. She groaned and shook as she came, driving her face into the ground, her teeth finding one of my fingers, closing, breaking the skin.

She twisted away and turned to face me and grasped at that suddenly exposed part of me that was slippery and cold, covered with her internal fluids. I felt the orgasmic heat start to build deep within, and this was the beginning of the end. But she slipped and fell into the hole, disappearing into the dark. She rose up, her side orange and her front blue, and took my glistening orange erection into her mouth. It started to happen quickly, unstoppably, and it was only as I sensed the gathering of the first muscular spasm that I realised where I was, and I thought about her teeth closing on me again. I pulled out of her mouth and it was immediately then, as I started to turn away, that the thick white seed flew from my body, arcing across to her side, falling, always falling, and vanished into the black pit. I watched it and I thought, that came from inside of me.

I looked at my bleeding hand.

It felt like a long time before either of us spoke. During the silence I watched the gush of blood coming from the dead bodies diminish to a slow trickle, and then stop. I looked back at Jennifer.

Why hadn't she attacked me before, though? Why hadn't the other werewolves moved in and gutted me? Maybe because I was hers now, for her to use as she wanted. For sex. For whatever else these things needed or wanted. Were those the answers? Things started to make some sort of sense. That was why she had not suffered the same kind of breakdown that I had. That was why she had not told me the truth about Kenny penetrating her. Because she hadn't wanted to explain how he had overpowered her without biting her and turning her into one of them. Because he *had* bitten her.

I walked backwards, and the lantern light was being reflected from pools and puddles all over the ground. I had not realised that there was so much blood. They had bled so much, our friends. The pools behind the pit were glowing orange, and those between the pit and the barn door were glowing blue, and Jennifer was in the middle, her torso rising from the landscape like she was sprouting out from underground, her breasts and face streaked with dirt and pale in the moonlight.

'Where are you going?' she asked.

'Come with me,' I said. 'We're not finished yet.'

She climbed up and followed as I walked out of the barn, and the whole valley was visible from the archway, and beautiful. Some astral light illuminated faint wreaths of woodsmoke that hung up above us and above the landscape, and the mountains seemed somehow peaceful and safe, and between the stars the sky was deep blue, and the lake was bright, like mercury.

'This way,' I said, and took her hand. I led her around the side of the barn and stopped by the outhouse and opened the door and turned on the light. I picked up the hacksaw and threw it backwards.

'Here,' I said. 'Sit on that chair.'

'OK,' she said. 'What are we doing?' She sat down and shivered at the contact of cold metal against her most sensitive skin, and she smiled at me.

I turned off the light and slammed the door and clicked the padlock shut.

She screamed and roared and hammered and shrieked so loudly and so hoarsely and so fearfully and so angrily that she sounded like an animal, and maybe she had changed shape in her fury. I would have to reinforce the door, because as a wolf she might have been able to just beat it until it broke, or even just tear it up over time.

Jennifer. You must understand that fear makes us do things. I do not want you to forgive me. But I do want you to understand. I'm sorry.

Back in the barn, the bloody, meaty butcher's-shop smell was stronger than before, and I could hear Jennifer through the wall. She howled and sobbed and scratched and fell silent and then started again. She didn't sound human. I had done the only thing that I could have done. I had not killed her, so the situation was reversible if I was wrong. But I was not wrong. If I had not taken the steps I had taken, she would have killed me. Maybe not immediately. Maybe not until she was bored with me. But there would have come a time.

As I picked up the shovel again, I heard her smash her whole body weight against the door to the outhouse. I sighed and dropped the shovel. The grave-digging would have to wait.

Luckily, my car was not blocked in by all of the cars of our dead guests, so I drove it round and parked it outside the outhouse, mashing the side of the vehicle into the wall and the door so that it could not be opened. That would have to do for the time being. I left the key to the padlock in the glove compartment and returned to the barn.

Outside, I could hear things moving. The wind rising quickly and crashing through the dead orchard and clanging the gate against stone, and the sorrowful croaking of the big black birds. I could even hear the flapping of their wings, although, no, that would have been too quiet for me to hear in there. But the caterwauling of lovesick felines as they coupled until they bled, dragging their claws across each other's backs, I could hear that clearly enough. The sick dripping of light as it leaked down from the stars. The beginnings of decomposition in the bodies piled up beside me – small rustles and gurgles. The smell of death was thickening. I picked up the shovel.

I dug and I dug and I dug.

The shovel hit something. I had driven it with such force that the obstruction sent an unbearable shock up through my arms. It sounded like I had hit metal. I rubbed my right elbow with my left hand, then I knelt and scraped earth from around the object. My head was aching anyway but the sudden jolt had made it worse and it throbbed now, like a beating heart. It was the feeling of the brain being too big for the skull, forcing itself against the walls of bone. I scraped at the thing in the ground, and I picked the shovel back up and found myself not just digging a pit, but excavating something buried. A coffin, I thought.

I found more of it, and gradually uncovered a curved shape. I was wrong; it was not a coffin. And even though I had something more pressing to be doing in burying the bodies, I had to see what this thing was.

During the excavation, I started to find bones. Human bones. This was part of some story that I didn't know. Teeth and femurs and gaping eye sockets and yellow vertebrae and splintered tibiae.

I had to dig almost the whole of the thing out of the ground before I understood, partly because the torch batteries were running out and the lantern was running out of oil and it was getting darker in there, and partly because it was the last thing I was expecting to find six feet underground beneath an empty barn half-way up a fellside.

Once I saw it I leant back against the side of the hole. I had no idea what time it was. The lantern had gone out and I was shining the feeble torchlight downwards so that I could see the thing at the bottom of the hole. It was the only thing I could see in the whole world.

At my feet was an upturned rowing boat. The shovel had struck the metal oar-bracket. Were the bones somehow related to the boat? Was that what had grown from the seed I spilled? Had I fertilised that bloody soil?

I think I must have started to drift off as I stared at it, because I started to imagine myself rowing it out across the lake, accompanied only by some rolled-up bedclothes. The image didn't make any sense to me. I shook my head and tried to clear my mind, tried to wake myself up a bit.

I heard Jennifer start screaming some more and I wondered if she was only human after all. Maybe she was screaming because she was only human and she thought that I was one of them.

I looked at the hole, at the boat, and thought that it was probably deep enough. I put a hand to my head, hoping somehow to ease the pressure.

The bodies were just the weight I expected them to be. I lifted and carried and dropped them, still naked. I was finding strength and endurance that I didn't know I had. Internal organs and thick, tacky strings of viscous saliva hung down my back. The damage that had been done to those people.

If only I could have been like the happy, selfish creatures by the lake. Not to have to feel pain or fear or guilt. My head ached. I imagined my brain looking purple and smooth, like a blueberry, or a full sheep tick on the point of bursting, and I looked at my hand. The bite wound had nearly healed completely.

Nearly healed completely. Already! I dropped the shovel. She *must* be one of them, so maybe I was too, now – that could be the only reason that my skin was growing back so quickly. Something scrabbled on the roof of the barn, and I could hear dripping, leaking, wet sounds.

The barn door squealed briefly, and then stopped. I turned to look and it started squealing again, being dragged open by somebody who stepped through into the barn once the door was open wide enough. He wore a long black cloak that seemed to change shape in the flickering light and a black, tricorne hat. Two huge dogs crept in alongside him, stomachs to the ground, and it was only as he got closer I saw that they were really wolves, noble and beautiful, and their eyes were slate-grey and calm, and their teeth were sharp and clean. Their coats were almost white at the sides, darkening to black along their spines. They made no sound at all. They just looked at me.

The man standing in between the wolves tipped his hat back so that I could see his scarred, tanned face, which was thick with black stubble. Black hair hung down from beneath his hat, and his eyes were as grey as the wolves' eyes. He was the man that I had seen holding Taylor by the throat. He smiled, widely.

'Evening, friend.' His voice was rough, raspy and low. 'Looks like you're in a bit of a pickle here.' He laughed, and it sounded like one of the birds that roosted in the dead orchard. 'What would your authorities say, eh?'

'Who are you?'

'I'm just doing some business for a friend,' he said. 'Someone who could be a friend of yours, too, if you were willing. Bearpit is what they call me these days, ever since that last fight in the pit.' He looked down at my hand. I didn't ask for elaboration on the origins of his name. 'Looks like you've had a bit of a biting. Maybe just a delicate little peck from your pretty little lass, but a bite is a bite is a bite, isn't it, eh?'

I looked down at my hand. There was no way he could have seen the bite-marks from where he was. My hand was shaking too much, anyway.

'You're one of them, aren't you?' I said. 'From down by the lake.'

'You could say that. Not how I'd like to be addressed, mind. Especially considering as I've come up here just to help you. And double-especially now that you could say that you're one of us too, now, eh?' He laughed again.

'Am I?' I said. The wolves sniffed and nuzzled at the remaining dead. He got a little closer, so that he was maybe only four or five feet away. His cloak was brushing the puddles. He smelled like dead leaves.

'Well,' he said. 'It's complicated. More complicated than most people imagine, to be frank. You been bitten, now, so you got it in you.' He pursed his lips. 'You got the wolf,' he whispered over-dramatically. He grinned again, too widely. 'But to really *use* it, there's more to it than a nice

400

little nibble from your lady friend. You've got to give something *back*.'

'Wh-what?' I managed to say.

'The soul, Jack. The *self*. And seeing as we've cut straight to the chase – how about it?'

'You know my name.'

'I know all kinds.'

'I don't understand. What if I don't give it?'

'Nothing, really.' He sniffed. 'Not the kind of thing that can be taken by force, see. You'll be all for giving it up soon enough though, see. Francis would've come begging if he'd lasted long enough. Not even a werewolf can survive having its head pressed flat.'

'I have plans for my soul already.'

'Yeah, I know,' he said. 'You and your girl. You think you need it for her. For what? A long and happy life? Don't make me laugh. What if she were to go and die, like that fine red-haired piece your Taylor friend got so cut up about? What if she got some cancer, eh, some uncontrollable gathering somewhere inside her? What would you do then, with nothing left to give? May as well get something for your money, is all I'm saying.'

'Like you said,' I replied, 'I've already been bitten.'

'Yeah, but you're not in control of it, are you? Don't quite know how to go about changing shape. Not to mention the guilt, Jack. You'll find the guilt is the killer. What I'm offering is a way of enjoying your life, Jack, because it's going to last a very long time now. No diseases, no old age. As long as that clever old brain of yours is intact, you'll be able to bounce back from anything. But trouble is, with all that soul of yours, you'll just spend all your time worrying, feeling rotten about yourself.'

'No,' I said. 'I'm not going to change my mind.'

'Well you're a fucking idiot then, Jack,' he said, and laughed again. 'And I'll be getting off. There's all kind of fun I could be having down by Wastwater. Just remember this. I've offered you what you've always wanted. You think you've got it, but you don't know. You just don't know what's coming.'

'I don't want this.' I gestured towards the bodies and the blood. 'I don't want to do this. I know what I want now, and that's Jennifer.'

'As long as she submits herself to you completely, and just does whatever you want, you mean?' he sneered. 'As long as she's locked up nice and secure so she can't get out and live the life she wants to live, eh? As long as she gives herself to you?'

I didn't say anything.

'Your soul wouldn't amount to much anyway,' he said. 'Never do these days. Don't really know yourselves, do you? Everything you lot have got to give is piss poor. Lot of poor fucking surface-dwellers, that's you. Well, you'll regret it. And I'm glad.'

He turned and left. The wolves followed without saying a word. Without making a sound.

The next day I woke to a pack of wolves howling their sad, lonely howls, but as I slowly regained full consciousness I realised that there was only one voice out there, and I had dreamed the rest. It was Jennifer in the outhouse.

I had to do something about the noise.

I found a working clock and saw that I had slept through to midday.

I fried some bacon and put it on a plate for Jennifer, and I started frying some for myself but then just pulled it out of the pan and ate it still raw, and eating felt more desperate than usual, less enjoyable, more functional. I thought about trying to find some jeans, but it seemed like such an effort for something so unnecessary, so I took Jennifer's food out naked. The sky was grey and the day was cold.

I opened the car door on the driver's side and saw that the seat was covered in the bloody mud of the barn. I didn't mind, as I was still covered in the stuff myself. I reversed away from the door and then drove back in front of it, but this time leaving enough of a gap to open the door slightly. I stopped the car and got out. I took the padlock key from the glove compartment and the plate of bacon from the passenger seat and put them on top of the car. Then I climbed on to the roof and slid across to the door. There was not enough room for Jennifer to get out.

I could hear her crying.

I took a deep breath and leant down and unlocked the padlock.

The door burst open and smashed into the car and she

tried to force herself out of the narrow gap, face first, but she couldn't fit. Her face twisted and contorted and the corner of her mouth got caught on a nail that stuck out from the wood of the door. As I watched, her face started to narrow and elongate in order to get through the space and her mouth stretched wider as the nail held one corner of it in place and the rest of it moved forward. There was something inside her struggling to get out, and it emerged from between her lips, which stretched like a foreskin. Gradually, a new, misshapen head squeezed through the widening hole and into the inches of air available, and she caught sight of me above her. Long, scrabbling arms emerged, broken and thickly furred, flailing wildly. I stayed where I was on the car roof. There was no way she could get out, no way she could fit. Not quickly, anyway; maybe she could have warped her body into ever thinner forms, elongating herself into a bony, hairy worm-thing that could have wriggled its way through anything. To think that I was fantasising about us having children! Could a normal healthy child really be born from the thing that tore and broke itself below me? What if she gave birth to another one and I had to keep them both locked up?

Maybe I should just have given in and tried to transform myself. The two of us could run through the wilderness like animals, free and innocent in our hungers. Would she ever forgive me? My head ached like cold metal.

I pushed the door shut with all that was left of my strength, hoping that the pressure on her arms and neck would force her to retreat. It did, eventually, and I managed to get the padlock shut. The transformation must have been new to her. She could still get a lot stronger.

I went inside and gathered up all of the books that I could. I had a huge collection of folklore, myths and legends, half of which I had never properly read. I had historical accounts of monsters and hauntings. I had eyewitness accounts. I had psychology and psychiatry books on beliefs and interpretations of beliefs of the supernatural. I had novels, short stories, epic poems. I had translations of Nordic sagas. I had literary examinations of the uncanny, of the phallus in fiction. I had books on the cultural significance of horror, fantasy and science-fiction writing. I had bestiaries. I had old role-playing games' rule books. I had encyclopaedias of faeries, dragons, aliens. I had spotters' guides to the flora and fauna of various different countries and different regions within different countries. I had shelves full of The *Fortean Times*. I had stubble, and was covered in dried blood. I threw all the books on the floor in the room that I had once thought of as my study and found some paper and a pen. The paraphernalia of my earlier life seemed stupid and simple and hopeless and sad. The pictures on the wall were just reminders.

I didn't know where to start. I picked up the nearest book. *The Folklore of the Scottish Highlands* by Anne Ross. I started a pile of possibly useful books to my right. *Fairy Tales and Feminism: New Approaches* by Donald P. Haase. I discarded it. The books were everywhere. Some useful, some useless. I ploughed on through.

The Tsathoggua Cycle (Cthulhu Mythos) by Robert M. Price. *The World's Greatest Mysteries* by Colin Wilson and Joyce Robins. *Into the Unknown*, edited by Will Bradbury. *The Vampire Encyclopaedia* by Matthew Bunson. *The Book of Werewolves* by the Reverend Sabine Baring-Gould. *The Trials of Life* by Sir David Attenborough. *Science Fiction After 1900: From the Steam Man to the Stars* by Brooks Landon. *The Lore of the Land* by Westwood and Simpson. I kept getting up and walking around. *The UFO Casebook* by Kevin D. Randle. *A Delusion of Satan: The Full Story of the Salem Witch Trials* by Frances Hill. Something, a bird, it must have been a bird, flew into the glass of the window and bounced off, squawking. I gritted my teeth. I had to work more quickly, but as I sorted the books and magazines and studies into either useful or useless piles I increasingly got the impression that none of this knowledge would help. Having all that knowledge was not going to help at all. *Alien Constructions: Science Fiction and Feminist Thought* by Patricia Melzer. I grew frustrated. *Fantasy: The Liberation of Imagination* by Richard Mathews. I threw the book across the room in disgust.

Having all that knowledge wasn't going to help. The words were stuck in my head. I was repeating them as a mantra. Having all that knowledge wasn't going to help. There was only one thing I needed to know, only one thing. One little thing. How did you reverse it? How did you go backwards? How did you exorcise the wolf from the human? Was that what had Francis told Taylor? What had they been saying out there? What had Graham and the axe prevented Taylor from telling me? One thing I was sure of was that I was not going to find the information anywhere in all those books. Outside the sky grew darker.

One little thing.

Having all that knowledge wasn't going to help at all.

Books all around, paper written on, screwed up, torn and strewn across the floor. The light bulb was unreliable, despite being modern, and flickered from time to time, dimming and glimmering. This was one of the few rooms that did have curtains, but they must have been torn down as part of the clean-up because now the glass of the window was naked and the darkness outside looked straight through into me. There was a smell throughout the house. We had scrubbed and scrubbed but evidently there was enough bodily matter left for the decomposition of it to raise a God-awful stink, enough left in between the floorboards and soaked into furniture and hidden behind and underneath everything that we could perceive. It had trickled into every gap, crept into the spaces that separated things. It was everywhere. It was in everything and around everything that we could see. It was almost as if it was inside me too, having clotted into some internal presence, some silent observer.

And I'm sorry, Jennifer. I'm sorry. I wish that I was religious enough and devout enough to be owed some sort of miracle, if that's how it works. I don't know how it works.

You were making that sound again, that sound like a whale far away underwater and in pain, in agony, a keening, a sad old animal song, like something huge and innocent. Perhaps innocent was the wrong word. Perhaps not. But you were making that sound again and it drew me to the window. It reminded me of Erin and her fear of whales; her nightmares of alien giants moving slowly through the deep murk of ancient oceans. She didn't seem dead to me. I couldn't believe that she was really dead. I found myself looking out over the darkened yard. The sky was black with cloud that night.

No. I had to find a way.

There was this recurring figure in the stories, in the werewolf stories that I had gathered there, and in those I had read before. The tall dark stranger, or a 'dark spirit', or the 'Lord of the Forest'. And though the Shepherd may have watched his flock by night He missed the cold stranger on a horse – the Lord of the Forest come to promise the flock the power to avoid hunger and pain for ever and ever by turning into a wolf. Who would refuse a gift like that? A kind of true freedom? Except it was not a gift. It was a deal, as far as I could make out. It was always only ever a deal. In the stories, the Devil – or one of His demons – came and offered the power in exchange for the person's soul, like Bearpit did with me. And the power – it wasn't really *power*, it was more just a kind of nihilism. It was the removal of your conscience and your compassion and your capacity for emotional attachment. Coupled with the ability to change at will. So yes, there was power in it, of a kind. It seemed there were two steps. First, there was being bitten, which turned you into a kind of unpredictable, schizophrenic wolf-man, and then there was making the deal, which took you to the next stage.

Pain burrowed through my brain again. My vision blurred and the wind carried Jennifer's howling in waves to my window. The metal impact of the gate rang out like some semi-intelligent creature was playing with it, delighting in the noise, attempting something like rhythm. Also, I could hear the awful shrieks of the cats as they raped each other, and small wings against the window and talons scraping around on the roof. I couldn't find the answer. I couldn't find it.

I woke up slumped over the pile of books, grey light stroking my eyelids with dusty fingers. White mist pressed its faceless self against the window. There was always something at the window. Something trying to get in.

Outside, the yard and the barn and the house were hazy through the fog, and everything was reduced to just a vague shape, the suggestion of itself, with indistinct edges. I was just the shadow, the silhouette, the idea of a person.

Through the mist, Jennifer keened, and the sound was sharp despite the clogged-up air and the wooden door between us. I made my way across the grey yard and caught sight of the gate as a bank of fog rolled back momentarily. I realised that I was still naked. I was living through a steady reduction of whatever it was that defined me as human. Leaving the house with no clothes on by accident. I shook my head and instead of going straight to the outhouse, as I had planned, I made my way over to the big barn door.

The barn door squealed as I pulled it open, and I imagined animals everywhere lifting their heads as they heard the sound, baring their teeth, breaking into a run at the high-pitched pain. I imagined people, if there were any left in the world, turning pale and shuddering, locking the doors and drawing the curtains. I imagined the dark red sky that I had seen from the window during my delirium.

Inside the barn everything was as grey as the world outside, but darker. My jeans lay on the ground, hard and crusty with filth. I picked them up and struggled into them, looking around as I did so, and I realised that the uneven patch of ground over there, the place where I had buried all the bodies, was not really ground at all – it was just the bodies: limbs and joints and other bits level with the surface, some almost broken through. I couldn't tell one from the other. It could just have been one many-limbed thing from deep down, worming its way up to our world.

I turned to leave.

I closed the barn door behind me and turned to fasten

it, and then stopped dead, a huge panic blossoming in my stomach and throat like smoke.

The axe was leaning against the wall. The last time I had seen the axe had been when Taylor and Graham were fighting.

One of them must have been here.

I took the axe and held it firmly in both hands, across my body like a bar. The mist was cold and impenetrable. I moved slowly around the back of the barn towards the outhouse, and saw that the car had been moved away from the door.

The door was wide open, swaying gently to and fro.

The mist turned to ice on my bare skin and I gripped the axe tightly.

My head was thudding with the flow of my body, each heartbeat carrying the impact of a battering ram, although making no sound at all – everything was completely silent.

I didn't want to be there and I didn't want it to be like this.

Jennifer. The house. A future together. I had wanted it to happen but not like this. I'm sorry.

I heard fast-moving feet behind me and turned to see a huge four-legged something looming through the air towards me. I lifted the axe and the wolf landed on me, knocking me to the ground, but also smashing its throat against the handle of the axe. It fell back, choking, saliva raining from its huge mouth, and I stood, feeling stronger than I ever had before, and brought the axe down on one of its hind legs. There was a splintering sound and a long,

411

high scream. I cut again, and was astounded to see the leg come away from the body. My heart swelled with pride as the wolf limped away, and I bent to pick up the severed limb.

By the time my hand fastened around the hairy thigh, it was not hairy, or even a thigh. It was the lower part of a human leg; it was the lower part of a female human leg. I looked up at the wolf to see Jennifer, crying, lying on her stomach, thick blood pouring from the stump of her right leg, truncated at the knee. 'Oh,' I said. 'Oh. I'm sorry.'

'Jack,' she said. She pushed herself up from the ground and rolled over, so that she was sitting up. Already the flow of blood was slowing.

'Jennifer,' I said. 'What happened?'

She managed to laugh, painfully, through her tears. She was naked in the fog. 'What kind of question is that, really?' she asked. 'After everything?'

'How did you get out?'

'The door was open. I think it was Balthazar.'

'Balthazar? Who's Balthazar?'

'You must remember, Jack. Our snowman. Don't tell us you don't remember. He'll be offended.'

'Ha ha!' I said, my voice and face cracking. 'Glad I'm not the only one to have had some sort of mental breakdown!'

She shook her head and grimaced with the pain. 'It's worse than you think,' she said. 'You shouldn't be joking.'

'Mm,' I said, and shivered. I hadn't been joking. I hadn't

even meant to laugh. The cold ate into me. 'Oh God, Jennifer. I'm so sorry,' I said. 'I'm sorry about the outhouse. I'm sorry about crushing you in the door. I'm sorry about your leg and everything and I just don't know what to think.'

There was a silence.

'Is that an explanation?' she asked, eventually.

I looked back down again, focused on the dim sheen of moisture covering a cobble. 'No. An apology.'

'Would you be apologising if I was still locked in that little cell?'

'You attacked me.'

'Anger does funny things to you,' she said. 'And I can't help but wonder what you were planning to do with that axe if I hadn't got out. Maybe crush my skull. Or sever my neck.'

'I hadn't thought that far ahead,' I said. 'Jennifer. Why didn't you just kill me before I had the chance to lock you up? Why aren't you killing me now?'

'I wouldn't have killed you!' She shook her head again, exasperatedly. She had stopped crying now, and didn't seem to be in so much pain. The bleeding had stopped. 'There are so many fundamental things that you don't understand. When I am human, I am human. I only change into the wolf when I choose to.'

'You made the deal?' I asked. 'You gave them your – your soul?'

'Of course I did,' she said. 'You should have seen it, Jack, down by the lake. All of the music and dancing and the drinking and the laughing, and all of the sex. The honesty. To be able to control it – it's a gift, Jack. Not to mention easier. Imagine how you'd feel if you came to one morning and found you'd been out killing people. If you'd made the deal, then you would have known what you were doing and you wouldn't feel guilty. If you hadn't – well.'

'So why didn't you kill me?' I asked. 'If you could – could change shape at any moment? If you wouldn't suffer any guilt?'

'Why would I have killed you? I had no reason to kill you.'

'For the house.'

'I already had the house.'

'But—' I couldn't think of anything to say. A kind of heat emanated from within, like the precursor to some sort of life-changing wave of relief. 'But – so we're OK? You can stay human if you want to?'

'I don't know how human I feel right now,' she said. 'When I am human I am human, but you have hardly treated me like a human being, have you?' She showed sharp teeth through a humourless smile. 'Besides. I don't think this is over yet.'

I took a step backwards.

'You're trembling like an injured kitten, Jack,' she said. 'I used to have a kitten. It was one week old and tried to eat the food we put out for the dog. The dog didn't even see the thing as he went to eat his food; just bit through it. His tooth went straight into the kitten's eye. You've never seen such shaking. Was it fear or pain or brain

414

injury, do you think, Jack? The end when we see it is a pitiful, trembling thing.'

'I don't understand,' I said.

'Nothing to understand. It's just a story.'

'If you're going to kill me, let me ask some questions first.'

'You're shaking, Jack,' she said. 'Why are you shaking? I'm not going to kill you. I'd have to wait for my leg to grow back, and that'll be hours yet.'

'Why did you say Balthazar opened the door?' The pain in my head.

'There is another world,' she said. 'He is a part of it. He is here, now. Look.'

I followed the direction of her pointing finger to look behind me, and sure enough I saw the sad-faced mound of snow. Balthazar. He lifted a cold, numb arm, slowly, to wave.

'The house,' I said.

'Belongs to our world,' she said. 'The other world. It is that simple. It is our house. Our kind have always been here. The Lord built it and it is His house and it shall be His house forever.'

'The Lord,' I said.

'He will take your soul in return for the gift,' she said. 'Or send somebody else to do it for Him. You know who He is. Even if you haven't met Him yet.'

'What do you mean when you say "soul"?' I asked.

'I don't really know,' she shrugged. 'But I don't miss it.'

'Not yet,' I said.

'I won't ever miss it,' she said. 'How can you miss what you never knew you had?'

'What about Taylor?' I asked.

'Taylor made the deal too.'

'Kenny,' I said.

'Took me and bit me and we fucked.'

'But he's a creep,' I said. 'You're so much better than that.'

'Sure, as a human he's a creep,' she said. 'Time and misery and guilt had made his human aspect a creep. But when we're *wolves*, Jack. You have no idea what it's like. Pure physicality. Pure emotions. No mediation, no guilt, no worry, no politics. All of us, when we're wolves, are beautiful.'

'You weren't a wolf when we found you,' I said.

'We were lost. We didn't know what we were by that point.'

I looked around at the mist. After a short while, I said, 'Erin.'

'Francis ate her.'

'And Francis?'

'Francis loved me,' she said. 'But I didn't love him back. Before you ask.'

'You just fucked him.'

'Yeah,' she said. 'And now I miss him. And I miss Erin too.'

From out on the fellside, the faint sound of a fiddle drifted.

'How can I make it better?' I asked.

She looked down and shook her head. 'I have to be honest, this isn't how I imagined things would end up. I don't think you can make it better now.'

'Jennifer,' I said. 'I'm sorry.'

'I know,' she said. 'So'm I.'

'One more question.'

'What?'

'The Leaping,' I said.

She looked up at me and shook her head slightly, narrowing her eyes. 'I don't know,' she said. 'What's that?'

'The Leaping!'

'No,' she said. 'I've never heard of it.'

'It's terrible,' said a wet voice from behind me, and I turned, and saw that Balthazar was standing next to us. He was tall and bulky and looked ill, because his head was too big and was covered in strange lumps. 'It's a contest. And woe betide the loser.' He nodded at me, slowly.

'Why are you helping me?' I said.

'You both helped build me, after all,' he said. 'Helping you now is the least I can do. So listen to me: go. You both have to go now. As fast as Jennifer is able. I don't know if you can escape it. But you have to try. You must.'

'OK,' I said. 'Thank you.' I went over to Jennifer to help her up, but she waved me away.

'We have to change,' she said. 'I'll be faster that way.'

'Won't you attack me again?'

'Not if I don't want to.'

I didn't say anything.

'Thank you, Balthazar,' she said. 'Now, Jack. You just close your eyes – and let all the fear rise up. And let yourself grow, transform and shift. Break open. Split. Splinter. Crack and rupture. Open up and burst. Mutate. Fall apart. Change.'

It rose up out of the earth and into me, ancient, like God.

Falling apart.

Coming back to myself, I realised that I felt badly put together inside. I tried to stand and choked with the pain, only managing to get half-way up. I felt something lodged behind my ribs, something restricting my breathing, and it was heavy and sticking into my lungs. I hit myself on the chest again and again, trying to dislodge it. I tried to stand a little straighter and felt it slip and fall into my abdomen, where it felt right. The pain eased and I stood up tall. I thought it was my stomach. And I knew that couldn't be right, couldn't really be medically possible, but the science that governed such things had been lifted from me and now I had this new freedom. No longer bound by natural law.

'Jennifer,' I said, as she changed back beside me. I helped her up and she stood with her right arm around my shoulders. Her leg was coming back, but was not nearly fully grown yet. I thought back to the werewolf we had captured on the fellside. Maybe the speedy regeneration came with time. There was so much to look forward to.

I looked around and we were still in cloud, on a shallow

rocky slope, still on the fell, or at least one of the fells, or at least still on *a* fell, for I had no way of knowing how far we had run. The clouds there were not clouds so much as grey skies that just came down low. The whole world might have been beneath that cloud.

I wished I could remember how it felt to be the wolf, to be truly powerful and free. But that memory loss didn't stop the steadily increasing flow of warmth and relief and hot light from flooding through me, growing inside me. I started laughing again, happy, relieved, happy, immortal! And Jennifer was still there, still with me, despite everything, and even if she left me, then maybe I would cross her scent on some grassy hillside on some summer's day a hundred years from now or maybe a long-forgotten mossy pathway through deep green woodland where only the animals go. We could run together through the rocks, the fells, the rivers, the firs, the pines, the evergreens, the snow, the driving rain, the never-ending sun, the day, the night, the dark, the fells, the meadows, the flowers like stars in the earth, beautiful red deserts, the night above us, stars like wolves in the sky, great burning wolves with white fiery eyes howling between solar systems. We would run over the great plains, ancient and noble and wise and cruel and everlasting, and we would make love for days, bodies locked together, molten and eight-legged and snarling and animal, making love with the northern lights above us. We would run with our pack, hundreds of us, thousands, swarming over the forested peaks and the misty valleys and the bleak moors and the red deserts and the great plains and the verdant meadows and the green fields and the frozen rivers and the sleepy villages. We would howl and the sleepy villagers would rise up and join us and we would take on the towns and the cities and the IF NOT YOU, WHO? graffiti and the IF NOT NOW, WHEN? graffiti and the towering offices like old gods made of glass and stone. There would be snapped wires and broken windows and blood in the gutters and all things running through the streets and overturned cars and burning horizons and blackouts over and over again and then the dark. And we would move on. And I would run by Jennifer's side. And she by mine.

And sometime, somewhere, would be the Leaping. The Leapings.

And the dancing, and the stars, and the trees, and the snow, and the fires, and the wolves, and the Lord, and the fiddle and the pack and the clean air and the clean earth and the open sky at night.

That was the world that we would usher in.

Taylor was sitting on a rock just in front of us, drifting in and out of my vision. He was tall and crooked. He had put his suit back on. His face was human although it stretched backwards, pulled backwards, and swept up into two black and pointed ears that protruded from the top of his head. Wolfish ears. His legs were crossed and he rested his right elbow on his right knee and his chin on his right fist. In his left hand he held some sort of ball and he was looking at it.

'Taylor,' I said, my voice faint. 'Taylor.'

'Jack,' he said. 'Jack and Jennifer.'

'Where are we?' I said.

'The shore,' Taylor said. 'We are on the shore.'

'Of what?'

'Of the lake,' he said. 'What else?'

'Taylor,' I said. 'I had a dream about Erin.'

He was silent for a long time.

'What kind of dream?'

'You know what kind of dream.' Another long silence. The mist obscured him and then revealed him. The ground was wet and the stones shone.

'That kind of dream,' he said.

'Yeah,' I said. 'But I don't think dreams mean that much. I don't think they mean anything whatsoever.'

'I don't know if what we think matters at all,' Jennifer said.

'I just thought I should tell you.' I turned to Jennifer. 'I just thought I should tell him.'

'I wish you hadn't,' she said.

'Erin was with me not too long ago,' Taylor said. 'Her ghost.'

'What happened to her?' Jennifer asked.

'She moved on,' Taylor said. 'The ghosts move on.'

'Where to?' I asked.

'How would I know that?' He looked at me and even through the pale haze his eyes glinted.

'I thought – I thought you, um, we, I thought we were all part of the same thing,' I said. 'The same world.'

'No,' he said. 'No. Most ghosts move on. She moved on.

She's gone. We are not part of the same thing. If you have a soul, it becomes a ghost when you die. Just like everybody always believed.'

'I'm sorry,' Jennifer said.

'Don't be,' Taylor said. 'I remember a short period of incredible emotional agony, but it all went away. I don't care. I don't even have the capacity to care. I gave all that away and do not regret it for a second.' He grinned at me and it was the most terrible thing that I had seen in all of this, in all the blood and the things and the killing, Taylor's smile, his slow smile, his considered smile, his eyes looking past me, at nothing. Because it was a smile that Jennifer had hidden from me so far. 'I gave it all away.'

The thing he was holding was Graham's head. My heart swelled into my ribs.

'But so did I,' I said. 'So did Jennifer. She bit me. She changed me. We're like you too now. Like you too. Werewolves.' I whispered the word.

'No,' he said. 'You, Jack, have some sort of disease. You are a human that changes shape and forgets what you really are. You are nothing like me. You made no exchange. You sacrificed nothing. You are in debt. And you still feel. You are still basically a wreck.' He threw Graham's head into the air and caught it again. 'Jennifer, on the other hand. Jennifer was seduced as I was, albeit for different reasons.'

'Taylor,' I said. 'We have to leave now. The Lord and all of the others are having some sort of contest – the Leaping

– and we have to be away from it. We have to go. I thought we were so far away. But I can't hear them. So we still have time. We have to go.'

'You know why you can't hear us?' Taylor said.

'Why?' I asked.

I looked around me and the mist started to thin, and it seemed that I was not on the barren shallow rocky slope that I originally thought, but in the middle of a thicket, surrounded by trees. I looked back at Taylor. I didn't understand.

'I don't understand,' I said.

He smiled.

They were not trees or ordinary living things at all. It was them. They were there already. I realised that they had always been there, just waiting, standing silent all around.

'I thought there was some potential here,' I said, my voice shaking. 'I thought there was some element of power. We could escape to another world, Taylor, if we knew how to use what we have. We could bring that world back.'

'It is typical of you to think that,' he said, 'but nothing is ever the way you think it is.' He threw his head back and barked a laugh, an explosive exhalation. 'Maybe that is the single lesson, the single truth that you can take away from this whole thing. This whole sorry mess of a party. Or maybe even that is a fallacy. And maybe you won't take anything away with you, Jack. Maybe you won't get to take anything at all.'

Behind Taylor there was a taller figure, standing with

his hands on his hips. Taylor's smile disappeared and he looked me in the eye.

I looked down at the ground.

'You should not have dreamed of her,' he said. 'There was a moment up there after we found Jennifer. I learned something. A way for you to get out of all of this. I was going to tell you it.' He fell silent, as if thinking.

I didn't interrupt him.

'You should not have dreamed of her,' he said, again.

I didn't say anything for a long time.

Then I said, 'So. The Leaping.'

'Yes,' said the figure standing behind Taylor, and he walked forward. I realised that it was him, the fiddle-player, the Lord, and without fully intending to I fell to my knees. 'Oh,' he said, 'you are too kind. Get up.'

I stood. I looked up at him. All around us the mist had more or less gone and I saw that we were surrounded by hundreds of them, the werewolves, and there was almost a cloud of other beings around them, less physical things, faeries almost, spirits, beings made up of colour and air, and it was as if the werewolves emanated a passionate light full of living sparks. Everything was so beautiful. Bearpit stood near the front of the throng, further back behind the Lord. The Lord himself seemed near ten feet tall and wore a long black cloak and ragged black trousers. He did not have his boots on, and he did not have feet but round hooves, dark and tattered. His skin was pale. His head was a man's head, with short grey hair and a down-turned mouth and thin lips and high cheekbones and hollow cheeks. His ears were sharp and lay flat against the sides of his head and his pupils were black, horizontal ovals, like they were just stab-holes made with a thick knife, or coin slots. The whites of his eyes were a milky yellow like those of a farm animal. His chest heaved in and out and his mouth was frowning and his fists were clenched. His arms were bulky with muscle and he wore a solid black bracelet. He was the clever vicious creature that you always thought was outside waiting for you in the dark, waiting for the lights to go out or for the river to freeze.

'The Leaping,' he said, and he reached behind him and lifted the fiddle from his back. His voice was uneven, like two bits of metal scraping together, like he was made out of metal, like he was some prehistoric machine. He drew the bow across the fiddle strings and the resulting screech echoed across the valley and the surface of the lake, which was visible behind the crowd. He waved the bow at the pale, indistinct glow that indicated the location of the distant, indifferent sun, and it seemed to fall to the western horizon and set the whole thing aflame. Tongues of orange licked up from behind those fells and the sky above them turned red. 'The Leaping,' he said again, and every cell in my body was vibrating. I wanted to die. 'It happens when it happens for no good reason and no good shall come of it. The pack falls upon the being which makes the most pitiful attempt. Do you understand?'

The sound that the pack made in affirmation was one of grief, almost, a long, low howling that was the sound of the red sky, the voice of a dying fire. It faded and then came back, falling and rising, as various members of the gathering paused to listen and draw breath and start again. It went on and on. I could have stayed there listening to it forever.

Jennifer was howling too.

I opened my mouth to join them but could not; my voice was merely human, lacking the timbre and tone and power of theirs. I closed my mouth again and just looked at the grey rocks beneath my feet. Until I couldn't bear it any more, and then I closed my eyes.

Eventually, of course, the chorus stopped, and after a second of utter silence, or maybe two, the Lord brought the bow down on the fiddle and the furious music was fast and high and mad. They all surged towards Wastwater. Jennifer leaned on my shoulder and we moved slowly. I had thought I was finding a way out. I had hoped my whole life to find another world and another way of living and I came so close. I was shaking. All around me, humanoid shapes were gradually becoming other things. Handsome, quadruped things.

'Jack,' Jennifer said, into my ear. 'We have to change.'

'Yes,' I said. 'OK.'

'Jack,' she said. 'I'm going to lose. I can't jump, Jack, I can't run.'

I looked behind me and the Lord was following me, grinning, and playing his fiddle.

'I'm sorry,' I said.

'I'm sorry too,' she said.

'I love you,' I said.

She just looked at me and bit her lip and closed her eyes and shook her head. 'You didn't open your present.'

The change came more easily this time. My vision buckled as my body twisted into a new and more agile shape. It hurt but the pain seemed to fall behind somewhere in time and the others were howling with joy and laughter at the game. I saw those in front of me leaping at the shore, reaching incredible heights, their changing shapes silhouetted against the bloody heavens. Some of them looked almost human at the apex of their flights. More and more of them were getting to the lake and jumping, so that the sky was filling up with their energy and their beauty.

All that wasted power. They could have gone so far.

I turned around. Ran away from the lake. Turned around again. Music. Dancing. A thousand different scents. Meat and fireworks. Cold wet stone. Jennifer. My beautiful Jennifer. She looked at me. Big eyes. Stars set in her face. Stars in the sky like the eyes of wolves. We ran. Stars wheeled past like the sky was melting. The water bubbled and lapped. Wolves roared across space. We ran. Cold air. Hot breath. We ran.

We leapt. The lake fell. We rose. We flew. We shook. Everything shook. The fells shook and started to fall. We spun. We howled.

We started to fall. Planets span out of orbit and fell. The stars in the sky all started to fall. The red light in the sky started to fall. The rocky shore fell. The black water

427

fell. We fell. The Lord fell. God fell. The machines fell. The wolves fell. The cities fell. People fell. The young fell. The old fell. The houses fell. Fell House fell. The castle in my dream fell. The green walls fell. The deserts fell. The trees fell. The rivers fell. The sun fell. Fire fell. Bombs fell. TV fell. The war fell. Heaven fell. Hell fell. The barn fell. The boat fell. The bodies fell. Balthazar fell. Taylor fell. Francis' naked-skulled body fell. Graham fell. Erin's ghost fell. Jennifer fell. I fell. We all fell.

We fell into the lake and we kept on falling through the water and the earth and the whole thing started to crack open and break, huge plates falling off and revealing something hot and liquid inside. We fell through the various layers towards the centre, the very centre of the falling earth, and we fell and the earth fell through the falling space and everything was rushing together and we fell towards the centre now, all things fell towards one point like an ending of some sort, but we wanted to KNOW, we wanted to know what was there right at the middle, right at the centre, right at the end. I twisted and burned and screamed and grinned and we wolves rushed past each other like wind and my mind flew backwards, further back, a silver train running along a perfectly straight track, accompanied by a beating drum, taking us back, a beautiful bolt of silver in the dark, running backwards, back to a long time ago, before, and I like to think that we were all very happy then.

*

The grey stones of the shore knifed into my all-too-human hands as I hauled myself over them. Once my feet were clear of the hungry, lapping edge of Wastwater I rolled on to my back and looked up at the cold, red sky. I could hear laughter and singing and small groups of wild, happy monsters playing discordant music. I could hear fires, and the splashing of hairy, sharp-toothed people emerging from the lake triumphant. But I just looked up at the sky. It went on forever.

A figure moved into view, standing over me. Looking up I couldn't tell whether the head was lupine, looking down, or just human. Either way, though, I knew it was Taylor.

'Taylor,' I said. 'Are there any clothes I can wear?'

'Jack,' he said. 'She lost.'

I closed my eyes.

'With her only having one proper leg and everything,' he said. 'If only you'd known what was coming, hey? I almost regret bringing the axe back. I should have known something like this would happen.'

The insides of my eyelids were sky-red. I opened my eyes again and sat up. The mountains rose into sharp, irregular points all along the horizon. The surface of the lake was rippling, choppy, disturbed. It slapped back and forth just beyond my bare feet. Taylor sat beside me.

'Why did you?' I asked.

'Why did I what?'

'Why did you bring the axe back to Fell House?'

'I was coming to help Jennifer. I thought I'd heard her

howling. But the door was already open. So I left the axe, and I rushed back down here.'

'Where is she?' I said.

'She's with the Lord now.'

'Is there any way out of this?'

'No,' Taylor said. 'I don't think so.' He turned and looked behind us, away from the lake. 'They're coming,' he said. 'They're coming over here.'

'Jack,' the Lord said, in his ancient metal voice. He arrived and stood above us, one hand on Jennifer's shoulder steadying her. Her leg was still weak, embryonic. 'Get up.'

I stood, shakily. He was nearly twice as tall as me now, his tattered black vestments fluttering in the gathering wind. His violin was slung across his back again. His yellow eyes pointed downwards at me, disapprovingly. 'She is injured,' he said. 'You injured her.'

'I know,' I said. 'I'm sorry.'

'I should let her live and punish you instead.'

'Yes.' I looked up at him. 'Yes, please do that.'

He frowned at me, his brow dipped and wrinkled, his eyebrows slanting, his eyes narrowed and blank, his mouth downturned. His whole frame was trembling.

'Please do that.' I shook my head and looked down. 'Please.'

He threw his head back and burst into mad laughter, loud enough to silence the crowds of lycanthropes all around. It rolled back from the fells, echoing as if there were a hundred Lords, a hundred Leapings, a hundred jagged shorelines. In opening his mouth so widely he revealed a long, wide purple tongue and long narrow teeth that tapered to sharp, flat edges.

'No,' he said, bending forward again. 'No, I don't think so. I was only joking. Besides, I'm not entirely sure of your motives, young man. I can't help but think that dying is the preferable option.'

'To what?'

'You'll see.' He smiled.

'She doesn't deserve to die.'

'No,' the Lord said, and looked down at Jennifer, pressed against his side. 'She doesn't, does she? She's been an all-round remarkable girl.' He laughed again. 'Although I don't know what *deserving* has to do with dying, Jack.'

'I could give you myself,' I said. 'Instead. My – my, uh, my—'

'Your *soul*?' he asked, leaning in closer and raising his eyebrows. 'Is that what you're offering me, Jack?'

'Yes,' I said. 'Yes, it is.'

'No, I don't think so.' He straightened. 'It would only make things easier for you in the long run, boy. And I don't want that. The pure cold avarice, the nihilistic *apathy* that remains after making such an exchange – it's a gift. It's a gift that I'm not going to grant you.' He grinned. 'You, ah – you don't *deserve* it!'

He laughed again, and this time the whole assembled host laughed with him, Bearpit behind him laughing the loudest of all. They were huddled all around us, their

431

strange bodies mutating with mirth. I was suddenly acutely aware of my nakedness.

I waited for them all to stop laughing.

'Why are you doing this?' I asked, once they had done.

'Doing what?' he asked.

'All of it,' I said. 'The Leaping. The killing.'

'Oh.' He appeared to consider his answer for a moment. 'It happens for no good reason,' he said, at length. 'And no good ever comes of it. It can come from nothing; it can arrive from nowhere. There's no knowing who it might kill. None of us really understand it.' He paused. 'I hope that's a satisfactory answer.'

I didn't say anything. I looked at Jennifer. Her eyes were squeezed shut. The Lord's hand was cradling the back of her head, his fingers entwined in her hair at the nape of her neck. Her hair was still wet with the lake. She was still naked. It looked like she had hit her head badly, maybe when she fell. Both her knees and both her arms were cut and bleeding. Her leg was nearly fully regenerated now. She was more beautiful than anything I had ever seen. My Morgana le Fay. Tears were rolling down her cheeks.

'So then,' the Lord said. 'We've dilly-dallied long enough. My friends here are all expecting a little taste of our Jennifer here, but I'm afraid they're going to be disappointed.' He turned to address the audience. 'I'm sorry,' he said. There was no response, other than disappointed wolf-eyes moving to follow him. The silence was complete. He turned back to face me. 'It's just that seeing as Jack

432

here was so desperate for her, so desperate to own her, so desperate to make her his, so desperate to have her and to hold her that, well, it would be a shame to deny him that, at least.' There was low laughter. The Lord smiled at me. 'It's not as if he'll get another chance. So, Jack. Here we are.' He pushed Jennifer forward, towards me, roughly. She stumbled and then stood by my side, facing away from him. She still had her eyes closed. 'Eat her,' said the Lord. 'She's all yours.'

'What?' I said.

'Eat her.'

'No,' I said. 'No.'

'Eat her,' he said.

'No. Or – or what will you do?' I said.

'I'll take you both back to hell with me when I go,' he said. 'It's far worse than this.'

The air was now bitterly cold. My breath was misting. Jennifer's too. My jaws were crashing into each other as I shivered and shook. Jennifer was a goose-pimpled statue beside me. Her lip-rings were long gone. I thought about her standing by the curtains in my bedroom in Manchester. That strip of early-morning light. Blue milk. I could not control my lips or my eyes. At least she was not really conscious. At least she was not aware of any of this. I had to kill her quickly. I had to kill her straight away, before she came round. I had to get a stone and hit her hard. I moved my hand a short distance, but stopped. I didn't know what to do. I couldn't do it.

'I can't do it,' I said.

The Lord didn't say anything. He just looked down at me.

I had to do it while she was unconscious. I put my hand around her waist and bent my knees slightly, in order to pick up a stone.

'Jack?' Jennifer said.

'Yes?' I said. I closed my eyes and my stomach started to crawl around inside me. 'Jennifer?'

'Oh,' she said. 'I'm glad you're here.'

'Really?'

'I've been dreaming again.' She put her arms around me and talked into my neck. 'It was a bad one. We had a party, or something.'

'Oh,' I said, looking past her at the smiling Lord and all of the gathered lycanthropes. 'Those dreams. It's the house. Maybe we should move.'

'I think I'd like that,' she said. 'Maybe I should try to buy Mum's house back. I could make an offer, hey?'

'Why not?' I said. 'You should do that. Moving up here was a nice idea but maybe we just weren't ready.' I hoped she wouldn't notice that my hands were shaking.

'I miss her,' she said. 'I really miss her, Jack.' She lifted her head away from my neck and, eyes still closed, stretched.

'Lie back down, Jennifer,' I said. 'Here.' I put my right arm around her shoulders and then bent down to press against the back of her knees with my left arm, so that I could lift her. I laid her down on the stones.

'This doesn't feel right,' she murmured. 'Not very

434

comfy, Jack.' She wriggled and opened her eyes. She saw me, dripping wet, the red sky behind me. She frowned a little bit, her lovely eyebrows lowering, her lips pouting ever so slightly. 'Is everything OK?'

'Yes,' I said, and I forced myself to attempt a smile and nod. I wasn't sure that I managed it. 'As long as you're OK, everything is fine.'

She looked scared, and started to try and sit up and look around. I found myself forcing her back, putting my weight on to her shoulders, trying to keep her head still by kissing her. But already the change was upon me, and I was closing my teeth on her neck.

'Where are we, Jack?' I heard her saying. 'What are you doing?'

EPILOGUE

JACK

I hid for a long time. The police were all over the valley for years, picking up bits of information. Sometimes they heard rumours about a wolf that might have escaped from some reservation in Scotland, but that was as close as they got to the truth.

Now I'm back, insects and spiders and small animals are starting to move in to Fell House with me. Often I watch spiders spinning their webs across open doorways, the silver threads delicate and perfect. Over time, further webs are built, and then they all catch the dust and thicken, and the dust starts to accumulate and cling to itself and form bridges and webs of its own, and all these fragile edifices start to knit together as if the house is somehow healing. The roof still leaks when it rains, and the plaster is still damp. It keeps on falling off in chunks and breaking on the floor. I leave it there. The birds still perch up on the roof, spaced so regularly they could be part of the architecture.

I lean against the door-frame between the living-room and the kitchen and look at the floor.

There are green forests and clear rivers to be found out there beyond all the shit, I used to think, and this was supposed to be about finding them. This was supposed to be about running across the fells on all fours beneath a starry night. Stripping away all the crap that we wrap around ourselves in order to reveal the true creature beneath. I always thought that the creature beneath would be somehow noble, being natural, somehow stronger and more honest than the people we pretend to be, but I'm finding out, now, what I am when I am alone and I am only me; no physical props, no social-feedback loops, nobody to distract me or lose myself in. And I am not what I thought I was. I have thrown all the mirrors out of the window.

I remember more now than I did immediately afterwards. Images come back to me when I'm trying to fall asleep. I remember hanging above the surface of the water, surrounded by red light; the water reflected the sky above so that it was like being suspended in a uniform void. Some hungry bodily hollow, ringed by mirrored mountains like teeth grasping in all directions at once. I remember plunging downwards, and the pure, sudden blackness of being inside the lake, the clean feeling of it, the joy of unadulterated sensation. I remember hot blood on my fine-boned, pale-haired face. The taste of her comes back to me sometimes, and I salivate. When I remember this, though, I need to forget, so I turn myself into the inhuman thing that is said to haunt Fell House, the twisted, narrow thing that slips across the fells and picks off sheep and lost climbers, the shadowy four-legged thing that screams and howls throughout the valley when the sunset turns the sky that blazing red, the warped lupine thing that growls and pants and chases its tail on the shore of Wastwater, turning around and around and around, looking for a way backwards.

When I am not remembering or forgetting, I am a person of sorts. I huddle in the corners of my peeling rooms, picking at carcasses that lie opened up like books, with ribs like lines of text. The ribcages are always empty by this point, eviscerated, with the beating hearts and important parts and meaningful aspects of the beings all removed. They're hollowed out. Little voids.

I've taken all the birthday presents I never unwrapped out of the bag now and laid them around me on the kitchen floor, having pushed the bones and whatnot out of the way, into a corner. Outside it's raining, and the clouds make the day so dark I can't tell what time of day it is. Water runs down the wall behind me and splashes on to the slates. The presents are dim shapes in the dark. I want to open them, to see what Erin and Taylor and Graham and Francis and Jennifer thought I might have liked. I pick up the heavy purple one, the one from Jennifer, and hold it in both hands. It is such a simple shape. Six-sided, with three pairs of sides the same size, each side having four edges, each edge shared with another side, and the whole thing having eight corners. Cuboid, but not a cube. It could be a box of some sort, holding something well-packed inside it. Or it could be a big heavy book. My fingertips flirt with the folded edges of wrapping paper. The wrapping paper is faded now, and slightly mouldy. Whatever is inside it is probably slightly mouldy too. I want to open it. Through the window I can see the big black birds swooping through the storm as if it isn't there. The house creaks. The golden ribbon is still curly. I remember seeing Jennifer running one arm of the scissors along it, pressed against her thumb.

I put it down again. Unopened. The outside of it is enough.

ACKNOWLEDGEMENTS

Thanks very much to Alan Bissett for the initial encouragement, to Sarah and Sally for lending me their laptops right back near the beginning, to Sarah Hymas and Flax for publishing some early pieces in *Before the Rain*, to Nicholas Royle for being an excellent friend, mentor and agent, to Kirkby and Dick for reading several drafts, to Nick Johnston at Quercus for his enthusiasm and his priceless advice, to my family for their unwavering support and to Beth, my wife, for just about everything.

THE THING ON THE SHORE

Tom Fletcher

COMING IN SPRING 2011

Artemis Black (from *The Leaping*) is assigned by a mysterious multinational corporation called Interext to manage a call centre in Whitehaven, on Cumbria's grim post-industrial coastline. The isolation and remoteness of the place encourage him to implement a decidedly unhinged project.

Soon one of his employees, Arthur, becomes aware of an intangible landscape inside the labyrinthine systems of the call centre – a landscape in which he can feel some kind of otherworldly consciousness stirring and in which, perhaps as a result of his father's increasingly alarming eccentricities, he feels that he could find his recently deceased mother.

Arthur takes refuge in this belief as his father, his job, and his house slowly deteriorate around him. He begins to conflate the mysterious, interstitial region that exists down the phonelines with the sea, as that was where his mother drowned. In a way he is right – Interext's activities have attracted something, it is just not as benevolent as he thinks...